PRAISE FOR

PRIDE AND PREJUDICE AND ZOMBIES

By Jane Austen and Seth Grahame-Smith

"A delectable literary mash-up . . . might we hope for a sequel? Grade A-."
—Lisa Schwarzbaum of *Entertainment Weekly*

"Jane Austen isn't for everyone. Neither are zombies. But combine the two and the only question is, Why didn't anyone think of this before?"
—*Wired*

PRAISE FOR

PRIDE AND PREJUDICE AND ZOMBIES: DAWN OF THE DREADFULS

By Steve Hockensmith

"A must-read for the growing legion of alternate-Austen fans."
—*Booklist*

"Mixing taut horror-movie action with neo-Austen meditation on identity, society, and romance, this happy sacrilege is sure to please."
—*Publishers Weekly*

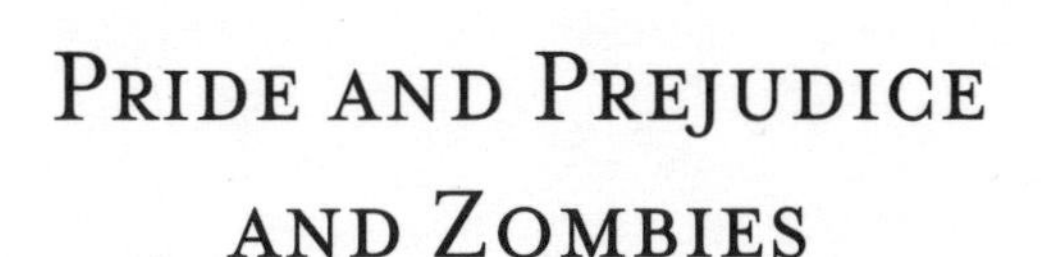

Pride and Prejudice and Zombies

Dreadfully Ever After

BY STEVE HOCKENSMITH

ILLUSTRATIONS BY PATRICK ARRASMITH

QUIRK BOOKS
PHILADELPHIA

Library of Congress Cataloging in Publication Number: 2010942862

ISBN: 978-1-59474-502-7

Printed in Canada

Typeset in Bembo and Mrs. Eaves

Designed by Doogie Horner
Cover painting by Lars Leetaru
Cover art research courtesy the Bridgeman Art Library International Ltd.
Interior illustrations by Patrick Arrasmith
Production management by John J. McGurk

Quirk Books
215 Church Street
Philadelphia, PA 19106
www.quirkbooks.com
10 9 8 7 6 5 4 3 2 1

LIST OF ILLUSTRATIONS

CHAPTER 1

As his beloved Elizabeth shattered the nearest zombie's skull with a perfectly placed axe kick, Fitzwilliam Darcy saw in her eyes something that had been missing for a long, long time: joie de vivre.

Much as he would have liked to revel in it—to bask in the rekindled warmth of his wife's delight—he could not. She was already ducking beneath another dreadful's clumsy lurch, for one thing. And then there were the three unmentionables that were closing in on *him*.

Although one couldn't say the creatures had joie de vivre, both *joie* and *vivre* being long beyond them, they were undeniably enthusiastic in their quest for succulent flesh. His. Which he denied them—temporarily, at least—with a backward flip that delivered him safely out of their reach.

Darcy landed directly behind the tallest of the dreadfuls. He drew his katana and, with one stroke, made it the shortest. The others whirled on him howling as even more zombies clambered out of the abandoned well in which they'd apparently wintered.

Darcy danced back a few steps and then stopped and set his feet, readying himself for the onslaught.

Something pressed up against him from behind.

"I'm so glad you suggested we check that well for dreadfuls," Elizabeth said, her back pushing harder into his with each panted breath.

"I thought it might bring you some amusement."

"Oh, it has. More than I've had in quite a while."

"So I noticed."

Mindless as they were, the unmentionables could be instinctively wary, and, rather than rushing in one at a time, they spread out around the couple, encircling them. Darcy raised his sword.

Elizabeth, being a married lady, had left the house unarmed.

"Would you like to borrow my katana?" Darcy asked.

"Oh, that wouldn't be proper, would it?" Elizabeth replied, sounding sour. Then she took in an especially deep breath, and her tone brightened. "At any rate, I can make do."

Darcy had little doubt she could—to a point. Elizabeth was no longer a warrior, but she sparred with him and his sister every day. Her way with the katana, longbow, musket, flintlock, dagger, mace, pike, battle axe, blow dart, and (most fortunately of all, at the moment) death-dealing hands and feet were nearly as sharp as the day he'd wedded her.

Yet that was in the privacy of the dojo; she hadn't faced a dreadful since becoming Mrs. Fitzwilliam Darcy four years before. Now they were surrounded by a dozen of the creatures. Her wedding ring would be no replacement for the saber or throwing stars she couldn't, as the wife of a gentleman, be seen wielding.

Their only hope, Darcy knew, was that the unmentionables would prove every bit as out of practice with killing. These were the first zombies of spring, still stiff from the long months they'd spent packed together in hiding. Some were men, some women, some whole, some disfigured, some as new to death as the previous autumn, some little more than rag-wrapped skeletons. One thing could be counted on, though: They would all be hungry. That never changed.

As if at some silent signal, the unmentionables charged en masse.

There was a bloodcurdling shriek, but it wasn't a scream of terror or the fabled zombie wail. It was Elizabeth unleashing the warrior's cry that had been bottled up within her for so long.

"HAAAAAAAAAAAAAA-IIIIIIIIIEEEEEEEEEE-EEEEEEEEEEEEEE!"

Darcy lopped off one head, and another, and split a third dreadful down the middle. And then, to his surprise, he was able to just stand back and watch.

Elizabeth had gone spinning into the pack like a whirling dervish. Her first kick turned everything above one girl-zombie's gray flap-skinned chin into an exploding plume of foul-smelling scarlet. She let her momentum twirl her into another unmentionable, a tottering collection of old bones, and snapped off its arm, using it to bat its head clear off its shoulders. A couple more swings and two more zombies fell, their crowns crushed. By then Elizabeth's bone-club had snapped, and she jammed the jagged end through the next dreadful's face. Two more ghouls, twin males, latched onto her wrists, but she was able to yank her hands free and use them to smash the unmentionables' heads together, the identical faces merging, for a moment, into one. The last two survivors of the pack turned to flee. Elizabeth stopped one—permanently—with a hefty hurled rock, while the final zombie she simply beat to a pulp with a branch hastily broken from a nearby tree.

"More!" she cried, whipping this way and that. "More! *More!*"

"You can stop now," Darcy said.

Elizabeth turned on him, still clutching the branch, the almost feral look on her face saying, *Why would I want to do that?*

"They're all dead," Darcy said, ensuring the truth of it by casually hacking at whatever necks were still attached to something resembling a head.

Elizabeth watched him a moment before tossing aside her branch and dusting off her hands.

"So the unmentionables are beginning to awaken," she said, suddenly sounding bored. "My, can it be that time of year again, already? I suppose we should return to the house and tell Charles what we've found. It would seem his gamekeeper has been unforgivably lax."

"Indeed."

Darcy offered Elizabeth his arm, and side by side they strolled back toward Fernworthy Manor, home of Mr. and Mrs. Charles Bingley and family.

As they walked, Darcy tried to recall what he and his wife had been discussing when, on a whim, he'd suggested they check the old well. Yet there was no conversation to resume, he remembered now. Until they'd left the safety of the lane, their walk had been free not only of zombies, but of chatter as well.

And so it always was these days when the Darcys visited the Bingleys. Elizabeth, usually so spirited and free in discourse with her husband, became sullen and withdrawn. She hid it from Mrs. Bingley—her much-loved elder sister, Jane. And she doted on her young nieces. Yet whenever out of sight of the Bingleys, she became muted, broody, and it took a week back at Pemberley for her spirits to lift. Even then, they never seemed to rise to the same heights they'd once known.

Upon returning to Fernworthy, Darcy and Elizabeth found Bingley in the drawing room playing Stricken and Slayers with the twins, Mildred and Grace, while little Millicent toddled around chewing on one of her mother's disused garrotes. As Darcy began telling his old friend of the unmentionables he and Elizabeth had encountered on the grounds, his wife excused herself, retreating upstairs to check on her sister and the household's newest addition, five-day-old Philippa.

"I'll send someone out to burn the bodies," Bingley said when Darcy finished his account. "Good thing you were here to deal with the wretched things. I can't tell you how sick I am of shooting them. At times I almost wish Jane would pick up her Brown Bess again and spare me the trouble!"

Mildred and Grace had been fighting over a battered wooden practice sword, each declaring herself the slayer and her sister the stricken, but suddenly their quarrel ended.

"Has Mumsy killt lots of zombies?" Mildred asked.

"Language, dear heart," Bingley chided gently.

"Has Mumsy killt lots of zed words?" Grace said.

"Yes. She has."

"But Mumsy don't kill zombies now?" Mildred asked.

"*Language*, dear."

"But Mumsy don't kill zed words now?" Grace said.

"No. She does not."

"Why?" Mildred asked.

"Yes? Why?" said Grace.

"Because Mumsy is Mumsy, and mumsies don't kill unmentionables."

"But Auntie Lizza did," Mildred pointed out.

"Aunt Elizabeth is not a mumsy." Bingley peeked over at Darcy, his ruddy face losing some of its color. "I mean, not yet. And your aunt doesn't *usually* go about killing unmentionables. This was a special—Millicent!"

Bingley leapt toward his second-youngest daughter, who was now sitting on a chaise longue teething on a dueling pistol she'd swapped for the garrote.

Not long afterward, the Darcys said their goodbyes and set off for home. Their own estate, Pemberley, was half a day's coach ride away. It was half a day that dragged past almost entirely in silence.

As the road began snaking up out of the shallow wooded valley before Pemberley House, Darcy signaled for the driver to stop.

"We'll walk from here," he said.

A moment later, the landau was rolling on without them.

"Again, you make me hike today," Elizabeth said as they started toward the house. "I fear you think I'm growing stout."

Darcy almost smiled. When he looked over at Lizzy, however, his grin wilted. There was no spark of impish mischief in his wife's dark eyes. She was simply staring dully at the winding road before them, her face slack, her usual crisp gait a grudging trudge.

"I know how fond you are of long country walks," he said. "And it seems to me we've had, while indulging in them together, many of our most heartfelt talks."

"There is something you wish to speak to me about?"

"Certainly. Unfortunately, I don't know what it is."

"Then, I don't see how I can be expected to hold forth upon it. Perhaps we should settle on a topic we can put a name to. Would you prefer the weather or which parent young Philippa takes after?"

"Neither!"

The word came out more sharply than Darcy intended—more sharply, in fact, than any words he'd spoken to Elizabeth since the time, years before, they'd come to blows over his first, botched proposal. Their tempers burned hotter in those days, perhaps fueled by the passions they had to hide deep inside, and they were lucky indeed that on that long-ago day, one or the other hadn't ripped out and eaten the very heart that would, in due time, be so gladly given.

"Dearest Elizabeth," Darcy went on softly, "I pride myself on less than I once did, but on one thing my self-satisfaction has never wavered: the forthrightness of my relations with the wife I so treasure. There has been, for some while now, a cloud hanging over you, and I have waited patiently for you to put a name to it. I had faith that you would do so in your own good time. Yet that time never seems to come, and the cloud has only darkened—until today, when I saw it part, however briefly, during our battle by the well. These four happy years there have been no secrets or lies or subterfuges between us. You know I find such things intolerable, as do you. So I will put it to you directly and trust that your answer will reflect all the frankness and honesty we both so value. Lizzy, what is wrong?"

Elizabeth wrapped her arm more tightly around her husband's, pulling him closer as they walked. It was, Darcy felt, a promising beginning. Then she spoke.

"I don't know."

"You don't know? If ever there was a woman who knew her mind, it was you."

Elizabeth loosened her hold on him and moved a little bit away.

"I harbor no secrets, I assure you. I simply find myself at a loss for words."

"A first," Darcy said, pulling her to his side again.

Elizabeth looked up at him and tried to smile. That she didn't succeed pained him, yet the attempt was reassuring. This was still the Lizzy he loved—the woman who, once upon a time, could behead a hundred dreadfuls with a grapefruit spoon and still have the good humor to tease him for only doing away with ninety-nine. There was no difficulty they couldn't overcome, Darcy felt, as long as they faced it squarely, together.

"The moods seem to come upon you most strongly when we visit Fernworthy," he said. "Does it have something to do with the girls? The fact that your mother and father can visit no such grandchildren at Pemberley?"

Elizabeth gave him an uncertain nod. "Yes. That is part of it."

"But we've spoken of that before. You know how I feel. We will be blessed as have Jane and Charles if only we continue to—"

"You misunderstand," Elizabeth broke in. "I do not envy Jane. Quite the opposite, in fact. Do you know—?"

This time she cut herself off, and half a dozen strides were taken in silence before she spoke again.

"It is too horrible a thing to say."

"There is nothing you could think that would be so horrible it couldn't be shared in confidence between us."

"You didn't say that the last time I told you what I'd like to do to your aunt."

"If you'll recall, it was only what you planned to do with the head that I found shocking. And upon reflection, even that I came to appreciate as a truly novel—perhaps even tempting—idea. Come. There is nothing you need hide from me."

"You say that *now*."

"And I mean it now. And always."

They took more quiet steps together up the hill. By this time,

Pemberley House wasn't far off, its high ramparts and swooping roofs making it look like a palace out of a Japanese tapestry, which was exactly the intended effect.

"When I see little Philippa nursing at her mother's breast, do you know what I think of?" Elizabeth said.

"Tell me."

Elizabeth took in a deep breath, and Darcy could feel the muscles of her hand and arm tense. It was as though she were preparing herself for some great exertion. Or a duel.

"A dreadful," she said. "A monstrous parasite intent on sucking the very life from the living."

Darcy stifled a laugh.

"Is that what this is about?" he almost said. "I'll grant you Philippa hasn't begun life as comely as her sisters, but she's not so unsightly as all that!"

He caught himself just in time.

His wife's black humors had begun long before the birth of her youngest niece (homely baby though she was). So it wasn't just this particular child that perturbed her.

"Are you saying you don't like *children*?" he asked.

"No! Yet I do find myself feeling unaccountably—"

Elizabeth grimaced as if she'd just discovered something unbearably sour in her mouth. Then she spit it out.

"—*relieved* that we haven't had any of our own."

Somehow Darcy managed to keep walking, though his mind had gone numb. No blow from a nunchuck or bo staff had ever struck him so dumb.

"You are appalled that a woman should have such thoughts," Elizabeth said. "Aghast. Disgusted. I can tell."

"No. I'm merely surprised."

Elizabeth stared at him dubiously, and he couldn't blame her. He wasn't sure if he believed it, either.

He was still focused inward, trying to divine his own feelings, when a small figure stepped out of the forest just ahead. Darcy was so distracted he didn't even think when he recognized who it was before them. For here was Andrew, youngest son of his steward. Darcy stopped and leaned forward, hands on his knees, as he always did when greeting the lad.

"And what brings you so far from the house, young master Brayles?"

Young master Brayles answered with a growl, and too late Darcy noticed the odd tilt to the boy's head and the gray pallor of his skin and the smell of death and feculence that drifted with him onto the road. By the time all that had registered, the dreadful had hurled itself at him and was sinking its little teeth deep, *deep* into Darcy's neck.

CHAPTER 2

There was no timepiece on earth fine enough in its workings to measure how long Elizabeth stood by motionless, in shock, as a zombie chomped into her husband. One tick of a clock would have been an eternity by comparison. Yet Elizabeth judged herself unimaginably, *unforgivably* slow to act.

She grabbed the little dreadful by its lacy collar and jerked it away. The ghoul-child stumbled back still chewing furiously on a stringy chunk of flesh torn from Darcy's neck. It showed no emotion as the rest of its supper stumbled off a few steps, hands clasped uselessly over a gushing wound. It merely swallowed and stepped forward again, ready for another bite.

Elizabeth swiveled and aimed a kick at its head that could have split a boulder. But Andrew Brayles had been young—just six years old.

"YOUNG MASTER BRAYLES ANSWERED WITH A GROWL."

He'd been nimble in life, and he was new to death. No sleepy-slow half-hibernating dreadful was this. His reflexes were fast, his muscles strong.

The zombie dodged under the kick and headed directly for Darcy.

"Elizabeth . . . I . . . ," Darcy gasped, and fell to his knees with his fingers still pressed to his throat. His white cravat and shirt-front were dyed red. His face was ashy gray.

The unmentionable reached him and bent in toward Darcy's neck, irresistibly drawn to the enticing sight of so much flowing blood. Before it could taste any again, however, its feet were pulled out from under it, and the zombie found itself swinging through the air. It screeched and flailed, but to no avail.

Elizabeth had hold of the creature by the ankles and was spinning away from her husband like a Scots highlander about to hurl a hammer. She didn't let go until after the dreadful's head had whirled into—and was completely splattered upon—a particularly sturdy tree on the opposite side of the road.

Elizabeth sent the rest of Andrew Brayles's lifeless body twirling into the forest. Then she turned back to Darcy, experiencing a sensation that had been unknown to her for many a year: fear.

She'd faced legions of reanimated cadavers without flinching. She hadn't batted an eye while dueling her Shaolin masters on tightropes stretched over poison-tipped punji sticks. She'd killed a dreadful with a pebble, a pair of ninjas with their own toes, and a bear with nothing but a long hard stare, all without sinking so low as to break a sweat.

Yet every time her sister had gone into labor, Elizabeth had found herself reacquainted with dread. At such times, Death wasn't something she could defeat with a well-executed Striking Viper or thrust of her katana. If it chose to take Jane, she'd be helpless—just as she would be if her husband's wound was half as bad as it looked.

By the time she reached his side, it looked even worse. Darcy was on his hands and knees, the blood that splashed onto the sloping road already starting to trickle in little rivulets down the hill. The only cause for hope (ridiculous as it was to have hope at such a moment) was that the blood was dark and came in a steady stream. It didn't squirt out in heart-beat spurts, nor was it the vivid crimson that issues from a torn artery. Darcy might yet be saved. Perhaps. For a time.

Elizabeth knelt beside him and helped him straighten—better to keep the wound elevated, above his heart. Then she lifted her skirts and tore a long strip of muslin from her petticoat.

"Keep applying pressure," she said, pushing the wadded cloth into his fingers and lifting his hands back to the side of his neck. "Don't let up, no matter what."

"Elizabeth . . . you must . . . "

She silenced him with a gentle kiss—for all she knew, their last.

"Tell me later," she said. Then she was hoisting him onto her back and beginning the sprint up out of the valley.

It wasn't so different than one of Master Liu's old disciplines during her training at Shaolin. Only now she wasn't dodging arrows, and it was her husband's weight upon her shoulders rather than a sack of bricks tied to her back.

She wasn't as strong or as fast as she'd been in those days. Yet she knew she was strong and fast enough. She *had* to know it.

Doubt, Master Liu always said, *is death*.

Ten minutes later, she had the great jade door of Pemberley House in sight. It flew open as she staggered across the lawn toward it, and the housekeeper, Mrs. Reynolds, bustled out as quickly as her bound feet could carry her.

"Oh! Oh! Oh!" she cried, waving her hands over her head. "What-ever has happened to Mr. Darcy?"

"An accident," Lizzy panted.

"Oh! Thank heavens!"

"Send for Dr. Oxenbrigg at once."

"Oh! Yes! Of course! Oh!"

And with another "Oh!" for every scuffling step she took, Mrs.

Reynolds scooted off. To anyone unfamiliar with the strange plague, the relief on the woman's face would have been unfathomable. Her master was riding piggy-back on her mistress, head lolling, eyes rolling, blood everywhere. At least he hadn't been bitten, though. At least he wasn't damned. Or so Elizabeth had led her to believe.

More servants came swarming out of the house, and three grim-faced footmen gently lifted Darcy off Elizabeth's back. She was shocked when she saw him again. As she'd run, she'd taken comfort in the steady thump of his heart against her back, but now she could see it had merely been emptying her husband of life. His skin had gone a pale beyond white, as if milk flowed through his veins. Certainly, there couldn't be much blood there anymore.

By the time they laid him on his low, palletlike tatami bed upstairs, Darcy was no longer moving, except to breathe. He'd closed his eyes as well, for which Elizabeth was grateful. They'd gone glassy, empty, and looking into them made Elizabeth feel dizzy, as if she were on the edge of some precipice staring down into a dark abyss.

A young chambermaid knelt next to her and reached for the clump of muslin she was pressing to Darcy's neck.

"I'll hold it!" Elizabeth snapped.

The girl jerked back. "I'm sorry, Ma'am. I thought you might like to rest."

"No. Just bring me the angelica root and fresh dressings, and I will attend to my husband myself. The rest of you may leave."

The servants were shuffling out glumly when Georgiana Darcy came bursting in.

"They say my brother is—no!" She rushed to the bed and threw herself to her knees beside Darcy. "Just look at him! Lizzy, how did this happen?"

"An accident," Elizabeth said, lowering her voice as she glanced meaningfully at the open door. "You must remember your training."

The younger woman nodded solemnly, and Elizabeth was grateful for the moment she took to compose herself. As Georgiana straightened her spine and wiped any hint of emotion from her face, Elizabeth did the same. Both had been trained to be warriors. They'd been taught to suppress their feelings, to squelch anything like fright or dismay. Yet Elizabeth felt that, so far that day, she'd utterly failed.

"Your brother has been bitten," she whispered, "by one of the sorry stricken."

Georgiana looked down again at Darcy, and in particular at the blood-soaked wad of cloth pressed to his neck. Despite her best efforts, her eyes widened.

"Then he is doomed," she murmured.

"Not necessarily."

"But the wound is—"

The chambermaid came hustling back in with a jar of flaky brown Kampo herbs and a roll of bandages. She set them on the floor (the room's spartan Japanese style accommodating nothing as decadent as a bedside table) before curtsying and scurrying out again, closing the door behind her.

"What happened to Andrew Brayles?" Elizabeth asked before Georgiana could finish the thought she'd started.

"He went missing a few days ago, just after you left for Fernworthy. Mrs. Leech was the last to see him. He was playing down by Dragon Bridge." Her gaze flicked to the bed again. "Not little Andrew."

Elizabeth nodded. "He must have fallen somewhere in the woods and broken his neck."

"Then this is my fault! I should not have rested until the boy was found and properly dealt with!"

"We can indulge in self-recriminations later. For now, there is work to be done. I set Andrew's soul free, but the body remains. You must find it and destroy it at once . . . without letting anyone know what you're doing."

"I don't understand. You want it kept secret that—?"

"*Quickly*, Georgiana! It is your brother's only hope!"

The young lady sprang to her feet. "Where will I find the carcass?"

Elizabeth told her and Georgiana bowed, pivoted crisply, and went striding away.

Through it all, Darcy stirred not once, nor did he open his eyes or move over the course of the next hour. Not when Mrs. Reynolds or one of the other servants popped a head in to tearfully inquire about his condition. Not even when Elizabeth smoothed back his dark hair and kissed him on his clammy forehead.

When Georgiana returned, she was accompanied by Dr. Oxenbrigg, whom she'd encountered on the road as she headed back to the house. The doctor was a withered, bald, eye-patch-wearing, sixtyish man who was no stranger to the dangers of the dreadful plague: Legend had it he'd plucked out his own eye after it was scratched by an infected patient. Whether or not that was true, one eye was all he needed to recognize a zombie bite when he saw one.

"An accident?" he said after slowly lowering himself next to Darcy and pulling back the bandages around his neck.

He shot Elizabeth a scowl.

"There are many kinds of accidents," she replied. "Is there anything to be done about this one?"

Dr. Oxenbrigg grunted and leaned in again over his patient.

Darcy remained motionless save for shallow, irregular breaths.

"No. It's hopeless," the doctor announced. "What am I supposed to do? Amputate his neck? There's no way I could dig out enough flesh to ensure the plague won't take root." He nodded at the black leather valise he'd left at the foot of the bed. "I've brought my hacksaw, if you want a professional to handle the coup de grâce. I know how you people feel about your fancy swords, though."

A little whimper broke through Georgiana's stone-faced facade.

"You'll have to excuse me. I'm sure I must seem horribly callous," Dr. Oxenbrigg said. "The heart hardens when you've sawn through as many necks as I have." He looked back down at the bed and shook his head. "I am sorry, though, Miss Darcy. Your brother was a good man."

"*Is* a good man," Elizabeth said. "Tell me, Doctor. Have you ever known the Darcys to shirk their responsibilities?"

"No. No one could say anything of the sort."

"Then if I were to ask you to keep this unfortunate matter to yourself, could you, trusting that we would do what needs to be done when the time comes?"

The old man gave her a long, monocular squint before answering. "You know what the Dreadful Act says."

"Of course. You're bound by law to see that my husband's head is removed and his body incinerated. I am asking you, as a favor to the family, to let us handle all that in private. In our own way, in our own time."

"And you presume to speak for the Darcys now, do you?" the doctor said. His one rheumy eye swiveled back and forth in its socket, swinging his gaze from Elizabeth to Georgiana and back again.

Oh, Elizabeth thought. *He's one of* those.

Not everyone in Derbyshire had accepted the warrior woman of inferior birth who had married their precious Fitzwilliam Darcy. Even after years at Pemberley House—years in which she'd never once worn her katana in public—she still caught the occasional whiff of disapproval. The resentment seemed to stir up most whenever her mother visited, yet Elizabeth could never be certain when it might arise. And here it was again at just the moment it might do the most harm.

Elizabeth didn't just have two responses to choose from. She had two Elizabeths: the former warrior who would bend the mulish old fool to her will by sheer force, and the gentleman's wife who could try to coax and wheedle her way to what she wanted.

Georgiana spoke before Elizabeth could make her choice.

"She doesn't *presume* to speak for the family, Doctor," the young lady said firmly. "*Mrs. Darcy* simply *does*."

Dr. Oxenbrigg let his glower linger a moment on her and then shrugged.

"I am a healer, not a butcher. It is no hardship for me to leave my hacksaw in my bag. I will do so now, with my pledge of silence."

"Thank you, Doctor," Elizabeth said.

The old man waggled a gnarled finger at her. "Don't make me regret it. If I hear Mr. Darcy has been running around picnicking on people's brains, I will be seriously put out."

"Of course," Elizabeth said. "I have but one more question before you go: If his wound hadn't been from a dreadful, might Mr. Darcy have lived?"

Dr. Oxenbrigg heard the hint about going; he rose to his feet grumbling and snatched up his bag. "He's lost much blood, some skin and sinew, too, but nothing vital. A strong man like him, in excellent health? Yes. He'd have pulled through."

"Thank you again."

The doctor grumbled something about sending a bill, bowed to Georgiana, and shuffled away.

"I do not understand, Elizabeth," Georgiana said once he was gone. "Do you mean to contrive some more honorable death for my brother?"

"No."

Georgiana blanched. "Then I should go and fetch your katana?"

"No."

Georgiana seemed to sway a little, as if she were standing on the deck of a ship rocking gently on the sea.

"And no—I do not mean for you to fetch yours, either," Elizabeth said. "There is hope yet. One alone, and very dim, but it exists." She allowed herself the indulgence of a sigh. "We must send for your aunt."

"Lady Catherine? Why, even if there *were* something she could do to help . . . well . . . "

"Would she?"

Elizabeth went to her husband's side again. His face was so waxy he could have been one of Madame Tussaud's famous creations—a lifeless simulacrum of himself. Yet breath still passed through his parted lips, and his eyes seemed to be darting this way and that behind closed lids.

"That is what we must find out," Elizabeth said. "Lady Catherine's hatred for me runs deep . . . but does her love for your brother run deeper?"

CHAPTER 3

Lady Catherine de Bourgh didn't bother sending a reply to Elizabeth's letter. She simply sent herself.

Just three days after Elizabeth's note was dispatched—barely enough time for it to have reached her ladyship's estate in Kent—a chaise and four came charging up the drive toward Pemberley. Despite the swiftness of the carriage's arrival, there could be no doubt who was inside. The horses' armor-plated harnesses, the steely-eyed ninjas serving as coachmen, the distinctive rose-and-crossbones crest upon the doors—all announced the coming of Fitzwilliam Darcy's aunt. And Elizabeth Darcy's greatest enemy.

Elizabeth and Georgiana waited on the front steps as the carriage came to a halt and the ninjas went springing off in all directions. The black-clad assassins bounced around the nearest hedgerows and parapets, frightening the gardeners with their somersaults and back flips. Just a few years before, Elizabeth had killed a dozen such men not far from that very spot. It had been a week to the day after her wedding, and they'd been sent to kill her.

Once the ninjas were sure the area was secure, two of them rolled out a red carpet from the coach while a third placed a black stepstool under the door facing the house. When all was in readiness, the ninjas lined up along the carpet and lowered their heads and the one nearest the coach opened the door without looking at it. Only then did Lady Catherine de Bourgh deign to grace Pemberley with her presence.

An exceptionally tall woman, she had to stoop mightily to make her way through the carriage door. Once her feet touched the ground, she straightened to her full height—an act she performed with such grave, stately deliberation, it seemed (to Elizabeth, at least) to go on for minutes. When she was fully erect, Lady Catherine seemed to tower over the coach itself. Indeed, she projected the air of one who rose above everything and everyone, and she came gliding up the carpet as slowly, smoothly, and unstoppably as a windblown cloud. Her gaze never once strayed, remaining locked firmly on the door just beyond Elizabeth and Georgiana.

"Your ladyship," Elizabeth said as she approached, "I cannot tell you how grateful I am that you—"

"I would see him," Lady Catherine interrupted. She stopped in front of Elizabeth, but her cold gray eyes remained on the door. She in no way acknowledged her niece, who had committed the cardinal sin of accepting, and even embracing, her brother's low-born wife.

"Of course," Elizabeth said, leading the way inside.

"What is his condition?" Lady Catherine asked. She was looking at the top of the staircase now, and she kept her gaze there as they started up the steps.

"He has shown little improvement since the accident," Elizabeth said. "He remains extremely weak, and consciousness comes and goes. When he is sensible, he has great difficulty speaking."

"He seems to be plagued by horrible nightmares," Georgiana added, keeping her voice low to avoid being overheard by the genuflecting servants down in the foyer. "He sometimes struggles and cries out in his sleep."

"So," Lady Catherine said, "it has begun."

As they approached Darcy's bedchamber, she slipped nimbly around

Elizabeth and darted through the door.

"I will speak to you in the drawing room," she said, whirling around to look Elizabeth in the eye at last. "Alone."

Then she firmly closed the door, leaving Elizabeth and Georgiana in the hall.

"She has not forgiven us," Georgiana said as they walked away.

"Forgiveness, I suspect, is one of the few things her ladyship is incapable of. As is mercy."

"Yet here she is."

"Yes," Elizabeth said. She couldn't help feeling, however, that forgiveness and mercy had little to do with Lady Catherine's decision to come.

After sending Georgiana off to Pemberley's Shinto shrine to meditate and pray, Elizabeth settled in the drawing room and waited. And waited. And waited.

The last few days had been torture. Keeping her impassive mask in place, hiding her torment from Georgiana, lying to the household staff and the worried friends who'd come to call. "Disguise of every sort is my abhorrence," Darcy once said to her, and now his final days might be nothing but disguise, untruths, deception.

And the biggest lie of all, Elizabeth feared, was the one she kept telling herself: that, should Lady Catherine fail her, she would end her husband's fall into darkness with the stoic calm of a warrior. That her heart wouldn't shatter forever as she put her sword through his neck.

It occurred to her, as she pictured that moment against her will, that Darcy's aunt might have taken the responsibility upon herself—might in fact, at that very moment, be revenging herself upon the nephew who'd disobeyed and disappointed her. The old woman was a widow and thus free to walk about with her sword at her side. She'd gone into Darcy's room with a katana. Is that why she'd insisted on going in alone? Would she come downstairs and announce that she'd done what Elizabeth, ever the unworthy wife, had foolishly put off?

To look at Elizabeth, one would never have known this tempest of doubt raged within her. She merely sat upon a divan, eyes closed, hands clasped in her lap, and tried to focus on the image that most soothed and centered her *ch'i*: her darling Darcy on their wedding day. When even that brought only more heartache and agitation, she instead pictured Lady Catherine de Bourgh's bloody, broken body at her feet. It proved a more comforting thought.

Eventually, the real Lady Catherine appeared. Elizabeth rose and stood silently while the old woman claimed the room's largest, most thronelike bergère. Once she was sitting, she signaled, with a downward jerk of the chin, that Elizabeth could seat herself as well. Then she spoke.

"I am most displeased."

To Elizabeth's relief, her self-control was complete. She did not raise an eyebrow. She did not say what first leapt to mind: *Aren't you always?* She'd been waiting for more than half an hour to learn what the future held. She could wait another few seconds.

Lady Catherine gave her a long, imperious glare before continuing.

"My nephew was once one of the greatest warriors England has ever produced. Then he spurned me. Spurned my daughter, his true intended. And what comes of it? He is laid low by a stricken *child*."

Elizabeth had to suppress a flinch. Her letter hadn't mentioned the specifics of the attack that had—perhaps—damned her husband to living death. She'd simply said he'd been infected and time was of the essence. Lady Catherine must have examined the wound and somehow seen the truth. Say what one would about her (and there was much Elizabeth could never say, inappropriate as such language was for a lady), few people in the world knew the dreadfuls better than Lady Catherine de Bourgh.

The old woman shook her head in disgust.

"I told him the path he chose would end in ruin."

"Must it, though?" Elizabeth said quietly, careful to sound neither too demanding nor too weak. Both could bring the full weight of Lady

Catherine's considerable contempt down upon her. "Years ago, you were able to help my friend Charlotte Collins after she contracted the strange plague. You delayed her dark descent by months. I pray that you have since perfected the serum you once used on her."

"I have not. I have no cure." Lady Catherine paused, lips pursed, obviously gauging Elizabeth's reaction.

Elizabeth refused to give her one. Here was one butterfly who wouldn't writhe for her ladyship's pleasure, no matter how cruelly pinned.

"However . . . ," Lady Catherine finally said.

Thank heavens! thought Elizabeth, though her face remained as still as a stone Buddha's.

" . . . that does not mean no cure exists. I merely lack access to it at the moment. Procuring it would require me to extend myself. Substantially. And I'm not certain I should make the effort on behalf of those who have treated me with such insolence and disrespect."

"What must I do to sway you?"

Beg, that was what Elizabeth expected to hear in reply. But Lady Catherine had something else in mind. Something more.

"You know that I have always considered you an exceptionally presumptuous and obdurate creature," the old woman said. "So I must ask myself whether your pride will allow you to save the man whom you have seduced into dishonor and disaster. If I told you there was but one path to his salvation—and it was also the path to your utter degradation—would you, I wonder, be able to bend that stiff neck of yours and do what you must?"

"What is it you propose?"

Lady Catherine was silent. And so she remained until Elizabeth realized what she was waiting for.

"Yes," Elizabeth said. "I will do whatever you ask, if it might save my husband."

A look of grim satisfaction came over Lady Catherine's wrinkle-creased face, and her puckered lips spread slightly into what might have been the beginnings of a smile.

"Good," she said. "Then the first thing you must do is give him to me."

CHAPTER 4

For days, Darcy dreamed of sausages. Blood sausages packed with pig meat straight from the grinder. Uncooked. In his mouth.

He dreamed, too, of liver pâté. And haggis, of all things. And oysters he slurped from the shell, one after another. And sashimi from his beloved Japan served so fresh it was spongy with blood.

He dreamed he was a wolf eating a man alive.

He dreamed he was a man eating a wolf alive.

He dreamed he was a man eating . . . oh, now his skin *really* crawled! His dream had shifted in that sudden, lurching way of the worst nightmares, and everything had changed.

He found himself in his bed, his neck and left shoulder burning as his fearsome old aunt, Lady Catherine de Bourgh, sprinkled crimson liquid on him from a small glass vial. Then she was bringing the little bottle to his lips, pouring an acidic trickle down his throat, saying as he coughed, "Not so bitter as what I've had to swallow from *you*."

Then it was back to the haggis, only the stomach it was being served in wasn't a sheep's. It belonged to his wife . . . and it was still attached to her by slimy ropelike cords of flesh. "Eat up, my dear," Elizabeth said as he chomped in, and she reached into her abdomen and pulled out a glazed ham. "There's plenty more where that came from."

Darcy felt as if he would throw up. Yet, in his dreams, he kept eating and eating and never was full.

Eventually, the queasiness subsided and he stopped dreaming about food; his eyes fluttered open. He was in his bed, as in his nightmare, and his neck and shoulder hurt in just the same way, too. He reached up and touched the side of his neck and found what felt like bandages there.

Then he remembered.

"Oh, thank God," someone said.

He turned—how difficult it was just to swivel his head a few inches to the left—and saw Elizabeth kneeling next to him.

"I was afraid I wouldn't even get a chance to—" She stopped herself and smiled. "But here you are. How do you feel, my love?"

"Why am I still alive?" Darcy croaked.

His wife's smile faded.

"We have hopes the infection can be stopped."

"How?"

"I have sent for your aunt. You remember what she did for Charlotte Collins."

"I do. I remember what became of Charlotte Collins as well. I remember her—"

He coughed, unable to go on. But in Elizabeth's eyes, he could see her remembering, too.

Her old friend eating leaves; picking and licking at her own open sores; losing the ability to speak or think coherently; in short, deteriorating into a grotesque mockery of humanity.

Elizabeth brought a goblet of water to his lips, and as he took a soothing sip another memory returned: Lady Catherine forcing him to drink something that made his tongue tingle and his throat constrict. It had been no dream, he now knew.

"There have been improvements in the serum in recent years," Elizabeth said. "Your aunt believes it might cure you entirely if we act quickly enough."

"And I have already received my first dose?"

"Yes. The first of many—more than Lady Catherine was able to carry with her. She has asked that you be taken to Rosings to continue your convalescence there."

"I see. When do we leave?"

"Immediately. In fact, her ladyship's ninjas will be up shortly to collect you." Elizabeth paused, and when she forged on her words sounded strained, forced. "Georgiana will be going with you."

"Just Georgiana?"

"Yes. Jane has taken a turn for the worse, I'm afraid, and I must return to Fernworthy to look after her and the baby. It pains me no end that I cannot accompany you to Kent, but it is a comfort to know that your sister will be by your side and that your aunt has high hopes for your recuperation."

Again Elizabeth's voice struck Darcy as tight, her manner stiff and unnatural.

"Is it because of my aunt that you are not coming to Rosings?" he asked. "A renewal of the hostilities between you?"

Elizabeth shook her head. "No. If anything, she and I are more in accord than ever. Neither of us wishes for anything so fervently as your full recovery."

There was something about his wife's reassurances that Darcy found extremely *un*reassuring. It was a new sensation, not believing her, and he didn't care for it one bit.

He reached out and took her by the hand. "My dearest . . . please . . . is there something you're not telling me?"

"Has there ever been any deceit between us?" Elizabeth said. "A time when either of us was anything but entirely forthright?"

Well, technically, yes, Darcy could have answered. *Years ago, when your sister was in London looking for Bingley, for instance. The way I held back my true feelings for you for so long as well. And if we had both been more forthcoming about George Wickham all those years ago, we might have spared your family and others much unpleasantness.*

Darcy lacked the strength to say as much, however. Besides, Elizabeth was already leaning in to kiss him right between the eyes.

"I love you," she said, and this Darcy did not doubt—even as she shocked him by whirling and hurrying away. She kept her face turned to the side, as if there were something there she didn't wish him to see.

"Elizabeth—?"

"I will tell her ladyship that you are ready."

And she rushed from the room, leaving the door ajar behind her.

Darcy started to rise to follow her, but his head swam and his vision blurred and he ended up flat on his back, panting and nauseous. As he lay there, waiting for his strength to return so that he might try again, he heard the telltale *shush-shush* of tabi boots in the hall, so soft that no one untrained in the deadly arts would ever hear the sound. At least his ears remained as sharp as ever.

He managed to push himself up onto one elbow just as his aunt swept in with six ninjas at her heels.

"Fitzwilliam," the old woman said.

"Lady Catherine. It is good to see you, though there is nothing good, I'm afraid, about what you find here to see."

"No matter. What did the warrior monk Benkei say about failure?"

"It is but the longer road to triumph."

"Precisely. Wise words." The lady leaned in over her nephew's bed. "I find more truth in them all the time."

She pulled a handkerchief from her sleeve and pressed it over Darcy's nose and mouth. It felt moist and reeked of acrid fumes, and with his first startled intake of breath Darcy sucked in a biting flavor not unlike exceptionally strong coffee. Bitter though it was, it didn't taste like the serum she had administered earlier. It was something different—something Darcy would have recognized as undiluted laudanum, had he ever sampled any.

He reflexively pawed at his aunt's hand, but he was too weak to pull the handkerchief away. He grew weaker every second it stayed in place.

"This will help you travel," Lady Catherine said. "We have a long way to go together, you and I."

Soon after, Darcy was asleep.

This time, for a while at least, he didn't dream.

CHAPTER 5

It took four days to find them. Elizabeth hadn't even realized she'd been looking for them until she stepped into a pasture and spotted them feasting on a still-kicking cow they'd somehow managed to bring down.

Dreadfuls. Lots of them.

Just what she needed.

Every day since Lady Catherine whisked Darcy and Georgiana away in her carriage, Elizabeth had passed the daylight hours tramping up and down the lush wooded hills of Pemberley. She could do nothing but wait, for her ladyship had shared no details of the disgrace that apparently awaited her. Instructions would come once all was in readiness, she'd been told. There was nothing she could do to prepare—except, the lady had hinted, to practice swallowing her pride.

So she'd taken refuge, as she so often had in her life, in long, solitary walks. Only she hadn't wished them to be *so* solitary, she knew now. She'd been hoping for a particular kind of company.

Elizabeth sauntered toward the zombies, an opened parasol perched on one shoulder.

It had been difficult, these past four years, watching Darcy ride off to war whenever the summons came, waiting in futile frustration for news of distant battles she should have seen—and claimed heads in!—firsthand.

Georgiana had been free to join her brother, and often did. Even Elizabeth's own sisters, Mary and Kitty, occasionally fought by his side, for neither had taken a husband. (And neither ever would, if Elizabeth's mother had any say in the matter. They could be wedded to but one thing: caring for the aging matriarch of the Bennet family.)

Unmarried ladies taking up arms could be tolerated (barely) as long as Britain remained in peril. Yet for a wife to wade into battle would be an affront not just to her husband, whose duty it was to protect her, but to all English manhood. Elizabeth, despite her formidable skills, could be seen in public wielding nothing more deadly than a lace-fringed parasol.

Of course, she wasn't in public now, for no one was around to see her but a pack of dreadfuls and a few scattered cows, and they didn't count.

At last, one of the unmentionables spied her. It had been gnawing on a rubbery length of bowel, but now it dropped its meal midchew and staggered toward her. Though animals would do in a pinch, there wasn't a zombie alive (so to speak) who'd choose one over fresh homo sapiens.

The other dreadfuls took notice, and soon the whole bunch was scuttling in for the kill. They were a motley assortment, fresh next to rancid, rag-shrouded beside fashionably clothed, all united in the democracy of death.

When the nearest of the ghouls was about thirty feet off, Elizabeth stopped and calmly lifted the parasol from her shoulder. A single tug on the handle simultaneously released the razors running along the ribs and the small sword hidden in the shaft. With her left hand, she sent the top of the parasol spinning through the air to remove as many limbs as it might, while with her right hand she brought up the sword, having already picked out the first three necks it would slice through. After they were seen to, she would improvise.

It all went smoothly enough . . . to Elizabeth's disappointment. Aside from one particularly dogged and shrieking she-zombie who kept flailing at her, even after both forearms and most of her face were littering the

"SHE SENT THE TOP OF THE PARASOL SPINNING THROUGH THE AIR TO REMOVE AS MANY LIMBS AS IT MIGHT."

grass, there were no surprises, and Elizabeth was unable to lose herself in battle as she'd hoped. It was just like the day Darcy fell, when he'd tried to cheer her with a little nostalgic slaughter. It hadn't worked then and it wasn't working now. Even as she hacked and slashed and vaulted and kicked, her thoughts kept returning to the road not far away where her husband had fallen to a single unmentionable child. Because of her moodiness. Her perverseness. *Her.*

When the last of the dreadfuls lay in pieces at her feet, Elizabeth reassembled her parasol (a cherished wedding gift from her father) and strolled back to the manor, still plagued by all the guilt and apprehension she'd sought to escape. How many more days would she have to endure?

The answer was waiting for her at Pemberley House.

"There you are, Ma'am!" Mrs. Reynolds cried as Elizabeth stepped out of the woods. The housekeeper came scurrying down the front steps holding an envelope aloft. "I've been looking for you everywhere! We've received a message from her ladyship!"

Elizabeth darted forward, took the letter, and started to tear it open while Mrs. Reynolds hovered anxiously nearby. All that the servants knew was that Darcy had been taken to Kent to be cared for by his aunt's personal physician. With each day that passed without news of their injured master (or of the missing boy, Andrew Brayles), the household slipped deeper into gloom and despair.

Elizabeth pulled out the message—then remembered what it might contain.

"Thank you, Mrs. Reynolds," she said, stuffing the letter back in its envelope. "I'll be meditating if you need me for anything else."

She left the housekeeper to wring her hands and furrow her brow on the front lawn.

Once Elizabeth was settled in the Shinto shrine that took up most of the east wing, she sat on the floor, crossed her legs, and took in forty soothing breaths while reciting her mantra exactly eighty times. Then she looked at the envelope in her hands.

It was addressed to "Elizabeth B.-D.," and the pages inside contained no greeting line at all. "Elizabeth Darcy," "Mrs. Fitzwilliam Darcy," "Dear Elizabeth"—Lady Catherine obviously couldn't bring herself to write any of it. Even that "B." she had to slip in so as to somehow negate the "D."

In lieu of empty pleasantries, her ladyship began her message with a warning.

Read quickly and commit all you see to memory, for you will have no record of what I tell you in but a few minutes' time. You are about to learn secrets no one of your station has ever been privy to, and even a personage as high-born as I would lose everything—including my very life—if certain parties in London learned I had enlightened such as you. Should the undertaking I lay before you end in failure and your true intent be revealed, I will deny having told you anything of what follows, will accuse you of acquiring your knowledge of it through subterfuge and guile, and will, in fact, possess the loudest voice calling for your immediate execution.

If you now find your fortitude faltering, screw your courage to this: Darcy lives, but there can be no doubt that the plague is in him. Just this morning, I found him gnawing on his own toes in his sleep, and when I roused him he told me he'd been dreaming of eating boeuf bourguignon. His slide into the service of Satan has begun, and the serum will only slow that so long. If you still intend to honor your pledge to me, you must act immediately and in unswerving compliance with my instructions. If you do not so intend, stop reading here and begin planning your husband's funeral.

First, the facts. The serum I once used on your friend, the unfortunate Mrs. Collins, was not, as I told you at the time, of my own creation, nor was it administered at its full strength. In truth, the elixir is made available, in miserly amounts, only to those of special interest to the Crown. Though its provenance has been kept secret even from them, there have been whispers in recent months that it has been improved to such a degree that, at long last, it might serve as an actual cure. These rumors inspired me to make my own private inquiries and, through much effort and expense, I have learned that the serum is the handiwork of one of the king's personal physicians, Dr. Sir Angus MacFarquhar, and is most likely produced within the confines of the infamous cesspit of insanity and squalor he oversees—Bethlem Hospital. Though once open to the public, Bethlem today is a virtual fortress, and the loss of many a ninja has taught me that the place is impregnable. We must try a different tack if we are to acquire the cure before my nephew succumbs to the strange plague. We must go through Sir Angus himself.

This is the plan of attack: You shall take up residence in town posing as a nouveau-riche widow, you will throw yourself into Sir Angus's path until a connection is established, and you will work your way into his confidence so completely that he will, intentionally or unintentionally, willingly or unwillingly, give us what we want. You will, in short, seduce and betray him. I have little doubt this task is within your power, for I'm told Sir Angus is a widower in desperate need of money, and what's more you have already proved once before that you possess formidable skill when it comes to entrapping a man of rank high above your own.

If you intend to honor your side of our bargain and proceed along the path I propose, you need send no reply to say so. I have eyes everywhere. Your immediate departure for London will be assent enough. Enter the city at the Northern Guard Tower, name yourself at the gate as Mrs. Mathias Bromhead of Manchester, and you will be taken in hand from there. I, of course, will be engaged at Rosings, doing all in my power to save the life we both hold so dear.

You must do the same in London. No matter how shameful you might find your own actions to be, they are necessary, and that, as always, should trump either warrior's pride or the squeamishness of weaklings.

You can have your precious honor or you can have your precious Darcy. One or the other must be set upon the pyre. Which it shall be I leave to you.

If you have reached these final lines without singeing your fingers, I would suggest depositing this letter in the nearest fireplace and standing back, for—

The pages in Elizabeth's hands began to smoke of their own accord, and a split second after she dropped them, they burst into flame. By the time they'd finished their fluttering flight to the floor, there was little left but swirling ash and cinders.

Everything was rapidly crumbling to dust at Elizabeth's feet, it seemed. Everything.

CHAPTER 6

Oscar Bennet was a man who appreciated peace and quiet. Yet for years his library had been the only place he could find either. Out in the green fields of Hertfordshire were the shambling, ever-ravenous escapees from Hell that it was his sworn duty to return to Satan in as many pieces as possible. His home, meanwhile, had been invaded long ago by more alarming creatures still—a swarm of strong-willed females. One foe he fought fearlessly. In the face of the other, his preferred tactic had been, most frequently, retreat to his book-lined safe hold.

Things had changed in recent years. Oscar Bennet had peace, of sorts, if not always quiet. (His wife's silences were like those of the battlefield: rare and brief and offering no relief, for they only gave one time to wonder what nerve-fraying onslaught might rain down next.) The dreadfuls still had to be dealt with, but the far fouler curse—that of unwed daughters and an estate entailed to a male relation—had been lifted. The Bennets' eldest girls had been joined in marriage to wealthy men, and no longer would worries of dowries and entailments weigh on the family.

Scandal, too, was something Mr. and Mrs. Bennet no longer needed to fear, for their youngest daughter, Lydia, had also been successfully married off—the match being "successful" only in the sense that a ring was on her finger before a child was in her womb. Mr. Bennet considered this a great triumph, given Lydia's character, which had been her own particular entailment from her mother. Lydia had always been a wild child, as much a slave to her impulses as any unmentionable, and it was a thing to savor that a husband, rather than her father, was accountable for her capriciousness. As Mrs. George Wickham, she was free to fill up the world with offspring as feckless and reckless as she, and this she had immediately set to doing. And if none of them looked a jot like *Mr.* George Wickham, what was that to Oscar Bennet?

Huzzah! Sweet freedom!

Yet Mr. Bennet had discovered something surprising about freedom from fear. It can be rather boring. Without challenges or strife or the struggle for something better and new, peace and quiet could seem very much like stagnation. It was, after all, peaceful and quiet in a grave. Or had been, once upon a time.

There was always an easy way to liven things up, though, especially in the spring when the undead emerged from the holes and caves and other hiding places in which they weathered the cold winter winds that stiffened them like snow-covered statues. One could go on patrol.

"I have yet to see a dreadful roosting in a tree," Mr. Bennet said.

His second-youngest daughter, Catherine "Kitty" Bennet, was near the top of a particularly tall elm at the time, swinging from branch to branch like a gown-wearing ape.

"I'm merely looking for the best vantage point from which to survey the area," Kitty said.

"You are merely showing off," her sister Mary replied. It was not really her place to criticize, Mr. Bennet thought, for she had spent the last hour idly spinning her katana with her right hand while holding up Mary Wollstonecraft's *A Vindication of the Rights of Woman* with her left. She knew the roads and footpaths of Hertfordshire so well she'd covered the last mile without once looking up from her book.

"Why would I bother showing off for you and Papa?" Kitty snipped back even as she did a double back-flip that sent her spinning to another branch.

"Because no young gentleman is around to show off for instead," Mary said.

"Simply exercising one's abilities is not showing off. At any rate, what respectable gentleman would take an interest in a girl who can do this?" Kitty grabbed a branch and swung around and around until the bark started chafing off under her calloused hands. "Or this?" She let go on an upswing, flinging herself to the top of the next tree. "Or this?" She executed a perfect swan dive, plummeting to within feet of the ground before grabbing the last available branch and slinging herself back to where she started.

Mary never stopped reading.

"Why should you care what a man makes of any of it?" she said.

"Because, unlike you, within me there resides a beating human heart, not an abacus for tallying the faults of others."

"If you read more books like this"—Mary gave Wollstonecraft's manifesto a little shake—"and fewer of those wretched novels you love so dearly, you would know the difference between the true concerns of the heart and the sentimental drivel peddled by romantic fantasists."

"You just say that because you gave up on romance years ago. Why, I haven't seen you give the handsomest man a second glance since Master Hawksworth went and—"

"Now you are being ridiculous!" Mary snapped.

Ridiculous or not, Kitty seemed to realize she'd gone too far. She ended the conversation with a groaned, "Oh, how I miss Lydia."

As always, Mr. Bennet stayed out of the fray. It made him uncomfortable when Mary and Kitty discussed anything related to *amour*, for there was a reason such things remained, for them, hypotheticals and conjectures and not the stuff of real experience.

With three of the Bennets' five daughters safely ensconced in the bonds of matrimony, his wife had abandoned the arranging of marriages and devoted herself instead to the preventing of them. She was determined that her unmarried daughters should *remain* her unmarried daughters—and, more important, her companions and nursemaids in her "declining years" (a phrase Mrs. Bennet was fond of repeating, even though, to judge by sheer verbiage, she was, if anything, on the incline). Mr. Bennet had much more faith in his wife's abilities as a matchbreaker than he'd ever had in her as a matchmaker. Indeed, a mere five minutes in a drawing room with her had driven off more than one would-be suitor. As a result, Mary and Kitty had, for years now, no new suitors to drive off.

"Do you know what I've just realized?" Mr. Bennet said. "It has been forever since we checked the quarry at St. Albans. Do you remember the herd we found crammed into the old clay pit? All they could do was moan as we dropped rock after rock on them. Why, they were packed in together like a bunch of frozen kippers!"

Kitty gave her father's jest (and his obvious attempt to change the subject) a half-hearted "La!"

Mary simply said, "To St. Albans, then?" But then she lowered her book and turned her head to the left.

Up in the treetops, Kitty stopped her acrobatics and turned to face the same direction.

Mr. Bennet didn't hear the sound for another few seconds, but finally it penetrated his age-weakened ears: gasps and struggling and the creaking of strained rope.

Without a word, the Bennets followed the sound deeper into the forest. It wasn't long before the smell came to them: Dead flesh lay ahead. The kind that gets up and walks around and tries to make more dead flesh.

Mr. Bennet raised the crossbow he'd been carrying. Mary tucked her book under her sword belt and put both hands on her katana. Kitty dropped out of the trees with her pistols drawn. A moment later, they reached the clearing. In its center was a single, ancient oak. From its thickest branch hung a woman with bulging eyes and a swollen purple face. She'd been dead about two days, Mr. Bennet judged. Time enough for her to decide she'd like to come down.

Zombies being zombies, of course, she wasn't meeting with much success. Along with losing all scruples about eating other people, the undead awoke without the capacity for reason. All this particular dreadful could do was thrash and kick and spin in sad circles, dangling on its death rope.

When it saw the Bennets, it thrashed and kicked all the harder.

"See, Papa?" Kitty said. "They *do* sometimes roost in trees!"

"It's Julia Goswick," Mary observed.

If Kitty had been about to unleash another "La!" it never left her lips.

"Oh. So it is," she said, sounding subdued (for her). Julia Goswick had been one of the Bennet girls' prime romantic rivals, once. "I should have recognized that horrid morning dress straight off. I must say, she did quite a nice job with the rope. I would not have thought her capable of tying her own bonnet."

Julia Goswick's mortal remains swiped angrily at them every time its face spun in their direction.

"Do either of you have any idea why Miss Goswick would do such a thing to herself?" Mr. Bennet asked.

He got the answer he was expecting.

"She had been disappointed in love," Mary said.

"People were starting to call her an old maid," Kitty added. "She was four and twenty, you know."

"I see."

Kitty was twenty-one, Mary twenty-two.

"Foolish, emotional woman," Mary spat with no shortage of her own emotion. "Mary Wollstonecraft says—"

"*Mary*."

Kitty's one word sufficed. Her sister fell silent.

"Well," Mr. Bennet said, and he brought up his crossbow and shot a bolt through the rope holding Julia Goswick aloft. She landed on her feet, her ankles and knees splintering with audible pops. Kitty raised a pistol as the unmentionable staggered toward them on wobbly gelatin legs, its mouth gaping wide for a zombie roar that was strangled by the noose still tight around its neck.

Before Kitty could pull the trigger, Mary slipped in front of her and charged the zombie alone. She ducked under its first clumsy grab and then straightened and swung her katana.

The dreadful's head slid slowly backward off its neck.

"I thought it might be best to be discreet," Mary said as body followed crown into the underbrush, "without gunfire to explain to those who might overhear it."

Mr. Bennet walked over to the corpse. "Good thinking." (How very long it seemed since he'd said anything of that kind.) He removed a small flask from his pocket and liberally drizzled the contents over what was left of Julia Goswick. "We shall spare the family the shame of a suicide. Allow them to hope that she ran off to Edinburgh with some young rake."

"Yes. A likely story," Kitty said as the burn-acid did its work, the body bursting into hot, nearly smokeless flame. "And who could blame her?"

The Bennets waited silently until nothing remained but chunky ash. Then they cut down the rest of the rope and, by unspoken consensus, turned and headed for home. Kitty kept her feet on the ground all the way, Mary's book remained closed, and no one spoke a word.

As was his way before heading into the house (and the company of his wife), Mr. Bennet sent his daughters ahead, retiring alone to his modest garden dojo for a quarter hour's meditation. He sat on the floor, crossed his legs, closed his eyes, and silently repeated his mantra ("The soaring eagle sees all, hears nothing") until he felt the serenity he needed to venture inside.

He got only as far as his second "soaring eagle," however, when a swirl of air, the slightest breeze stirred by furtive movement, blew across his face. Opening his eyes, Mr. Bennet found lying on the floor before him an envelope inscribed with his name. He looked around the dojo, leapt to his feet, and then dashed to the doorway, but the messenger was already gone.

Hears nothing, indeed. Someone practiced in stealth—a ninja, no doubt—had been hiding in the rafters or a weapons locker and managed to slip past him almost undetected.

He was getting old.

Mr. Bennet walked back to the envelope, picked it up, and opened it. The letter inside read thusly:

> *If you value the happiness of your daughter Elizabeth, you will come to London immediately. The life of her husband, my nephew, Fitzwilliam Darcy, hangs in the balance under circumstances that require the utmost secrecy. Should you reveal the reason for your journey, it would surely doom it to end in disaster—and would condemn you, I promise, to the death by a thousand cuts, each of them inflicted with no great haste by my own sword.*
>
> *You may share the truth with but one person, for she is required in London also: that daughter of yours who has been favored both with my name and, I can only hope, enough discretion and skill not to dishonor it. Bring her with you to Massingberd's, Colebrooke Row, One North, and your role in Mr. Darcy's salvation will be made plain.*
>
> *Fail to heed me, and you bring ruin upon not only him to whom you owe so much but also the daughter who has inveigled her way into his good graces and my ill.*

The letter was unsigned, but there was no question from whom it came. Mr. Bennet read it quickly and then simply let it go, having recognized the smell and feel of Shinobi flash paper. He didn't even glance down as the magnesium bound into the parchment reacted to the air and the oil on his fingers and ignited with the flickering white light of a shooting star. He would not dignify the spectacle with his attention. As far as he was concerned, the flash paper was a cheap, high-handed, melodramatic ploy—and, being designed to impress and intimidate him, it was entirely unnecessary. He was impressed and intimidated already.

Lady Catherine de Bourgh was a great warrior, a national hero, a living legend, and, by all accounts, a monumentally vindictive bitch. She was neither someone to be trifled with nor, given her bitterness toward Elizabeth, someone to be trusted. His daughter had married the man Her Ladyship had chosen for her own. Perhaps she intended to avenge herself with some perversely roundabout trap.

But, if so, why bait *him* into it? With Kitty? In North London?

In the end, two things decided him. One of Lady Catherine's silent assassins had been in his dojo while he meditated, utterly oblivious, and had merely left him a message rather than take his life. If the lady had wanted him dead, there was no need to command him to London to see it done. And whether she was lying about the danger to Darcy, this much was certain: Elizabeth needed his help.

He would do as the letter instructed.

Once his decision was made, he found his concern for his favorite daughter tinged by something that felt very much like excitement. Ashamed by the emotion, not understanding it, he sought, in the best English manner, to ignore it. There were more important things to consider than his own mixed feelings—the campaign he had to plan, for instance. His foe would be wily and tenacious, yet it was crucial that he outwit her.

How could he get Kitty to London without Mrs. Bennet learning of it and insisting on coming along?

Mr. Bennet settled himself back on the floor, closed his eyes, and thought again of the soaring eagle seeing all and hearing nothing. He didn't rise until he, too, was ready to soar once more.

CHAPTER 7

The first thing Darcy became aware of was the fact that he was aware. This was a change of pace.

All was blackness and had been ever since . . . something. Somewhere. Somewhen. The difference now was that he knew the blackness for what it was. He remembered the possibility of light.

His consciousness dragged itself from the abyss a little more, enough for him to feel surprise that he was alive. If this was living.

A nameless dread stirred deep within him. If he wasn't alive, then what was this? Damnation? Limbo? What else was there that wasn't life but wasn't death?

An image flashed into his mind, obliterating all thought: a steak and kidney pie, the crust golden brown and steaming, the minced center bloody and raw and liberally garnished with . . . were those fingers?

His stomach growled.

His eyes opened.

Still, all was black.

No. Not *all* black. The more he stared into it, the more he could make out black-black and gray-black and brown-black in patterns that remained indistinct yet strangely familiar. There was a comforting quality to it all. It felt almost like home.

Surely, he *was* home, for out of the corner of his eye he noticed the outline of a slender woman at his bedside. She had dark hair and dark eyes and seemed to be wearing the black mourning dress of a widow. Or a widow-to-be.

"Elizabeth."

He reached out and took her by the hand . . . a cold, bony hand that could belong to his wife only if she'd spent the past week fasting in an ice house.

Darcy tried to snatch back his hand, but skeletal fingers clamped tightly over his.

"It's all right, Fitzwilliam. You're safe. You're with *me*."

The woman leaned closer, her face piercing a stray shaft of moonlight cutting through the room, and Darcy found himself holding hands with Lady Catherine's daughter, his cousin, Anne de Bourgh.

She looked as gaunt and sallow as the last time he'd seen her. *Exactly* as gaunt and sallow, in fact. She hadn't changed a bit in the past four years. She was a ghostly, ghastly, listless little thing, and at one time Darcy would've guessed that the slightest breeze from a drafty window would be enough to puff her into the afterlife. She'd obviously managed to survive if not thrive, however, carrying on in her immutable, enervated way, like an old tortoise or a spindly tree.

"You have nothing to worry about anymore," she said. "Nothing to fear."

Her words only served to remind him what he did have to fear, even if the details remained hazy. He brought his free hand up to his neck. The bandages were still there. "I wish I could agree with you."

"Oh, but you should. Even the strange plague is no match for Lady Catherine the Great."

"You know what's happened to me, then?"

Anne nodded, her eyes filled with compassion rather than the revulsion Darcy would have thought his due.

"Yes. I know. It doesn't bother me. We're all family here."

At last Darcy realized where *here* was and why it had seemed so familiar. He had awakened in a bed he knew well—the one in his favorite guest room at Rosings. The memory of his last conversation with Elizabeth came to him then as well. Darcy found himself eager to forget it again.

He managed to free his hand from his cousin's icy grip. The fingers had gone numb.

Anne retreated, and her features were swallowed by darkness, turning her again into little more than the muddled outline of a woman. In a way, that was how Darcy was used to seeing her—though the shadows in which his cousin eternally dwelled had, in the past, been cast mainly by her mother.

"Is Georgiana here?" he said. "I . . . I seem to remember that she was with me during the journey from Derbyshire. I should very much like to speak with her."

"She's asleep. She has been for hours."

"What time is it?"

Anne's silhouette shifted, seemed to grow and then contract.

She was shrugging.

"Three? Four? I can't remember the last time I heard chimes from downstairs."

"Three or four? What are you doing in my room?"

Anne giggled. The coquettishness of it caught Darcy off guard. He'd known this woman all her life, yet her laughter seemed like something new and strange to him.

"I'm watching over you, silly," she said.

"Aren't you tired?"

"Always . . . and never. Sleep hardly seems to make a difference. I certainly haven't missed it tonight."

"It was very kind of you to keep vigil. You need not trouble yourself any longer, however. I think I'll sleep all the more soundly in solitude."

"I understand." Anne rose to go. "I will always be near if you need me. You can rest assured of that."

She bent over Darcy and brushed his forehead with lips that were as cold as her hands. It was like being kissed by a granite slab. Then she turned and left without making a sound.

She was so quiet, in fact, and the room was so dark that Darcy couldn't be sure she'd really gone. Indeed, her presence seemed to linger in the air, hovering like the must of mold and decay in a cobwebbed attic. No matter how long he lay there, perfectly still, perfectly silent, Darcy couldn't quite feel he was alone.

Anne had promised to stay near him, and somehow Darcy knew she meant it. It did not, however, help him "rest assured."

He didn't sleep again all night.

CHAPTER 8

The worst thing about being a master of the deadly arts, Kitty Bennet thought, was the wardrobe. Sparring gowns, battle gowns, executioner's gowns—it didn't matter. They were all dull dull *dull*!

A warrior's clothes had to be sleek, simple, functional; she understood that. No one wanted to trip over their own train just as they were about to disembowel an enemy, and there was no way to justify white kid gloves when armored gauntlets would be more apropos. Still, what would be so wrong with a little color? A little allure? A little lace trim or show of décolletage? She'd put flowers in her hair the second morning of the Battle of the Cotswolds, and you'd have thought she'd reported for duty in nothing but her petticoat, her father was so furious.

"If you want to keep these soldiers' respect," he'd growled, "you won't go prancing up and down the lines looking like an Alsatian milkmaid."

"I'd have thought the number of notches on my sword hilt would be enough to ensure respect."

"You have more kills than any one company here, it's true." Her father reached out, gently drew a daffodil from behind her ear, and then crumpled it, letting it fall to the blood-soaked ground. "Yet you'll always have more to prove, too."

So here she was, on her way to London—during the Season, even!—and rather than a fashionable spencer and a new shawl, she was draped in plain, shapeless, gray muslin with a katana hanging at her side. Just when she should be turning heads, she was instead dressed for removing them with as little fuss as possible.

To make matters even worse, she and her father were traveling by stagecoach rather than the family's own carriage. The convention of crossbow manufacturers to which they were going was being held in the tiny village of Wapping-on-the-Dunghill in Lincolnshire, Mr. Bennet had explained, and he had it on good authority that there remained no reliable liveries in the area with room for their horses. (It was only later, once they'd left Hertfordshire, that Mr. Bennet discovered he'd misread the convention invitation and their destination should be, instead, London.)

Not only was the coach cramped and crowded and stuffy, without even the ventilation to dispel the various smells generated by the other passengers, but each time a new spring flock of unmentionables staggered onto the road, all eyes turned to the Bennets. By the time they reached the city's Northern Guard Tower, Kitty and her father had put down no fewer than thirty dreadfuls. And they were thanked for it, yes, but always a little stiffly, sometimes even begrudgingly, as one might thank an unexpected guest for a gift one doesn't want. It had been decades since the first Englishman took up the deadly arts—and only slightly less since Kitty's namesake, Lady Catherine de Bourgh, became the first English*woman* to follow in his footsteps—yet the citizenry as a whole still seemed to need convincing.

Even the handsome soldier who poked his head into the compartment to check for signs of the strange plague seemed to smirk when he saw her battle gown and sword, and as the coach rolled through the gate a moment later, Kitty began plotting ways to escape her father so that she might go shopping for *real* clothes in the fashionable boutiques of Four Central and Five East. She knew she wouldn't follow through on such plans, though. Not without Lydia there to give her strength . . . and better bad ideas.

Not thirty minutes after arriving in town, Kitty and Mr. Bennet were leaving their baggage at an inn and heading off to see the very latest in crossbows. To Kitty's surprise, her father instructed her to take her throwing stars and nunchucks in addition to her katana, and he had upon him his sword cane, a brace of pistols, a stiletto, and an American tomahawk of which he'd grown especially fond.

"Really, Papa. I don't see the need for us to attend this convention of yours," Kitty said as they walked up a bustling, storefront-lined road. "You've got a dozen perfectly good crossbows at home, and bolts enough to win Agincourt all over again."

"It was longbows that carried the day at Agincourt, my child."

"Longbows, crossbows, hair bows, rainbows—that's not the point. You don't need any new weapons, Papa. Why, just look at you. You're already carrying such an arsenal I'm worried you'll herniate yourself. La!"

Mr. Bennet winced, as he so often did when Kitty let loose with the little bark of merriment that had been her sister Lydia's sole contribution to the family (aside from acute dyspepsia).

"I suppose you'd rather we just ducked into one of these nice little shops, hmm?" he said. "Maybe see what we can find you in the way of an evening dress?"

"Oh, goodness, no! I was thinking nothing of the kind."

"I am relieved to hear it."

Kitty waved a hand at the haberdashery they were passing. "I couldn't go back to Meryton and tell people I'd bought a new dress in *One North*! Everyone would think me a perfect fool!"

"And they wouldn't be wr—" Mr. Bennet cut himself off with a sigh.

"That's neither here nor there. We have more important things to discuss."

"Crossbows?"

"No, my child. Not crossbows . . . though weapons may come into it. There is something I haven't told you, and it can be put off no longer."

This proved to be untrue, however, for he stopped suddenly and stared in puzzlement at a black box about twenty yards ahead. It was waist high, with three wheels—two on the sides, attached by an axle, and a third protruding from the back. A small leather harness was bolted to the front, but it lay on the ground, limp and empty.

Bookending the box were two mongrel dogs sitting with such perfect stillness it was only Kitty's Shaolin-sharpened senses that allowed her to detect the shallow in and out of their breathing.

"Odd sort of box," Mr. Bennet said. "I could've sworn I saw one just like it at the gate as we entered the city."

"I didn't notice anything."

"You were still leaning out the window to admire the captain of the guard at the time. You seemed to find him quite mesmerizing."

"Oh, don't be silly, Papa! I was merely, ah, studying the fortifications thereabouts."

"Yes, I'm sure you were."

As they drew closer to the box, Kitty spied a narrow slot cut across the front, toward the top. A handbill, painted with such clumsiness it could barely be read, had been tacked crookedly beneath it. "VETERAN," it read. "I LOST MY LIMBS. YOU CAN SPARE A SHILLING."

They were close enough to hear the rasps emanating from inside and see the rheumy, reddened eyes that peered out through the slit.

Kitty had stood her ground before scores of putrid ghouls still chewing on their last victims. Yet *now* she wanted to flee.

Her father stopped directly in front of the box.

"Good afternoon," he said.

The voice that answered was whispery and sibilant, just as the serpent must have sounded when it tempted Eve.

"If you say so," it said. "I awake each morning dreaming that the dreadfuls had finished making a meal of me all those years ago instead of stopping at my arms, legs, ears, and nose. All that remains of me is a lumpy blob for which there is no use but this: sitting on street corners reminding children to say their prayers at night so that God, in His infinite mercy, might spare them the fate he didn't spare me. Yet you, Sir, pause to wish me a 'good afternoon'? Well, I shall try my best."

There was a thumping from inside the box, and the clink of metal on metal.

"I have jumped for joy, Sir," the man in the box said. "Please give generously."

Mr. Bennet removed a coin from his pocket and slipped it through the slot.

"A sovereign, Sir? Indeed, the afternoon *has* improved. Ell, Arr—wag your tails for the gentleman and his lovely daughter."

The dogs did as they were told.

"Come along now, Papa," Kitty said, taking her father by the arm. "We don't want to miss a single shooting demonstration, do we? They might run out of unmentionables before we get there."

Mr. Bennet carried on with her up the street, but his pace was slow, his expression troubled.

"What is it, Papa?"

"I don't know. I have the nagging feeling there's something I should be remembering, but I can't think what."

"I know! You were about to tell me that we're off to Four Central to shop for bonnets!"

"Most assuredly not. It had something to do with . . . " Mr. Bennet glanced over his shoulder and then shook his head and shrugged. "At any rate, I was just about to tell you where we *are* going. I have good news and bad news, my child. Which would you like to hear first?"

"Oh, always the good news, Papa! Always!"

"Of course. Well, then . . . there is no crossbow convention."

"What? Then why are we here?"

"That, I'm afraid, is the bad news."

Mr. Bennet stopped again. To their right was a winding street so narrow it could barely pass as a tunnel, let alone an alley. Unlike the broad, busy avenue the Bennets had been walking along, this one was dark and deserted, with rubbish heaped against the buildings like snowdrifts and but one shop sign poking out into the shadows about forty feet off.

W. W. MASSINGBERD
BUTCHER, POULTERER, PURVEYOR OF WILD GAME
CAN'T AFFORD A PHYSICIAN?
INFECTED LIMBS REMOVED AT HALF THE PRICE

Mr. Bennet looked at the sign and sighed.

"We came all this way to meet a butcher?" Kitty asked.

"That remains to be seen," her father said. "Here is our state of affairs: Either your brother-in-law Mr. Darcy is in some grave danger and we have been enlisted to help save him or *we* are in grave danger and will, quite soon, be fighting for our lives."

"You don't know which?"

"No." Mr. Bennet raised his cane and pointed it at the sign. "But I do know where we'll find out."

"All right, then," Kitty said, and without a second's hesitation she tugged her father toward the butcher's shop. "Why didn't you tell me about Mr. Darcy sooner?"

"Because discretion was called for, and with some, the only way to ensure it is through complete ignorance."

"I resent that, Father."

"As well you should."

The old Kitty—the one who was but an extension of Lydia, a pale shadow cast by the stronger spirit—would have done more complaining. And the new Kitty did indeed put on a prodigious pout. Yet she did so silently. Unlike her younger sister, she didn't enjoy the sound of her own voice so much that she couldn't deprive herself of its mellifluousness, if need be. And something told her need was.

At Shaolin Temple on Mount Song, she'd been taught to listen with such intensity that the falling of grains in an hourglass resounded like the cascade of a waterfall. She was used to the silences of the glens and meadows: It was easy to pick out the shuffle of a dreadful's gait when all that might obscure it was the singing of starlings and the rustling of windblown leaves. But this was London, and echoing up and down the narrow lane were the sounds of clattering hooves and rumbling wagons and bellowing street peddlers.

Mixed in with the din was something softer that came and went too quickly to be pinpointed, leaving in its wake nothing more than a tingle across the back of the neck. Kitty was straining to catch it again when a high whiny sound, like the drone of small wheels rolling over cobblestones, bounced up the street from behind them. Both she and her father looked back, but nothing was there.

When they turned toward the butcher's shop again, they found four men before them, dressed all in black from head to toe. Kitty heard another noise behind her—a shushing thud, this time—and she didn't need to look around to know more ninjas had dropped from the rooftops to cut off their escape.

"Well," her father said. "It seems we have the answer we sought. I'm sorry, my child."

"Oh, that's all right, Papa. But if we live out the day, you shall owe me a new cashmere shawl at the very least."

One of the ninjas stepped closer. Like his comrades, he hadn't drawn his weapon, though his right hand rested on the hilt of a katana.

"You will give us your weapons," he said.

Kitty gave him her sweetest smile instead.

"With pleasure." She whipped up her right arm, and a dagger popped out of her sleeve and into her hand. She jerked her left arm sideways across her body, and two throwing stars were instantly in her fingers. "Which ones would you like first . . . and where?"

CHAPTER 9

Elizabeth wasn't traveling alone. There was the coachman, of course, as well as the musket men who sat atop the Darcys' brougham, popping off the occasional shot at unmentionables lurking near the road. Yet that was hardly company, and Elizabeth, on her own in the passenger compartment, had never felt so alone.

It didn't have to be. There'd been a moment, as she was sending word of her trip to Fernworthy, that she'd been tempted to tell Jane of her troubles. Elizabeth knew what her sister would do: drag herself from bed and insist on accompanying her.

Which was why, when she finished her note to Jane, it made no mention of Darcy's condition or the incredible, disgraceful course of action Lady Catherine had proposed for saving him. Jane was too weak to be much help, and, what's more, Elizabeth could not have accepted her aid had it been offered. Her sister had found a contentment that Elizabeth feared she could never share. She would do nothing to imperil that happiness. She would shoulder her burden alone.

The dreadfuls posed a serious problem only once during the journey to London, when they stormed an inn at which Elizabeth had stopped for the night. They were few in number, and most were still stiff and sluggish from their winter's sleep. Elizabeth stood back while the villagers beat them to mush with the cheap clublike "Zed rods" that had of late become popular with the yeomanry.

At least when I am a widow, she thought, *I will be free again to do more than watch*.

She was so mortified to find herself thinking such a thing that she immediately retired to her room and administered the first of the seven cuts of shame. But she stopped there. Best to pace herself. She knew that, in the coming days, there would be much, much more to shame her.

As the coach sped south the next morning, a gray blob on the horizon loomed ever larger. The lower half was "Britain's Barrier"—the Great Wall of London. The upper half was the vast cloud of smoke that hung over the city thanks to the factories and crematoria continuously belching ash into the dreary sky.

The brougham came to a stop while still far away from it all. A line of coaches and wagons more than a mile long stretched from the Northern Guard Tower, and it took hours just to be near enough to spot the red-coated soldiers stationed at the gate. The queue was full of merchants and peddlers and performers, all drawn to town by the upcoming recoronation of George III. The king, finally cured of his "nervous exhaustion" (otherwise known as "insanity" when it afflicts those of lower rank), was about to reclaim his throne. The Regency was ending, and London was set to host such celebrations as hadn't been seen in a generation. Which meant, of course, that there was money to be made, and on a grand scale. It irritated Elizabeth to be stuck there among the fortune hunters, but she knew her timing might have been even worse: It wouldn't be long before the tourists started pouring in.

At long last, the brougham reached the gate, and the captain of the guard appeared alongside. He was a man of just the type Lydia and Kitty found so irresistible: young and brightly uniformed, with bland good looks unmarred by either scars or excessive character.

"Name, place of residence, and reason for entry?" he said.

"I am Mrs. Mathias Bromhead of Manchester, and I have come for the king's recoronation."

Elizabeth knew by heart all the questions that should follow. Did

“A LINE OF COACHES AND WAGONS A MILE LONG STRETCHED OUT FROM THE NORTHERN GUARD TOWER.”

she have among her baggage any cadavers or body parts? Had she come into contact with an unmentionable within the past fortnight? Were there upon her person any festering bites or scratches? Et cetera. Then the officer would wave the brougham through with a lazy flap of the hand.

Not today.

"To the side, if you please." The soldier pointed to a candy-striped sentry box off to the right. "Over there."

"What's this about, Mrs.—?" the coachman began.

"Just do as he says, Gregory," Elizabeth broke in. "I'm sure it's all quite routine."

"That's right, Madam," the officer said. He looked as if he were suppressing a smile. "*Quite.*"

Once the coachman had finished maneuvering the brougham off the road, there was nothing to do but wait again. The captain of the guard had disappeared.

Elizabeth passed the time watching the other soldiers go about their work—poking through the contents of farmers' carts and drays with churlish lassitude while sending the most resplendent carriages ahead with hardly a glance. They moved with the indolence born of infinite boredom, like the dreadfuls themselves when they sense nothing around to grab and tear and eat, and Elizabeth had to wonder if even an unmentionable in their midst would rouse them from their torpor.

She wasn't expecting an answer, but she got one nevertheless.

A commotion rose up in the queue, and when Elizabeth turned she saw two soldiers dragging a man from one of the big mud-splattered stage coaches waiting to roll into the city.

"Thith ith a horrible mithtake," the man was saying. "Therth nothing wrong with me but a wee cold. Gwarr!"

He was about Elizabeth's age—no more than twenty-five years old—and he might have been handsome not long before. Now, however, he was sallow and twitchy, with rings under his eyes and dark hair matted down in sweaty clumps.

The soldiers were hustling him toward a section of the wall that was pocked with small holes.

"That thquirrel ith . . . gwarr! . . . eathily ekthplained. I am a takthidermitht, you thee. I wath going to mount the little fellow . . . gwarr! . . . I thwear."

One of the soldiers snorted. "How'd them tooth marks get on it, then?"

The man's back was against the wall now, and the soldiers released him and moved off a dozen paces, reaching for the muskets strapped to their backs.

"Oh, all right. Yeth. An unmentionable did give me the thlightetht little nip on the ankle the other day, and ever thinthe I've come over all peckith for . . . well. But I hear there are . . . gwarr! . . . cureth to be had in the capital. Phythicianth who can—"

"All lies, Sir," the other soldier said. "There's only one cure for the plague."

He brought up his Brown Bess and took aim. His comrade did the same.

"Oh," the man said. "Can I at leatht have my thquirrel back firtht?"

Both musket balls caught him in the forehead, and the back of his skull exploded onto the wall, along with the majority of his brains.

A moment later, the soldiers were beheading the body and stuffing it into a burlap sack. Four more such sacks, already full, were stacked up against the wall nearby.

The sorry stricken would find no pity here. And neither would Darcy, Elizabeth knew, if anyone learned of his plight before she found the cure—the one the soldier was so sure didn't exist.

"Mrs. Bromhead?"

Elizabeth turned toward the voice but couldn't believe she was seeing its source. The tone had been deep, the *R*s rolled regally, the accent as English as the Union Jack and buttered scones. Yet walking up to her carriage was a slightly built young Asian man dressed in the tidy but unassuming black and white of a gentleman's valet.

"Yes?"

The man stopped, offered her a shallow bow, and then swept an arm toward the gateway into the city.

"If you would be so good as to step down and come with me," he said—and yes, it was with *that* voice.

"But my carriage—"

"Will not be needed."

"My servants—"

"Will not be needed."

"My things—"

"Will not—"

Elizabeth silenced the man with an upraised hand.

When she stepped out of the brougham, she took only one thing with her: her parasol.

"It will not be needed, I know," she said. "Yet I hope I shall be permitted this one little nonessential."

"Of course, Ma'am."

"Thank you."

And with that, Elizabeth said her goodbyes to her astonished servants and followed the little stranger through the gate into the biggest, grandest (and dirtiest, wickedest) city on the face of the earth.

CHAPTER 10

Of course, Georgiana Darcy was relieved to see how much her brother was improving. If only he'd stop talking in his sleep about lungs and livers and kidneys and brains . . . and then licking his lips.

Whenever he awoke and found his sister sitting at his bedside, he would look abashed, and if she asked what he'd been dreaming of he deflected her questions with those of his own. About the bitter, crimson liquid their aunt poured down his throat twice a day. About Jane Bingham's supposed descent into dire illness. And, most of all, about Elizabeth and her decision to stay behind in Derbyshire.

Georgiana did her best to bat these queries aside with still more, but there are only so many times one can say, "Fancy another round of Crypts and Coffins?" or "I brought my Sun Tzu with me—shall I read another chapter?" Still, despite the awkwardness, she rarely left her brother's side. And she knew that, if she did, he would not be alone long, for their cousin Anne was ever ready to continue the vigil. Which made Georgiana uneasy. There was something about the way Anne watched over Fitzwilliam that reminded her of a vulture perched near a battlefield, waiting patiently for the moment when the fighting ended and the wounded stopped moving.

Anne had never been a favorite of either Georgiana or Fitzwilliam, though she'd been capable of a rousing game of Spank the Dreadful once upon a time and seemed destined for the same training in the deadly arts as they had received. Yet she'd changed drastically about age fourteen or fifteen, withdrawing into shadowy corners and dark moods and the black dresses of a Spanish contessa, sometimes even donning a veil. It was as though all vitality had been siphoned out of her, and Fitzwilliam once said he knew who the succubus was. While some—his Elizabeth, for instance—had the kind of strength that not only nourished but was nourished by the strength of others, Lady Catherine de Bourgh's strength fed on weakness.

Still, Anne seemed to have regained a measure of her old vigor, though she remained a quiet, lurky creature given to inexplicable smirks and cryptic comments.

"Ahhhh, fresh meat," she'd said when a servant entered Fitzwilliam's room bearing a bloody slab of undercooked beef that Lady Catherine had sent up. "Just what we've needed around here for so long."

Another time, Georgiana checked on her brother in the middle of the night only to find her cousin hovering over his bed, so motionless she could have been a dressmaker's mannequin.

"Back again?" she said as Georgiana stepped up to the bedside. She reached out and pressed a clammy hand to Georgiana's cheek, and it was hard to tell if Anne was gazing at her tenderly or trying, in her langorous way, to slap her. "What need has Fitzwilliam of anyone else when such a sister as you is with him?"

Then she'd turned and swept soundlessly out of the room.

The next day, Anne looked up from her breakfast—the same small dollop of red roe and salmon sashimi she took every morning—and said, apropos nothing, "How many unmentionables do you think you've killed?"

"Oh, not so many. Only two hundred and seventy-three." Georgiana thought a moment and then added: "And a half."

"Only?" Anne glanced at her mother, who was glowering at her from the head of the table. "Of course. Not so many when compared to some. Still, you've been in battle after battle, Georgiana, and your reflexes must be finely honed, indeed. So honed, in fact, it makes me wonder if you can entirely control them."

"I don't think I understand you."

"Anne," Lady Catherine said.

"It's just that you've been spending so much time with your brother," Anne went on. "Even as he improves, there will certainly be moments when he will behave erratically, alarmingly, perhaps even like a—"

"Anne!" Lady Catherine gave the table a thump with her fist that sent every plate and cup jumping. "This is neither the time nor the place!"

If the downward-looking kimono-wearing servants shuffling around the room showed any sign of noticing the exchange, Georgiana didn't see it. As far as she knew, none of them spoke English, for Her Ladyship populated her household staff entirely with imported Japanese peasants.

"I bring it up only out of concern for Fitzwilliam," Anne said coolly.

"You warriors are always so eager to kill, I should think it would become something of a habit. An impulse barely held in check. And I would hate for something tragic to happen if your little potion didn't work quickly enough."

"Not the time," Lady Catherine grated out. "Not the place."

"Fine."

Anne returned her attention to her meal, albeit with a strangely serene smile upon her face. She plucked up a single roe with her chopstick and glanced over at Georgiana before sliding it between her thin lips.

The proper time and place for the conversation to continue, Georgiana couldn't help but think, was whenever she wouldn't be around to hear it. And, indeed, Lady Catherine did all she could to arrange many such times, pressing her young niece to spar with her ninjas and sample the exotic weapons in her vast armory and make use of the small flock of dreadfuls she kept on hand for target practice. Yet always Georgiana resisted and, aside from those moments when she slept or bathed or ate, she stayed at her brother's side. She would not leave it willingly unless Elizabeth herself asked her to.

And then she did.

One of Lady Catherine's waiting geishas brought the letter to her in Fitzwilliam's bed chamber. Fortunately, her brother had plunged into a deep slumber after taking his morning medicine, so he couldn't inquire about the mud-speckled envelope that had just come, it seemed, all the way from the Yorkshire Dales. Georgiana didn't open it until she was alone in her own room.

My dear Georgiana,

I have not the time to tell you everything that has happened since your departure from Pemberley. Suffice it to say this: Our situation is more desperate than ever. The physician who holds the key to curing the strange plague has, I have just learned, left London for Aberdeen! He has there, I am told, a laboratory like a fortress, and only within its high stone walls will we find what we seek.

I have already begun the long journey north. Our only hope, I am convinced, is to strike immediately, taking the cure either by stealth or by force. In either case, my paltry peasant skills are unequal to the task at hand. I need assassins versed in the noble Shinobi ways of death. I need you, Georgiana, along with as many of your aunt's ninjas as she might spare! Let us rendezvous at the Seasick Sheltie Inn in Aberdeen, and together we shall snatch your brother back from the very gates of Hell!

Yours etc.,
Elizabeth

Georgiana didn't linger over the letter. She read it through just once and then dashed downstairs to find Lady Catherine. Her Ladyship was giving her kitchen staff their midmorning beating, but paused to hear Georgiana through. She immediately agreed to send a small force of ninjas to accompany her to Scotland.

"I wish I could go along myself," Lady Catherine said. "But I must remain here to continue administering the serum to Fitzwilliam. Only I, of all of us here, have some inkling as to its properties and proper use."

"I understand entirely. And how grateful I am to have you for an aunt in this hour of need!"

Georgiana turned and started to hurry off, but Lady Catherine called her back.

"Where are you going?"

"Why, to pack my things. And I shall want to say goodbye to my brother, of course."

"And where is it you will tell him you are going?"

"Well, I . . . I hadn't thought about that."

"That is obvious."

Her Ladyship approached, not stopping until she was *too* close—her chest mere inches from her niece's, her eyes glaring down over a sharp nose that would, with but the slightest nod, poke the younger woman in the forehead.

"Georgiana, do you know why I asked your sister-in-law not to tell Fitzwilliam that she is in search of a cure?" She didn't pause for a reply. "It is for the same reason I will ask you not to speak to him now: We must preserve his peace of mind. His very soul is in flux. All that is good in him is weakened, dying, while unspeakable urges grow ever stronger. We mustn't upset or agitate him, lest we tip him all the more quickly into the dark pit that looms before him. He rests now, and that is good. Would you disturb that rest to tell him that his sister and wife are risking their lives to save his? No. Just go, and I will find the best words to explain your absence."

"Oh, but surely I couldn't—"

"Just." Lady Catherine narrowed her eyes. "Go."

"Yes. All right. If you really think it's for the best. . . ."

Not a quarter of an later, Georgiana was hurrying out to a carriage already loaded with clothes and ropes and grappling hooks and an array of weapons from Her Ladyship's arsenal. Riding up top were four ninjas dressed in coachmen's livery.

Anne de Bourgh was standing by the carriage door. Georgiana rarely saw her cousin venture outside, and her jet-black dress made her seem somehow incongruous in the full light of day, like a shaft of coal jutting from a glass of milk.

"I understand you must leave us," Anne said.

"Yes. It pains me to quit my brother's sickbed, and with such suddenness, but I fear it must be done."

Anne nodded.

"Well, I, for one, am glad to see you go," she said, "knowing that when you return, all will at last be set to rights."

She gave Georgiana a hug that imparted no warmth and then stepped aside, smiling. Once the carriage was rolling off up the drive, she reentered the house.

As Anne took her young cousin's place at Fitzwilliam's side, curling from one of the chimneys came smoke that had been, not long before, the *real* letter Elizabeth had sent Georgiana from an inn on the road to London.

CHAPTER 11

"There is one more thing you will no doubt tell me that I don't need," Elizabeth said as she and her mysterious companion passed through the Northern Guard Tower and into London. The soldiers, she noticed, let them stroll by without question. "Your name. Even if, by your reckoning, it is not required, it would still be nice to know."

The young Asiatic who'd met her at the gate—surely another of the Japanese servants Lady Catherine so favored—pulled an envelope from his coat pocket and handed it to her.

This is Nezu, the note inside read. *He will guide you in my absence. You will find him to be an invaluable tool. Trust him in all things.*

This time, Elizabeth wasn't caught by surprise when the paper began to smoke. She let it drop to the ground, and within seconds it was but more swirling soot in a city that produced it by the ton.

"If you have any further messages from Her Ladyship, I'd appreciate knowing so in advance," Elizabeth said. "I should like to have a bucket of water at the ready."

"There will be no more notes from the mistress. Anything else you need to know will come from me."

"Wonderful. You've been so loquacious so far."

Nezu said nothing.

A dark barouche was waiting just beyond the gate, and, upon reaching it, Nezu opened the door and motioned for Elizabeth to climb in. As she started to oblige him, her eye caught sight of something odd: a grotesque parody of the very carriage she was stepping into. It was a squat black box, perhaps four feet high, careening around a corner up the street. Pulling it were two small, scruffy dogs in harness.

"Did you see that?" Elizabeth asked.

"See what?"

He didn't even bother following her gaze.

"Never mind," Elizabeth said. "Perhaps I didn't see it, either."

Once she was seated, Nezu hauled himself up next to the driver—another stone-faced Asiatic who seemed no more garrulous than he—and with a snap of the reins they set off down the narrow streets of Section Fourteen North.

Years ago, before the partitions were erected and London was sliced into perfect squares like some colossal cake, the area had been known as Camden Town. Once an unimportant district on the fringes of the growing metropolis, it was now more or less a rampart protecting the affluent sections of the interior. Only the meanest sorts of shops—most of them for "used" (that is, stolen) clothes and jewelry and Zed rods and swords—would take up residence where, so many times, the dreadfuls had broken through. Indeed, the buildings looked as though they'd been burned down and rebuilt before the charred planks had finished smoking. The other elegant barouches and phaetons and landaus coming through the gate shot down the filth-poked avenue with teams at full gallop, the whip-snapping drivers desperate to reach Four Central or Six East before their passengers could peek out and have their delicate sensibilities bruised by the sight of such squalor.

More than once, Elizabeth had made this same mad dash through North London, bound for the Darcys' town house in Mayfair (now Two Central). The route they followed was the old familiar one she knew well until they reached the City Road, at which point they turned abruptly east rather than continuing into the heart of socially acceptable London. Soon they were winding their way through the side streets of what

Elizabeth guessed to be Section One North, formerly Islington. It was by no means the most fashionable part of town, but the long rows of tidy white-terraced homes was evidence that the merchant class, at least, was willing to make it their own.

The coachman finally brought the barouche to a stop in front of a house that was identical to its neighbors in every respect but one: scale. The bay windows were taller, the front door wider, the stucco entryway arches higher, the ironwork balcony broader and more ornate. It was the very picture of size substituting for style; the perfect London home for a vulgarian parvenue from the hinterlands. As "Mrs. Bromhead," it seemed, was supposed to be.

Nezu climbed down and opened the carriage door.

Elizabeth remained in her seat. She'd caught a glimpse of someone peeking out one of the windows and now found herself reluctant to enter the house with these men—minions of the woman who once threatened to cut her into chunks and use her for zombie bait.

"Remind me," she said. "Why would a wealthy widow such as I choose to settle, alone, in so grandiose a home in One North?"

"I'm sure you will remember quickly enough once you are inside," Nezu replied. "The others should be waiting in the drawing room."

"The others?"

Nezu simply held out an arm toward the house.

If he was trying to be discreet, he need not have bothered, for the "other" whom Elizabeth had seen watching the street suddenly threw open the front door and came bounding down the steps.

"Ursula! Ursula!"

"Kitty?"

Elizabeth scrambled from her seat, and the moment her feet were on the ground her sister was upon her, holding her tightly.

"Oh, *Ursula*—sweet *Ursula*!" Kitty cried. "I have been so worried about you! Just let me look at you." She stepped back, clasping her hands, and sighed. "You are a vision, as always. Still the prettiest of the Shevington sisters—though now, of course, you are a Bromhead, *Ursula*."

"Come, come, Avis," Elizabeth heard her father say. "You speak as though your sister needed reminding of her own name."

Oscar Bennet appeared beside Kitty and leaned in to kiss a stunned Elizabeth on the cheek.

"I apologize for the theatrics," he whispered in her ear. Then he kissed the other cheek and whispered again. "Your sister is a tad overexcited."

Kitty seemed to find the kiss-whispers an irresistible idea, for she jumped in to try some herself.

Cheek one: "We were assured you were safe."

Cheek two: "But we didn't know whether to believe it."

Forehead: "Just give the word, and I'll take this little wretch's head."

Elizabeth retreated a step before her sister resorted to kissing her nose.

"I am overjoyed to see you, too . . . *Avis*," she said.

Nezu—"the little wretch," to judge by the petulant glare Kitty bestowed upon him—sidled in and cleared his throat.

"Perhaps it would be best if your reunion were to continue inside." His gaze flicked left and right, sweeping over the neighboring homes. "In private."

"A capital idea." Mr. Bennet took Elizabeth by the arm and began leading her toward the house. "No doubt these last days have been long and wearying for you, my dear. But fear not. Whatever comes next—"

Kitty hustled up and attached herself to Elizabeth's other arm. "You will face it with us at your side!"

Elizabeth gave her sister the grateful smile she seemed to expect. Yet, though she was deeply pleased to see Kitty and her father, a part of her wished they'd stayed far away.

Already the Darcy family teetered on the brink of calamity. Now, if things went as badly as they might, the Bennets would be swept over the precipice with them.

CHAPTER 12

The Bennets hadn't been in the drawing room half a minute before Kitty noticed it. Her father was giving Lizzy *that look*—both affectionate and respectful, tender yet twinkling with wry amusement. And it brought the old feelings right back.

Kitty didn't want to call it jealousy. So much so, in fact, that years ago she had consulted Dr. Roget's thesaurus in search of a more palatable word for it.

Envy, no. Jaundice, no. Invidiousness, no. Horn-madness . . . *what*?

In the end, she decided that "covetousness" would have to do. She didn't resent Lizzy. She simply wanted what her sister seemed (to her) to have won so easily. A father's esteem. A good man's love.

In the days when she and Lydia were so close that they shared between them not just ribbons and jewelry but one impetuous and petty personality, she would have stamped her foot and declared, "It's not fair! Lizzy always gets what she wants!" But she was older now and trying to be wiser, and her sister needed her help. The time had come for Kitty to prove she was worthy of what she coveted.

"You should have seen the Fulcrum of Doom I gave that first ninja!" she cackled. "I thought his eyes were going to pop out of his little black pajamas!"

Elizabeth offered her a rather strained smile. "Master Liu would be proud."

"Yes. Well. Carrying on," Mr. Bennet said. "Once they saw that we would not surrender our weapons voluntarily, they went to the extraordinary length of *explaining themselves*."

Nezu was standing not far from the elegant divans upon which the Bennets had settled themselves, and Mr. Bennet paused to arch an eyebrow in his direction.

"I can understand the likes of Lady Catherine de Bourgh demanding obedience even when cooperation might be won by a moment's consultation, but when their lackeys act with the same presumption, it only leads to trouble."

"And to a good Fulcrum of Doom! La!"

Kitty couldn't help but notice the degree to which she was ignored—which was total—and she immediately resolved to "La!" no more.

"As I explained earlier to your father and sister," Nezu said to Elizabeth, "none of you can be seen carrying arms into the house. It is a black mark against the Shevingtons already that they are new to wealth and lack obvious social connections. They would not curry further disfavor by displaying too bold a fondness for combat. I'm sure I need not remind you that, with a few notable exceptions, those who practice the deadly arts in England are largely viewed as eccentrics or outsiders . . . especially when it is a woman who picks up the sword."

Kitty bridled. Who was this presumptuous little man to call *her* an eccentric outsider?

She held back her devastating retort, however. Not that she'd thought of one yet. But, she realized, there was no point in trying. He was right.

"So that is why you were summoned here," Lizzy said to her father. "We are all to be Shevingtons."

Mr. Bennet nodded. "It seems each of us has a part to play in the little melodrama Lady Catherine has arranged. What I don't as yet know is *why*."

"Yes, Lizzy, you must tell us! What has happened to Darcy?"

For the first time in as long as she could remember, Kitty thought her sister might cry. Elizabeth Darcy had emotions after all! She felt something other than satisfaction at an enemy's death or amusement at another's foibles! It was a revelation.

Lizzy quickly composed herself and began pouring forth the sad tale: how Darcy, distracted by a disagreement between them, had been bitten by a dreadful where no amputation could save him.

"A cure? After all these years?" Mr. Bennet said when Elizabeth told of Lady Catherine's visit to Pemberley. "I can only pray it's true. Although, if it is, then why hasn't it been shared with all of England? Why hasn't the strange plague been ended once and for all?"

He, and then Lizzy, and then Kitty turned to stare at Nezu.

"There are some things even Her Ladyship does not know," he told them.

Mr. Bennet looked dubious. "And this charade she's arranged will somehow grant us access to the serum?"

"Perhaps," Lizzy said, and she continued her tale, explaining about Dr. Sir Angus MacFarquhar, and how she was supposed to get the cure from him.

When she was done, Kitty realized another reason Lady Catherine had wanted the Bennets disarmed before entering the house. If they still had their swords handy, her flunky Nezu would have been puréed on the spot. Kitty had never seen her father so furious. Although, being a controlled and even-tempered man, even now his rage was revealed only by a reddening of the face and a narrowing of the eyes. For Oscar Bennet, however, that was as good as a spittle-spewing roar.

"So my one daughter is to play seductress," he said to Nezu. "What of the other? Why is she here?"

"Sir Angus has a son."

Mr. Bennet's face shifted from hot pink to purple.

"Bunny MacFarquhar," Nezu went on. "He is a foolish, superficial young man who spends all his time—and considerable sums—on drink, clothing, gambling, the theater, carriages, horses, and every other waywardness one can think of. He has done much to erode his father's social standing as well as his fortune. A sizable dowry would solve many of the resulting problems. If Sir Angus does not provide an avenue to our prize, perhaps his son will."

"So Kitty is to be more bait," Mr. Bennet said.

"Just so."

"She is to be thrown into the snake pit of London society in the hopes that she might ensnare this young popinjay."

"Precisely."

"I see. One more question. . . ." Mr. Bennet rose to his feet. "Tell me, if you would, why I should not rip out your oily entrails and throttle you with them?"

"I can give you three answers," Nezu replied with such coolness that Kitty had to admire him. He seemed to remain utterly still, unflinching, and yet she could sense a coiled tension about him, too, like a spring wound tight. The man wasn't simply composed. If Mr. Bennet wasn't swayed by his answers, he was *ready*.

"First," he said, "you would not succeed. Second, even if you did, you would be killing the one person in London who can or would aid you in any way. And third, Mr. Darcy has been bitten by a dreadful, and you are in no position to quibble with *how* he is to be saved *if* he is to be saved. Lady Catherine has offered this one path to salvation, and this one alone. Step off it, and your son-in-law is damned to living death."

Mr. Bennet stared a moment at the younger man. Then he sighed and sat down.

"That was four answers," he said.

"I considered the last more of a summation."

"Ah." Mr. Bennet slumped back into the cushions. "In any event, two would have sufficed."

"You're saying it's decided, then?" Kitty asked. "I get no say, even when it's my own disgrace that's being debated?"

Mr. Bennet sat up straight again. "Oh, my child, I am sorry. It's just that—"

"I am not a child," Kitty shot back, much to her father's surprise, and even more to her own. "Certainly not when something such as this is being proposed. I am being asked—no, told!—to become a jezebel, a vixen, a temptress so that I might beguile some young gentleman I've never even met. And yet so inconsequential is my opinion that it's not even asked for when it's my very character that is impugned and imperiled!"

"You are correct, of course, and I apologize," her father said. He jerked his chin at Nezu. "If *you* wish to kill this dog who has insulted you, that is by all means your right."

Kitty turned to face Nezu as if she were thinking it over. He simply looked back at her, as impassive—and fearless—as ever. This was no mere valet, that much was clear. He was something . . . more. And Kitty found she enjoyed trying to stare him down. It took some effort to pull her gaze away and look at her sister.

"The choice is yours," Lizzy said, in answer to her unasked question. "It is, as you so rightly say, your honor that is at stake. Taking part in this ruse is something you must do only if you think it right."

Kitty nodded gravely.

"Thank you, Elizabeth."

And then she could hold back her grin no longer, and she felt a "La!" coming on despite herself.

"As it just so happens," she said, "I think it sounds like fun!"

CHAPTER 13

The hunt for the MacFarquhars began the next day in Section Three Central—Hyde Park. This was the afternoon playground of the elite, where the fashionable went to see and be seen. Elizabeth wasn't anxious for the former and dreaded the latter, even with the new look she'd been given by the waiting geishas supplied by Lady Catherine. A preparation of yogurt and powdered henna had turned her dark hair red; meticulous plucking had reshaped her eyebrows into thin, elegant arcs; a padded petticoat gave her a rounder, fuller shape while obscuring the tautness of her well-developed muscles.

Her father and sister declared her to be utterly transformed, yet Elizabeth remained unconvinced. How long would it be before someone recognized her as Mrs. Fitzwilliam Darcy?

"Longer than you might think," Nezu told her. "In my experience, the English see the rank more clearly than the person. Change the one, and the perception of the other is altered in kind."

Elizabeth wasn't so sure. It comforted her more to know that she was by no means a perennial in town. Not long into their marriage, she'd convinced her husband to stop spending the Season there. It hadn't been hard: They both preferred the bucolic simplicity of Derbyshire to the venom of London's so-called polite society. Elizabeth hadn't been a pariah, as Lady Catherine had predicted before she married Darcy, but she wouldn't have entirely minded if she had been.

When they reached Hyde Park, she found it just as she'd remembered, if a trifle more crowded in advance of the recoronation. The grounds were beautiful: lushly wooded and verdant, despite the long shadows of the towering walls all around. No one was there to admire the greenery, though; they were there to be admired themselves. Gentlemen bounced upon the broad backs of black-maned thoroughbreds that cost more than Mr. Bennet earned in a year, while carriages of every size and design whizzed up and down the park's paths, completing the same circuits over and over, going nowhere in the finest style.

"Oooo, is that the Prince Regent?" Kitty cried as their barouche passed a particularly resplendent chaise and four. "No? But that simply must be the Duke of York over there! No? Well, how about that gentleman? Surely he's someone important. No? Really? Why, just look how grand is his . . . is that a landau or a calash? I can never tell the difference. Oh, now that *must* be the Prince Regent. He looks so wonderfully fat and flushed . . . and so grumpy! I suppose I would, too, if I had to give up a throne."

"That is not the Prince Regent," Elizabeth said.

"Then how about that gentleman over—?"

Mr. Bennet put a hand on Kitty's knee. "You're getting too worked up, my dear. Remember, the point is to appear indifferent. If we are impressed by important people, how important can we be ourselves?"

"But the Shevingtons are supposed to be new to London. I can't imagine they'd be so blasé about . . . ooo, tell me that's the Prince Regent! Please, do!"

"If you wish," Mr. Bennet sighed. "It is the Prince Regent."

"It is not," Elizabeth said before her sister could wave to His Royal Highness (who was indeed looking fat and flushed and grumpy that day). "And, at any rate, it's not the royal family we're looking for."

"Oh, that's why *he's* here." Kitty said, fluttering a hand at the front of the carriage, where Nezu sat beside the driver. Both were dressed in the powdered wigs and silver-satin liveries of coachmen to the upper crust. "If Bunny MacFarquhar turns up, he can tell us."

"He'll be here," Nezu said. "His five o'clock appearance at Hyde Park is the only time he can be counted on to be punctual. And if the king decides to grace us with a visit from St. James's, it is a certainty that Sir Angus will be at his side."

"Ooooo! We might see the king?" Kitty squealed. "I didn't think they'd let him out in public for fear he'd start barking and chasing phaetons. I know we're all supposed to be so very glad he's not a loony anymore—as if it were the whole country that had gone mad, not just him—but I can't help wondering . . . Good heavens, who's that magnificent creature?"

She was looking at a large white carriage with but one passenger: a beautiful if (to Elizabeth's eyes) overrouged young woman luxuriating upon seats of plush red velvet. An honor guard of would-be beaux surrounded her on horseback, all of them jockeying for the best position from which to lean in and exchange pleasantries (and perhaps steal a peek down a décolletage so immodest, her charms might as well have been laid out on a serving platter).

"I don't recognize her," Elizabeth said, though she certainly knew the type.

"She's ever so popular with the gentlemen! I'm surprised, though, that she should be out unchaperoned."

Elizabeth and her father exchanged a chagrined look. Kitty had killed men on four continents, yet she remained an unworldly Hertfordshire girl at heart. Much of what she knew of society came from the novels and periodicals she loved so dearly, and the picture they painted was, to be charitable, incomplete. Elizabeth was in no mood to sketch in what was missing: that, in some circles, it was more acceptable for a woman to be a harlot than a warrior. So she simply changed the subject.

"Is Bunny MacFarquhar among the lady's admirers?" she asked Nezu.

"On most days, yes. I see nothing of him or his friends, however."

The ninja (and that's what the man's unflappable calm, watchful bearing, and smooth agile movements had convinced Elizabeth he was) glanced off to the left, his attention captured by a swirl of movement in a nearby copse.

"Interesting," he said. "That's not supposed to happen here."

Then the screams started.

"Dreadful!"

"Unmentionable!"

"One of them! One of *them*!"

A single, contorted figure was staggering stiffly out of the thicket. Not so long ago, it had been a man, if not a gentleman. Its coat and trousers were frayed, stained, rumpled—the clothes of a pauper. And one who hadn't died peacefully in his sleep, either, to judge by the grimace that twisted its gray face.

It raised its arms and roared.

Women shrieked. Men shrieked. Horses reared. Coaches scattered in every direction.

Elizabeth and Kitty sprang to their feet.

Their father grabbed each by the hand and pulled them back down.

"Think," he said. "What would the Shevingtons do?"

Nezu looked over his shoulder and spoke in his usual cool monotone. "They certainly wouldn't leap from their carriage and kill an unmentionable with their bare hands."

"What would you have us do?" Kitty asked. "Scream?"

"Yes," Nezu said. "If you wouldn't mind."

"I *would*, actually!"

"Swoon, then," Mr. Bennet said.

"I've never swooned in my life!"

"Neither has your mother, but you've seen her feign it often enough to know how it's done. *Swoon*."

"Oh, all right." Kitty put a hand to her forehead and fell back into Mr. Bennet's arms. "Is anyone even looking?"

"No," Elizabeth told her. "They're too busy running away."

"All of them?"

"All of them."

Kitty sat up again and took a look around. The cream of English society had fled, without exception.

Kitty folded her arms over her chest and frowned. "They ought to be ashamed of themselves."

Nezu nodded at the dreadful, which had gone loping off after the retreating bluebloods. "As should he—and he is every bit as likely to admit it."

Elizabeth noticed Kitty throwing the man an amused, admiring glance. It wasn't often one ran across a ninja given to wit. When they spoke English—which wasn't often—they usually limited themselves to things like, "My mistress sends her regards!" as they tried to poke sai spikes through your eyes.

"Well," Kitty said, looking away again, "I shall *make* him sorry if he keeps that up."

The zombie had lost interest in the other carriages and was now clumping toward the only one that wasn't speeding away: theirs.

Nezu reached under the driver's seat and produced a stubby carbine.

"I think it would be better, Miss, if you were to swoon again," he said. "Just in case anyone has collected themselves enough to look back."

"Oh, we're being watched, all right," Mr. Bennet said.

Then Elizabeth spied it, too: something long and tan and serpentine slithering through the grass directly behind the unmentionable.

"You tell us Sir Angus's son is a fool." Elizabeth pointed at the rope tied to the dreadful's leg. "Is he that kind of fool?"

Nezu nodded. "Very much so," he said.

The zombie was now no more than fifty feet away.

"I have an idea," Mr. Bennet said. "Nezu, if you would do me the favor of missing and alarming the horses, please."

"As you wish," Nezu said after only the slightest pause, and he murmured something to the driver in Japanese.

Mr. Bennet turned to Elizabeth and put a hand over hers. "Know by this, my dear, how fond I have grown of your husband . . . for if it were Wickham who'd been bitten, I would sit here laughing."

"I don't under—," Kitty began.

Nezu brought up the carbine and shot a bullet into the ground near the dreadful's feet. The horses whinnied and danced in their harnesses, and the carriage jerked forward.

Mr. Bennet took the opportunity to tumble out.

"Father!" Kitty cried, beginning to leap to her feet again. It was Elizabeth who held her back.

"Scream," Elizabeth said.

This time Kitty didn't hesitate to accommodate.

The carriage was rolling away from their father while the unmentionable was closing in.

"Ahh!" Mr. Bennet cried. "God have mercy on a helpless old man!"

He went hobbling off waving his arms over his head, and the zombie was soon no more than five steps behind him.

"Oh, my lumbago! I can barely move, I am so stiff!" Mr. Bennet threw a wide-eyed look back at the ghoul that was dribbling black drool practically on his heels. "Do you not understand? There is no tender meat for you here! Shoo! Shoo! Ahhhhhhhhhhhhhh!"

Mr. Bennet tripped over nothing and went sprawling face-first into the grass. He flipped himself over and screamed just as the dreadful lunged in for the kill—and was jerked backward by a tug on the rope wrapped around its right ankle. It roared in rage and went for Mr. Bennet again, but still the rope held it back. The zombie ended up making futile swipes at its intended dinner as it loomed over him on one leg.

"What—what is the meaning of this?" Mr. Bennet sobbed.

Raucous laughter could be heard from the grove from which the unmentionable had first emerged. A moment later, it was followed by half a dozen young men. Two were dressed in drab, dirty clothes not much better than those the zombie wore; they were the ones holding the rope. The rest were of the type never to have held so much as a length of yarn lest it scrape the pampered flesh on their soft palms. Their coats were long and black, their hats tall and glossy, their cravats extravagantly fluffed, their trousers so tight as to invite detailed study of the male anatomy. The uniform of the dandy.

Elizabeth didn't need to ask which one was Bunny MacFarquhar. It was safe to assume he'd be the strikingly handsome young man leading the huge, leashed rabbit. He was also guffawing the loudest of the bunch.

"It was a practical joke?" Kitty asked her sister.

"Yes. Though you do it a kindness to call it practical."

"Or a joke," Nezu added. The man was turning out to be rather loquacious after all.

"If Lydia were here," Kitty said, "she'd laugh and laugh." Elizabeth was pleased to see that Kitty herself wasn't even smiling.

"What an awful thing to do! You nearly scared us all to death!" Kitty called to the young gentlemen approaching their barouche. "It was horrid! Horrid!"

They stopped to stare at her, frozen in that undecided moment when they might shrink into po-faced shame or explode with more laughter.

Then Kitty's expression—her whole face—changed so completely that, for a moment, Elizabeth could have sworn she was looking at Lydia.

"You must tell me which one of you naughty monkeys thought it up!" Kitty said. "La!"

CHAPTER 14

Darcy didn't know if he'd been in his bed a week or a month, for he could no longer distinguish any division between day and night. The heavy curtains remained drawn, and the light that shone at their edges might have come from the moon or the sun, Darcy couldn't tell. It never seemed to him anything but dull gray. The only thing more unremitting than the room's gloom was the presence of his cousin Anne, who hovered constantly by his bedside, giving him all the more reason to keep his eyes closed.

Sometimes he slept, and dreamed. More often he lay awake, and worried. And more often still, he drifted in some nameless place between slumber and wakefulness. If there truly were such a place as Limbo, he knew what it was like—and he came to hate it.

So at last the day (or night?) arrived when, woozy or not, nauseous or not, he had to escape. And not with a pull on the bell rope. His cousin was giving him the rare gift of her absence, and he didn't wish to summon her or her mother or the cowering servants, with their downcast eyes and mottled bruises. This was something he had to do himself. With a monumental exertion of will, he swung his feet off the bed and stood.

Then he fainted.

Sometime later, he picked himself up off the floor and stood again. When he was satisfied that he could manage without fainting, he started shuffling toward the dresser.

Then he fainted.

When he regained consciousness, he started the process over. He stood, shuffled, fainted, stood, shuffled, found his clothes, fainted, stood, put on his trousers, fainted, put on his shirt, didn't faint, put on his waistcoat, didn't faint, put on his stockings, didn't faint, picked up his coat, fainted, stood, picked up his coat, fainted, stood, and finally decided he could live without the coat. After much (but faintless) effort, he had on his shoes and cravat and was at last ready to leave the little tomb in which he'd been interred for so long.

He moved slowly, cautiously, out the door and into the hall. There he found windows with no curtains drawn, yet the world outside still seemed dreary and dim. The sky lacked the absolute blackness of night, though nighttime it was, Darcy decided. There were no groundskeepers to be seen, no one walking or riding along the road just beyond the hedgerows, and he could hear no movement save for the distant ticking of a clock.

Darcy followed the sound through the murk shrouding the house. The clock stood, he knew, just outside the room he wished to visit. There was no getting away from Rosings—not with the strange plague still in him. But if he couldn't escape the place, he could at least leave the time and all its troubling questions. He would seek refuge in the past.

Lady Catherine always liked to remind him that he'd taken his first steps in her trophy room, wobbling from his mother to his father under the literally glassy-eyed gaze of hundreds of mounted dreadful heads. Her ladyship could tell you where and when and how she'd acquired each and every one, and as a lad he'd spent countless hours at her feet while she regaled him with tales of her victories in battle. Only one trophy would she never talk about, though it was mounted alone over the room's huge fireplace. It was the head of the first dreadful she ever killed—and of her first husband as well.

Darcy couldn't look at it without wondering whether another head might soon join it, should the cure fail. So instead he concentrated on the weapons along the walls. Yet even as he took down a favorite old katana (and found he could barely keep the blade aloft), his thoughts betrayed him again. He wanted to remember happier days—taking his first clumsy lunges with this very sword, waving it over his head as he and his sister played Stricken and Slayers, panicking when he accidentally halved one of the stuffed zombies that loomed in the room's four corners.

All he could think of now, though, was how much he'd like to share those memories with his wife and show her the sword that helped set him on the path to her. And that brought back all the questions, and all the pain; he replaced the katana on its rack and thought himself a fool for seeking solace in a place such as this.

When he turned to go, he nearly walked into the small black-clad figure that had planted itself directly behind him.

"Anne! I didn't hear you come in!"

His cousin's thin lips curled upward ever so slightly. "Going unnoticed is one of my specialties."

"What are you doing out of bed?"

"I could give the same answer as you." Anne looked past Darcy at the swords and maces behind him before lifting her gaze to the heads poking from the wall all the way to the vaulted ceiling high above. "I have been visiting old friends."

On the young woman's pale face was a curious mixture of fondness and revulsion. She wiped it away with a smile as she looked again into Darcy's eyes.

“WHEN HE TURNED TO GO, HE NEARLY WALKED INTO A SMALL BLACK-CLAD FIGURE.“

"It is good to see you up and about. I have been looking forward to the time when we might again walk the grounds together, as we did so long ago."

She offered him her right hand.

Darcy didn't take it.

"In the middle of the night?" he said.

"There is as much to admire in the nighttime as in the daytime."

"I still feel quite weak."

"You may lean on me, if need be."

"I would be afraid to crush you, you are so delicate a thing."

"I am stronger than I look."

She was still holding out her hand to Darcy, and he found himself taking it even as he said, "I will need a coat."

"No, you won't," Anne told him, and she moved in close to his side as she guided him from the room.

Once outside, they strolled up the gravel path to the rose garden. Anne was right: Darcy barely noticed the chill of night, and the lack of light didn't bother him either. The world was still bathed in the same dull gray glow he'd noticed from the windows, only now he could see small pinpricks of glistening brilliance spread throughout it. Not overhead in the sky—these weren't stars he saw. The twinkling was in the bushes and the grass and the trees and sometimes swirling in the air.

Darcy rubbed his eyes with his free hand, and the tiny white sparks disappeared.

"Are you all right?" Anne asked.

"Yes. It's just . . . the tonic your mother gives me is helping, I'm certain, yet I still feel . . . not quite myself."

"Surely, that will pass with time, though I wonder if you'll ever feel exactly as you used to. Going through such an ordeal could not help but change how you see yourself and those around you."

"Perhaps," Darcy said in a tone that did not invite further discussion. There was a truth to his cousin's words he could recognize even as he tried to evade it.

Anne let only a few steps pass by in silence.

"I'm glad you're here, Fitzwilliam. I'm sure that sounds strange, but I mean it. That you should end up at Rosings in your time of trouble almost seems like providence. Now we have a chance to get to know each other again. We haven't really talked, just you and I, in years, and we've both changed so much since then. I think you'll find that we have more in common now than we ever did as children."

"Yes, well . . . I do appreciate your attentiveness since I arrived. You've been extraordinarily understanding, given the circumstances. After all that's happened these past few years, I could hardly have expected you to show such concern for me."

"How could I not support my cousin when I find him on my doorstep in such need—and so very alone?"

If Darcy hadn't been trained to withstand every torture known to man, he would have winced.

Anne gave his hand a squeeze. It was a cold grip, but one Darcy found, to his surprise, not entirely unwelcome. It was good to have *something* to cling to when all else seemed to be slipping from his grasp.

"Ahh! Look! Isn't it beautiful?"

Anne stopped and leaned toward one of the bushes lining the path, pulling Darcy in beside her. Before them were half a dozen flowers in full bloom, though Darcy couldn't tell what color they were. They looked washed out and drab in the hazy half-light, and he could smell them not at all. It made him wonder what his cousin was admiring.

"I'm ever so fond of roses," Anne said. "They don't close their blossoms when the sun goes down like those haughty daisies and poppies. I think that's quite sporting of them, don't you? The night creatures deserve their beauty, too."

Darcy was about to make some neutral reply when he noticed a glimmer of light just beyond the nearest flowers. The little points of light were back—two of them, close together, hovering not a foot from him.

When he squinted at them, he saw that they were suspended on a lattice of thin, interconnected lines stretching from one rose stem to another.

He was looking at a web, and the lights were a spider and the cocooned fly over which it hovered.

Darcy felt the strange urge to reach out and touch them. Feel their radiance.

"Yes, I do dearly love them," Anne said. "Day, night—it's all the same to them."

The two glows seemed to merge for a moment; then the fly's flickered and went out.

The spider's light burned on all the brighter.

CHAPTER 15

Kitty Bennet had studied under four masters in her life. Her father and a young man named Geoffrey Hawksworth had introduced her to the deadly arts. Master Liu of Shaolin had deepened her understanding and broadened her skills through years of grueling training in China. Yet it was her fourth master—her final and yet also her first—whom she found herself most indebted to now.

Kitty was drawing upon all the lessons she'd learned during her years as an acolyte to her sister Lydia.

Bunny MacFarquhar and his dandified friends were gathered around her as their toadies wrestled away the dreadful that had cleared Hyde Park just minutes before. And Kitty was doing all that Master Lydia would have done in her place.

When the men made bad jokes, she laughed.

When they gave her long, leering looks, she simpered and bit her thumbnail.

When they made disparaging remarks about her father and the comical way he'd run screaming from the unmentionable, she said, "Oh, you're beastly!" in a tone that added, "And I just *adore* beastly boys!"

To her own dismay, it worked. With no dagger-dangling bandoliers or scabbarded katana or dowdy battle gown to hold her back, she could actually charm these wild young London bucks. Or Avis Shevington could, at any rate. In fact, it became obvious quite quickly that Avis Shevington could have a lot more fun than Kitty Bennet ever did.

Kitty had only ten minutes in Avis's skin, however. Then the soldiers began moving in from the guard towers, and Bunny called for a hasty retreat before their most excellent joke could be ruined by those twin spoilsports: responsibility and consequence.

"I do hope I shall be seeing you tomorrow at Ascot," Bunny said as he scooped up his rabbit, Brummell, and got ready to run.

"You can bet on it," Kitty told him, "and count on a better return on your investment than the races will bring!"

"Ho!" Bunny guffawed, and off he went, in the company of his little troop, scampering into the trees.

Kitty turned and walked back to the barouche from which Lizzy and her father had watched her impromptu debut into London society.

"Well, it would seem we're off to the races. La!"

"Indeed," Lizzy said. "Well done, Kitty."

Kitty climbed up and settled herself beside Mr. Bennet.

"It was my pleasure. Truly! Why, I'm half-tempted to stay Avis Shevington forever. Who would miss boring old Kitty Bennet anyway?"

This, of course, was a hint for her father and sister to exclaim, "We would! Never change, dear Kitty!"

They missed their cue. Instead, strangely enough, it was only Nezu who seemed to note the comment at all. He glanced back from the driver's seat with a quizzical look upon his face. But, just as he opened his mouth to speak, there was a thundering of hoofbeats and the crash of something tearing through brush.

A black ambulance was bursting out of the thicket nearby, and from the hoots and giggles coming from inside it was clear who the passengers were.

"Let us follow young master MacFarquhar's party," Mr. Bennet said. "I don't think answering a lot of questions would serve us any better than it would them."

At a word from Nezu, the coachman snapped the reins, and the carriage darted off before the soldiers could reach them. A moment later, they were following the ambulance as it streaked through the easternmost gate onto the streets of Section Two Central. Bunny apparently noticed who was behind them, for Brummell appeared at the ambulance's barred back window and (with the help of an unseen hand) waved one of his floppy paws at them.

Kitty waved back—and kept on waving for quite some time, for they ended up following Brummell northeast through London. Both Sir Angus's hospital and the MacFarquhar residence were near the home Lady Catherine had secured for the Shevingtons, Nezu explained, so their destination and that of Bunny MacFarquhar weren't far apart.

Mr. Bennet and Lizzy seemed to find this illuminating. Kitty could think little beyond, *I'm going to Ascot!*

When they returned to the house, Nezu had to rush off to make preparations—*for Ascot!*—while the Bennets went through their usual evening rituals: stretching, sparring, meditating. (*Ascot Ascot Ascot Ascot Ascot!* was Kitty's mantra that night). Then, after supper and a night of Ascot-filled dreams, Kitty was awakened at five in the morning to begin the journey.

To Ascot!

It took hours to make their way there, and Mr. Bennet passed the time napping while Lizzy, looking dour, merely stared off at the horizon. By contrast, Kitty was so excited she couldn't even concentrate on the novel she'd brought along. A little flirting at *the* event of the Season—the races at Ascot Heath—and they would soon put all their troubles behind them.

When she shared this optimistic thought with her sister, Lizzy replied only with a grim, "We shall see," while Nezu glanced back from the driver's seat and shot her another of his curious looks.

Soon after they were weaving their way around the hoi-polloi-packed omnibuses that clogged the last stretch of road to the racecourse. When at last they were close enough to step out of the barouche, Nezu led them through the crowds milling about outside the blinding white grand stands.

"What goes on in there?" Kitty asked, nodding at a row of nearby canvas tents. They were quite the hive of activity, with a constant stream of men (and only men) pushing in and stumbling out.

"Things beneath a proper person's notice," Nezu said. "I would suggest that you restrict your attention to the ladies' fine gloves and gowns."

"Now, look here. You might be Lady Catherine's proxy, but you are not Herself. When I ask you a question—"

Lizzy and Mr. Bennet leaned in on Kitty's either side.

"Gambling," Lizzy whispered.

"Gin," said Mr. Bennet.

"Dreadful baiting."

"*Worse.*"

"Oh," said Kitty.

None of the accounts she'd read of the races had mentioned any of that. The gloves and gowns, yes. The *worse* (whatever that was), no.

"Why, just look over there, Ursula," she said to her sister. "Have you ever seen such a magnificent hat?"

Just before they moved on into the stands, they passed one final distraction: A pair of zealots from the Society for the Prevention of Cruelty to Z_____s was being dragged out screaming the group's slogan ("Undead isn't inhuman!") as the leaflets they'd been trying to distribute littered the ground behind them.

"Let's see you prevent *this*!" someone called out (sounding as if he'd paid an especially long visit to the gin tent), and a pack of men fell on the SPCZed fanatics with drunken kicks and punches.

"This isn't as dignified as I'd imagined," Kitty said.

"Dignity one must sometimes bring to a thing oneself," Lizzy replied gravely. It seemed to be a thought she'd been pondering for a while.

At last, they reached the private box in the upper stands that Nezu had secured for them. The seats inside were perfectly situated for the viewing of the races—and the crowd's viewing of their occupants. Kitty's excitement to find herself in such an enviable spot faded quickly, however, once she noticed the sneers and nasty laughs being directed at them from those both above and below.

"Why are we getting such horrid looks?"

"You are social unknowns who have presumed to claim one of the racecourse's finest boxes," said Nezu, who was standing at the back of the booth trying to look like a servant awaiting orders rather than a puppeteer peeking out from behind his Punch and Judy. "You are no doubt being accused of making a tasteless, ostentatious display of wealth."

"As, of course, we are," Lizzy added.

"A calculated risk. We must pique the MacFarquhars' interest. To appear gauche is acceptable so long as you appear rich and ambitious in the process."

"Well, I don't see Bunny or his friends," Kitty said, leaning out to peer down into the crowd. "I can't pique a man if he's not here."

"I suspect MacFarquhar the Younger will have business to attend to in the tents before he comes in," Mr. Bennet said. "If so, so much the better, for we will find him all the more pique-able."

"Whatever do you mean, Papa?"

"Ah," her father said, looking away. "Our master of ceremonies."

Kitty turned to see a hulking, florid-faced figure entering one of the center boxes. There was a smattering of tepid applause, which the man acknowledged with the hoisting of a single hand. (The gesture was too apathetic to be called a wave.) The object of the crowd's not-quite adulation looked exactly like one of the men Kitty had mistaken for the Prince Regent in Hyde Park the day before, but this time there could be little doubt it was indeed George IV. His elegant clothes, his regal bearing, his sagging jowls and enormous protruding gut—all fit the descriptions Kitty had read in the ladies' journals and fashion magazines.

The man sat. Trumpets blasted a fanfare. There was a flurry of activity down on the track, and a great huzzah went up from the crowd.

The first Irishman of the day was off and running. Seconds later, the gates opened, and out charged the dreadfuls.

As always, a few zombies, catching sight of the great buffet arrayed in the stands, turned and rushed the high walls protecting the spectators. This was met with boos from those who'd wagered on them to win. The rest of the pack, meanwhile, galloped after the Irishman, their colorful silk tunics flapping as they ran. Kitty picked out an unmentionable to root for—a young female dressed in pink gaining quickly on the frantically fleeing bait. She cheered it on until it tumbled clumsily over a hurdle and impaled itself on the spikes on the other side. Soon after, the Irishman was scrambling up the rope that had been lowered for him at the finish line as the winner swiped and roared at him in futile frustration. After that, the unmentionables that could walk were lured back into their pens with fresh cabbages pulled on lengths of twine, while the rest (including Kitty's favorite) were put down with quick pistol shots to the head.

"Somehow I find all this less entertaining than I once did," Mr. Bennet said.

"I never found it entertaining at all." Lizzy stretched her already strained smile a little wider. "Now, however, is not the time to show it. Not if we are to entice—"

There was a knock at the door.

Nezu turned, slipped from the booth, and exchanged quiet words

"THE GATES OPENED, AND OUT CHARGED THE DREADFULS."

with someone just outside. When he returned a moment later, he was carrying Brummell the rabbit.

"I asked the gentleman to present his card," Nezu said. "He gave me this."

"Bunny!" Kitty exclaimed. "Come in here this instant, you rascal!"

Bunny MacFarquhar popped through the door, grinning. Kitty liked his smile. There was no guile about it whatsoever. Here was a man who smiled not to please those in his company but because he simply couldn't help it.

Of course, it didn't hurt that he had perfect teeth and an equally perfect face to frame them.

"You don't mind?" he said. "This is terribly forward without proper introductions, I know, but when I saw you up here I just had to . . . I say! How did you know my name?"

"Oh!" Kitty swiped a hand at him. "What a question!"

She turned toward Lizzy and her father, eyes wide.

"It was your calling card," Lizzy said with a nod at Brummell (who was now sniffing around her feet as Nezu retreated discreetly to the corner to brush several small brown pellets off his jacket).

"When one is the victim of a prank perpetrated by a man about town given to the company of rabbits, it is not altogether difficult to divine his identity," Mr. Bennet explained.

Bunny's eyes lit up with delight. It obviously pleased him to hear he had a reputation.

"Then you have the advantage of me." He tried to put on a serious expression but, lacking practice, failed miserably. "Which means I do not even know to whom I should be offering my most abject apologies."

"My name is Shevington," Mr. Bennet said, "and these are my daughters, Miss Avis Shevington and Mrs. Matthias Bromhead."

"It is a pleasure to make your acquaintance." MacFarquhar offered the family a bow. "I hope you can forgive me for my lapse of judgment yesterday. There was no malice intended. It was merely a lark carried too far."

"A lark to you—a humiliation to us," Mr. Bennet replied coldly. "We are new to London and eager to make the best possible impression on its leading lights. Yet I can't imagine anyone yesterday saying, 'Just look at the delightful way that old stranger screams and cowers. Let us have him and his lovely companions to dinner!'"

Kitty was caught off-guard by her father's gruff talk until Bunny showed it for what it was: bait. He took it.

"Your point is well taken, Sir," MacFarquhar said. "I believe there is but one thing to do: You must allow me to make amends for my thoughtlessness by offering entrée into the very circles you aspire to. I am not without connections, some extending to the very pinnacle of not just London society but of all the empire, if you take my meaning."

Just in case they didn't, he threw an insinuating nod at the royal box.

"Ahh," MacFarquhar said, shifting his attention to the track below. "They're loading the gates for the next race. I must say, you have here one of the finest spots for taking it in."

"And it would be rude to keep it to ourselves," Mr. Bennet said. He held out a hand to an empty chair beside Kitty. "Would you care to join us?"

"I should be delighted." MacFarquhar scooped up Brummell and seated himself with his furry mascot on his lap. "Actually, this isn't the first time I've admired this particular view. I've been in this box before. Did you know it's usually reserved for Lord Guernsey?"

"I did not," Mr. Bennet replied. "All I know is that I demand the best and pay accordingly."

"Ho! A capital policy, Sir! I subscribe to it myself . . . though I daresay I don't always manage the second p—"

MacFarquhar cut himself off with a cough and focused on the scraggly line of unmentionables that was now lurching around the turf after another Irishman.

"Better pick up your pace, Paddy!" MacFarquhar called out. "You've got one gaining on you!"

"La!" Kitty chirped.

"Ho!" MacFarquhar hooted.

They looked into each other's eyes, smiling.

Could it really be this easy to land a handsome man? Kitty thought. *If so, why didn't I try it ages ago?*

Then she remembered (*Oh, yes. The zombies. And Mother.*), just as movement in one of the other boxes drew MacFarquhar's attention away.

An old gray-wigged man, stout yet seemingly frail, was easing himself onto a thronelike chair beside the Prince Regent as beribboned attendants fluttered around him anxiously. Once the man was safely seated, the crowd broke into cheers as if he'd just won a great victory. Neither the old man nor the prince acknowledged the applause, the former because he seemed to take no notice while the latter scowled as if it were beneath his.

"Goodness!" Kitty exclaimed. "Is that the king?"

"It isn't the winner of the last race," her father said.

Kitty joined the applause . . . until she glanced over and saw that the man beside her hadn't.

MacFarquhar was gaping at the royal box as though a dreadful *had* just been seated there. Even Brummell seemed to sense something was amiss: The rabbit hopped off its master's lap and hid under his chair.

"Is everything all right, Mr. MacFarquhar?" Kitty asked.

"Yes . . . yes, of course. Why do you ask?" MacFarquhar said.

His face had lost all color.

There was a knock at the door, three quick and insistent raps, and MacFarquhar went practically translucent.

Nezu slipped outside again but was back almost instantly, trailing the tall broad-shouldered man who'd just pushed past him.

"No calling card is needed, forrr this is no social call," the man said in a heavy Scottish brogue. Though he was dressed as a gentleman, he had wild, graying hair, even wilder gray eyes, a thick mustache, and chin whiskers.

"Out," he said to MacFarquhar.

"But—"

"Out."

"But—"

The man didn't bother with another "Out." He simply took a step closer.

MacFarquhar jumped up and started for the door.

"Pleasure meeting you terribly sorry must dash thank you goodbye!"

"Don't forget your rrrrrrrabbit," the man growled.

"Again, pleasure meeting you et cetera et cetera!"

MacFarquhar spun around, snatched up Brummell by the scruff of the neck, and scurried from the box.

"Who are you? What is the meaning of this?" Mr. Bennet blustered.

The man just stared at him a moment and then turned and stalked out.

"I can tell you what it means," Elizabeth sighed.

Her father slumped in his seat. "You needn't bother."

"Well, I wish someone would," Kitty started to say. To her surprise, however, she found that she could work it out all by herself. All it required was something both Lydia and her mother had often counseled her against: thought.

"So," she said, "we have been snubbed by Sir Angus himself."

"So it would seem," Nezu said.

Kitty pretended to interest herself in the race, which was just then concluding with the Irishman hanging from the rope by the finish line while the winner hung from *him*. There were both cheers and boos as track attendants leaned out to poke away the dreadful with pikes before it could get a bite.

Despite all the excitement, Kitty noticed that part of the crowd wasn't paying any attention. Most of the people in the boxes near theirs were looking—and snickering—at the Bennets. The uppity nobodies had been put in their place.

They stayed for only one more race.

It was a very long, very quiet ride back to Section One North. They'd taken a bold step to attract the MacFarquhars' interest, and they'd been just as boldly and baldly slapped down. It was hard to imagine how the day could have gone any worse.

They pulled up in front of their house just as one of the servant/ninjas came flying out the front door. He rolled to a stop on the walkway and lay there in a bloodied, groaning heap.

A woman stepped out of the house after him but stopped when she saw the carriage.

"Oh, God," Mr. Bennet groaned.

"I doubt that He had anything to do with this," Elizabeth said.

They both looked over at Kitty.

Kitty cringed.

"So there you are. I was concerned," Mary Bennet said to them. "Now, would you be so good as to tell me what is going on?"

CHAPTER 16

Elizabeth had always been glad to have Mary with her in battle. Her sister was bold, fearless, the epitome of rectitude and unwavering self-assurance.

Which was exactly why Elizabeth was *not* glad to see her now, when boldness and rectitude might well ruin everything.

Take the bruised, moaning ninja-butler sprawled in front of the house, for instance. Here was Mary's handiwork, and already passersby were beginning to stop and stare.

"Oh, my! Poor Arnold's tripped down the front steps again!" Mr.

Bennet cried as he hopped from the barouche. "Come, Nezu. Help me get him inside."

"It is good to see you again, Miss Millstone," Elizabeth called to Mary. "I apologize for the confusion about the timing of our outing. Our trip to Ascot was *today*, you see, and it is tomorrow that we will be accompanying you and Colonel Plimmswood to Almack's."

Her steady stream of chatter worked. As she scrambled from the carriage and hurried toward the house, her sister never had the chance to say what she was obviously thinking: *Have you all gone mad?* When Elizabeth reached her, she hooked her by the arm and jerked her through the door.

There were two more battered ninjas lying in the foyer, and another hung over a nearby banister.

"Really," Elizabeth said, "did you have to thrash the whole household?"

"They wouldn't tell me where you were."

"Mary, I don't think any of them speak English."

"Ah. That would explain why the conversation was going so poorly."

"The drawing room!" Mr. Bennet barked. He let his half of "Arnold"—the top half—plop unceremoniously to the floor. "Now!"

When everyone was gathered in the drawing room a moment later, it wasn't Mary on whom Mr. Bennet fixed his glare. It was Kitty.

"All right, yes! I sent her a letter!" she blubbered. "I'm sorry! I couldn't help myself. I just had to tell *someone*. I was discreet, though, really! All I said was that our plans had changed and we were in London and awful and exciting things were happening."

Elizabeth turned to Mary and braced herself for an answer she didn't want to hear.

"Did Mother see the letter?"

"No."

Elizabeth and her father heaved identical sighs of relief. If Mrs. Bennet knew they were secretly in London, the "secretly" would only apply for roughly five more minutes.

"So far as Mama knows," Mary continued, "I have been summoned to Berkshire to root out an infestation of dreadfuls in Windsor Castle."

"And she let you go?" Kitty asked, incredulous.

"'Let' is not quite the right word." Mary thought a moment and then shrugged. "She couldn't stop me."

Mr. Bennet nodded gravely and then walked to the divan upon which Kitty sat and placed his hands on her shoulders.

"I am very fond of you, my child," he said, "but if you answer my next question incorrectly, I shall be forced to beat you unmercifully with bamboo rods. It will sadden me, without doubt, yet our revered Master Liu would assuredly counsel me to do far worse. Now, tell me: Did you also write a letter to your sister Lydia?"

"No."

Mr. Bennet tightened his grip. "Truly?"

"Well, did I *write* it? Yes. But I never got the chance to sneak out and mail it. It's still hidden in the dresser in my room."

Mr. Bennet leaned in and kissed his daughter on the forehead.

"You are saved," he said. "As is Mr. Darcy. If Lydia were to show up, too, our little ruse wouldn't last the afternoon."

"Mr. Darcy?" Mary said. "Is he in some kind of danger?"

Elizabeth sighed again and repeated her story for the benefit of her other sister. As she listened, Mary asked no questions and offered no commentary, save for a single "I'm so sorry" upon hearing that Darcy had been tainted by the plague. Once Elizabeth was done, Mary took a moment to coolly appraise each person in the room—her sisters, her father, Nezu (who didn't seem to feel the slightest discomfort about crashing a family conference)—before speaking again.

"And none of you considered other avenues by which the cure might be obtained?"

It was the reaction Elizabeth had expected: pious disapproval. She felt her face flush with shame—and not a little resentment.

"We would not even know the cure existed, nor would my husband still be alive to benefit from it, if not for Lady Catherine," Elizabeth said. "Our efforts here in London are made possible only through her. I see no choice but to proceed as she directs."

"Perhaps you are right," Mary replied with all the smugness that implies that a "yet" or "however" or "but" is coming. "Yet still I find it curious that Lady Catherine would see no better use for you and Kitty than as temptresses. The lady herself knows that women are capable of far more than mere allurement. Why would she not call upon the mastery of the deadly arts that has thwarted her so often in the past? Why resort to romantic entanglements and elaborate intrigues?"

"Because that is all Lady Catherine thinks we're good for," Elizabeth was about to say.

Nezu spoke first.

"If you are suggesting a more direct approach—such as, say, an assault on Sir Angus's laboratory—I can answer your question. My mistress has already made the attempt more than once. I would say that those she sent to Bethlem Hospital met the same fate as the many she once dispatched to Pemberley." There was the slightest pause as Nezu's frosty gaze slid over to Elizabeth. "But I don't know that for a fact. I only know that they were never heard from again."

"I see," Mary said, and again her tone told Elizabeth that a "however" or an "all the same" was on its way. Standing firmly on principle was one of her sister's few joys in life; once she took a position, she was as likely to change it as a marble statue was to change its own.

"All the same," Mary said, "I would point out that we are no one's minions. We are Shaolin warriors. Or *were*, in some cases."

She nodded at Elizabeth.

Elizabeth resisted the urge to show her just how sharp her Shaolin skills still were.

"What's more," Mary went on obliviously, "this reliance on roundabout—"

Nezu silenced her with a raised hand.

"Goodness!" Kitty giggled. "If only I'd known it was so easy. I'd have been doing that for years now!"

Mr. Bennet shushed her.

"You hear something?" he said to Nezu.

"Footsteps," Elizabeth answered for him. "Just outside. A man, long-legged, firm of purpose. He is about to—"

Someone knocked on the front door.

Nezu slipped quickly to the windows. The portico wasn't visible from there, yet one could look out on the road before the house.

"There is a carriage waiting," Nezu reported. "A landau. Very large. Very fine."

A moment later, a servant—one with a prodigious black eye—came in bearing a card on a silver platter.

He took it to Nezu.

"My mistress might be in Kent, but she has a long reach," he said upon reading it. "Gossip that she has planted about the presumptuous Shevington family and their lavish One North residence has reached the right ears."

"Sir Angus MacFarquhar's?" Mr. Bennet said.

Nezu nodded.

"Sir Angus is here? Now?" Elizabeth said. It was the sort of pointless regurgitation of news she usually disdained—like exclaiming, "His head? Bitten off?" when informed that an acquaintance has just had his head bitten off. She couldn't help it, though.

She wasn't prepared for this. Wasn't ready to play the part of seductress.

Really . . . would she ever be?

Her father seemed to know just what she was thinking.

"'Opportunities multiply as they are seized,'" he said, quoting Sun Tzu. "He is here. We must act. Steel yourself as you can. It might help if you were to reflect upon what we saw of the man earlier today. I don't think you'll have to play the coquette, my dear." He turned to Kitty and

Mary. "Avis, Miss Millstone, wait here."

Elizabeth was still puzzling over his advice as she followed him out to the foyer. She began to understand when she heard the angry snap in his voice once he saw Sir Angus.

"You again? Have you come to make off with another of our guests? There would be no audience this time, though I can gather the staff if you'd like."

Sir Angus narrowed his eyes, yet he didn't look affronted.

"Do you know who I am?" he growled.

He was asking Mr. Bennet, but it was Elizabeth who answered.

"We know your name, for it was presented to us on your card. We can infer that you are in some way related to our acquaintance Bunny MacFarquhar. Beyond that, we have only your conduct to judge by."

Sir Angus shifted his gaze to her and held it there. Elizabeth stared back in the way she hoped he'd most appreciate—openly, boldly, uncowed.

He was a proud, stern, hot-tempered man, her father had been reminding her. And such men often respect only those who are themselves proud, stern, and hot tempered.

Of course, sometimes they *hate* anyone who's as proud and stern and hot tempered as they. . . .

After a moment, the tiniest sliver of a smile appeared beneath Sir Angus's salt-and-pepper mustache, and he nodded in a way that suggested, "Touché."

"It is that conduct I have come here to discuss," he said. "Afterrr speaking to my son—forrr that is what young Bunny is to me—I rrrealized that some explanation was due to you. It was not my intention to insult you today, though I can see now that's exactly what I did. The plain truth is this: I do not approve of the dreadful races, would neverrr attend them were it left to my own scruples to decide, and have strenuously conveyed my feelings about them to my son. I was not expecting to see him at Ascot today, as obviously he was not expecting to see me. My angerrr was directed at him alone—though there was enough of it to spill overrr onto those who would keep him company while he flouted his father's wishes. And forrr that I should, and do, apologize."

"Apology accepted," Mr. Bennet replied. "Your plain speaking does you credit, Sir."

Sir Angus acknowledged the compliment with a slight bow, but his eyes were on Elizabeth again.

"I'm sure my father is sympathetic, for he knows the frustrations of willful offspring," she said. "As for myself, I share your objections to the races, if not your zeal for displaying them. My own late husband fell to the plague, and the thought of him chasing after Irishmen for the amusement of the masses is sickening, indeed. Why I let myself be coaxed into going I do not know, but I owe you my thanks for giving us reason to leave all the sooner."

Elizabeth did her best to sound civil, though not entirely appeased.

"Your plain speaking does *you* credit, Madam," Sir Angus said. "I bid you both good day."

He bowed again and then turned to go. Nezu had slipped into the hall to eavesdrop while pretending to wait for orders, and now he darted around the Bennets, trying to reach the front door to spare the gentleman the indignity of opening it himself.

"I know how to turn a doorrrknob, man," Sir Angus snarled, and he let himself out and stomped off toward the street.

"And so our second MacFarquhar of the day slips through the net," Nezu said.

Mr. Bennet and Elizabeth stepped up beside him.

"You are an extremely intelligent and observant young man, Nezu," Mr. Bennet said. "When it comes to *amour*, however, you are an utter blockhead."

"Excuse me?"

Out in the street, Sir Angus was hauling his tall, broad frame up into his landau. Once he was seated, he glanced back at the house—and, seeing that he was being watched, looked long and hard at one of the three figures in the doorway. Eventually, he pursed his lips, and though she was too far away to hear it, Elizabeth knew he was saying a single word.

"Go."

The coachman cracked his whip, and the carriage rolled off.

"No, he didn't slip away as cleanly as all that," Mr. Bennet said. "In fact, I daresay he's still ours to catch, so long as we don't draw in the net too quickly."

A burning queasiness churned in the pit of Elizabeth's stomach, and her hands began to itch as if chafing at nothing but their own skin. She didn't know if it was because she suspected her father was right or because, in spite of everything, part of her hoped he might be wrong.

CHAPTER 17

With more rest and ample servings of roe and sashimi and regular doses of his aunt's elixir, Darcy began to regain his strength. Yet the world around him remained a gray place draped in a dingy haze. Only occasionally did flashes of light and splashes of color cut through the gloom and warm him somewhere deep inside: in his dreams of tangy-fresh liverwurst and near-raw rashers and the red juice of undercooked beef running over his chin. Or anywhere there was life.

It gave him all the more reason to struggle out of bed, dress himself without fainting, and shuffle out the door, for his room now had the air of a tomb. To once again feel fully alive, he had to be among living things. Birds, insects, squirrels, people. It didn't matter which. The mere presence of life strengthened him—though he always felt compelled to get closer, to take from it something it wasn't giving, something hidden, hoarded. He was a hungry man always smelling a feast he couldn't see, let alone eat.

Which was why he ended up taking so many long walks with his cousin. Lady Catherine he saw only twice a day, when she administered his medicine and coolly inquired about his dreams and appetite and bodily functions. The rest of the time she was off "on patrol" or "attending to affairs." Her Ladyship's servants, meanwhile, were skittish, her ninjas standoffish. Besides, it would hardly be fitting for a gentleman to keep company with the help.

So Anne became his near-constant companion, and each day they rambled around the grounds together. They spoke of their childhoods and family members long dead or, for long stretches, merely strolled side by side in silence. Thus the conversation was kept to either the past or nothing. What neither ever brought up, by unspoken mutual agreement, was how the present was once supposed to look and what the future might hold for them.

Until, that is, one of their walks took them both farther and further than ever before. It was late afternoon, approaching evening, and they'd strolled so long Darcy no longer recognized where they were. The ground swept up and down in bramble-covered hills that felt like the cresting waves of a choppy sea, and the slant of the setting sun sent beams of radiance slicing through the trees while leaving the gulleys in shadows as dark—to Darcy, anyway—as any ocean depths.

"Perhaps we should turn back," Darcy said. "We have strayed far from the house, and the spring dreadfuls lack the sense to give Rosings a wide berth."

"Oh, I'm not worried," Anne replied blithely.

She was dressed, as always, in black, and with Darcy's vision muddled as it was, all he could see clearly of her was a pale face that floated along beside him, smiling serenely. She paused to admire something above them—a starling trying to stuff a fluttering moth into the upturned mouth of a cheeping chick, Darcy saw when he looked up—and then moved on.

"Perhaps the slightest bit of worry, or at least *caution*, would be in order," Darcy said. "I am in no condition to defend us should any unmentionables avoid Lady Catherine and her traps, and you . . . well . . . "

"I am a weakling untrained in the ways of death," Anne said. For some reason, her smile grew.

"I would not have used those words."

"Surely, I captured your sentiments, though."

They were heading down into another ravine, and the light grew so murky that Darcy was no longer certain they were on a trodden path anymore. Yet Anne walked with such a sure step, Darcy found himself carrying on beside her.

"Anne," he began.

"Tell me, Fitzwilliam," his cousin cut in. "Is that what first drew you to Elizabeth Bennet? Her skills as a warrior? Lady Catherine disparages them, but I can tell when she's talking simply to convince herself. Your wife's talents must be quite formidable for her to have withstood Her Ladyship's wrath."

"Elizabeth is a great warrior. Or *was* a great warrior. She's given all that up now, of course. But, no. That is not what intrigued me. It was her spirit. Her wit. Her intelligence. Her strength of character."

He almost stopped there. The conversation was already going places that made him uncomfortable. He couldn't help but add one more thing, however, because he'd been thinking of it much, and it was true. It bolstered something within him to say it aloud.

"And her beauty, too, of course. To be honest, it was that which I noticed first."

Anne laughed softly. "Oh, Fitzwilliam. You say that as though it's something to be ashamed of. All it really means is that you are a mortal man, after all. Flesh and blood instead of a paragon of virtue up on a pedestal. Your wife, on the other hand, sounds like quite the goddess! Is there any positive quality she doesn't possess, by your reckoning?"

"None I can name."

"Perhaps you lack my vocabulary."

"Do you accuse my wife of something?" Darcy snapped.

"Oh, no. Certainly not. How unfair that would be when she is not here with us to defend herself."

And there it was: the accusation made without being spoken. The list of Elizabeth's virtues was long, indeed, but the benefit of every one she was denying her husband now, for she'd sent him far from her at the very moment he needed her most. He didn't even have the cold comfort of a letter inquiring after his condition. No word from Derbyshire had reached him in the week he'd been at Rosings.

They were at the bottom of the gully now, and Darcy stumbled over rocks and twisted roots he couldn't see.

"If you're not ready to go back, at least let us walk where there is more light."

"Light is overrated," Anne said. "One misses so much when confined to it. Take this, for instance." She stopped and did a spin. "This is my favorite place on the whole estate."

"It is?"

All Darcy could make out was a small, dim glade that was remarkable only for a looming outcropping of stone that bordered it on one side.

"It's so wonderfully still here," Anne said, her voice hushed. She kept moving in a slow circle, her arms spread wide. "So tranquil. Especially now, at dusk. Does it seem to you sometimes that night and day are at war? That one must always obliterate the other? Here, now, however, it is neither night nor day. There *can* be something in between. There can be peace. That is why I love it here. It makes me feel . . . safe."

She stopped, facing Darcy, just as a breeze swept into the ravine and stirred up an all-too-familiar stench.

"Anne . . . "

Darcy heard a low, growling groan to his right—from the wall of stone that jutted up ten or twelve feet into the air. He turned toward it, squinting, and saw that the rock face wasn't as sheer as he'd first thought. There was a black crack in its center partially hidden by a mossy rise in the earth. It was perhaps six feet tall by three wide. The same size as a doorway. A path wound out of it—the kind worn into the ground by heavy, shuffling feet.

"We must go. Quickly," Darcy whispered.

"Oh, I think it's too late for that," Anne replied.

There was movement in the fissure—a blackness stirring within the blackness. Within the *cave*, Darcy now knew.

"Do as I do," Anne said.

She stepped back a few paces, raised her hands in the air, spread her fingers wide, and gazed off at nothing.

"Be a tree."

"*What*?"

"Be a tree," Anne said. "Or be supper."

The reek of rotten meat was overpowering now. The solitary groan had become a chorus. Darcy was too weak to fight, too blind to flee.

He brought up his hands and became a tree.

The first dreadful to stagger out of the cave moved slowly and awkwardly, even by zombie standards. Some mishap had twisted its head around on its neck so that it had to walk backward to see where it was going. It had been a woman, and it occasionally tripped on the hem of its tattered skirts. Its flesh was gray and frayed, its lidless eyes so wide they looked like they might fall from their sockets. Yet there was no sign it saw Anne and Darcy. The creature simply shuffled between the two "trees" and carried on out of the gully.

The next dreadful did the same, and the next, and the next. There were fourteen in all, some old, some fresh. One was still gnawing with literal absent-mindedness on an arm that had been torn from the zombie before it. Another seemed to be little more than strips of gnarled leather spackled here and there with matted fur. It looked like it had spent the last millennia pickled in a bog.

All the unmentionables had one thing in common: Darcy could see in them no hint of the spark that drew him to living things. Instead of light, they had at their core gray smudges of nothing.

As each one tottered past, Darcy silently repeated his new mantra: *I am a tree. I am a tree. I am a tree. I am a tree.*

And the zombies seemed to believe it. Or to find him unworthy of their attention, at least. Once the last one was past him, Darcy let himself breathe a sigh of relief.

He'd forgotten for a moment that trees don't sigh.

The dreadful at the back of the line turned and came toward him.

It was a male of perhaps thirty years of age when it had died—that death having taken place some weeks past, to judge by the putrefaction. It had upon it not a single stitch of clothing to hide the advanced state of its decay or to stifle the attendant odors thereof. Its skin was black, its limbs bloated, its burst belly a cornucopia of dangling viscera.

It stopped directly in front of Darcy and stared at him with eyes ringed by writhing maggots.

I am a tree. I am a tree. I am a tree I am a tree.

The unmentionable leaned in close, and something rough yet moist moved up Darcy's neck. It was only after the zombie turned and lurched off again, growling, that Darcy realized that the something had been a tongue.

The dreadful had tasted him and found him not to its liking. All the same, Darcy waited a long, long time before sighing again.

"I told you this place was special," Anne said.

She was no longer a tree. She was a woman again.

One who was laughing.

CHAPTER 18

The day after Sir Angus's call on the Shevingtons, a servant arrived bearing a note from him.

Dear Mr. Shevington:

My son tells me that your family is new to London. I propose, then, that a tour is in order. I hope you will allow me, an immigrant to this great city myself some years ago, to be your guide. It would go some ways further, I feel, toward making amends for the presumption and rudeness you might still associate with the name MacFarquhar. Send word if you intend to accept my offer, and my son and I will collect you and your daughters at a time of your choosing.

Your humble servant,

Sir Angus MacFarquhar

"You were right about having him in the net," Nezu said to Mr. Bennet.

"So it would seem. Shall we begin hauling him in?"

Mr. Bennet turned to Elizabeth.

She nodded.

Four hours later, the MacFarquhars were in front of the house in their open-topped landau. Mr. Bennet and Elizabeth and Kitty joined them as a glummer-than-usual Nezu—who, try as he might (and did), could offer no valid excuse for accompanying the party—watched from the portico. Mary, meanwhile, lurked out of sight inside. At first, Elizabeth had feared she might want to come along as a heretofore unseen Shevington. Instead, she'd announced her intention to spend the day "meditating on the other ways I might prove myself useful."

"Splendid, my dear, splendid," her father had said, and it was obvious to Elizabeth that, in his mind, the greatest use Mary could make of herself was to keep on meditating—preferably in a closet—until their unsavory business in London was done.

Unfortunately, it wouldn't be concluding anytime soon. As the driver guided the MacFarquhars' landau through the streets, it quickly became apparent that he was taking them southwest. They were headed back to the more fashionable, well-protected sections far from the city's fringes. Which meant they were headed *away* from Bethlem Royal Hospital. Sir Angus's laboratory wouldn't be on the tour.

Mr. Bennet noticed, too—and, unlike Elizabeth, couldn't resist commenting on it.

"I've been told, Sir Angus, that you're one of the administrators of the famous 'Bedlam' Hospital. I do hope a visit is on today's itinerary."

"The days when one could come in and gawp at the Bedlamites arrre done," an icy Sir Angus replied. He hadn't been particularly warm before then, either, though Elizabeth suspected his chilly disposition had less to do with his guests than with Bunny's giggly fawning over Kitty and the miniature coat, cravat, and trousers in which his son had dressed Brummell that day. "The hospital's no longerrr open to the public. At any rate, it's in Section Twelve Central. And if you'd everrr been there, you'd not wonderrr why I don't take you and your daughters there today."

Mr. Bennet clamped his lips together in a way that promised not another word would be said on the subject. Satisfied, Sir Angus launched into a detailed history of the watch towers scattered along St. John Street Road. His travelogue expanded to include each wall, moat, and gate they passed, and he even (delicately, of course, and employing much in the way of metaphor) talked about the extensive new sewer system that had been necessary when so much of the city was cut off from the river it had for centuries used as its communal chamber pot.

Despite his incessant stream of trivia, Elizabeth didn't think Sir Angus a bore. He struck her more as a man who took his obligations seriously: He'd promised them a tour, and by gad he was going to give them one. Elizabeth heard little she didn't already know, yet she wasn't annoyed. In fact, she came to find the low, growling roughness of Sir Angus's rolled *R*'s strangely soothing, like the purring of an especially large cat.

Kitty, on the other hand, could have learned a great deal had she been paying the slightest bit of attention. She and Bunny were facing each other, and the two quickly fell into whispered jokes and half-muffled giggles that were interrupted only when Bunny wanted to point out a favorite shop or lift Brummell for a friendly wave of the paw at an acquaintance in another carriage. Sir Angus and Elizabeth and Mr. Bennet ignored them with the same studied obliviousness that falls over a dinner party when the host makes the sort of noise people of good taste insist doesn't exist.

The two separate parties—Sir Angus and Elizabeth and Mr. Bennet, Kitty and Bunny and Brummell—splintered even further when the tour reached its climax: the Vauxhall pleasure gardens in Section Four South. Bunny dragged Kitty and Brummell off toward one of the far arbors, where a hot-air balloon would be making an ascent into the dingy-dull late afternoon sky. Mr. Bennet, meanwhile, feigned enchantment at the sound of Handel floating through the air, and he drifted off toward the orchestra pavilion looking as entranced as any sailor hearing the siren's song.

At last, Elizabeth was alone with Sir Angus . . . alone with her *prey*, she couldn't help thinking. It filled her with such sudden, overpowering self-loathing, every conversational gambit she'd concocted was forgotten. To lure this man into a dalliance would only confirm everything Lady Catherine ever accused her of. So she simply strolled silently by his side, thinking of Darcy, trying to draw from her love for her husband the strength she needed to both betray and save him.

Up ahead, Bunny and Kitty were pausing by one of the gurgling cascades dotting Vauxhall's tree-lined paths. Bunny jammed a hand into a pocket and threw a handful of coins into the water. Some witticism apparently followed, for so, too, did a "Ho!" from the young man and a "La!" from his female counterpart.

Elizabeth was aiming an appraising glance over at Sir Angus just when he pointed one at her. Their eyes met, and they both smiled ruefully.

"I am not a betting man, Mrs. Bromhead," Sir Angus said. "But I would wagerrr that you and I were just searching for the same thing."

"And did you find it?" Elizabeth asked.

Sir Angus tilted his head this way and that, as if examining her face from a variety of angles.

"Around the mouth a little, maybe. And the ears. Otherrr that that, no. No family rrrresemblance at all."

"Avis takes after my mother . . . in more ways than one," Elizabeth said. She cocked her head as Sir Angus had, making a careful study of the man's wavy gray hair and prominent forehead and strong, blocky features.

"You can look all you want," Sir Angus said. "You won't see much of Bunny in me. It's as with your sisterrr. He's his mother's child. He *is* his mother, rrreally." His smile, not large to begin with, faded to nothing. "When my son came into the world, my wife's soul left it, and thus some balance was rrretained. God knows, His creation couldn't have survived the two of them at once."

"Your wife was a . . . formidable individual?"

"Formidably silly, yes. And formidably beautiful. It's a combination that often appeals to a man, when he's still young and silly himself."

Sir Angus looked off again at Bunny and Kitty. The balloon ascent had apparently been forgotten, for they were still by the little waterfall, Kitty cackling as Brummell (with some help from Bunny) tossed another coin into the foam.

"In that way, perhaps, there's a bit of me in Bunny, afterrr all," Sir Angus said. He glanced over at Elizabeth and smiled again, warily this time. "If you'll pardon my saying so."

"You can have my pardon if you want it, but it isn't needed. I take no offense. My sister *is* spectacularly silly. You merely speak the truth, without artifice. I find that admirable in a gentleman."

Sir Angus offered Elizabeth a small bow.

"Since you praise forthrightness, I hope I may say without being thought overrrbold that I feel the same admiration for plain-spoken ladies."

"You may."

"Then I do."

A tittering couple suddenly darted between them, separating them before veering off onto one of the shadowy "dark walks" that were, Elizabeth knew, so popular with young lovers seeking privacy. The little shrubbery-shrouded path was even darker than usual, for dusk wasn't far off, and attendants had only just begun lighting the thousands of paper lanterns strung throughout the gardens. The couple faded into the murk, their silhouettes merging as a final, lecherous laugh echoed out of the gloom.

The interruption seemed to sober Sir Angus, for when he resumed conversation, he did so with a somber expression and a very different subject.

"I understand your fatherrr is an industrialist of some kind. Has he experimented with Zed laborrr, as have others in the north?"

"No, though he sees potential profit in it, of course. What factory owner wants workers who insist on sleeping and eating and who complain when ground up in the gears? He hasn't brought in any unmentionables, however . . . largely because I won't stand for it."

"You object on the same grounds you disapprove of the rrraces?"

Elizabeth nodded. It wasn't hard to feign a silent upswell of emotion. In fact, when she thought of Darcy and what some would do to him, if they could, she wasn't feigning at all.

"I wonderrr, Mrs. Bromhead," Sir Angus said, watching her in a way that suddenly seemed wary and calculating, "are you a memberrr of the Society for the Prevention of Cruelty to Zed-dash-dash-dash-dash-dashes?"

Elizabeth stifled a bitter laugh. Few in England had shown the dreadfuls less mercy than she.

"No. The SPCZed goes too far. I accept that the unmentionables must be dealt with firmly. Decisively. Yet that doesn't give us the right to . . . is something wrong?"

Sir Angus wasn't looking at Elizabeth anymore. He was scowling at something just off the path they'd been sauntering along. Elizabeth followed his angry gaze.

Bunny and Kitty, she saw, had joined a small group of young men in a circle of crumbling Doric columns—faux-Roman ruins that had been installed in the gardens a few years earlier. The gentlemen were all dressed as stylishly as Bunny, though the styles varied wildly. In fact, that's what seemed to separate them. The young bucks closest to Bunny (several of whom Elizabeth recognized from his lark with the zombie) wore trousers and frock coats and boots tailored in snug, straight lines and sober hues. The men facing them, by contrast, were adorned with so much frillery—large, lacy cuffs and powdered wigs and morning coats of pink and purple satin—that any one of them, with just a few alterations, could have passed for a Parisian courtesan.

The two groups were lined up like skirmishers facing each other on the battlefield. Elizabeth couldn't hear what any were saying, but the way the men alternately glowered and laughed told her insults were being volleyed back and forth.

"Such foolishness," Sir Angus grumbled as he stomped toward them. "With all the turmoil in the world, they have to create morrre out of buttons and silk."

Up ahead, Bunny was escorting Kitty back a few steps and putting Brummell in her arms before turning and striking a stiff pose: chin high, chest out, arms raised, fists clenched. Bunny, it seemed, was a practitioner of Britkata, a bastardization of the deadly arts that emphasized English dignity above all else. He'd struck the Affronted Noble stance. His comrades did the same, while the men facing them all assumed the Haughty Vicar.

"They're going to fight?" Elizabeth asked. "But why?"

Sir Angus quickened his pace. "My son and his friends arrre dandies."

"And the others?"

"Fops, of course."

Elizabeth recalled again why she'd given up on London.

"You therrre!" Sir Angus barked. "Don't you darrre!"

It was too late. The fight had begun.

Bunny threw the first punch—if merely straightening one's arm and poking at empty air could be called a punch. To Elizabeth's eyes, it looked more like he was practicing the offering of flowers to potential paramours. His friends waded in with jabs that were equally weak, and even when they connected—which was infrequently—they seemed to have no effect at all. The worst injury any of their foes sustained was a slightly loosened wig.

The fops, meanwhile, were far more accurate with their face slaps and back-handed smacks, and the battle quickly turned into a rout, with one dandy after another staggering back with monogrammed hankie pressed to bloodied nose. Bunny was the last dandy standing when an unlikely ally charged in to save him.

Actually, Brummell didn't so much charge in as fly. Despite Kitty's cry of "No! Come back!" it wasn't the rabbit's choice to go to Bunny's aid. Kitty had flung him into the fray and then dashed after him, squealing, "Brummell, stop! Someone will step on you!"

She grabbed at the rabbit and "accidentally" head-butted a fop in the gut.

She spun after a darting Brummell and "accidentally" sent another fop sprawling with her hip.

She chased Brummell in a circle, "accidentally" crushing fop toes, elbowing fop faces, and (Elizabeth could but pray she alone noticed) kicking a heel backward into one unfortunate's most foppy parts.

Only when all the fops were stretched out on the ground, whimpering or (in some cases) weeping, did a seemingly oblivious Kitty snatch Brummell up and admonish him with a finger-wagging, "Bad rabbit!"

"Oh, I beg to differ, Miss Shevington!" Bunny cried giddily. "Good rabbit! *Great* rabbit! And you're rather magnificent yourself!"

He was leaning in to kiss either Kitty or Brummell when a hand on his starched collar jerked him back.

"We'rrre leaving," Sir Angus said.

He gave his son a shove toward the pleasure garden's central path—and the crowd that had gathered there to gawk and whisper and giggle. As Bunny went slinking off through the throng, Sir Angus turned to Elizabeth, looking more anguished now than enraged.

"Mrs. Bromhead, I . . . I . . . "

His gaze flicked over to Kitty, and all emotion drained from his face. When he continued, his tone was cold and controlled.

"I'll have the carriage brought rrround. If you would be so good as to collect your fatherrr and meet us out front."

Then he, too, stalked off into the onlookers. The crowd had the good sense to part for him.

Kitty stepped up beside Elizabeth, Brummell still cradled in her arms.

"And I used to think *we* caused a lot of scenes," she said. "We're nothing compared to the MacFarquhars."

"Oh? You don't think you made a spectacle of yourself just now?"

"I was ending a spectacle, not starting one. And it wasn't me. It was—"

"Don't blame the rabbit," Elizabeth said.

Bunny's friends were milling about dazedly, heads back, crimson-stained handkerchiefs still jammed to their faces. The fops, meanwhile, were starting to get back to their feet.

"Let's go," Elizabeth said. "If there's to be another Britkata demonstration, I want us to be as far away as possible."

"Good idea. I don't think I'd be able to keep from laughing a second time."

As Elizabeth and Kitty moved through the spectators, one among them—a short, slender man who slipped out from behind a particularly broad-beamed lady—started walking with them.

"Your lack of discipline might have ruined everything," he said to Kitty.

It was Nezu.

"And you are so overstocked with discipline that you can criticize?" Elizabeth snapped back at him. "When *you* risk everything by speaking to us where the MacFarquhars might see you?"

Nezu bowed slightly and then slowed his pace until he was behind the ladies, following them at a distance—as, it seemed, he'd been doing all afternoon.

Kitty threw him a look over her shoulder that started out as a pouty glare before transforming into something more confused, and perhaps even amused.

"Well put, Lizzy. Who is he to pass judgment on us?"

Elizabeth said nothing, though she knew the answer.

Who was he to pass judgment?

The one who was right.

CHAPTER 19

Mary let all of half a minute pass after her father and sisters rode off in the MacFarquhars' landau. Then she joined them on the streets of London.

Not the same streets, though. Not for long. She had her own destination in mind.

She wasn't just leaving the house. She was walking away from the role she'd been assigned both as a woman and a Bennet. Second fiddle. Nursemaid. Lady in waiting who was never supposed to do anything *but* wait.

Well, she wasn't waiting any longer. She'd come all the way from Hertfordshire to help, and help she would.

The nearest shop was a small bookseller's around the corner, and Mary marched in and asked the way to Bethlem Royal Hospital.

"That's two questions you're really asking, Miss," the man behind the counter said. He was a roly-poly fellow with spectacles sliding so far down the bridge of his nose they seemed in imminent danger of falling into his mouth. "*Could* I tell you the way? Why, it's but a twenty minute walk from here down to the grounds of the Foundling Hospital, where they moved old Bedlam after the Siege of '97. So that's a yes for you, young miss. Yes, indeed. But *will* I tell you? *Can* I, in good conscience? Nooooooooo. No, indeed."

"Why not?"

"Because, Miss, Bethlem Royal Hospital is in Section Twelve Central, and if I were to send you there I would be as guilty of murder as whichever footpads or unmentionables got hold of you first."

The shopkeeper leaned over the counter and popped his eyes wide on the word "murder," saying it as one would "Boo!" to a small child.

"And what if I were to tell you," Mary replied coolly, "that the footpads and unmentionables have more to fear from me than I do from them?"

The man scratched the lowermost of his several chins. "Then I do believe I would laugh, Miss, very much like this." He cleared his throat. "Ho ho ho!"

Mary had never snapped a living man's neck, but this was a day for new experiences, and she was momentarily tempted to give it a try.

"Will your scruples allow you to sell me a guidebook to London?"

she said instead.

"Oh, yes. Yes, indeed. What a lady does with a guidebook is no business of mine, once it has been paid for."

"Then I will take one."

"I recommend this." The shopkeeper reached under the counter and produced a slender volume. "*London: Being a Complete Guide to the British Capital; Containing, a Full and Accurate Account of its Buildings, Commerce, Curiosities*—"

"I will take it."

"—*Exhibitions, Amusements, Religious and Charitable Foundations, Literary Establishments, Learned and Scientific Institutions: Including a Sketch of the*—"

"I will take it."

"—*Surrounding Country, with Full Directions to Strangers on Their First Arrival.*"

"I said I will take it."

"By John Wallis."

"Yes, yes. I will take it."

"I have not yet quoted you a price."

Mary found herself gritting her teeth in a way she hadn't done since her sister Lydia left home.

"How much is it?"

"One shilling and sixpence."

"*I will take it.*"

"There's no need to be snippy, Miss," the shopkeeper said, but at last he held out a pudgy hand, palm up.

Mary reached into her reticule, careful to avoid the pistol inside lest she be tempted to make use of it.

Once book and coins had changed hands, Mary said, "Do you also have in stock Mary Wollstonecraft's *A Vindication of the Rights of Woman*?"

The shopkeeper nodded, half-smiling, as if her question answered one of his own.

"Indeed, I do. Two shillings. But wouldn't the young lady prefer a nice frothy novel, instead?"

Mary put the coins on the counter.

"I'm not buying the book for myself," she said. "Be so good as to give it to the next young lady who comes in looking for a nice frothy novel."

Mary walked out of the shop so absorbed in her guidebook that she didn't even notice the scruffy dog sitting patiently beside the door. Nor did she notice that it hopped up and darted around the corner the moment she passed, as if it had been waiting for her to emerge.

She was too busy plotting her course. While her father and sisters practically circumnavigated the globe to get to Bethlem Hospital, she would go there in as straight a line as possible.

Her first major zig came at the north gate to Section Twelve Central: The soldiers there refused to let her pass.

"I had daughters myself, once," said the captain of the guard, a grizzled man with only one of nearly everything—hands, ears, eyes, nostrils, legs—that God granted in pairs at birth. "No other father shall be deprived of his on my watch."

With a simple zag, however, Mary was back on course: After circling around to the east gate from Section Eleven Central, she was able to carry on toward Bethlem Hospital. In fact, this time the guards let her pass with nary a question, waving her through almost as if they'd been expecting her. (If Mary hadn't been consulting her guidebook again, she might have noticed the dogs watching her from behind the sentry booth and the squat black box they flanked.)

"The accompanying map we provide only out of obligation to comprehensiveness," Mary read from the brief chapter on Section Twelve Central. "If you value your life, you will make no attempt to use it. Study instead the maps of One North and Eleven Central, so that you will know well the roads leading *away* from what you see depicted here."

It struck Mary as melodramatic, all this humbug about the hellishness of Twelve Central. She'd just walked along the edge of One North and Eleven Central entirely unmolested, and how much difference could a few feet of limestone make?

She looked up from her book and found her answer.

A lot.

Passing through the gate hadn't just brought her to a different part of London. It seemed to have transported her to a different time—somewhere in the Dark Ages, perhaps.

She had to assume that the street before her was paved with cobblestones, as were the ones she'd just left behind, for it was so covered with mud and garbage and the vilest filth of human making that she couldn't see the street at all. The creatures along this wretched avenue were dressed in shabby fourth-hand clothing or mere rags or, to Mary's dismay, nothing at all: She spotted several naked children, empty bellies protruding before them like little drums, staring at her with glassy, sunken eyes from alleys and doorways. Here and there bodies lay in the gutters before the ramshackle buildings, some with the heads removed or crudely crushed, others ready to reawaken to darkness at any moment. Two slow-moving men were collecting them, tossing the corpses onto the back of a dray already heaped high with more of the same. Something squirmed and moaned at the bottom of the pile, but whether it was someone in their last moments of life or their first of undeath would soon make no difference, for Mary could see where the cart's cargo was headed: the chimneys of a crematorium that spewed black over the nearest rooftops.

It was then that Mary knew the secret of the city's walls. They were as much for locking this horror in as keeping the dreadfuls out. And not only was she supposed to stay on the right side of the stones, she wasn't even meant to know how very, *very* wrong the wrong side really was.

A true lady would turn and flee.

Mary straightened her spine and started up the street.

As she weaved around the largest mounds of muck, the men loading the dray paused to gape at her, the stiff carcass of a woman stretched between them, its severed head resting on its stomach.

"You've picked a poor time to come sightseeing," one of them said. "Unless you want a dose of cholera to go with the bad memories."

Mary could think of no reply, and so made none. She did, however, give the bodies lining the streets a wider berth.

Even with her map, navigating Twelve Central proved difficult, for the street signs (where any existed) were so blackened with soot they were unreadable, and what passersby Mary encountered answered her queries with snorts or shakes of the head or, most frequently, some variation on "Bedlam, eh? That's certainly where you belong when you chose to wander around *here*." Eventually, however, a sandy-haired, apple-cheeked boy in tattered clothes offered to lead her to Bethlem Hospital for two farthings.

"That seems quite reasonable," Mary said, and she fished out the coins and handed them over. "You will receive four more if we're there within a quarter hour."

"A whole penny?" the boy exclaimed. "God blind me, let's go!"

Mary followed him up the street, around the first corner, and then into a narrow darkened alley—both ends of which were quickly blocked off by grime-smeared men wielding Zed rods and knives.

"'Allo 'allo, fancy lady," said the burliest, dirtiest of them. "Are you a reformer, then? Come to improve our miserable lot? Well, me friends and I can make some suggestions as to how you might start."

Mary sighed. Kitty had gone on and on about the way Lady Catherine's ninjas had ambushed her and Papa in an alley a few days before, and now she'd walked right into the same sort of trap. Certain details would have to be omitted when she told her sister about all this. And she was certain—for it didn't occur to her that there might be reason to think otherwise—that she would be telling her sister about all this at the end of the day. That the end of her *life* might be at hand never crossed her mind.

"You have sacrificed your gratuity, young man," she said to her guide.

The boy just grinned as two of the men moved past him, closing in on Mary.

"Oh, he'll get 'is. I reckon we all will." The big ruffian looked Mary up and down. "Ten bob for the dress, five for the shoes, maybe a tanner for the purse—not to mention whatever's in it—and then thruppence for dragging another bogey to the furnace. Yeah, there'll be plenty to go 'round by the time we're through."

For the first time in her life, Mary found herself envying her sister Elizabeth's wit. She racked her brain, but the gang was nearly on her—two from the front, three from behind. All she could think to say was, "Yes, well, perhaps, perhaps not."

She whipped out her pistol and shot the first thug through the forehead. As he toppled over, she quickly clubbed the stunned man beside him with the smoking barrel while kicking backward. She felt her foot crush half a ribcage, and when she spun around she found, quite incongruously, that the other two hooligans behind her were being attacked by mongrel dogs. As the men kicked at them, screaming, Mary turned again and hurled her pistol end over end at the ringleader. The stock thunked into the man's thick skull, sending him reeling.

The two footpads still on their feet fled toward the street, the dogs at their heels, while the little boy darted off down the alleyway.

Mary strolled over to the gang's leader, who was on his knees, head in hands, and flattened him with a casual snap kick.

"Less expenses," she said.

The man blinked up at her, barely conscious. "Huh?"

"That's what I should have said before. When you were calculating what you might earn from robbing . . . never mind." She put her foot on his throat. "Tell me how to get to Bethlem Royal Hospital—*truthfully*—or my first step away from here will be through your esophagus."

He told her.

"Thank you," Mary said, and she pivoted crisply and went on her way.

"Miss? Oh, Miss?" the thug called after her.

She stopped and turned.

"You wouldn't want to come work for me, would you?" the man wheezed.

A strange sensation came over Mary's face. Her lips tightened. Her eyes crinkled.

It took her a moment to realize she was smiling.

"I am flattered by your offer," she said. "But no, thank you. I find myself quite gainfully employed already."

It was about time, too.

Less than five minutes later, she was at the gates of Bedlam.

CHAPTER 20

No matter how many times Darcy asked, Anne wouldn't tell him where she'd learned the tree trick.

"Actually, I had no idea any dreadfuls were even in that cave," she said as they walked back to the house. "I just thought you'd look smashing with branches."

"Anne, *please*. I really would like to know."

"Oh, it's simply a parlor trick some friends taught me. And that is all I care to say about it at present."

"Fine. If you feel you don't owe me a serious explanation after what we've just been through. . . . "

"I am being serious. Or don't you think I could have friends?"

"No, no!" Darcy said. "That is, yes, yes! Of course, you could. That's not what I meant."

Anne finally lost the smile she'd been wearing for the last ten minutes. "I didn't, you know. Have friends of my own. Not for the longest time. All I had was Lady Catherine. Do you think that should have been enough?"

"No. I don't."

"Good. So it wasn't just me."

Darcy looked into his cousin's eyes as the two of them kept walking side by side. Night had fallen, yet he could see Anne more clearly—and pick his way through the forest with more ease, it seemed—than when the sun had been shining down through the trees.

Before he could speak again, a loud thumping sound drew Anne's attention, and he followed her gaze to find a hazy radiance moving toward them. As it neared, it grew sharper, gained definition, until Darcy could see his aunt riding toward them on one of her enormous Scottish-bred chargers. To his eyes, both glowed with a dull light that cast no shadow, and he found himself wishing to bask in it, bathe in it, wallow in a warmth that wasn't even there.

Lady Catherine stopped her horse before them. Her mount seemed nervous, stamping its heavy hooves and dancing in a semicircle. As its great haunches turned, Darcy could see a cluster of oval shapes strung to its side like an enormous bunch of grapes.

Anne stiffened beside him.

The shapes were freshly severed heads. Darcy recognized among them the puffy black face of the putrid unmentionable that had tried a taste of him not a quarter hour before.

"What do you think you're doing?" Lady Catherine snapped. "You know it's dangerous out here this time of year."

She was looking at her daughter.

"Oh, there was nothing to worry about. We were perfectly safe. Weren't we, Fitzwilliam?"

She wrapped her arm around Darcy's.

"Yes," he heard himself say. "Perfectly."

Her Ladyship kept her gaze on Anne. "Your cousin is not well. It is foolish to take him so far from the house."

"DARCY COULD SEE A CLUSTER OF OVAL SHAPES STRUNG TO ITS SIDE LIKE AN ENORMOUS BUNCH OF GRAPES. THE SHAPES WERE FRESHLY SEVERED HEADS."

So far from me, Darcy suspected she really meant.

"It seems to me," Anne replied, "that Fitzwilliam will end up going further faster if he is not limited to the confines—and the close company—of Rosings. A little more fresh air and freedom, and who knows how quickly he might come 'round as we'd like?"

Lady Catherine narrowed her eyes and jutted out her jaw and flared her nostrils. It was a look Darcy knew well. He'd seen battle-hardened soldiers wither under it like an ant burned by the hot focused light of a magnifying glass. He'd only been its locus a few unhappy times in his life; he'd never seen it pointed at Anne. To his surprise, she withstood it without blinking or looking away.

"I will see you back at the house for supper," Lady Catherine said. "Don't dawdle. Kochi is laying out eel from the Great Stour, and you know how much better that is when it's fresh."

She wheeled her stallion around and galloped off, the heads tied to the horse's flank clunking against each other like muffled castanets.

"I've never stood up to her before," Anne said. "Not about anything." She squeezed Darcy's arm. "I think *I'm* the one growing stronger now . . . thanks to you. You're the only one of us who ever dared defy her."

"It was not something I took pleasure in doing."

"Yet you did it all the same, because you felt you had to. I wonder if I would have passed the test as you did." Anne stared off into the shadows that had quickly swallowed up her mother. "Perhaps someday we will find out."

She looked back up into Darcy's eyes and smiled in a way that was somehow warm and cold at the same time, like a sip of chilled sake. Then she started toward the house, still latched to his side.

In the dining room, they found Lady Catherine already sitting stiffly at the head of the table while Kochi, her favorite sushi chef (for the moment), stood ready at his work table nearby. At the man's feet was a bucket of churning water. Kochi greeted the newcomers with a bow and then plunged a hand into the bucket, plucking out a furiously squirming black eel. Within seconds, it was slapped onto a cutting board, beheaded, sliced into slivers, and presented to the dinner party on small mounds of white rice.

Kochi stood stiffly beside Her Ladyship as she took her first bite. The man did his best not to look like he was bracing for an elbow to what was once known—before the term was appropriated for something deemed even more horrifying—as his unmentionables. If his sashimi didn't rise to the heights his mistress demanded, he would know quickly. And painfully.

"The unagi is . . . ," Lady Catherine began in Japanese.

Kochi fought to keep his hands at his sides, but Darcy could see them inching together involuntarily, creeping toward those appendages he might soon be clutching in agony.

" . . . acceptable."

Kochi let out a deep breath, bowed again, and scurried back to his work station.

Darcy already had a piece of glistening red eel meat pinched in his chopsticks, and now that his aunt had pronounced judgment, he was free to take a bite.

He'd never eaten sawdust, but now he felt he might as well have. He could barely keep himself from retching on the glob of flavorless paste he found himself chewing.

And then, an explosion of not just flavor but warmth radiated from his mouth to the whole of his being. It was the accursed rice! It had blunted the taste of the fish. Now the juices were reaching his tongue, and the little brick of fresh thick-cut flesh was tearing apart between his teeth. With each bite, he could taste more of not just the fish but its strength, its drive to hunt and kill and spread its seed, the riverbed it had been slithering along not long before. Its very life.

Darcy felt almost woozy with pleasure, and his eyes rolled back in his head. He became aware of a guttural groaning that grew louder with each chew.

Then he realized it was coming from *him*.

He blinked and swallowed and peeped over at his aunt and cousin to see if they'd noticed. He found them staring back, Lady Catherine looking revolted, Anne seemingly stifling a laugh.

"Don't worry," Darcy said, dabbing at his face with a napkin. A thin trickle—he could only hope it wasn't drool—had escaped his mouth and run down his chin. "I shan't be yanking fish from Kochi's bucket and gobbling them down whole."

"You may if you like," Anne said. She turned to her mother, grinning. "Isn't that right?"

Lady Catherine was not amused.

"On second thought," the old woman said gravely, "there is a mealiness to this eel. You must be more careful when cutting against the grain, Kochi. I can only hope the next piece is more satisfying."

Kochi went as white as his spotless chef's smock.

Darcy picked up another piece of sashimi with his chopsticks but set it back down again. The next time he took a bite, he wanted to be ready. He distracted himself from the thwarted rumbling of his stomach with the question he asked his aunt every night around this time.

"Any word from Derbyshire?"

He got the same answer as always: "No" and a quick change of subject. ("I can taste the vinegar in the rice, Kochi. You know I don't like that. Come here.")

There was something different about this latest "No," however. It came out as blunt and brusque as always, yet Lady Catherine's gaze never met his. Instead, it jerked toward Anne. As the two women looked into each other's eyes for all of a second, Darcy could sense a change in them he couldn't put a name to. It was as if the light he sometimes saw in living things flared for a moment. Then Lady Catherine was turning her attention to Kochi, and the moment passed.

Darcy had suspected, and now he knew, though he couldn't explain how. Something was being kept from him. Something to do with Derbyshire—and Elizabeth.

There was a yelp from the head of the table, followed by the sound of a man falling to his knees while gasping out apologies in Japanese. Yet Darcy didn't even notice. He was carefully peeling a lump of eel from its bed of rice even as he began planning how to strip away the secrecy that surrounded him.

He was weakened, unsteady, confused. Yet he was still enough of his old self to get to the truth. Or so he had to hope.

He popped the raw meat into his mouth and tried very, very hard not to moan.

CHAPTER 21

If someone had described Section Twelve Central as "hell" that afternoon, Mary could not have disagreed. Now that it was night, however, she was discovering an unpleasant truth: Even hell can get worse.

Her dealings at Bethlem had been brief yet promising, and afterward she'd lingered a while nearby, observing the comings and goings of the hospital staff. Nezu had suggested the place was heavily guarded, but the wooden watch towers at each corner of the grounds stood empty, and the only sentry was a jumpy old man at the front gate. Mary was hoping Sir Angus would drop in for an evening inspection (or whatever it is "administrators" do): If he did, she would accelerate her plan and follow him inside. Somehow. Yet he never arrived, and when at last it became too dark to see anything of Bethlem but candlelight shimmering dimly through a few barred windows, Mary started back toward One North—and began her second tour of Twelve Central.

As earlier, the streets were lined with bodies awaiting collection.

With the corpse wagons gone till dawn, the piles were all the higher, and more of their jaundiced contents had begun to twitch and groan. Here and there, small groups of men attended to the newly awakened with Zed rods, and the cobblestones were slick with pulped brain glistening in the moonlight. For the most part, however, the living of Twelve Central had retreated into their filthy gin shops and tenements, and more than one leaned out an upper-story window to offer commentary as she passed below.

"Ooooo! Looks like a do-gooder went and stayed too long amongst the unwashed. I do hope she's alive in the morning to bring us back more alms!"

"Could you tell the soldiers to pop 'round on your way out, Your Highness? I've a dead chimney sweep stuck up my flue, and he's starting to make an awful fuss."

"You don't want to be out on them streets alone, Milady. Why not come up 'ere and spend the night safe an' sound with ol' Bill?"

Sometimes all Mary heard was a hiss or growl from the shadows, as if even the dreadfuls were heckling her. Yet despite the ghastliness all around, she walked on unafraid. It wasn't just because she had supreme confidence in her own abilities—though that she did. She also knew she wasn't alone. She had an escort, as she had on her way to Bethlem Hospital hours before. There would be a difference this time, though: Soon, she would know who that escort was.

Ambushes weren't really Mary's specialty. If she'd had one before then, it was noting the errors of others. Now, however, she intended to learn from her own experience.

She turned a corner and dodged a few steps down an especially narrow alley, much like the one in which she'd been waylaid earlier that day. Then she stopped and waited.

Within seconds, she heard the pitter-pat of clawed paws on pavement and the soft hum of well-oiled wheels. Both sounds grew louder, louder—and then broke off abruptly just as they seemed to be reaching a crescendo.

Years before, at Shaolin Temple, Master Liu had taught her to track the passage of a cockroach across the floor with a blindfold over her eyes and straw stuffed in her ears. So while the dogs were obviously well trained—there was no whining or whimpering, no fidgeting, no scratching at fleas—she could still hear their shallow pants as clearly as the ringing chimes of a London church bell.

"You can pretend you're not there, and I can pretend I'm not here, but there's really no point in it, is there?" Mary said. "Here we are, so we might as well acknowledge each other. At any rate, I merely wish to thank you."

A dark snout slowly poked around the corner and took a tentative sniff before the rest of its face followed. It was by no means a pretty dog: The wiry hair was patchy, half of one ear had been sheared off clean, and a pink scar ran across its forehead. It inspected Mary with such wary intelligence, however, she almost expected it to speak.

Which, in a way, it did. The dog chuffed out a single, gruff, breathy sound—more than a snarl, less than a bark—and a moment later Mary heard the squeak of leather. Reins were being loosened.

The dog stepped into the alley with another, even scruffier dog at its side. With them came the small, black, coffinlike crate to which they were tethered.

"Why should you thank me?" said the Man in the Box.

He had a hoarse, gravely voice, yet underlying it was both a softness and a vitality. Whatever had happened to his throat (and the rest of him), he wasn't old. Mary peered at the narrow slit that ran across the front of his little enclosed carriage, hoping for a glimpse of his eyes, but all she saw was darkness.

"You've been of such service to me today," she said. "Sending your friends to help when I was delayed by those ruffians; escorting me back to One North now; seeing to it that the guards at the gate from Eleven Central let me pass on my way in. That last is an assumption, by the way.

Please correct me if it is in error."

The Man in the Box said nothing.

"Would you mind explaining *why* you've been helping me?" Mary asked him.

There was more silence. Then, eventually, "Yes."

"Then I shall have to do more assuming. You are another agent of Lady Catherine, like Nezu, and have been tasked with aiding my family in its undertaking here in London."

There was a raspy sound within the box—perhaps a husky sigh.

"You are as skilled with your assumptions as you are in the deadly arts," the Man croaked. "You have the gist of things, if not all the particulars."

One of the dogs—the one with the scar—perked up its ears and stared off into the blackness of the alleyway. The other dog quickly followed suit.

Mary heard footsteps shuffling somewhere far behind her, though not as far as she would have liked.

"Perhaps we should move on together," she said.

She didn't wait for the Man to agree. She simply started walking. Soon enough, the dogs joined her, bringing their master with them.

"As much as I respect your abilities," the Man said, "I was about to suggest moving along myself. I have never seen Twelve Central so bad, and it is always abysmal. Even as seasoned a warrior as you might find herself inconvenienced."

Mary felt an unaccustomed warmth rise to her cheeks. She resented it the second she realized what it was.

It wasn't often—never, in fact—that anyone paid her a compliment. And this was a *Man* in a Box, not a Woman. And a Young Man at that.

Still, though . . . "in a Box"! And why should she care what any man, boxed or unboxed, thought of her?

So she did the English thing. She changed the subject.

"It is quite clever how you've trained your dogs. It reminds me of an army officer I once knew who was similarly unable to autolocomote.

He got around with the help of two soldiers and a wheelbarrow."

"Such a man was my inspiration. Only I, of course, have no privates at my command."

"You have no—? Ah! Yes, of course! I see what you mean."

Mary coughed, her cheeks not tingling now but burning. She found herself so desperate to change the subject (again) that she committed the sin she most frequently accused her sister Kitty of: lack of tact.

"Was it the dreadfuls who rendered you thus?"

"Oh, goodness, no. I cut myself shaving."

A long moment passed in silence.

"You are being facetious," Mary finally said.

"Indeed. I hope you will forgive me. It is a bad habit I have acquired in recent years. Since being *rendered thus*, you understand."

"Now you mock me."

"No, Miss Bennet. I *tease* you. There is a significant difference."

"There is?"

Mary resolved to look it up when she got back to the house, assuming she could find a copy of Dr. Johnson's dictionary. It seemed to her that she'd been mocked, teased, jeered, derided, scorned, disdained, and pooh-poohed her entire life, yet she'd never paused to separate one from the other or gradate them in any way.

A scream cut through the night, ending in the kind of choked gurgle that could mean only one thing: somewhere nearby was at least one happy zombie.

The dogs picked up their pace. Since the party was still more than a quarter mile from the gate to Eleven Central, Mary was in complete agreement with her canine companions.

She started walking faster, too.

"I am shocked to find any part of London in such a state," she said. "I am not often in the city and don't know it well, I admit, but never would I have imagined the dreadfuls could have such a toehold within the Great Wall."

"London is walls within walls. A city of boxes. A person can stay safely in one and never fear—or know—what's in the next. Or so those in the snuggest of such boxes like to think. It is my experience that what one hopes to lock away in a box will not be content to stay there if it has any kind of life left. Even the dead kind."

The more the Man spoke, the more Mary began to find his throaty, warbly voice less grating than . . . textured. Even pleasingly so.

"You are quite the philosopher," she said.

"I have much time to think. For instance, this afternoon I had hours to ponder upon you and your journey to Bethlem Hospital. You set off for Twelve Central only after Nezu and your father and sisters had left the house. No one escorted you, you did not seem to know your way, and Nezu had made no arrangements for you to pass through the gate from One North. I could reach but one conclusion: You came of your own volition, without the permission or even the knowledge of Nezu or your family."

"And you disapprove?"

"Not at all. I applaud your nerve. Metaphorically, of course. Courage is the trait I have always admired most in your . . . sort."

"My *sort*?"

"Warriors, I mean. True warriors. Those with not just the skills to deal death but the fortitude to face it unafraid."

"You would pronounce me to be such a person after just one afternoon's observation?"

"I have seen enough to judge."

"I must say, you speak to me very freely, Mr. . . . ?"

There was a long pause—so long, in fact, that Mary threw a questioning glance over at the Man. All she saw, of course, was the flat black top of his box.

"Quayle," he said at last.

"Well, I say again, Mr. Quayle: You speak to me very freely."

"And you object?"

"No!" Mary replied with a fervor that both surprised and embarrassed her. "I mean, no. Why should a man and a woman not converse freely? If discourse were more open and minds less narrow, many an injustice might be undone. What I find surprising is that you should be so very complimentary, given your mistress's feelings toward my family, which she has made plain through not only her statements but numerous assassination attempts as well."

"I may be Lady Catherine's creature, Miss Bennet, but I am not her," Mr. Quayle said. "When men and women speak freely together, surely they are free to hold their own opinions of each other as well."

"You are right, of course."

"As I said, I have much time to think."

They continued for a while without speaking. The only sounds were the *tap-tap-tap* of the dogs' claws against the cobblestones, along with the occasional burst of distant laughter or screaming.

How long had she and Mr. Quayle been talking? Mary wondered. Five minutes, at most. Yet she couldn't remember the last time when a conversation with anyone outside the family had gone on so long. Once upon a time, she'd been able to take her thoughts to the local vicar, the Reverend Mr. Cummings. But then he'd thrown himself off Colne Bridge, and his replacement was always out when she called (even when she'd seen him scuttle into the vicarage just a moment before). Since then, her lengthiest and liveliest discussions had been between herself and whatever straw men she set up in her own mind.

She had the feeling things weren't much different for Mr. Quayle. Once they'd moved past his initial reluctance, he seemed keen to talk—and did so with such quick (and, yes, presumptuous) familiarity. It was almost enough to make her think he'd *wanted* to be caught following her. If she had little experience talking to men, she could only imagine he had even less talking to women, at least since being boxed up in pinewood.

Why not gratify him? Wouldn't that be the charitable thing to do?

An act of compassion?

And anyway, she was rather proud of what she'd done. It would be a shame to tell no one.

"Do you know why I went to Bethlem Hospital today?" she said.

"I know what it is you seek there," Quayle told her. "I have no idea, however, how you sought to attain it. Despite our obvious disadvantages, Ell and Arr and I can sometimes manage 'inconspicuous'; 'invisible' remains beyond us. Once you walked through the gates of Bedlam, we could only wait for you to walk out again."

"I see. And you have been ordered to assist my family?"

"I have been ordered to *watch* your family," Quayle said, "but I wish to help."

For some reason, Mary liked that answer far better than a simple, "Yes."

"Good," she said. "Then I will tell why I went to Bethlem, Mr. Quayle—and why you and I must return tomorrow."

CHAPTER 22

For once, Kitty was glad that the closest thing "the Shevingtons" had to a dojo was the attic. Yes, it was hot and dusty and cluttered, and if she tried a Leaping Leopard or a Flying Dragon she'd probably brain herself on the low ceiling. Yet the fact that it was so cramped was an advantage now, for it discouraged anyone else from coming up to train with her.

She wanted to be alone with her thoughts. They weren't good company, but better them than her father or Lizzy.

The ride back from Vauxhall Gardens had been painful in a way none of her Shaolin training had prepared her for. Shove bamboo under her fingernails, and she would laugh. Slather her in honey and tie her over an anthill, and she would tap her toes and whistle "Oh Dear! What Can the Matter Be?" But thirty minutes in a carriage with two brooding MacFarquhars had proved sheer torture. There had been no more history lessons from Sir Angus, only scowls directed at the son who sat slumped in a corner sullenly stroking his rabbit.

That left it to the Bennets to smooth over the general unease with small talk. But Elizabeth hadn't been up to it. In fact, she looked no happier than Sir Angus. So, all the way from Section Four South to Section One North, Kitty had synopsized her favorite romance novel by the writer Mrs. Radcliffe (whom Mr. Bennet usually referred to as "the noted twaddlemonger Mrs. Rotwit"). The outing ended with cursory farewells and no mention—and little hope—of another engagement involving the MacFarquhars and the Shevingtons.

"Well, it didn't end on the best note," Kitty said, "but it could have gone worse."

"Indeed," her father replied. "At least none of us were *eaten*."

And then he and Elizabeth came at her in a crossfire.

"You couldn't steer Bunny away from that ridiculous brawl?" said Lizzy on her left.

"You simply *had* to thrash all those fops?" said her father on her right.

"You could think of nothing better to talk about than *The Mysteries of Udolpho*?"

"Didn't you notice me trying to change the subject? I think Sir Angus couldn't decide whether to hurl you under the carriage wheels or himself."

"I'm sorry I've ruined everything!" Kitty cried. "But what else would you expect from the silliest girl in all England?"

She ran into the house feeling sillier than ever. It was a good thing she didn't encounter Mary as she bolted for the stairs. One more condescending comment and someone was going to get a Striking Viper where it would hurt the most.

Once Kitty reached the attic, there was no dearth of distractions from which she could choose. Days before, when she and Lizzy and their father had first explored the house, they'd found an entire arsenal up there: ninjatos and nunchucks and hand claws carefully laid out on the floor, throwing stars and daggers pocking the walls. After rushing through a quick warmup, Kitty stalked over to a sword that had caught her eye that first day—a beautifully crafted katana with a white-oak grip and a gently curving Tamahagane blade inscribed with Japanese letters—and began practicing her slices and lunges and spins.

She was graceful, she knew. She was deadly. Yet did that make her any less silly? Perhaps it just made her more so. She tried to imagine her wizened old Shaolin master, the stern and imperious Liu, simpering and tittering and batting his eyes at . . . well, whoever a one-hundred-and-five-year-old Chinese man would bat his eyes at.

She couldn't picture it. She couldn't even envision a young Liu doing it. Or a young Oscar Bennet or a young Lizzy Darcy, for that matter.

Perhaps it wasn't something a person grew out of. One was either silly or one wasn't, and Kitty would go from being the silliest girl in England to the silliest woman. No, more than that. She'd be the silliest *spinster*. One who not only frittered away her own chances for love, but helped doom her sister's as well.

"Hoooooooyyyyyyaaaaaaaaaahhhhhhhhh!"

Kitty hurled herself into a furious, twirling butterfly kick that ended with her right foot smashing into—and through—the attic wall.

"Uhhh . . . may I join you?"

Kitty turned to find Nezu watching her warily from the stairs.

"Yes. Of course," she said with all the dignity she could muster (the mustering being hindered by the fact that she was ankle-deep in splintered wooden slats and shattered plaster).

Nezu came up the steps and, with a gallantry Kitty didn't expect, turned his back to her and pretended to inspect the weapons lined up along the other side of the room. He didn't face her again until she'd managed to free her foot from the wall.

"I see you like Fukushuu," he said.

"Excuse me?"

Nezu nodded at the katana Kitty was holding. "Fukushuu. My father's sword."

"Oh. Yes. It is truly beautiful." Kitty admired the long blade and then gave the sword another swing to appreciate its perfect balance. "Of course, I never would have drawn it had I known it was your father's. Not without your permission. I am not *completely* without discretion, you know."

"I didn't, actually," Nezu said. "Which is why I find your reassurances so comforting."

Kitty's grip tightened on the katana. More disapproval. More disdain. But what better way to show the jibe was unjust than to let it pass without losing her temper?

"La!" she forced herself to chirp. She walked across the room and returned the sword to its scabbard. "A droll ninja! I would have thought that about as likely as a vegetarian dreadful."

"Then you have much to learn about ninjas," Nezu said. "Which is something I *did* already know."

"A-ha! So you don't deny it! You're one of Lady Catherine de Bourgh's assassins!"

"Why should I deny something I've never tried to hide?"

"Because ninjas are—"

Sneaky, deceitful little snakes, Kitty was about to say. And *dirty, dishonorable, back-stabbing curs*, too, if she could have gotten the words out uninterrupted. And maybe even *despicable, underhanded, pajama-wearing worms* as well, had she really worked up some momentum.

She stopped herself and changed tack.

"—not great favorites of ours," she said instead. She felt quite proud of herself for having managed an understatement, for once.

"That is no surprise," Nezu said, "seeing as your sister Elizabeth has killed so many."

"Well, there is that, yes." Kitty picked up a pair of nunchucks and began nonchalantly slinging them around her waist and over her shoulders. "What did you come up here for, Nezu? I have many drills to finish before I retire for the night."

"I wished to speak to you about the incident today."

"La! You will have to be more specific. We Bennets are unmatched when it comes to generating incidents."

"I was thinking of the pleasure gardens. When you attacked those young men."

Kitty began flinging the nunchucks around her body so quickly that her back and upper arms would be bruised black and blue. And she didn't care.

"You presume to criticize?"

She stepped toward Nezu, coming so close that the breeze whipped up by the flying fighting sticks ruffled his thick black hair.

The rest of him, meanwhile, remained utterly still.

"Yes," he said blandly. He didn't retreat or even blink as the nunchucks began swinging past, no more than a foot from his face. "First, it would have been better had you not intervened. And second, your intervention lacked finesse."

"Lacked finesse? *You* try being finesse-ful or finesse-ish or what-have-you while holding a two-stone rabbit!"

"The word would be 'subtle,' and it is not something that is as hard to achieve as you seem to think. For instance . . . "

Suddenly, Kitty's hands were empty. The nunchucks were now whirling around Nezu. He'd snatched them away without once moving his gaze from her face.

"Impressive," Kitty said. "If you'll recall, however, the idea at the time was *not* to look subtle. I had to appear clumsy, ungainly. Speaking of which—" She leaned to the side to peer past Nezu at the stairs. "Now you, Mary? At this rate, we'll soon have the whole household up here."

Nezu didn't look over his shoulder. He didn't have to, though. His one quick peek at the floor—searching for a shadow that wasn't there—was all the opportunity Kitty needed. She snatched the nunchucks from him and went cartwheeling away.

"Well, goodness me," she said as she popped to her feet and began twirling the nunchucks around herself once more. "I seem to have your little sticks again. Who would have thought an oaf like me could manage something so *subtle*."

"I did not say you were an oaf."

"Oh, thank you! I stand corrected!"

Nezu looked chagrined. Somehow Kitty had the feeling it wasn't just because she'd tricked him.

"You show remarkable skill. Remarkable potential," he said. "It is discipline and gravity I do not see in you."

"Perhaps you simply are not used to seeing them in moderation."

"What does that mean?" Nezu beetled his brow and cocked his head, and Kitty couldn't help but smile. She was finding she enjoyed cracking through the man's impassiveness. He hadn't been wearing a ninja's hood the past week, but he may as well. Each time she managed to put an actual expression on his face, it was like she was able to peek beneath a black mask.

"I mean," she continued, "that you're so overblessed with gravity, it's a wonder you can stand up. Tell me, do ninjas never smile? Laugh? Sing?"

Nezu turned and walked off a few steps and then pulled out one of the throwing stars lodged in the wall.

"Not Lady Catherine's ninjas."

He idly balanced the six-pronged star on his right index finger. Kitty could see a tiny speck of red where the tip bit into his flesh.

"What is there to laugh about when you are born and raised only to kill and, inevitably, be killed? Our fathers lived and died at Her Ladyship's whim, and so it shall be with us. I suppose if any of us could smile, it should be me, for at least I've been granted this little holiday with your family first."

Nezu tossed the star into the air, caught it by one of the blades, and, with a half-hearted flick of the wrist, threw it across the room. It was a weary gesture, jaded and full of disillusionment. And it didn't fool Kitty for a second.

Her eyes were supposed to follow the star's flight. Instead, she was watching Nezu as he rolled across the floor toward her and sprang up, grabbing for the nunchucks.

She let him have them, though not in the way he wanted. As he bounced to his feet, Kitty wrapped the nunchucks around him, pinning his arms to his sides and jerking his body against hers.

"How subtle of you," she said. "But not subtle enough."

"Nicely done, Miss Bennet. Very nicely, indeed."

Nezu looked down, avoiding Kitty's gaze, but jerked his head to the side when he found himself staring into her décolletage.

"Nezu," Kitty said, "are you *blushing*?"

"You have shamed me."

Kitty pulled back harder on the nunchucks, crushing Nezu's chest more firmly against hers.

"You're not going to run off and commit hara-kiri, are you?"

The flush of color on his cheeks darkened until it looked almost like a bruise.

"No," Nezu said. "Even if I were so inclined, that would not be an option. I have too much yet to do. Would you release me now, please?"

"Well . . . "

For some reason, Kitty couldn't bring herself to let the man go. A part of her wanted to show him—show somebody—that *she* could be in control. Another part of her . . . well, another part of her was just enjoying itself too much.

"Miss Bennet, I know how to break your hold on me, but I'd rather not do so."

"Meaning, you don't want to fight me?"

"I do not wish to injure you."

Kitty laughed. "You're so sure you could?"

"Yes, reasonably. And I do not think Bunny MacFarquhar would find you quite as attractive with a black eye and a limp."

"Oh, is that what you're worried about? Me and Bunny? Well, then. Let us strike a bargain. I will let you go if you answer just one question: Why were you following us this afternoon?"

Kitty could feel Nezu suck in a deep breath.

"I have been tasked with guiding you, ensuring that either you or Mrs. Darcy forge a quick and intimate bond with one of the MacFarquhars. It was important that I monitor your progress."

"Truly? That's it? You only tagged along because you're so desperate to see me in Bunny's arms?"

"Miss Bennet," Nezu said, sighing. And then the toes of Kitty's left foot were squashed beneath his heel. When she jerked forward in surprise, he brought the crown of his head up hard into her face. He kept going as she stumbled back, stripping the nunchucks from her hands while flipping himself backward beyond her reach.

"I came up here to speak with you about self-control," he said when he was again flat on his feet. He dropped the nunchucks to the floor and then turned and headed for the stairs. "Unfortunately, I find that I came far too late."

Kitty was stunned, nearly blinded with pain—and, for no reason she could say, smiling again.

"Too late for whom?" she called after Nezu as he started down the steps. "Me or you?"

He'd already answered her one question, though, and this other he chose to ignore.

CHAPTER 23

It was easy for Darcy to wait for Lady Catherine and her servants to retire for the night. Sleep was no temptation for him. He didn't desire it. He didn't even feel he needed it anymore. What he wanted was a little time in Her Ladyship's study. Alone.

Alone wouldn't be so simple, however. Not with Anne roaming the house and grounds at all hours. That night, after a long game of piquet in the drawing room (the usual round of Crypts and Coffins being, under the circumstances, in poor taste), she'd asked if he'd accompany her on another of her nighttime strolls. He'd declined. Being treated like a candy cane by a walking corpse had cured him of any desire to wander around out of doors, he explained. Perhaps tomorrow he'd be in the mood again.

Anne had nodded and patted his hand and said, "I understand," in a strangely patronizing kind of way, as if being licked by zombies was simply an acquired taste and she felt sad for—and a little superior to—those prudes who couldn't yet appreciate it. Then they'd exchanged goodnights, and Darcy went to his room . . . where he stood now, propped against the door, listening intently for any sound.

He heard nothing, but he knew that was no guarantee where Anne was concerned. She didn't so much walk along the halls as float, moving with a smooth silence any ninja would envy.

Still, he couldn't just stand there all night. Well, perhaps he could, if he tried, but that wouldn't get him the answers he so desperately wanted—and dreaded. Another two hundred breaths, tallied with the infinite patience of one trained in the ways of the Shinobi, and then he'd risk it.

On breath one hundred and twelve, he heard the opening and closing of a far-off door—a heavy jade one, as indicated by the tortured squeak of its hinges and the dull *thunk* as it swung shut. Darcy slipped into the hall and hurried to the windows overlooking the large barnlike structure that served as dojo and armory and barracks for Her Ladyship's private army.

Soon enough, he saw it. A shimmery-gray shape moving through the black of night: Anne walking to the dojo. Darcy had spotted his cousin heading that way twice before, both times, as now, in the middle of the night. It was enough to make him wonder if she had a lover among the ninjas. Such things simply weren't done, of course, and Darcy could imagine the fate that awaited any of his aunt's assassins who dared an indiscretion with her daughter. After all, this was the woman who, that morning, had taken a whip to the entire kitchen staff because she'd been served a currant scone.

Lady Catherine de Bourgh loathed currants.

Come to think of it, though, Anne did sometimes mention slipping out to visit "friends." In fact, she'd said it was a friend who taught her how to go unnoticed by dreadfuls. And who better to perfect such a technique than ninjas, for whom concealment and deception were akin to a religion?

Whatever it was her cousin did in the dojo, Darcy hoped it made her happy. He was growing fonder of his cousin, strange though she was. She seemed to understand him instinctively, to sympathize with his plight in a way he wouldn't have thought possible, given their past. For years, she'd simply been the sickly, dreary girl he knew he *wouldn't* marry. Now, she was . . . more. What exactly that made her, though, he wasn't sure.

When she finally disappeared into the darkness, he started downstairs.

When Darcy was a boy, the fact that his aunt had declared her study off limits to everyone made it, of course, the very place he most wanted to be. During his many visits to Rosings, he'd spend entire nights tinkering with the intricate locks on its door, slowly mastering each in turn until only one thwarted him. He finally decided to give up when he came downstairs one morning to find footmen carrying out a dead ninja.

"It appears Hashimoto was either a sneak-thief or a spy," Lady Catherine told him. "The locks on my study door did not stop him, but one of the booby traps beyond them did."

Darcy could only hope he'd get the chance to risk those booby traps himself. It had been fifteen years since he'd last tried to break into the study. Even if his aunt hadn't changed the locks, he might not remember how to get past them, and there would still be the one he had never bested.

The study was just off the trophy room, so Darcy had an audience as he examined the door: hundreds of dreadful heads staring out from the walls. Their eyes were glass, their heads stuffed with sawdust, so no one was truly on hand to see Darcy's first smile in weeks. It was a grim smile, one of relief and satisfaction rather than cheer, and it was gone in an instant.

All the old locks were still in place. If he was patient and cautious and very, very lucky, he might soon know the truth that would, without doubt, break his heart one way or another.

It took just five minutes with a handful of hairpins (pilfered at great risk from his aunt's boudoir) to get through the first six locks. The seventh had always been a particular challenge, but after another five minutes' work, Darcy felt the springs lift, as if at the turn of a key.

And then, to his dismay, the door moved. Just a fraction of an inch, giving way to the slight pressure he'd been putting against it as he worked at the lock. But it was enough to tell him he'd finally succeeded where his younger self had so often failed.

He gave the door a push, and it swung slowly open. The last, lowermost lock—a mysterious brass disc with a thin slot in the middle, as opposed to the simple keyholes above it—hadn't been fastened.

He'd been patient and he'd been lucky. Now it was time for the caution. It would be a shame to have come so far only to be carried out in the morning stretched between two footmen.

He stepped over the tripwire stretching out from the door to its frame, walked around the pressure-sensitive plates that created shallow depressions in the Persian rug, ducked beneath the razor wire that was visible only because a spider had helpfully begun spinning a web from one end, and moved with special slowness past the portrait of Lady Catherine herself—and the small holes in the pupils that would no doubt spit poisoned darts if the breeze stirred by his passing should cause even the slightest quiver on the canvas.

At last, he reached Lady Catherine's compact cherry wood *bureau à gradin*, and he paused to look up at the lone head mounted directly above it. Darcy had known its owner well: It belonged to Sir Lewis de Bourgh, Lady Catherine's second husband, Anne's father. The circumstances of his death had always remained vague, and Darcy once overheard a colonel joking that Her Ladyship had simply lopped off Sir Lewis's head so that, as a widow, she would be free to keep the sword in her hand. Unfortunately, Lady Catherine also overheard the jest (if such it was), and the last time Darcy saw the colonel alive, he was an ensign leading a patrol into a Scottish bog infested with unmentionables.

Darcy hadn't given the incident a second thought until now, years later; looking up at his uncle's waxy face, he found himself searching for any sign the man hadn't been dead when he died (so to speak). The greenish tint to the skin looked right for a dreadful, but couldn't that be a taxidermist's trick? Sir Lewis and Lady Catherine had always seemed comfortable enough with each other, yet Darcy knew from hard experience that Her Ladyship wasn't one to take being thwarted lightly. If she felt herself more warrior than wife and mother—and surely she had and did—what wouldn't she do to reclaim her destiny?

It made him think of someone else who faced the same dilemma. Someone he already had been thinking of almost every waking second (which seemed like all of them, these days). Someone who was the whole reason he'd risked death to be standing where he was.

He began going through the papers on his aunt's desk.

There were communiqués, maps, government white papers on this or that new strategy or weapon. And there were more booby traps, too. An asp in a portmanteau. A drawer filled with gunpowder and a lucifer, rigged to explode when opened. A toxin-coated scroll.

Darcy didn't find what he was looking for, though: the letters to him from his wife. The letters his aunt said didn't exist. His heart sank as he began to accept that she might not be lying.

Then he found proof that she wasn't, and his heart did more than sink. It plunged like an unchained anchor bound for the darkest depths of the abyss.

Underneath the leather desk pad were four faint lines arranged in a square. With some experimentation—pushing one corner, then another, then two at once, then all four—Darcy unlatched the hidden springs that held the little board in place. It covered a shallow compartment containing a single, neatly folded piece of paper. When Darcy picked it up, he found that it was a report, written in Japanese, from one of Her Ladyship's ninjas.

Highest One Who Is unto Me Like the Sun, the Brilliance around Which All Revolves, the Source of All Light, Whose Righteousness Burns the Unworthy without Mercy:

It is as you suspected (of course, as always, Infallible One). Mrs. Jane Bingham made a fast and full recovery from the delivery of her child and is not ailing in any way. Her supposed illness was an excuse concocted by her sister, She Whose Name Would Befoul This Paper. I did not confront The Dishonorable One with this, but I did convey your latest request that she come to Rosings to minister to her husband as he struggles to overcome the strange plague. Once again, she refused. Her words (which were seared into my memory like the sizzlings of acid they so sounded like) were this: "If I did as your mistress asks, I would be far more likely to behead Darcy than to offer him succor, for he has been tainted by the very vileness I once devoted myself to destroying. Her Ladyship may attempt to cure him if she must, but in my mind he has been forever befouled, and it matters not whether he begins drooling on himself and eating the servants. Fitzwilliam Darcy is dead to me, as is whatever love I once felt for him. That will not change." As you ordered, I did not kill her immediately, but I stand ready to repay her perfidy with sharpened steel whenever you command it.

Yours in abject insignificance,

Nezu

Darcy felt his knees start to buckle, and he staggered back toward the chair he'd pushed away from the desk a few minutes before.

"Don't!" Anne cried out. "You would be dead in seconds!"

She was watching from the doorway. Her wide, sad eyes moved from him to the chair and back again.

"In the seat cushion are pins tipped with scorpion venom."

Darcy blinked blankly at her and then stared back down at the letter. "Why didn't Lady Catherine tell me?"

"She was trying to protect you. A blow like this, when you are so weak . . . it might have finished you."

"Finished me? What a capital idea," he joked grimly.

Or was he joking?

He looked at the chair behind him.

"I suddenly feel so weary, Anne. More weary than I have in days."

How easy it would be to simply sit down and . . . rest.

His cousin scurried toward him, zigzagging around every death trap with swift, practiced ease. When she reached him, she took his hands in hers and held them tightly, as if he were dangling from some great height and she alone could keep him from falling.

Don't worry, Fitzwilliam, he almost expected her to say. *I've got you.*

CHAPTER 24

Time and again, as the night crawled with agonizing slowness toward morning, Elizabeth thought of the one thing that might soothe her enough to sleep: Jane Bingley's hair. Elizabeth felt anxious, frustrated, angry, guilty, and, despite the sisters and father slumbering soundly in the rooms around hers, alone. She longed to steal up the hall and slip into one of the other bedchambers and whisper, "Jane? Are you awake?" And whether she had been or not, Jane would sit up and say, "Yes." And they would talk and talk as they had those many nights when they were girls brushing each other's hair before bed, untangling—or trying to—the mysteries of life and love.

Only Jane was at far-off Fernworthy recovering from the birth of yet another child, and thinking of her only reminded Elizabeth of one more thing she had to worry about . . . and regret. If she hadn't been so honest with Darcy about how her young nieces made her feel—if she hadn't had those feelings to begin with—perhaps she wouldn't be lying here now in a strange bed in a strange house in such a strange, strange predicament.

The outing with the MacFarquhars had been a disaster. The way Elizabeth and her father had thrown the blame on poor Kitty afterward had been shameful. And Elizabeth couldn't even brood properly at first, for when they entered the house Mary was nowhere to be found. Only after an hour wasted on anxious pacing did her sister return, smug and (for once) mute on the subject of her own whereabouts.

It was almost a relief not to sleep after such a day, for what would that have brought but nightmares?

At long last, the black of night gave way to the dull gray glow of dawn. Elizabeth rose from bed and dressed herself and went downstairs . . . only to discover that she wasn't the first of her family to awaken. Nezu stood in the hallway, head bent over a slip of paper. He held it out for her without a word. When she had it in hand, he walked out the front door.

Elizabeth read.

Independence, Mary Wollstonecraft tells us, is the basis of every virtue. If this is correct—and I believe little that comes to us from Mrs. Wollstonecraft is not—then I, who have so long fancied myself a peerless judge of personal quality, have, in fact, none of my own. On scruples I could lecture all day, while of initiative I have known nothing. No more. I am a Shaolin warrior, and I should act—act!—accordingly. "The beginning is always today," Mrs. Wollstonecraft wrote. For me, it was yesterday. Today, it continues.

M.B.

"Oh, Mary," Elizabeth groaned.

Why did her sister have to be so sanctimonious?

Why did she have to be so mulish?

And why did she have to be so *right*?

Elizabeth walked out to the portico and saw Nezu looking up and down the street. He wasn't at it long before he headed back toward the house.

"We will soon know where she has gone," he said as he and Elizabeth went inside again.

"Oh? How?"

Nezu closed the door and turned to Elizabeth, speaking as if her question hadn't been asked.

"Whatever your sister has set herself to doing, we are unable to stop it now. Fortunately, she does not strike me as a reckless or capricious girl

. . . unlike some. I think, therefore, that we may continue with our current course of action."

"You mean, we should simply wait here for one of the MacFarquhars to come calling or, at most, connive to put ourselves again in their path."

"Yes."

Elizabeth shook her head. "That is the course of *in*action, and we can't afford to take it another day."

"There is no need for undue haste, Mrs. Darcy. Her Ladyship assures me that your husband has grown no worse, and if we force the issue—"

"These assurances would mean more if they had come to *me*," Elizabeth interrupted. "From Miss Darcy. And even if they had, hearing that my husband 'has grown no worse' is hardly an inducement to do nothing."

"Biding one's time is not doing nothing. And, at any rate, the wrong kind of something could jeopardize all our plans. I hardly need remind you that there are rules in polite society by which one must abide."

"Indeed. You do not have to tell me that which I know so well. All the same, my mind is made up. I am through waiting for a chance at a cure that might not even exist. We will pay a call on the MacFarquhars."

"That would be extremely forward."

Elizabeth shrugged. "The Shevingtons are like that, I suppose. Good thing they're rich enough to ignore the rules when they choose. Now, why don't you go make sure breakfast is ready while I tell my father and sister to prepare themselves for a morning call."

Nezu stared at Elizabeth for a long, silent moment. She had the feeling he was playing out a conversation in his head—one that began, "I'm sorry, Your Ladyship, but . . . ," and ended with his mistress's knee going where no knee ever went with good intentions. Though he eventually bowed and said, "Very good," the expression on his face seemed in no way in agreement with his words.

Within the hour, Elizabeth was setting off with Kitty and Mr. Bennet. Since the MacFarquhars lived just six blocks away—and because

Elizabeth wished (rather perversely, she knew) to deny Nezu an excuse to tag along as a coachman—it was decided that the party would walk. As they sauntered off, Nezu watched from the portico, a strangely forlorn look upon his face. Elizabeth almost expected him to howl like a hound watching its master ride away. To her surprise, Kitty glanced back and smiled in a way that seemed both comforting and cruel.

"There's just something about people who take themselves *so* seriously," Kitty said when she noticed Elizabeth watching her. "I can't help but tease them a little."

"Our young friend Nezu certainly isn't what anyone would call frivolous," Mr. Bennet said.

"Oh, no! He makes Mr. Darcy seem as giddy as Lydia!" Kitty giggled with a very Lydia-like giddiness, and then took her sister's arm and gave her an apologetic pat. "Not that I'm saying your Mr. Darcy lacks for humor. It's just . . . " She grinned and looked back again at Nezu. "Oh, he's like a male Mary!"

"Mary's like a male Mary," Mr. Bennet said.

"Papa! You're simply horrid!" Kitty shot back, but she was laughing as she said it.

"It's nothing to make light of," Elizabeth said, not laughing at all. "Whatever it is Mary's doing, at least she's—"

A man ran around the next corner screaming.

"That never bodes well," Mr. Bennet said.

There were more shrieks, followed by more fleeing men and women.

The Bennets kept walking toward the corner.

"I do wish someone would scream a *word*," Mr. Bennet said.

"You know what that kind of scream means," Elizabeth replied.

A phaeton came careening around the corner, the galloping horses wide-eyed with panic.

"Dreadfulllllllllllll! Dreadfulllllllllllll!" the coachman bellowed.

"That's more like it," Mr. Bennet said. "I just prefer when people are clear about these things."

Even forewarned, however, the Bennets couldn't have predicted what they found when they rounded the corner: *four* dreadfuls hunched over a still-twitching body.

The zombies all seemed relatively fresh. The skin was still taut, not bloated or shriveled, and it had the jaundiced pallor of illness rather than the green or gray of decay. They all shared the same fiery red heads of hair as well, and their clothes were similarly tattered and smeared with muck. Two were adults, a male and a female, and two were children, a boy and a girl.

This had been a family.

At present, they were enjoying a meal together: a well-dressed middle-aged man whose ample belly the children were in the process of emptying into their mouths. Father, meanwhile, was gnawing on an ankle while Mother doggedly bashed the dead man's skull against the cobblestones in an attempt to crack it open like a walnut and avail herself of the sweet meat within.

"How did *they* get here?" Kitty asked as the last screaming ladies and gentlemen sped past them. The street was now deserted except for the unmentionables and their main course.

"They certainly don't look like residents of Section One North, do they?" Mr. Bennet said.

Elizabeth eyed the wall and watch towers that loomed over the houses half a mile away.

"However they got past the checkpoints," she said, "it will be quite some time before any soldiers arrive to attend to them."

Mr. Bennet shook his head. "The Shevingtons don't fight dreadfuls, Lizzy. We shouldn't involve ourselves."

"Oh, Papa?" Kitty said. "I think we're about to get involved."

Papa Zombie apparently found ankles less than satisfying, and, rather than move on to the juicier flesh of the calf or thigh, it stood and started lurching toward the Bennets.

"We should run," Mr. Bennet said.

"I will not run," Elizabeth replied.

The dreadful was no more than forty paces away now, and it was gaining speed with each step.

"Really, Elizabeth," Kitty said. "We *should* run."

"I will not run."

Papa Zombie opened its mouth and roared, and Mama Zombie, as if still playing the dutiful wife, dropped the gentleman's head and staggered off after its mate.

"You should run," Nezu said.

Elizabeth hadn't even noticed the man slip up beside them. By the time she did, he was already off again, charging Papa Zombie. He started at a sprint and then flipped himself end over end—ninjas and their incessant hand springs!—until he was soaring into the air toward the unmentionable. At the apex of his flight, he pulled a katana from a back-scabbard hidden beneath his cutaway coat, and as he fell back to earth the blade bit into the dreadful's head. It stopped slicing downward only when it had reached the creature's collarbone, and the skull and neck split open like the blooming of some viscous red blossom. The zombie ran a few more staggering steps before pitching forward and tumbling, cleaved head over heels, along the cobblestones. It finally flopped to a stop at the Bennets' feet.

Nezu, meanwhile, never slowed. His momentum carried him forward into another roll, and then he was sprinting and springing, springing and sprinting toward the other unmentionables. Mama Zombie he cut in half in his haste to reach the youngsters, who (in a display of the instinctive self-preservation that sometimes presented itself even in those with no more self to preserve) were retreating up the street. Once their heads were in the gutter, he could stroll back to the matriarch of the family at his leisure, and this he did with a casual calm and absolutely no sign that his acrobatics had winded him in the slightest. The zombress—or the top half of her, anyway—slithered toward him, hissing and clawing at his feet, but he was able to finish her off with an upward-arcing slice of the sword, not unlike a Scotsman swinging his "golf" club.

Watching him, Elizabeth had to respect the man's formidable skills even as she resented that her own remained untapped.

"Well, I don't know about you," Kitty said, "but I'm impressed."

She looked it, too. In fact, she was gazing at Nezu with such smiling delight, Elizabeth almost warned her not to applaud.

"Ooo," Kitty cooed, "he is a marvel with Fukushuu."

"Fukushuu?" her father asked.

Kitty nodded at Nezu and the sword he was resheathing as he walked toward them. "His katana. He told me it belonged to his father."

Mr. Bennet looked around Kitty at Elizabeth.

She nodded. She knew what it meant. The word, anyway. Living with Fitzwilliam Darcy, how could she not have picked up a little Japanese?

Fukushuu meant "revenge."

"Next time," Nezu said as he swept passed them, "*run*."

Behind him, long red fingers stretched out from puddles of blood, creeping their way toward the grates in the gutter and, below, the new sewers that ran under all of London.

CHAPTER 25

At first, Mary didn't mind the stares. In fact, she rather relished them. So she was a lady walking through a respectable neighborhood beside two mangy dogs and a black box. What of it? She could choose her own company. If she should decide to go for a stroll with a flock of geese while pushing an orangutan in a purple perambulator, who had the right to stand in judgment?

She had released herself from the shackles of propriety. She was free!

Still, the gentlemen's frowns, the ladies' scowls, the children pointing and laughing—she wasn't entirely immune to it. There was freedom, and then there was making a spectacle of oneself.

So Mary tamped down her misgivings and kept up her nerve the best way she knew how.

"Mary Wollstonecraft tells us," she said, "and I quote: 'Women are systematically degraded by receiving the trivial attentions which men think it manly to pay to the sex, when, in fact, men are insultingly supporting their own superiority.' How true! It is one of the reasons I have never much missed such attentions. If one is pursued by suitors, let's say, is that really a thing to be envied? For what is the purpose of pursuit but capture, imprisonment, destruction even? Better, I think, to be left alone to one's *own* pursuits—those that elevate spirit, mind, and body—rather than wallow in sentiment."

Here, Mary remembered to pause (something she'd been mostly forgetting that morning) to allow Mr. Quayle the opportunity to either demonstrate his intelligence by agreeing or expose his ignorance by dissenting. She heard nothing from the little crate rolling along beside her, and after a moment she began to wonder if Mr. Quayle had been listening at all—or was even awake. Ell and Arr certainly seemed to know the way, turning crisply at all the right corners without any apparent pulling on the reins that disappeared into the slot of Mr. Quayle's box. For all Mary knew, the man inside was slumped against a pillow, snoring contentedly until a yap from his dogs alerted him that they'd reached their destination.

So she decided to try a test. She would ask the question her mother always claimed either put men to sleep or sent them fleeing.

"Have *you* ever read Mrs. Wollstonecraft?"

"I mean"—she quickly threw in before Mr. Quayle could answer (or not)—"*did* you ever read her? Before your . . . change in circumstances?"

"Oh, I still manage to keep up my reading," Mr. Quayle replied, sounding as chirpy and cheerful as one could when speaking (it seemed from the rasp of it) through a throatful of scars and sand. "I've trained Arr and Ell to shave my face, load a flintlock, and prepare and cook an entirely satisfactory shepherd's pie. Turning the pages of a book was nothing. Yet I have, alas, never sampled Mrs. Wollstonecraft. I recently read her daughter's novel, though."

"Oh," Mary said. "*That.* Yes, I read it as well. Mrs. Wollstonecraft died soon after giving birth to Mrs. Shelley, you know. I wanted to see what her sacrifice had begat."

"I take it from your tone that you did not find Mrs. Shelley's work worthy of her heritage."

"Most novels are worthless, Mr. Quayle. *Frankenstein* has the added defect of being perverse. I can only take solace from the fact that Mrs. Shelley's little grotesquerie will soon be forgotten, allowing her mother's legacy to live on, unsullied and immortal."

Mary almost stopped there, pronouncement complete, but she was overcome by the sudden urge to add four more words she had, up to then, rarely spoken.

"What do *you* think?"

"I'm afraid I must differ. The story aroused my sympathies in the deepest way imaginable. Though, thanks perhaps to my unique 'circumstances,' those sympathies often lay with the monster, not its creator. As to the book's perversity, yes, I will grant it was intended to shock, in some ways. But, given the things you and I have seen—"

Mr. Quayle's voice trailed off, and for a moment he fell silent.

"I found it quite diverting," he finally finished.

"Ahh, but a book should do more than divert!" Mary declared. "It should do the opposite, in fact. It should focus one's consideration on that which is real and important. It should strive for uplift. Inspiration."

"I try to take those things from *life*, Miss Bennet. It has not been easy, I grant you . . . though of late I find I've had a bit more success than in years past. And here we are."

They'd arrived at the gateway from Eleven to Twelve Central. When they tried to walk through, however, the soldiers there—the same ones who'd let Mary pass without any questions about her intentions (or sanity) a mere twenty-four hours before—looked tense and sweaty. The captain of the guard came over to ask if she and Mr. Quayle really, truly, absolutely, without question, no matter the consequences, being duly forewarned and absolving him of all responsibility, *had* to keep going.

Mary said yes.

"All right, then," the man mumbled with a twitchy nod. "But I'd stay close to the soldiers, if I were you."

"Soldiers?" Mary asked. The officer had already turned his back and stalked off, however, as if suddenly anxious to wash his hands.

On the other side of the gate, they found a crowd of clamoring, shabbily dressed people pressed around a squad of soldiers stretched along the roadway. Mr. Quayle had to set Ell and Arr to growling and barking to clear a path through the throng.

"You've got to let me out!" a man was roaring at the soldiers as Mary moved past. He lifted up a wailing baby swaddled in a canvas sack. "For my wee one's sake! She needs a doctor!"

"I don't know who you got that from, Coogan," replied a soldier wearing a sergeant's chevrons, "but you may as well take it back and get a refund, because you're not getting through this gate."

"You can't do this!" another man shouted, and others joined in with, "For God's sake!" "It's an outrage!" and the like.

"This is the last time I'm saying it!" the sergeant bellowed back. "New orders. No one gets out without work papers. But don't get your pantaloons in a bunch! Once the recoronation's over, everything'll get back to normal."

"With one difference," Coogan said over the squawks of "his" wee one. "We'll all be dead!"

"And who liked 'normal,' anyway?" a woman threw in.

"Yeah!" half a dozen others called out.

A dark-skinned man wearing a red turban and an immense black beard turned and glared at Mary just as she cleared the edge of the crowd. It wasn't often one saw foreigners in England anymore, for who would come willingly to the Land of the Dead? The fact that most proved immune to the strange plague only made them more resented in a country that was never particularly fond of outsiders to begin with. What remained of the old immigrant populations was rarely seen outside deepest London.

"And how about her?" the man asked in a heavily accented singsong, and he stabbed a finger at Mary. "Will you be asking the lady and her pets for papers when they want to leave? I think not! They'll be free to come and go while the likes of us stay trapped in here like rats."

The soldier who'd been doing all the talking waded into the mob and drove the butt of his Brown Bess into the outlander's stomach.

"Keep a civil tongue and don't forget your place." The sergeant turned toward Mary as the bearded man doubled up in pain beside him. "I do apologize for that, Miss. All sorts of unpleasantness you're bound to encounter here today. Even more so than the usual, I mean. You won't be staying long, will you?"

"Just long enough," Mary called back, and she and Mr. Quayle and the dogs carried on up the street.

The unpleasantness they'd been promised presented itself quickly enough: More bodies had been left out for collection, the heaps reaching as high as Mary's chest in spots, and here and there soldiers worked in teams of two, collecting the heads of the dead and the dead-ish with heavy sabers. Even where the corpses were starting to get frisky, the soldiers never fired a shot. Instead, one would pin the stricken in place with a bayonet or pike while his partner finished the job with his sword. The practice conserved powder and musket balls, of course, but Mary suspected that wasn't the only reason for it.

The walls would spare respectable London the sight of an epidemic, but even stones and mortar twenty-five feet high couldn't blot out the sound of so much gunfire.

"We were lucky to get in . . . depending upon one's definition of 'lucky,'" Mr. Quayle said. "Tomorrow, without doubt, the quarantine will be total. No one in or out."

"Agreed. Which makes it all the more imperative that we act immediately."

"Agreed."

They turned a corner and found themselves moving up a street that had yet to see its morning visit from the soldiers and body wagons. The locals had done what they could with their Zed rods, and the cobblestones were coated with fresh-pulped brains and bits of shattered bone. Still, there were stirrings in several of the corpse heaps, and Ell and Arr slowed and bared their teeth and growled.

"This is intolerable," Mary said. "How could they allow it to become this bad?"

"Of which 'they' do you speak?"

"The authorities, of course. The government."

Mr. Quayle's box let out a little squeak.

"That was a shrug, Miss Bennet," Mr. Quayle said. "Of the cynical, world-weary variety. Section Twelve Central and all such sections like it will always be tolerated, no matter how appalling they become, because it is easy to tolerate that which one ignores. And, at the moment, the authorities—and those who keep them in power—have all the more reason to focus their attentions elsewhere. There is a king to be recrowned. There are balls and banquets and jubilees to plan. The only thing that would be intolerable would be spoiling the fun."

Mary looked down at the box rolling along the blood-slimed street and wondered, not for the first time, what the man inside it looked like.

"You have a didactic streak, Mr. Quayle," she said.

"My apologies."

"You misunderstand me," Mary said, and for perhaps the first time in her adult life, she gave in to an impulse: She rested a hand atop Mr. Quayle's box, the fingers spread wide. "I meant that as a compliment."

"Ah. It has been so long since I received one, I failed to recognize it for what it was."

Mr. Quayle's voice was even gruffer than usual, and for a long while the only sound that came from his box was the rumbling of the wheels over the cobblestones.

Eventually, they reached the abandoned brewery Mr. Quayle preferred when keeping watch on Bedlam.

"It offers more seclusion than the alleyway you used for your observations yesterday," he explained as they made their way past cobweb-covered casks and vast copper vats streaked with grungy green. "A kidsman and his gang of thieves have claimed the place as their den, but they shan't disturb us. We came to an understanding long ago, they and I."

"That understanding being . . . ?"

"That if I am left to my business, they are left to theirs, including the business of breathing."

"A happy arrangement for all."

"Quite."

"One thing puzzles me, however."

They stopped in front of a staircase leading up to a walkway lined with shattered windows. Long wooden boards had been placed end to end from the bottom of the stairs to the top, creating a convenient gangplank for Mr. Quayle. Above, more boards led to a crate placed by a window that, Mary assumed, afforded the best view of the hospital grounds.

"Nezu told us that Lady Catherine's ninjas have attempted to infiltrate Bethlem in the past," Mary said. "And here I find that you have a cozy observation post that has seen no little use. Yet Mr. Darcy was tainted with the strange plague only two weeks ago."

"You wonder why Her Ladyship would take such an interest in Sir Angus MacFarquhar *before* her nephew was infected."

"I do, indeed."

"I have wondered the same thing. My mistress has not seen fit to tell me, however. Nor have I felt quite suicidal enough to ask."

Ell and Arr joined the conversation now, growling in harmony as they raised their wet black noses and snuffled at the brewery's musty air. Mary copied them (minus the growling), tilting back her head and sucking in a long, deep breath through flaring nostrils, as Master Liu had once taught her. ("You cannot taste what is on the wind with a dainty sniff. You must fill your throat, your lungs, your whole being! Now try again—with these crickets up your nose this time.") The fetid stench of rotting wood and yeast and barley lay like a waterlogged blanket over every other scent, however, and Mary could smell nothing else.

After a moment, she began to *hear*. It started as a rustling sound and then became a scraping and pawing, all of it strangely echoey and metallic.

Mary looked at the top of the farthest beer vat just as a pair of hands appeared there. Rising between them came the scowling face of a sunken-eyed child. The boy hauled himself over the side and dropped to the floor, and within seconds more came spilling out after him, as though the vat were a cauldron boiling over with angry, rag-wrapped children.

Ell and Arr wheeled around to face them, snarling and snapping.

"Solomon! Solomon, where are you?" Mr. Quayle shouted. "Come out and call off your dogs, and I shall call off mine!"

"I think your understanding with Mr. Solomon is no longer in effect," Mary said, "for his wards are now beyond any understanding at all."

Another boy came crashing to the floorboards with what looked like a large reticule in one hand. It was, in fact, a man's head, clutched by the long grey beard that grew from the pain-contorted face. The eyes were rolled back in their sockets to point at a smashed crown dripping blood and morsels of brain.

"Mr. Solomon?" Mary asked.

"Mr. Solomon," Mr. Quayle replied.

The cholera had swept through the thieves' crib, it seemed, and now Mr. Solomon's gang was interested less in picking pockets than in emptying skulls.

The boys were already loping forward toward the intruders/buffet.

“MR. SOLOMON’S GANG WAS LESS INTERESTED IN PICKING POCKETS THAN EMPTYING SKULLS.”

"Let's see if this drives off the little guttersnipes," Mr. Quayle said, and at a cluck of his tongue Ell and Arr slipped from their harness and stepped aside.

A panel opened near the base of Mr. Quayle's box, and a long dark tube slid out.

"Very impressive," Mary said.

She was looking down at the barrel of a pistol.

"I told you Ell and Arr could load a gun," Mr. Quayle said (before adding a mumbled, "Just don't ask how I fire it").

Then he did whatever it was he had to do, and there was a boom and a puff of smoke and a distinct "Ouch!" from inside the box.

One of the zombie-boys pitched backward and lay still.

The rest—half a dozen in all—kept coming.

Mary had already drawn her own pistol, and she brought down another slavering waif just as the diminutive mob reached her. Using the cloud of gunsmoke as cover, she spun to the side and let the dreadfuls hurl themselves fruitlessly into the swirling gray haze. By the time the smoke began to clear, she'd swept the feet out from under two of the unmentionables and had sent the butt of her pistol smashing through their foreheads. Ell and Arr, meanwhile, had brought down another dreadful in tandem and were working with frenzied, frothing fervor to chew through its neck before it could rise again.

Mary whipped around, looking for the last two zombies, and found them hunched over Mr. Quayle's box, which they'd knocked backward onto the floor. Despite the clumsiness of their clawings, one or the other had managed to trigger some hidden spring, and the front of the black case swung open.

"Uhhh, Miss Bennet. If you might oblige?" Mr. Quayle said.

Mary was already moving. With a warrior's cry so shrill it seemed to startle even the unmentionables, she hurled herself into a double-handspring, flipping end over end over end over end. She landed directly behind the dreadfuls, unleashed another screech, and then grabbed the tousle-haired heads and slammed them together. Three quick thumps and they cracked like eggs. With the fourth, black goo began to spew this way and that. By the seventh, there was little left for Mary to beat together, and she finally let the bodies drop to the floor.

"Mr. Quayle, are you—?"

"Ell! Shut!"

Ell came bounding over and dipped her furry head under the door to Mr. Quayle's case. Before the dog flipped it closed, Mary caught the quickest glimpse of a dark-haired man, impeccably dressed despite having no need for trouser legs or sleeves, his face turned to the side and pressed into the plush red velvet that lined the inside of the box.

"You're obviously a woman with a strong constitution, Miss Bennet," Mr. Quayle croaked. "Gazing upon me, however, would no doubt sicken even you. Arr! Up!"

Arr stopped chewing on the snapped zombie spine he'd been enjoying and padded over to join Ell. Through a series of complicated though clearly well-practiced steps—one dog nosing slowly under the back panel, the other pulling gently on the reins—they began righting Mr. Quayle's box. Of course, Mary could have done it for them in seconds, yet, with an instinctive sensitivity that hadn't before been her forte, she knew to leave them to it.

"I do believe that was the finest example of Satan's Cymbals I've ever seen," Mr. Quayle said, his wheezy voice turning breezy in a way that suggested a desperate desire to change the subject. "Complete destruction of both crania and all their contents in less than ten blows. Superb, Miss Bennet. Simply superb."

Mary was grateful Ell and Arr hadn't finished getting their master off his back. With his view-port pointed at the ceiling, he wouldn't see her blush.

"You know Satan's Cymbals?" she said. "So you were trained in the deadly arts, then."

"Oh, yes. I once fancied myself quite adept . . . though the skills came more easily to me than the disciplines, if you follow me."

Rather than pause to see if she did, Mr. Quayle pressed on quickly.

"And what of your training, Miss Bennet? What masters can claim credit for so skilled a student?"

"I was introduced to the ways of death by my father and a man named Geoffrey Hawksworth. But the bulk of my training was in China, under the Shaolin master Liu."

"Liu. Yes. Of course. The man is a legend among those who follow the Shaolin path. This Hawksworth, however. What can you tell me of him?"

Mary felt her blush deepen. There was what she *could* tell of Geoffrey Hawksworth, and what she *would*.

"I don't know much about him, really. Eight years ago, he came to Hertfordshire to train my sisters and me. He only stayed a matter of weeks. That was at the time of the Return, you see, and he . . . he seemed to abandon us to the dreadful hordes."

"*Seemed* to?"

"He fled, yes, and my family has always taken that as proof of his cowardice. Yet Sun Tzu tells us of the importance of timing. The wise warrior strikes as the falcon swoops on its prey: only at the precise moment that action will lead to success. Without knowing what became of Geoffrey Hawksworth, I cannot say with certainty whether he was running away or merely seeking another, more prudent path to victory."

At last, Ell and Arr managed to right Mr. Quayle's one-man carriage, and as the springs and wheels squeaked and creaked under the shifting weight of its occupant, Mary heard another sound coming from inside: a gruff chuckle.

"You find my faith in my old master amusing?" she snapped with a vehemence that surprised her—and, even more surprising, seemed to please Mr. Quayle.

"Not at all, Miss Bennet," he said as soothingly as his sandpaper voice allowed. "Rather, I find it uplifting and inspirational. Now, we have work to do." He gave a little two-note whistle, and Ell and Arr lifted their right front paws off the ground. "After you."

"Thank you," Mary said, and she acknowledged the dogs' good manners with a nod before starting up the stairs to the windows overlooking Bethlem Royal Hospital.

CHAPTER 26

It had been a quarter hour since Nezu dispatched the zombie family in the street, and Kitty Bennet's heart was still pounding. Which she was beginning to find odd, since it took a lot to get her heart to pound. A three-mile sprint, say, or the slaying of two or three dozen dreadfuls.

Yet there it was, thumping away in her chest as she thought of Nezu and his display of deadly prowess. He'd moved with such control, such economy, such grace, such *beauty* even, but with power, too. It didn't just fill her with admiration. It excited her somehow.

Yet why should it? Nezu hadn't done anything she and her sisters couldn't have done blindfolded. Just because now it was being done by a man—a lean, lithe, exotically handsome man—that shouldn't have made any difference.

She knew what Lydia would say. The Bennet women and their weakness for warriors! Both Lizzy and Mary had once developed an unhealthy attachment to their young master, Geoffrey Hawksworth, and of course Lizzy had gone on to marry one of the most skillful zombie killers in the home counties. Lydia, meanwhile, had flirted with half the officer corps of the King's Army before settling on the worst of the bunch to run off with. Their mother was little different even as dotage approached, still going noticeably fluttery and flushed around every red tunic and shako hat. Only sweet Jane seemed to be immune, choosing for her mate a man so amiable and benign it was hard to imagine him taking a blade to so much as a grapefruit, let alone an unmentionable.

Still . . . Nezu? Even Lydia wouldn't stoop so low as to pine for a ninja. And the man was so unbearably humorless and stiff—not at all the sort she was supposed to be drawn to. Not at all, to be precise, like Bunny MacFarquhar. If her heart was going to pound, let it pound for him.

She pushed aside all thoughts of Nezu, fixing Bunny's image in her mind as she and Lizzy and their father walked up to the MacFarquhars' door.

Not only did Kitty's heart stop pounding, it seemed almost to stop beating altogether.

Just as Mr. Bennet reached for the knocker, the door swung open, and a burly bald man barreled out carrying a stopper-topped vase the size of a cannonball.

"One side, old man," he said as he pushed past the Bennets. "Lady comin' through 'ere."

Another, even brawnier man was on his heels, this one grinning lasciviously at Kitty and Lizzy as he strutted out with Brummell cradled in his arms.

"Oi . . . anyone for *hasenpfeffer*?" he said with a wink.

The two men were guffawing as they carried on up the street.

"Whatever could that be all about?" Kitty said.

There was a decorous clearing of the throat from inside the house, and a footman appeared in the doorway. He was a portly saggy-jowled man who carried himself with a great, grave dignity that was all the more impressive for the fact that his collar was half torn off and his powdered wig was on sideways.

"Who may I say is calling?" he drawled.

"Mr. Shevington and his daughters Miss Shevington and Mrs. Bromhead," Mr. Bennet replied, offering a card supplied by Nezu. In no way did he acknowledge the servant's disheveled appearance or the two callers who'd just made off with a smallish vase and a largish rabbit. As was so often the case, good manners demanded a certain judicious blindness.

"If you would wait here," the footman said. But before he could go see if anyone was at home (which is to say whether anyone chose to be at home for the likes of Mr. Shevington and company), Bunny poked his head into the foyer. His hair was tousled wildly, and the flesh around his left eye was bruised and swollen.

"Ah! My dear friends the Shevingtons! What an unexpected pleasure! I feared you would never again grace us with your company—and you, the very people I most wished to see! Do show them in, Scroggs! Do, do!"

Rather than step out to greet them, however, their host disappeared, and as Scroggs the footman led them across the foyer, Kitty could hear the sounds of frantic movement from the room Bunny had ducked back into: hurried footsteps, furniture being righted, hard shards of something or other scraping over floorboards, as if being kicked beneath a convenient settee.

When Kitty and Lizzy and Mr. Bennet joined Bunny in the drawing room, however, they found him seated nonchalantly in an armchair, the only hints that he'd just hurled himself there being the beads of sweat on his forehead and the flattened flowers and shattered crystal he hadn't completely succeeded in shoving under a rug. Like the rest of the house, the room was large and elegantly appointed—and grungy and musty, with that entropic air of decay that inevitably sets in when dusting and mopping stop but living carries on apace. Though they'd seen no more than a vestibule and some stairs and one room, Kitty could sense the vast cavernous emptiness of the whole house, and she knew then that Scroggs was the last servant the MacFarquhars had left.

Bunny slowly rose to his feet and offered them a slight, almost blasé bow completely at odds with the anxiousness he'd displayed just a moment before. He was making a stab at decorum so transparent it only highlighted what he wished to hide: that he was desperately afraid the Shevingtons would turn and leave.

Once all the usual greetings had been exchanged and everyone was seated and Scroggs was sent off to whatever dusty cupboard he kept himself in, Bunny favored his guests with a small smile and said, "Well. . . . "

Then he hunched over, plunged his face into his hands, and started sobbing.

Kitty sprang from her seat and rushed to his side.

"Bunny! Bunny, what's the matter?"

Bunny howled out something that sounded like, "Tha too brummah a mutha!"

He tried again as Kitty patted his back and his sobs subsided, and after seven or eight repetitions his words took shape.

"They took Brummell and Mother!"

"We saw those men leaving with Brummell," Kitty said. "But . . . 'Mother'?"

"The vase," Mr. Bennet whispered.

Kitty glanced back at him blankly.

"The *urn*," Lizzy said.

"Oh! Oh, my!" Kitty cried. "How horrible! Why would anyone do such a thing?"

"Collateral," Bunny said, wiping the tears from his face with the back of a hand. "Those men claim I owe them money. And if I don't pay them. . . . "

Bunny began sniffling again, but Kitty's hand on his shoulder seemed to calm him.

"These scoundrels burst into your home to extort money?" Mr. Bennet thundered. "Assaulted you and your servant? Made off with precious possessions they expect you to ransom back? It's an outrage! You must take the matter to Bow Street immediately!"

"Yes, well, I would, but . . . they do have some basis for their claim, I'm afraid. A chit I signed. For a friend, of course! For a friend! An old school chum with a fondness for faro and the rottenest luck. He reneged on his obligations, and now I—faultless, foolhardy, innocent me!—I have been left in the lurch."

"Oh, you poor, poor dear," Kitty said, giving Bunny another pat. He looked up at her with eyes so round and moist and begging for affection, she almost expected him to purr. "All because you tried to help a friend."

"Yes. The purest of motives, and an example to the rest of us," Lizzy said. She stood and turned to Mr. Bennet. "We must speak to those men."

"No, you mustn't!" Bunny blurted out. "I mean—I doubt very much they are the kind to heed pleas for mercy."

"Then we will not plead with them," Lizzy replied coolly. "We will talk terms."

Bunny blinked at her a moment, mouth agape.

"But the debt. It is not insubstantial."

"Neither are our means. Right, Father?"

Mr. Bennet came to his feet as well. "Indeed. I'm sure one way or another, we can persuade those men to end this insufferable harassment. Avis, you stay here with Mr. MacFarquhar. I think he is, quite understandably, too upset to be left alone."

"Yes, Father."

Bunny was still gawping at Lizzy and Mr. Bennet as they strode from the room.

"Come," Kitty said, taking him by the hand, "sit next to me."

She led him to a nearby divan. When they settled themselves upon it, they kept holding hands and, even more scandalous, one of Kitty's knees was touching one of his.

Kitty waited for the thrill of illicit contact, the naughty tingle that would surely come from a stolen moment alone with a handsome young gentleman. This wasn't just the opportunity for which her family had been so desperate—a chance for seduction, at last—it was, supposedly, the very thing she had been dreaming of for years. What Lydia would have done were she on that divan! Within a minute, there would have been fodder enough for the ruining of a dozen reputations.

Yet Kitty couldn't help but notice the errant locks of hair that sprouted at awkward angles from the young man's head, the tear tracks that still glistened beneath the wet and puffy eyes, the faint snuffling sound coming from his thin nose, the general expression of simpering vacuity upon his face. And she felt nothing but disgust—though for Bunny or herself, she didn't know.

"You are so kind," he said. "*Too* kind. That your family would go to such lengths on my behalf . . . it astounds me."

Kitty forced herself to smile. "It is, as you said, what one does for a friend."

"I have to be honest with you. The friend I mentioned . . . "

Kitty nodded reassuringly, anticipating the words "he does not exist." At the last second, however, Bunny seemed to reconsider: He didn't *have* to be honest. Not completely.

"I do not think he would do the same for me," he said. "Nor would any of my other friends."

"What about your father? Surely, with all his connections, he could have dealt with this handily."

"Ah, yes! Sir Angus and his precious connections," Bunny spat with a bitterness Kitty had not seen in him before. For a second, it almost made him seem interesting again. "He's at St. James's Palace this very moment, you know, making certain old George is ready for his recoronation. I'm sure those two have much to commiserate over together—them with their profligate sons. It is precisely because he's allied himself with the king that father's position is so precarious. How the Prince Regent and his toadies in court would revel in our downfall! That's why I'm so blessed to have new friends like you. People of means but not—"

Bunny stopped himself and offered an abashed grin that indicated he'd been about to say something even he knew was stupid. "Rank," perhaps. Or, more likely, "importance." Or even "quality."

He chose to paper over the resulting awkwardness in a surprising way: He took Kitty in his arms and kissed her passionately.

Once again, Kitty waited patiently for the throb of pleasure, the raging inferno of ecstasy, the swoony blooming of forbidden bliss, *anything*. All she felt was a vague discomfort that grew greater in tandem with a single thought: "What *is* he doing with his tongue?"

Kitty had been kissed before, of course. There was that peck on the cheek she'd allowed Ensign Denny after a Netherfield Park ball and the time another young soldier had taken a quick liberty—a hurried mashing of lips against hers—before marching off to be slaughtered in the Great Stonehenge Massacre. This, however, was something very different. Bunny's mouth was so . . . active. He seemed to be trying to swallow her chin or perhaps clean her teeth. In the absence of actual gratification, it became almost comical, and Kitty had to distract herself to keep from giggling.

I wonder if his father has a laboratory in the house, she thought. *Or a study in which he keeps his medical journals. When Bunny's done with his slurpings, I shall find a way to ask. Perhaps I could even get him to take me there. "For more privacy," I could say. Why, by the time Lizzy and Papa return, maybe I'll even have the cure, assuming there really is one. Wouldn't that be a surprise for dour, disapproving little Nezu? I—the silly, reckless, irresponsible one—land the prize? No doubt he's slinking around outside somewhere this very moment, keeping watch on the house. Lord knows you can't keep a ninja from skulking and lurking and spying at any given opportunity. So much the better! I could saunter down the front steps and wave to him and say, "Did you get an eyeful through the drawing room window? What did you make of Mr. MacFarquhar's technique? Perhaps you'd care to show me how ninjas do it? La!"*

And then, sweeping in like a sudden storm, there it was. More than a mere tingle or throb. A great thunderclap of pleasure, a swirling whirlwind of exhilaration.

"Ooo," Kitty couldn't help but say. And then, for the first time, she didn't just let herself be kissed. She kissed back.

"Oh, Avis," Bunny moaned a moment later, when pausing for a quick gulp of air. "I knew you were a saucy one the second I saw you."

The voice nearly ruined everything. Because it wasn't the right one.

"Shut up," Kitty growled, and she put a hand on each side of his face and jerked his lips back to hers.

She had him. He would answer any question, reveal everything, do anything. All she had to do was kiss him like this. Kiss him while thinking of the man she *wasn't* kissing.

If this was being a jezebel, it really wasn't all that bad. A little awkwardness, a little titillation, a lot of shame later, no doubt. But in the moment: success! Mr. Darcy was as good as cured.

"What the devil is going on herrre?" a gruff voice barked, and Bunny spun away so quickly, Kitty was left with her head tilted and her eyes closed and her lips parted, kissing empty air.

When she opened her eyes, she saw Sir Angus MacFarquhar standing in the doorway, his hands on his hips and his eyes, flashing with rage, on her.

CHAPTER 27

"It won't take both of us to deal with those ruffians," Elizabeth whispered as she and her father left Kitty and Bunny alone in the drawing room.

"I should hope not," Mr. Bennet whispered back. "And with Sir Angus gone—"

"My thought exactly. Do you have a preference?"

Mr. Bennet nodded. "The ruffians. I wish to show them what this 'old man' is still capable of."

He hustled out the front door at a pace just below a sprint. The thugs he was after had a significant head start, but Elizabeth was confident he'd catch them quickly enough. They didn't seem the types to have a carriage waiting, and there's only so quickly one can walk while cradling a giant rabbit.

Elizabeth stopped in the middle of the foyer and for the next minute did nothing, not even breath or blink, but listen. At first, she feared the sound of the door opening and closing would draw out the footman, Scroggs, to investigate. The servant never appeared, and eventually she satisfied herself (by the occasional squeak of a floorboard overhead) that he was occupied upstairs. Kitty and Bunny, meanwhile, were still murmuring in the drawing room. Otherwise, the house seemed to be empty.

Perfect.

Elizabeth moved swiftly yet silently through the first floor. It didn't take long. Though elegantly (if dustily) appointed, the MacFarquhars' town house wasn't large, and once she'd made a quick circuit of the dining room, kitchen, pantries, cloak rooms, and servants' quarters (abandoned but for one), she was back in the foyer having seen nothing that looked like a laboratory or study. She would have to try the second floor.

That was riskier. There would be no excuse if she was discovered.

Oh, I was just trying to get back to the drawing room and I guess I went up the stairs by mistake and then I stumbled into Sir Angus's chambers and—oopsy!—I seem to have begun accidentally rifling through his things. . . .

So the first questions to settle: Where was Scroggs and what was he doing?

Elizabeth hopped atop the banister— in her experience, balustrades were far less likely to creak than steps—and glided up the spiral of the staircase as gracefully as a skater sliding over ice. She slowed as she approached the top, focusing all her Shaolin-sharpened senses on the hallway just beyond. The footman was up there somewhere . . . as was, perhaps, the salvation she sought.

The rustling of fabric and the sound of someone humming told her where Scroggs was: in the first room to her right. The door was slightly ajar, and Elizabeth dropped soundlessly to the floor and crept toward it. When she reached the doorway, she peeked through into what looked like a lady's boudoir.

There was her dressing table topped with perfumes and powders and combs. There was her wardrobe, opened to reveal a veritable rainbow of gaily colored silk and muslin. There was her four-post bed, the white sheets so smooth and taut it would seem like sacrilege for someone to muss them by actually touching them.

And there was the lady herself, staring back at Elizabeth. She showed no surprise, however, as staring and being stared at were all she was capable of.

The portrait hung over the empty mantel that (Elizabeth assumed) had until recently held her urn. If the likeness was at all accurate, Mrs. MacFarquhar had been a slender raven-haired woman with rosy skin and sly, dark, wily eyes. Her full lips seemed to be tilting ever so slightly to one side, almost smirking, as if the painter had just offered her a cheeky wink.

Sir Angus had described his wife as "formidably silly," but Elizabeth found herself instinctively liking the woman. She looked like the kind who are so often dismissed as thoughtless merely because the follies of those around her move her to laughter instead of tears.

Her husband might not have appreciated her, yet he honored her all the same. Why else maintain this shrine to a woman dead these twenty-some years? The room was so perfectly preserved, it was as though death was but a day trip for the lady, a little outing from which Sir Angus expected her to return any minute.

If she'd walked in just then, she would have found more than just Elizabeth peering into her bedchamber. She would have come across Scroggs . . . doing what, exactly? Elizabeth could still hear him humming to himself and (from the sound of it) sorting through gowns in a far corner of the room. She couldn't quite see him, though, so she dared the smallest push against the door, all the while praying that Scroggs wouldn't let the hinges get too rusty.

Fortunately, no squeak emanated from the door, although Elizabeth almost let one loose when she saw what Scroggs was up to. Gore and horror she'd seen in a million varieties, yet nothing could have prepared her for the sight of a chubby footman trying on his dead mistress's dresses.

He wasn't wearing them, thank goodness. That might have been more than Elizabeth could take. Instead, he was merely standing in front of a full-length mirror pressing a particularly resplendent ball gown to his chest and bulging belly. He hummed a lilting waltz as he inspected his reflection, and Elizabeth assumed (because the alternative was unthinkable) that he was imagining himself dancing with a beautiful lady. The way he spread the skirts out around his legs and rump and turned to admire his profile argued for something less savory, however.

Either way, the man was occupied—engrossed, even—and this was a gift horse Elizabeth resolved not to look in the mouth (or, in fact, ever let herself think of again). She moved on to the next door.

Beyond it was the room Scroggs was *supposed* to be in, apparently. It was another bedchamber the same size as the first, only this one didn't double as a mausoleum. Indeed, it looked quite lived in, for the bed was unmade and a sleeping gown and night cap lay tossed across the rumpled sheets. On the bedside table, Elizabeth saw as she came through the door, was a half-melted candle and a bookmarked copy of *A Continuation of Facts and Observations Relative to the Variolae Vaccinae, or Cow-Pox, by Edward Jenner, M.D., F.R.S., F.L.S., Etc.*

Obviously, this wasn't Bunny's room.

On the other side of the bed a small writing desk was pushed against the wall, and the sight of loose papers upon it drew Elizabeth closer. Among the documents she found was the smudged draft of a letter dated the day before.

> *~~My dear Lord~~*
>
> *~~Dear Lord Dundas~~*
>
> *~~"Squidgy"~~*
>
> *Sir,*
>
> *The ~~curative~~ ~~restorative~~ ~~thing~~ item after which you once inquired*

is in readiness at last~~!~~. The final problem remains one of production. Procuring the necessary ingredients ~~involves the most revolting~~ ~~requires the blotting out of all human~~ has proved problematic and, in mass quantities, ~~impossible~~ ~~unacceptable~~ impossible. I must continue to move slowly and with the greatest ~~secrecy~~ discretion. You will have to be patient a little longer, ~~my friend~~ ~~Squidgy~~ good sir. I will see to it, however, that your ~~support~~ ~~fortitude~~ ~~supportive fortitude~~ patience is known to ~~the king~~ ~~you-know-who~~ He who shall soon be, praise God, again in the best position to reward it. Not all have shown your faith and loyalty. Some, in fact, have attempted to steal that which you have earned through fealty. They will still be waiting in vain long after ~~Miss Wilson~~ ~~your beloved Harriette~~ ~~your inamorata~~ ~~your "special friend" (wink wink)~~ the one you have so selflessly supported is fully restored to you as she once was.

~~Yours sincerely~~
~~Your humble servant~~
~~Yours in Christ~~
Yours etc.
~~Sir Angus MacFarquhar~~
~~"Old Haggis Breath"~~
A.M.

As she reached the end of the letter, Elizabeth found herself clutching the paper so hard, it was starting to crumple. She had to force herself to relax her grip and put the paper down and calmly smooth it out, all while silently exalting.

So it was true! There *was* a cure. Just a few more minutes going through Sir Angus's things, and she might learn exactly where to—

"What the devil is going on herrre?"

There was no mistaking the voice echoing from downstairs. Sir Angus had come home at the worst possible moment. It was easy to guess what had upset him: Elizabeth could hear him railing on about "shame" and "disgrrrace" and "prrroprrriety." Kitty should have heard him come in, of course; usually, it would have been impossible for so much as a ladybug to flap past her back undetected. But the lapse was understandable if she'd been buying time for her father and sister in the way Elizabeth suspected.

They were out of time now, though. There was no way Elizabeth could slip back down the stairs without being seen by Sir Angus or Scroggs or both. Yet if she stayed where she was, she'd be found out soon enough anyway—perhaps within seconds, if Scroggs decided to hastily make his master's bed, as he should have done hours ago.

She had no choice. She rushed to the windows.

They were French windows, glass doors leading out to a narrow terrace. Elizabeth hurried through onto the balcony, closed the doors behind her, and then turned to survey the street below.

Mr. Bennet was walking up to the house, Brummell tucked under one arm, Mrs. MacFarquhar's urn in the other. He'd apparently been whistling some jaunty tune, for his lips were frozen midpucker even as he stared up pop-eyed at his daughter.

Unfortunately, he wasn't the only person staring. Some two dozen others were scattered up and down the thoroughfare—gentlemen, ladies, children, servants, workers. It would be impossible to make her escape without witnesses.

At least she'd give them something worth seeing.

"Oops!" she said, and she pitched forward over the wrought-iron railing, spun end over end, and landed on her feet directly beside her father.

"My goodness," she said loudly, looking back up at the balcony as if in astonishment. "What an amazing stroke of luck I wasn't injured!"

"Yes," Mr. Bennet said, matching her volume. "We shall have to tell MacFarquhar that railing is dangerously low!"

Neither of them dared to glance back to see how their performance had been received. Instead, Mr. Bennet simply handed Elizabeth the rabbit and knocked on the MacFarquhars' front door.

"Trouble?" he said under his breath.

"Sir Angus came home unexpectedly," Elizabeth replied.

"Trouble," her father said, sighing.

Elizabeth peered down at the rabbit in his arms.

"Don't worry." Mr. Bennet wiped at the blood that speckled the rabbit's thick fur. "It's not his."

The door before them opened a crack, and Scroggs peeked out at them warily.

"Yes?"

"We've returned," Mr. Bennet said.

Scroggs refused to open the door any wider.

Mr. Bennet raised the urn in his hands. "With the lady of the house."

"So I see," Scroggs said, still not stepping aside. Obviously, he was in no rush to throw fuel on his master's raging fire. "If you would be so kind as to wait here while I—"

Before he could close the door, his master's voice boomed through it.

"I tell you, I will not tolerate such behaviorr in my home! I should throw you out on your earrrrrr!"

Someone in the drawing room let loose a sudden, girlish sob.

"Step aside," Mr. Bennet snarled. And snarled very well, apparently, for Scroggs hopped back to let the man pass.

A moment later, Mr. Bennet and Elizabeth were marching into the drawing room, where they found Bunny MacFarquhar doing all the sobbing. Kitty was slouched beside him on the couch looking even more embarrassed than she had the time a dreadful tore away the top half of her battle gown. A scowling Sir Angus was looming over them both as if they were vermin he was about to flatten beneath his boot heel.

"What is the meaning of this?" Mr. Bennet said.

Sir Angus turned his glare on him and then swung it down to the urn he was holding.

"I would ask the same of you, sirrr! By what right do you lay hands on the most prrrecious and sacred thing in this house?"

"I claim no such right," Mr. Bennet said, and he stalked to the nearest table and placed the urn atop it. "I was merely retrieving it from those who would."

Elizabeth, meanwhile, was returning Brummell to Bunny, who proceeded to kiss the rabbit repeatedly and deeply, drying his tears on its fur.

"Dirrrk?" Sir Angus said, turning to his son. Apparently (and unsurprisingly, given his father's disposition), "Bunny" wasn't the young man's given name.

"Some of Mr. Mugg's associates paid a call," Bunny said, still nuzzling his pet. "They were rather adamant about those accounts that need squaring. On behalf of my friend, you'll recall. When I couldn't satisfy them, they insisted on taking something as a guarantee."

Sir Angus pointed a shaking finger at the urn. "And you let them take *that*?"

"How could I stop them?" Bunny sniveled. "They already had Brummell!"

Sir Angus turned toward Elizabeth and Mr. Bennet, his anger giving way to something like horror. "And you went afterrr them?"

Mr. Bennet nodded brusquely. "Those two, at least, have been given an incentive not to bother you again. I cannot speak for their employer, however."

"I see."

Sir Angus's gaze shifted so that he was no longer staring at Mr. Bennet or Elizabeth but instead seemed to be entranced by some mote floating in the air between them. He was assuming, no doubt, that the "incentive" offered to the thugs was a bribe as opposed to a generous offer to let them escape with their lives.

"I am in yourrr debt, then," he murmured.

From the softening of Mr. Bennet's expression and the little twinkle of self-satisfaction in his eyes that only his daughters would recognize, Elizabeth knew her father was about to say something appeasing, soothing, conciliatory. They had Sir Angus where they wanted him. They could start another round of calls and outings and strained flirtations aimed at inching their way toward what they sought.

Elizabeth was no longer satisfied with inching. Not with the prize in sight at last.

"Unlike some," she said coldly, "we have no desire to acquire debtors. It is friends we hoped to find here in London—and friends, despite the embarrassment that has dogged our every encounter with you, that we thought perhaps we'd found. Yet to return just now, only to hear you impugning my sister's honor? It is more than we can bear." She turned to her father. "Let us go before we are further insulted."

"Perhaps you are right," Mr. Bennet said with a slow uncertainty that wasn't just for show. Elizabeth's gambit wasn't entirely to his liking. "Come, Avis. We should—"

"*Wait*," Sir Angus said. "Perrrmit me to explain, Mrs. Bromhead. When I came home a few minutes ago, I walked in on Miss Shevington . . . "

The man swallowed hard. He had a lot of pride to get down.

" . . . consoling my son. Finding her herrre without chaperone, engaged in such tenderrr intimacy, I misread the situation in a way that shames me. I let my temperrr get the betterrr of me and I spoke rashly, and for that I apologize with all my hearrrt."

"Apology accepted," Bunny said.

Everyone ignored him.

"You're rrright that I have insulted you," his father went on. "Again. So I must beg you to allow me the chance to make amends. I would offerrr you the highest honor it is in my powerrr to bestow."

Elizabeth's whole body went numb.

What could this privilege be? A tour of Bethlem Royal Hospital? A peek at Sir Angus's secret laboratory?

Or could it be a cure for the strange plague, made available only to the most select of a very select few?

"Mrs. Bromhead, Mr. Shevington, Miss Shevington," Sir Angus said gravely, and Elizabeth's heart began pounding so loudly she feared she wouldn't hear what the man said next. "Would you like to see ourrr king recrowned?"

CHAPTER 28

After discovering the letter from Elizabeth in his aunt's study, Darcy took to his bed for two days. He didn't just take to it, in fact. He may as well have become it.

He did none of the things one usually feels obligated to do when "taking to bed": sleeping for long stretches, moaning, writhing in sweat-soaked linens, crying out at fever-born phantasms, slurping spoonfuls of broth offered by anxious loved ones, vomiting said broth back onto ones who are, as a result, even more anxious and slightly less loving.

No. All Darcy did was lie upon his bed so still and silent that he could have been the stone effigy of himself atop his own tomb.

He did not sleep. When his aunt had food sent up to him—not broth but dollops of calf's brain, bloody chunks of Kochi's unagi, lumpy pastes it was impossible to identify except as "flesh" freshly minced—he did not eat. Even when Lady Catherine herself came up with his daily dose of serum, he only grudgingly consented to part his lips and swallow the astringent crimson liquid that kept him alive (more or less).

What need had he for more life? His appetite for pain was sated.

"I don't know that I should tolerate this disagreeable humor of yours," Lady Catherine said on the second day of his self-imposed internment. "Wallowing in self pity—it is beneath you. What do you have to moon about, anyway? With each passing day, up till now, you have gained more strength. There is every reason to believe you will make a full recovery."

"You see more reasons than I, then," Darcy muttered. "There is much I fear I shall never recover."

"You talk twaddle, Fitzwilliam. You are a warrior! Face this battle like one, and you will lose nothing you do not choose to."

The old woman's tone was harsh. Yet even as she snapped at her nephew, she laid a gentle hand on his shoulder. It was, Darcy knew, as warm and nurturing as Lady Catherine de Bourgh ever was.

How easy it would be to turn her tenderness into disgust.

Anne had helped him erase every trace of his entry into the study, so his aunt had no way of knowing he'd penetrated her sanctum. If he told her he'd seen the letter, he'd also be admitting that he'd violated her trust.

And how would Lady Catherine feel if she knew he hadn't been eating because the plates being placed before him held nothing he now recognized as food? The kitchen might as well send up bowls of sand. It was the light alone he hungered for. The light of living things—such as glowed even in the bony old fingers that rested on his shoulder, so tantalizingly close to his mouth.

Darcy looked up into his aunt's dark, piercing eyes and forced himself to smile.

"You are right, as always. Soon, I'm sure, I will be well enough to take up my sword again, and together we shall finally rid this land of its last dreadful. If this cure of yours works, no Englishman or Englishwoman need ever again feel the shadow of the plague fall upon them."

Lady Catherine returned his smile, though it was so tight and dry, it was a wonder she could pry her lips apart to speak.

"There. That is what I like to hear. Keep thinking of England, Fitzwilliam, and before long you will be strong enough to save it."

Darcy managed—just barely—to keep smiling until his aunt left the room.

How could he be expected to save England when he hardly had the will to save himself?

Not a minute after Lady Catherine stepped out, Anne slipped in.

She always managed to avoid her mother's visits. At first, Darcy had assumed it was because she didn't like seeing him take the serum; it would be a reminder of the foul pollution of his blood. Yet she'd proved so tolerant of his condition (unlike some others he could think of—and was, obsessively), he eventually concluded it was something far simpler: She didn't like Lady Catherine.

"Do you wish to keep brooding alone, or may I brood with you?" she said.

"I am managing it quite well on my own. I need no help."

Despite his words, Darcy found himself wearing the slightest sliver of a smile—a real one, this time. Anne returned it as she stepped closer, stopping at her usual spot. Darcy had started to think of it as her post: two steps from his side, halfway along the length of the bed. She could stand there tirelessly for hours. There was something of the gargoyle about her perfect vigilant stillness, and at first it had unnerved him. Now, he found it comforting.

"I believe I could teach you a thing or two about brooding," she said. "I have had much practice at it. In fact, I consider myself quite the master."

Darcy need not ask what reason his cousin had for brooding. To some degree, he was the reason. And now his heart—the one he'd given to another four years before—was as pained as hers must have been back then.

He could not have blamed Anne had she come to gloat, but she wasn't there to wound him further. She seemed ready to wait—for a thousand years, if need be—for him to heal.

"Perhaps I should take you on as an apprentice," she continued, "though I would hate to see you become as expert at self-torment as I. It is a skill I have been endeavoring to unlearn, and with some success, I'm pleased to say."

"What is the secret to your success?"

"Acceptance."

Darcy snorted and turned away. "I am not ready for that. I do not know that I shall ever be."

"I thought the same thing, once. Do you know why I took to wearing black so many years ago?"

Darcy turned toward his cousin again. He found her away from her post at last: She'd taken a step closer that he hadn't even heard.

She didn't wait for him to say, "No."

"I was in mourning . . . for myself. I thought my life—what I had of one—was over. What a little fool I was! Though with excellent taste in gowns, I must say." She looked down and ran a pale hand over the silky smoothness of her bodice. "I don't mourn anymore, but I do so love black taffeta."

"I am glad you no longer grieve. But it is different with me, Anne. My life as I knew it *is* over, unless perhaps . . . "

Darcy couldn't say it. The words—the hope—hurt too much.

"If I am to accept anything," he said instead, "it is that I am tainted. Impure. Untouchable."

"No!" Anne spat back with a ferocity Darcy found shocking. "You are special, rare, extraordinary—and all *for* being impure! What good is purity? We English once fancied our blood so fine that it would be a crime to blend it with anyone else's. Yet did that spare us the strange plague? No. For all we know, it brought it upon us. And even now, when that curse could be turned into a blessing, many such as my mother lack the ability to see it, for that would require an acceptance—an *embrace*—of the very 'impurity' they so hate."

Darcy had never seen his cousin speak with such passion (for he'd never seen her speak with any passion at all), and he gaped at her as he groped for a reply.

"Anne, I . . . I don't know what you're talking about. You're not making any sense."

"I will show you, then. And perhaps you will come to a new understanding of what does and does not make sense."

Anne held out her hand.

After a moment's hesitation, Darcy took it.

A few minutes later, they were walking into the large dojo/barracks of Lady Catherine's ninja army. Assassins were everywhere on the training floor—twirling nunchucks, sparring with swords and spears, scaling ropes, practicing their hand springs, painting pictures of rainbows and sad-eyed puppies (their tiny, meticulous brushstrokes honing the precision required to flick a needle into an opponent's eye or drop a poisoned pellet into a goblet while hanging upside-down from rafters).

Silence fell over the room as Anne led Darcy inside, and without a word the ninjas set down what they were doing and began filing out.

"Be sure to lock all the doors this time!" Anne called after them. "You remember how displeased Lady Catherine was when Rinsaku and Susumu forgot. I'd hate to see any more heads on pikes. Thank you!"

One by one, the doors of the great hall slammed shut, and Darcy could hear the scraping and clicking of bolts being thrown on the other side.

The ninjas were locking them in.

It wasn't the first time for Darcy. He'd trained there many a time in his youth, so he knew what usually came next. He couldn't believe his cousin had ever tried it herself, however, or that she would presume to doom them both to bloody, agonizing death by attempting it now.

"What is the meaning of this? Why have you brought us here?"

"Fitzwilliam," Anne chided him with a smile, "for a man who was content to spend the last two days staring at the ceiling, you are so impatient. I said I would show you, and show you I shall. Now, wait here, if you would."

She walked to one of the weapons lockers against the wall, opened it, and pulled out a drawer.

"Ohhh, poor dear," she said, reaching down for something Darcy couldn't see. "Just a little light left . . . but enough."

When she turned toward Darcy again, she was holding a tiny case about the size of a snuff box. As she carried it to the center of the training floor, she cooed down into it and said, "There, there. Almost over now."

Then she stopped and knelt down and tipped the little box until something short and thin—like the tip of a small stick—tumbled out onto the floorboards. It seemed to be black, though it was hard for Darcy to tell, for it glowed with the soft white radiance of a living thing.

"What is that?"

Anne was hovering over the whatever-it-was with a wistful look on her face.

"A butterfly," she said.

"A butterfly? But I saw no wings."

"Oh, I removed them. All that flapping around. It wouldn't do today."

She stood and started walking back toward Darcy.

For the first time he noticed how dark she seemed, for all her paleness. The luminescence he'd begun seeing in people and animals—it was nowhere in her.

She stopped beside him and wrapped an arm around his.

"Minoru!" she called out. *"Zombi o dashite yare!"*

Release the zombies!

Across the great hall, a section of wall started to slide aside. Beyond it was utter blackness.

"Anne, have you lost your mind?"

On the floor nearby was a pair of abandoned sai daggers, and Darcy started to turn toward them. He wasn't sure how much of a fight he could muster, but he would at least take a few dreadfuls to hell with him. A part of him was even relieved to have the opportunity. Perhaps this was the death he should have had in the first place, instead of dragging things out for weeks . . . and losing that which most made life worth living.

Darcy got no closer to the daggers. His cousin held him tightly to her side with a strength he never would have suspected she had.

"Remember the forest," she said. "The unmentionables from the cave."

"I hardly think they'll take us for trees this time. Thoughtless though the dreadfuls might be, they'll see us for what we are sooner or later. We must fight or—"

"Here they come," Anne said.

The first zombies shuffled out of the darkness of their holding pen.

A woman, green and bloated; an old man, desiccated and gray; a boy; a girl; something with only a blob for a face, a mass of mangled flesh from which stared one wide, lidless eye. And then there were more and more, all wearing plain white shifts with multicolored circles on the front and back.

This was Lady Catherine's practice stock, held in captivity for those moments when only a moving target would do. As such, most were missing hands or arms or ears, and several had great gaping holes in their gowns where chunks of flesh had been blasted or carved away. They all had their legs and feet, though. What good would they be otherwise? When a practice zombie lost the ability to run, it quickly lost its head as well.

Not that any of these unmentionables were running. They came shambling out slowly, almost uncertainly, as if blinded by the light of day. Their pace picked up as they neared the center of the training floor, though, and eventually one of them grunted and broke into a lope. The others quickly followed suit.

Again, Darcy tried to dive toward the daggers so near at hand. And again, his cousin stopped him.

The dreadful at the head of the pack hurled itself into a shrieking leap—onto the butterfly, which it immediately crammed into its mouth. The unmentionable closest on its heels tried to pry its jaws apart and pluck out the prize, but it quickly lost interest, as did all its brethren.

The bait that had drawn them from their lair—the butterfly's life-light—was gone. The zombies began milling about listlessly, obviously seeing nothing else of interest.

Anne and Darcy they ignored.

"We must find a way out," Darcy whispered, barely daring to so much as move his lips. "This trick of yours won't save us forever."

"It is no trick, Fitzwilliam," Anne replied. She spoke in a normal tone, not loud but not a whisper either. "I lied about that before, I'm afraid. It seems cruel now, making you pretend to be a tree, but I didn't think you were ready for the truth."

The unmentionables were still wandering around obliviously in the middle of the training hall. As Anne spoke, a few turned to look at her and then turned away again, utterly uninterested.

Anne took a step toward the dreadfuls. She tried to drag Darcy along, but he was the one anchoring her now.

"Come along," she coaxed. "Don't be shy."

"I'm not shy. I just have no desire to be eaten."

"But that's just it, Fitzwilliam. That's what I've been trying to show you."

Anne uncoiled her arm from his and set off quickly, practically skipping, toward the practice stock.

"Anne! Come back!"

When she reached the nearest zombie—a bearded male with the stretched neck and cocked head and bulging eyes of a recently hung thief—she reached up and playfully tousled its ginger hair.

"I call this one Mercury," she said. "Extremely quick on his feet. Two whole months he's been here without losing a single limb! I'm surprised he didn't get the butterfly. Perhaps he's slowing down. It happens sometimes, as the legs begin to rot."

"How can this be?" Darcy muttered. "How can this *be*?"

Anne hurried over to a corpulent femme-zombie that was contentedly munching on the maggots it scraped off its own face.

"Just look at Humpty go!" she hooted, and she gave the dreadful a mischievous poke in the stomach. "Dead all these weeks, and still she finds a way to keep eating. Watch out, my girl! All that fat will be the death of you—again!"

Laughing, Anne spun away and happily pranced in a zigzag through the herd. Darcy had never seen her so euphoric, so carefree, so . . . lively.

"Hello, Romeo! Good morning, Juliet! You're looking well today, Crusoe! And you, Gulliver! Goodness, Aphrodite, whatever happened to your hands?"

"These are your 'friends,'" Darcy said. "The ones you told me you visit at night."

"Yes. These are my friends." Anne leaned against the beautiful (if olive-tinged) dreadful she'd called "Aphrodite" and wrapped her arms around its neck. "The best I've ever had. They don't demand anything. They don't judge. Not like Lady Catherine. Not like that wife of yours."

Darcy flinched, but Anne didn't seem to notice.

"They think we're abominations," she snarled. "Ha! What we are is exceptional!"

And then Darcy understood. It snapped into focus with shocking suddenness, like a spider dangling so close to the eye it's but a smudge until you recognize it for what it is and wonder why you didn't see it all along.

"You were bitten, too. You take the serum. You've been taking it for years."

Anne nodded, and then she released Aphrodite and started back toward Darcy.

"So you see," she said, "I alone can truly understand what you're going through. I alone can help you come to peace with what you've become. I. Alone. But not alone any longer. For now we have each other. As it was always meant to be."

She stopped in front of Darcy and leaned forward into him, her arms encircling his neck just as they'd done with the zombie's a moment before. Darcy was so numb with shock and confusion, he neither returned her embrace nor broke it. "You took a vow to remain at Elizabeth Bennet's side till death did you part," his cousin said. "Well, death has parted you. It touched you, and now your wife rejects you as a result. But death need never come between us, Fitzwilliam, for already we are neither wholly dead nor wholly alive. And do you know what that makes us?"

Anne pressed herself harder against him, bringing her lips up close to whisper breathlessly in his ear.

"*Immortal.*"

CHAPTER 29

Mary's surveillance of Bethlem Royal Hospital went much as it had the day before, with a few notable exceptions. Again, she saw the occasional free-roaming gaggle of dreadfuls lurch down the streets around the hospital fence. Again, she saw the hospital's black ambulance roll off, only to return a few hours later with what seemed to be a new inmate for the asylum. Again, she saw attendants rushing out to help wrestle the madman inside. And again, the bedlamite-to-be seemed dark skinned and quite vigorous in his resistance, and his cries were either gibberish or something other than English.

What was different wasn't just that Mary saw all this more clearly (for her perch in the brewery was indeed an improvement over her hiding place of the day before). Now when she muttered, "Curious" or "Queer," there was someone beside her to say, "Quite" or "Indeed." And it wasn't just affirmations Mr. Quayle had to share, for he had packed in a compartment of his box a loaf of bread and an assortment of sliced fruits and cheeses, so that he and Mary (and Ell and Arr, both of whom proved surprisingly fond of stilton) could share a companionable picnic while watching the comings and goings down below.

"Look! At the south end of the fence," Mary said as she slid a crust of bread into the view-slot of Mr. Quayle's box. "There must be a dozen dreadfuls chasing that cat. I do believe that's the biggest band we've seen yet."

As the bread disappeared into the darkness, Mary thought she caught a glimpse of soft, moist lips and perhaps even, for just a second, a surprisingly perfect Roman nose.

There was a polite pause while Mr. Quayle chewed his food.

"Yes. It is alarming," he said finally. "I'm sure you know well how the danger grows exponentially. If nothing is done, it won't be long before such bands become herds. We can only hope the situation isn't worse elsewhere in the city."

"I find it hard to believe there could be anything worse than Section Twelve Central anywhere inside the Great Wall."

"I have heard things about other sections, Miss Bennet, that make Twelve Central seem a veritable Garden of Eden. Fortunately, my obligations never took me to such places."

"Because Bedlam is here."

Mr. Quayle's box creaked.

"I am nodding."

On the horizon, a new column of smoke was adding to the ashy canopy that hung over London. This one was different than all those around it, though: roiling black as opposed to the white-gray of the factories and crematoria. Even as Mary watched it, another serpentine spiral of black smoke began coiling its way into the sky nearby.

"I think the time for picnicking has past," Mary said.

Mr. Quayle's box creaked again, though at a slower, more mournful pace.

"Be careful, Miss Bennet."

"And you, Mr. Quayle." Mary turned to the dogs. "And you, Ell. And you, Arr."

The wagging of the mutts' stubby tails put a small smile on Mary's face. There was something to be said for this levity business, she was finding. Perhaps it was easier to appreciate when no one tagged a "La!" onto the end of every quip.

Moments later, she was circling around the block to approach the hospital from the main road, past the front gate. It would hardly do for Miss Mary Godwin to be seen walking out of a deserted brewery. And it was Miss Mary Godwin—of the Society for the Prevention of Cruelty to Lunatics and Village Idiots—who was expected to pay a call at Bethlem Royal Hospital that afternoon.

In the course of her walk, Mary had to brain one zombie with a brick and scramble up the side of a building to avoid a flock of ten more. Eventually, though, she was walking up to the hospital wearing her most unctuous look of disapproving piety—which, being so well practiced, would have done any prude in England proud.

Once Mary coaxed the attendant at the entrance from behind his guard box (where he spent most of his time cowering so as not to be spotted by passing zombies), the man unlocked the gate with frantic fumbling fingers and waved Mary through. He was so anxious to shut the gate again, he nearly slammed it on her rump, and within seconds he was scrambling back to his hiding place.

"You can just follow the drive up to the front door, Miss," he whispered from behind the guard box. "They're expecting you."

"Thank you."

Despite the squalor and chaos just outside the gate, the hospital grounds were immaculately manicured, with a wide, lush lawn and flowerbeds exploding with gay spring color. As she strolled up to the column-studded portico of the hospital's central facade, Mary could have been approaching the home of a blue-blooded country squire—a friend of Mr. Darcy's or Mr. Bingley's, perhaps. And, indeed, a well-dressed gentleman stepped out of the building to watch her approach, the condescending smile of a lord of the manor on his face. Drawing near, Mary could see that he was an unhealthy man, gray and gaunt, and if not for his smirk she might have worried that he was about to have a go at her brains.

"Sir Angus MacFarquhar, I presume?"

The gray man's smirk grew smirkier. "No. Sir Angus is occupied elsewhere today. I am Dr. Sleaford, assistant administrator of Bethlem

Royal Hospital. And you would be Miss Godwin of the SPCLVI?"

"That is correct."

"I received the note you left with my subordinates yesterday demanding a tour of our facilities. I'm sorry no one was available to accommodate you at the time, but I'm happy to see that you returned, as promised. I'm certain you will find that Bethlem lives up to the high standards of your fine organization."

"So you will allow me to inspect the hospital? With no restrictions?"

"If that is still your wish, Miss Godwin. We have been at cross purposes with the SPCLVI too many times in the past. It is the sincerest wish of both Sir Angus and myself that such quarrels should be put behind us. Despite its reputation, Bethlem is a happy place for all, whether they be merely a tad overeccentric or violently insane. I would urge you to take my word for this as reassurance enough, for despite the good cheer of life inside these walls, it can still be a shocking thing to see. If it makes a patient's day a little brighter to spend it *sans* clothes, for instance, we don't force the issue. Nor do we stand on ceremony if someone wishes to, say, smear themselves with feculence and chicken feathers and pass the time in spirited clucking. *Quisquis no vestri navis*, those are our watchwords here. 'Whatever keeps your vessel afloat.' It is a humane philosophy, but one that is not always the most pleasant to see in practice. Do you still wish to come inside?"

"I feel it is my duty."

"I see. Come this way, then."

Dr. Sleaford turned and headed toward the front door, and Mary started up the steps after him. How she would separate herself from him and locate Sir Angus's laboratory, she still didn't know. Yet it was thrilling to have the chance, at last, to improvise.

Dr. Sleaford opened the door and then stepped aside with a bow. "After you."

"Thank you."

Mary crossed the threshold into Bedlam.

The net came down over her head the second she was inside.

"I got 'er!" a man yelled.

A steely ring clamped around Mary's waist, pinning her arms to her sides, and she was jerked forward as the door slammed shut behind her.

Though her eyes had yet to adjust to the dim light, Mary could tell what was happening: Someone was trying to trap her with a zombie-catching net. She groped for the pole that led off from the binding ring at the bottom of the net, and, when her fingers found it, she grabbed hold and launched herself into a Whirlwind Kick that sent her spinning up into the air.

She heard several gratifying crashes and yelps as the pole was ripped from her attacker's grasp and whipped in a circle around the room, smacking anyone in range at more or less chin height.

"She's a flippin' tigress!"

"Dr. S said she might be tough, but oi!"

Mary followed the sound of the men's cries and, using the net pole like a battle staff, managed to jab one in the stomach and sweep the other off his feet.

"Gorblimey, Styles. What are you waitin' for?"

Mary's vision returned just in time for her to see that Styles was, apparently, the big bristle-faced man coming at her with another zed net. He brought it down over her and snapped it tight before she could dodge aside. When she tried to spin away this time, he was ready: The big man managed to keep his grip. Mary twisted as far as she could to one side, lining Styles up for the Fulcrum of Doom, when she noticed someone else darting in behind her.

"Not too hard, Topsy! Dr. S wants her brains still in 'er head!" And then Topsy brought down his sap just hard enough, and once again Mary couldn't see . . . or hear or smell or think or feel.

It was the smelling, of all things, that returned first. Mary became aware of the stench of excrement and mold and wet straw. Sound came next. She heard screaming and wild shouts and distant . . . clucking? Which brought back thinking, of a sort. Enough for her to wonder *Where am I?* And that's what opened her eyes.

She found herself in a dark, cell-like room. Along one wall was a long shelf topped with beakers and vials and what might have been either medical instruments or weapons, it was hard to tell which, for she saw the glint of metal blades both large and small, jagged-toothed and smooth. Across from all this was a squat door with a barred window through which passed the sounds of shrieking and moaning and insensible raving.

She remembered. She was in Bethlem Royal Hospital. And she wasn't leaving anytime soon.

She was lying on a large tilted table, her wrists and ankles held tightly by leather cuffs bolted to the wood. She began testing her strength against the restraints, but they were too thick to snap and too tight to writhe out of, even with all her Shaolin training. As she struggled with the manacles and fetters, the table beneath her wobbled and even seemed to roll a few inches across the floor.

"I see you have returned to us," someone said. "I am so glad."

Dr. Sleaford walked around the table to face her. Here, out of the sunlight, he looked even more cadaverous, though he still wore the strained smile of a patronizing host.

"I've been anxious to continue our conversation," he said.

"I can assure you that *this* is hardly necessary for conversation," Mary replied, nodding at the strap around her right wrist.

"Oh, I'm sure, I'm sure. But would the conversation be forthright?"

"Why shouldn't it be?"

"Because we have friends inside the SPCLVI, and they've never heard of any Mary Godwin."

"I am from the Hertfordshire branch. We are unaffiliated with the London office. Their standards have grown too lax, perhaps because they are overly friendly with the likes of you, Doctor."

"An honorable parry, Miss, but not convincing. You wish me to believe that you are such a zealot, you would travel all the way here, to Section

Twelve Central, and not be frightened all the way back to Hertfordshire by the bloody turmoil of our streets?"

"Yes. I *am* just such a zealot."

"I do not believe you."

"What an ungentlemanly thing to say."

"Yet it is true, and I shall tell you why. It strikes me as odd—*very* odd—that a busybody spinster reformer should have mastered the so-called deadly arts."

"What makes you think I have?"

"What my warders tell me, and the bruises and abrasions all over their bodies."

Mary tried to shrug but found, with her hands pinned, that she could not.

"I resisted when your men first tried to net me, it is true, but any injuries they sustained were merely the result, I'm sure, of their own clumsiness."

"Again, I might be inclined to believe you but for one thing. I have seen such injuries more than once in the past: on the soldiers who'd captured ninjas sent to infiltrate this hospital."

"Soldiers? I have seen no soldiers here, though surely you could use a few, with Twelve Central in its current state. Why were they here before and where have they gone now?"

Dr. Sleaford's gray eyes lit up with glee in a way that told Mary she had, once again, walked into a trap of his setting.

"*I* am asking the questions here!"

The way the man said it, it was obvious he enjoyed it—and that he'd had some practice at it.

"Now," he went on, "we know that someone has taken an untoward interest in us. What we do not know—and what you must tell me—is who that someone is."

"I will not," Mary said simply. She'd never much cared for amateur theatrics, and anyhow, the time for keeping up pretenses seemed to have passed.

Dr. Sleaford leaned in close (though not close enough for Mary to butt him or bite off his nose). "It would be so much more pleasant for everyone if you told me."

"No."

"Please."

"No."

"Really. Please. I beg you."

"No."

Dr. Sleaford straightened again. "Well, I did ask nicely."

"Yes, you did."

"I'm afraid I must be a little less than nice now." Dr. Sleaford turned toward the door. "Turvy! Bring in Subject Seven, if you please!"

Turvy had apparently been waiting in the hall, for the door immediately opened, and a man came in pushing a small cart upon which was strapped a glistening red skull and spine—both writhing.

Subject Seven was a zombie stripped to its essence. Just the central nervous system and some muscle and bone to hold it together. No hair, no skin, no organs but for the brain. It didn't even have a tongue, though Mary suspected that was by its own doing. The thing was madly gnashing its teeth, snapping at everything, as if it wished to devour all the world.

Turvy steered the cart to Mary's side. When he stopped, she and Subject Seven were only inches apart.

The dreadful locked its lidless eyes on Mary and began chomping at her frantically. Just one more push, the most minor adjustment of its trolley, and the thing's big yellow teeth would be sinking into Mary's hand or thigh or head.

"Anything to say?" Dr. Sleaford asked.

Mary considered for a moment and then nodded at the zombie.

"I should think that the Society for the Prevention of Cruelty to Zed-dash-dash-dash-dash-dashes would object to this. It is lucky for you that I am not a member."

She knew it wasn't as clever as whatever Elizabeth would have said in the same situation. Yet still she derived some satisfaction from it. If these were to be her last words, they were brave enough, if rather fatuous, and her only disappointment was that no one whose good opinion she valued was nearby to hear them. Mr. Quayle would have been particularly appreciative, she thought, and it saddened her that by the time he returned to rescue her with her sisters and father, she would be on her way to becoming a drooling ghoul capable of no speech at all.

"You do not relent?" Dr. Sleaford asked.

Mary just shook her head. Her last words were said.

"I anticipated as much," Dr. Sleaford said, sighing. "None of your predecessors were any more inclined to cooperate. You're all so anxious to 'die with honor,' you people! Fortunately, this time I have a little extra leverage. Styles! Our other guest, thank you!"

The door opened again, and in came the burly unshaven warder who'd managed to capture Mary not so long before. He, too, was pushing a small gurney upon which was secured a limbless form. This one, however, was graced with a full torso, clothed—not to mention skin and hair and a face that it seemed at pains to keep turned toward the far wall.

"Mr. Quayle!" Mary gasped. "Is that you?"

So much for her cool and composed final words. She'd never gasped in her life, and now her spotless record was spoiled with, most likely, just minutes to go.

"Over here, I think," Dr. Sleaford said, stepping away from Mary. "Both of them, lined up together. Where she can see."

As Turvy and Styles situated the trolleys side by side, Subject Seven took to nipping at Mr. Quayle's stubby body. Mr. Quayle, for his part, merely kept his face pointed away and said nothing.

Mary found herself straining to get a look at the man who had, till then, been just a voice from a box. She'd expected him to be scarred, disfigured, but the chin and temple and ear she saw seemed flawless—and strangely familiar. A band of white stretched from his mouth over his cheek.

He'd been gagged.

"Your friend made the most foolhardy attempt to come after you," Dr. Sleaford said. "If you care for him half as much as he apparently cares for you, then you'll tell me what I want to know, and quickly. I think the poor fellow's already lost every protuberance a man can lose . . . with one exception, perhaps. I'm sure you wouldn't want to see Subject Seven make a meal of *that*, now, would you?"

"Oh ooh ee, Ahhee," Mr. Quayle said.

"Oh, capital. Capital! Styles, Turvy. Do remove the gentleman's gag so that his pitiful pleas for mercy will provide further persuasion for the lady. You *are* offering up a pitiful plea for mercy, aren't you, Mr. . . . Quayle, was it?"

Being careful to keep himself from Subject Seven's snapping jaws, Styles slowly moved in and lifted Mr. Quayle's head. As he held it steady between his big hairy hands, the other warder worked to unknot the strip of linen tied tightly around the prisoner's mouth.

For the first time, Mary was able to look straight into Mr. Quayle's eyes. And before the gag even came away, she knew that they weren't Mr. Quayle's eyes at all. Because she recognized those eyes, and there was no Mr. Quayle.

When Styles and Turvy darted away again, it was Geoffrey Hawksworth, her first master, who gazed back at her.

"I was saying, 'Don't do it, Mary.'" Hawksworth smiled sadly. "As you know so well, I am not worth it."

CHAPTER 30

As Mr. Bennet and Lizzy and Sir Angus finished making arrangements for the next day—arrangements that would bring the Bennets into the presence of the loftiest lords and ladies in the land—Kitty sat silently beside Bunny and Brummell and brooded. Her soul was roiling, and though it was good to know she had a soul to roil (she'd sometimes wondered), it wasn't a pleasant experience.

Nor was it entirely a new one. Her soul had stirred first, if not churned, when Lydia ran off to become Mrs. George Wickham, leaving her sister with no clear idea who Miss Kitty Bennet was. And now Bunny MacFarquhar, of all people, had provided an answer. One she didn't like.

Miss Kitty Bennet was the kind of woman who kissed men she didn't love and loved men she couldn't kiss.

Well, "loved" was too strong a word. How could she love a man she barely knew? How could she love a man she could never know?

She was mistress; he was servant. She was Shaolin; he was Shinobi. She was English; he was Other. There were so many walls between them, she shouldn't have even noticed that she was a woman and he was a man. Yet notice she had, apparently, for when she'd been kissed by Bunny MacFarquhar—just the sort of fool she would have expected to fall for—she'd found herself thinking of Nezu.

Little Nezu, of all people! Even beyond the scandalous fact of his race, any match would be absurd. Love blossomed between kindred spirits. Lizzy and Darcy, Jane and Bingley, Lydia and Wickham—all were perfectly suited for each other because they *were* each other (with the necessary exception of certain anatomical details). One didn't add oil to water or axle grease to tea or zombies and ninjas to a romance. Like belonged with like.

And Nezu couldn't be more unlike Kitty. The man was stiff, distant, humorless, haughty. And agile, exotic, handsome, and very, very *standing right in front of her.*

Kitty was so lost in thought, she barely registered that goodbyes were being spoken or that she was walking out of the MacFarquhars' and up the street with her sister and father. Not until Nezu joined them, gliding out of whichever shadowy corner he'd been hiding in, did she stop brooding and start hearing and seeing again.

"One of you I saw flipping out of a window," the ninja said as he fell into step with the Bennets. "Another maiming two men in order to retrieve a rabbit and an urn. With such indiscreet public displays, I fear to even ask what went on inside."

"Well, don't then!" Kitty blurted out. "What matters is that Sir Angus is taking us to the recoronation tomorrow!"

"And he definitely has a cure for the strange plague," Lizzy added. "I saw a letter that confirmed it."

"So we may have been indiscreet, Nezu, but, more important, we were successful," Mr. Bennet said. "We can now be certain that Sir Angus has what we want—and trusts us enough to offer an opportunity to take it."

Nezu nodded solemnly. "That is progress. You're right. It should not matter how it was achieved."

He gave Kitty a long look that made her suspect—or perhaps merely hope—that it did matter. To him, anyway. As they carried on back to the Shevington residence, only Mr. Bennet and Lizzy continued talking, debating in low tones how best to steer Sir Angus toward a tour of Bethlem Royal Hospital, while Kitty and Nezu strolled with an abstracted air, saying nothing.

Upon reaching the house, they found to their surprise that Mary hadn't yet returned from the mysterious errand she'd slipped off to attend to that morning. Twilight was fast approaching, and the graying horizon was striped black here and there by ominous columns of dark smoke. They waited for Mary for a time in the drawing room, but at last Mr. Bennet could sit still no longer. He hopped from his chair and began pacing around the room.

"Perhaps your afternoon would have been better spent searching for Mary rather than spying on us," he barked at Nezu.

It had been years since Kitty had seen her father so much as cock an eyebrow when she and her sisters charged in to battle hordes of the undead. Yet he seemed shaken now. Perhaps it was because Mary had chosen her own battle, for once.

"I did not think it necessary to look for your daughter," Nezu said. "She would not have left the area unobserved or unescorted."

"In other words, you had someone spying on her, too," Lizzy said.

"Watching the house, yes. With orders to accompany any of you who struck off on your own."

"'Accompany,'" Mr. Bennet snorted. "You mean follow. Your trust in us is truly an inspiration, Nezu."

"It is not necessarily a sign of mistrust to take precautions."

"No. Not necessarily," Mr. Bennet replied. "Just usually."

"Nezu," Lizzy said, "if you've had someone watching us, then surely you know where Mary disappeared to yesterday. Wouldn't it stand to reason that she went back there today?"

"Indeed, it would . . . except that apparently she went nowhere. According to my agent—"

"Spy," Mr. Bennet said.

"—Miss Bennet simply visited a book shop and then spent the rest of the day aimlessly wandering the streets of One North."

"Indeed?" Lizzy said. "That doesn't sound like Mary."

"Oh? Who knows what she's capable of now?" Mr. Bennet muttered. "I should have known that Wellstonecroft woman's ramblings would lead her astray."

"Wollstonecraft," Lizzy corrected.

"Yes, of course. How could I forget, after hearing the wretched bore quoted ten times an hour for the past year? I tell you, I'd have rather seen Mary turn her mind to mush, like Kitty with her novels and fashion plates, than convince herself a young lady has the right to go charging off without so much as—"

"And you accuse *me* of talking too much!" Kitty cried, leaping off the divan. "Come! Let's go look for her!"

"Excuse me?" Mr. Bennet said.

Kitty was already headed for the door. "Lizzy, you and Papa work north from here. Nezu and I will cover the south."

"Why in—?" Lizzy began.

Kitty was ready for the question, or at least the question she imagined it to be.

"We can't have ladies the likes of Miss Shevington and Mrs. Bromhead seen roaming the streets alone," she said. "Bad enough that their houseguest 'Miss Millstone' has been doing it! Now come along, Nezu. If my sister is still meandering about through One North, I'd like to find her before midnight."

Kitty didn't look back to see if anyone was following her. She was afraid to. She just went striding out of the room and across the hall toward the front door, which Nezu reached first, sliding quickly by her in smooth Shinobi silence.

"Might I suggest you wear your cloak, Miss? London nights can be chilly."

He'd already taken the liberty of grabbing her long fur-trimmed wrap, and as he helped Kitty slip into it, she felt the reassuring weight of the throwing stars, nunchucks, and sai knives sewn into the lining. Once Nezu had shrugged into his own great coat—capacious enough to conceal a small cannon—they left the house together, with Lizzy and a grumbling Mr. Bennet at their heels.

"Happy hunting," Kitty said as they separated.

"And to you," Lizzy replied, giving her sister a queer look. She appeared troubled yet strangely amused, and Kitty was glad that by then it was too dark for Lizzy to see the flush she felt rise to her cheeks.

"This man you had following Mary yesterday," she said to Nezu. "Did he mention where, exactly, she did her rambling?"

"Mostly along Upper Street."

"Perfect. That's just ahead, is it not? We'll take it toward the gateway to . . . what's the section just south of here?"

"Eleven Central."

"So we'll follow Upper Street down to Eleven Central, and then, if we still haven't run across Mary, we can come back up that other big street. What-Have-You Lane."

"Liverpool Road?"

"Well, don't ask *me*. You're the one who's supposed to know everything. Isn't that why Her Ladyship put us under your thumb? Too bad you let one of us wriggle free. Don't worry, though. I won't tell the lady. Not so long as we find Mary safe and sound, and I can't imagine we won't. Don't let on that I said so, but I think she might be the most skilled killer of us all. Perhaps that's just because she's always soooooo serious. I mean, just listen to me prattle on. You'd hardly think I'd mastered three hundred and sixty-seven ways of dealing death, would you? All you might guess is that I could talk a man to death. La!"

Nezu didn't laugh along, of course. When Kitty glanced his way, she found him watching her intently, his brow so furrowed he might have been making a study of the Rosetta Stone.

"What?" Kitty said.

Nezu looked away.

"*What*?"

"I was just noting how very right you are," Nezu said. "I *can* hardly believe that you've mastered the deadly arts."

"Yet you know very well that I have," Kitty snapped back, stung. "For how else could I have bested you in the attic last night?"

"You did not best me."

"Why, you arrogant little—!"

"You matched me," Nezu went on, still perfectly calm. "Quite perfectly. Which is what confuses me. I cannot understand how someone who lives so close to death can remain so . . . "

Nezu searched for the right word.

Kitty braced herself.

Would he choose "frivolous"? "superficial"? "sallow"? Or her father's favorite: "silly"? Whichever it would be, Kitty had her answer ready.

"I see! So you would presume to pronounce me frivolous/superficial/shallow/silly merely because I smile and laugh and maybe talk a little too much," she would say. "Yet, as you have seen, I can do everything a warrior does. I have gone to every dark place a warrior can go. I *am* a warrior! Perhaps my mistake is that I do not frown and sneer and feign world weary self-seriousness. This leads some, I suppose, to take me for a fool, and nothing more. If so, then the question is, Who is more frivolous/superficial/shallow/silly—them or me?"

She wouldn't add that *she* was one of those who sometimes assumed she was a fool. It would hardly bolster her argument.

" . . . so . . . ," Nezu repeated, "human."

"I see! So you would presume to pronounce me—" Kitty gaped at Nezu. "'Human'?"

Nezu grimaced. "I have said too much. Let us direct ourselves to the task at hand."

"We can look for Mary and talk, too. She's not a dog. We don't have to walk around calling for her."

"All the same . . . "

Nezu pointedly began scanning the opposite side of the street.

"You're just afraid to let yourself be human, too," Kitty said.

Nezu still looked away.

"Perhaps we *should* try calling for her," he mused.

"Oh, don't stop now, Nezu. You made such a good start. Talk to me."

"And I wonder if searching in pairs is really such a good idea," Nezu said, still speaking as if to himself. "We could cover ground twice as quickly if we separated."

"Perhaps. But what fun would that be?"

"We are not here to have fun."

"No, but we're not here to be miserable either."

"Misery and happiness are two sides of the same delusion. All that is real is duty."

"La! That's the kind of twaddle they write on dojo walls."

"It is something my father once told me."

"Well, far be it for me to speak ill of your father, but he sounds like a dismal little killjoy."

"He was." An embittered flintiness came over Nezu's face even as his eyes seemed to lose their focus. "Yet he was my father." He shook his head, and his expression was once again impassive, blank. "I thought I'd ended this conversation," he said.

"Oh, you'll have to try harder than that with me!"

Hissing whispers and quick footfalls echoed from somewhere up ahead. When Kitty turned toward the sound, she found a middle-aged couple hurrying around the corner from Upper Street. They were huddled close together, speaking in low yet harsh tones that made it obvious they were taking umbrage at something. Everything about them—the well-tailored yet unstylish clothes, the fleshy builds of the stolidly prosperous, the looks of disgust on their round faces—seemed to tell Kitty that these were just the sorts who would object most vociferously to a young lady out late in the company of an Asiatic man.

Kitty slipped a hand under her cloak and gripped the hilt of a dagger. She wasn't going to use it on the busybodies—probably—yet she found the feel of it soothing.

"Imagine," she heard the man say. "In One North. It's unheard of."

Kitty's fingers tightened around the dagger.

"What are all the walls for if the horrid things can just go wherever they please?" the woman replied. Then she looked up and seemed to notice Kitty and Nezu for the first time. "I do hope you don't have reservations at La Langoustine Rouge. We were just there, and the scene is simply appalling."

"Scene?" Kitty said.

There was no need for the woman to explain, it turned out, for the "scene" was following them.

More than a dozen dreadfuls came lurching along on Upper Street. Most had blood and blobs of poorly masticated viscera ringing their gaping mouths. One was trying to gnaw through the shell of a lobster that had clamped its claws to its right hand. Another had, unaccountably, what appeared to be a fillet of sole on its head. And still another glanced to the left and saw fresh meat—Kitty and the others—and howled.

The whole pack wheeled around and charged.

"Oh!" the woman cried.

"That's it," her husband harrumphed as he hustled her into a run. "We're moving to Three East."

Nezu drew Fukushuu from under his coat.

"It appears we will have to postpone our conversation after all."

"Oh, Nezu," Kitty said. "Have you not come to know me better than that?"

She paused a moment to ready a fistful of throwing stars and study the creatures rushing toward her. Many of the unmentionables were skeletally thin, and they all had the sallow skin and dark-ringed eyes of plague victims, as had the zombie family they'd encountered that morning.

Somewhere in the city, Pestilence was raising an army for its fellow horseman, Death.

"When you say I've remained 'human,' you don't mean 'soft,' do you?" Kitty said, and she began flicking star after star with perfect precision.

The five nearest dreadfuls were instantly blinded by the triangular blades sunk deep into their eyeballs.

Nezu dived past them into the middle of the approaching pack, rolled to his feet, took off the next four zombies' heads with two quick swings, and then back-flipped out of grabbing-and-biting-and-disemboweling range.

"I meant 'alive,'" he said. "Your spirit has not been deadened by what we do."

"Ah." Now that the unmentionables were near, Kitty took to hurling daggers, aiming for the knees. The heavy knives brought down three more in quick succession. "So it is my joie de vivre that confounds you."

A withered and screeching she-hag of an unmentionable threw itself at Nezu. He calmly impaled it, flipping his katana around as the zombress flailed upon it. With a mighty jerk, he brought the blade up through the belly, up through the neck, and finally up through the skull itself. The neatly halved brain plopped out onto the street like a pair of soggy hot-cross buns.

"I suppose you could put it like that," he said.

Kitty was busy using her nunchucks to fend off a small group of zombies that had surrounded her.

"Well, I can see why you'd be . . . Thank you."

Nezu had beheaded the most nettlesome of the dreadfuls, and Kitty could now concentrate on braining those that remained.

"I can see why you'd be envious," she began again. "You ninjas seem to know nothing but *misère de mort*."

"Envious?" Nezu ducked under an especially tall zombie's swipe of the arm and then cut the unmentionable down to size by sending Fukushuu through its thighs. "What makes you think I'm envious?"

"Well, what word would you prefer?"

Only one dreadful was still able to walk and see, and Kitty had her nunchucks wrapped around its neck. With all her might she whipped the growling, thrashing ghoul first one way, then another.

"Intrigued? Admiring?"

At last the thing's head tore free, and the rest of the body went stumbling off into the street a few steps before collapsing and lying still.

"Infatuated?" Kitty said.

By now, Nezu was mopping up, coolly dispatching all the maimed and moaning dreadfuls that ringed them. There were so many loose heads bouncing around, the street looked like a monstrous billiards table.

"You used the word 'confound' a moment ago," he said. "That comes closest, I think."

Kitty retrieved one of her daggers from a zombie's leg and then plunged it into the top of the creature's skull, as if she were planting a flag.

With that, the "un" was removed from the last of the undead.

"So you admit you are confused," she said. "Perhaps I can clarify things for you."

She stalked over to Nezu, grabbed him by the lapels of his great coat, and pulled him into a kiss.

It was by far the most impetuous, scandalous thing she'd ever done. Which made the day quite notable, as the second most scandalous thing—letting Bunny MacFarquhar probe her gums—was but a few hours old.

"Mmph!" Nezu said.

It was interesting to learn that it was indeed possible to take the man by surprise. Even more interesting: He was a good kisser. Not that Kitty had much to judge by. But after a stunned moment just standing there stiffly, Nezu bent in toward Kitty and pressed his lips more firmly to hers and wrapped one arm around her back and it was heaven . . . even if she was standing in the spilled innards of a disemboweled dreadful.

Nezu started to raise his other arm, as if to complete his embrace. He was still holding his sword, though, and at the last second he seemed to realize he couldn't wrap his arms around Kitty without driving Fukushuu through her.

He broke off the kiss and jerked away.

"I will continue the search to the south, as planned," he said. "You should return to the house. It would not do for you to be seen in public."

"But—"

Nezu sheathed Fukushuu and glanced down at Kitty's blood-

"IT WAS HEAVEN . . . EVEN IF SHE WAS STANDING IN THE SPILLED INNARDS OF A DISEMBOWELED DREADFUL."

splattered cloak and gown.

"You are soiled," he said, and he spun on his heel and marched alone into the night.

"Nezu, wait. Nezu!"

If he'd looked back at Kitty—and he did not—he would have seen this: a slowly scuttling shape trying to make its escape into the storm drain behind her.

As Kitty's eyes filled with the tears a warrior was never supposed to shed, the lobster crawled over the grate, pulled itself into the inlet, and tumbled into the sewer below. It splashed into water mixed with blood and brain and sewage. But it was water, which was all that mattered. Crustaceans are incapable of sighs of relief, yet this one came as close as such things can.

A second later, a hand, the skin hanging from it in green strips, stabbed into the muck, wrapped itself around the lobster, and raised it to broken yellow teeth that were already smeared with a film of minced flesh.

CHAPTER 31

Dr. Sleaford let his pet dreadful nip at Hawksworth for a while, but after his sixth "And what if your friend were to be bitten *here*?" Mary realized it was all for show. Subject Seven wasn't going to sink its teeth into anybody, anywhere. Not yet.

She returned her attention to a matter of real concern.

"You remain admirably composed," she said to the man she'd known until minutes before as "Mr. Quayle."

He hadn't so much as glanced at the snapping skull as it was pushed within biting range again and again. He merely lay on the cart to which he'd been strapped, staring either at the stain-splattered ceiling or, from time to time, at Mary.

"When last I saw you," she continued, "you seemed to find dreadfuls . . . unsettling."

"You are generous with your choice of words," Hawksworth said. At the moment, he was in one of his ceiling phases. "Others might have said that I fled like a craven coward, abandoning you and your family to certain death."

"Others *have* said that."

"They were right to do so." Hawksworth looked into Mary's eyes. "It is true."

Dr. Sleaford cleared his throat. "I said, 'And what if your friend were to be—?'"

"My *friend*," Mary said, still holding Hawksworth's gaze, "is not going to be bitten anywhere until Sir Angus MacFarquhar has had a chance to interrogate us. No doubt your master will want the same power over us that you feign, and you could hardly spoil that for him by dooming us before he's even arrived."

"Oh, ho! You think so, do you? Well, what if your friend were to be bitten . . . here!"

Dr. Sleaford leaned in to point a long chalk-white finger at a region of Hawksworth's body that was never supposed to be acknowledged at all, let alone pointed at. His assistants, Turvy and Styles, obediently swung Subject Seven's gurney toward the area in question.

"Sir," Hawksworth said, turning away from Mary to glare at their captor, "as you can see, I have been bitten by dreadfuls before." He waggled what was left of his arms and legs, which wasn't much. "With enough repetition, even one's greatest fear loses its hold. So have your creature bite me *there*, if you truly mean to. Otherwise, end this charade now."

Dr. Sleaford glowered at the man a moment before blowing out what seemed to be a sigh of relief.

"All right, fair enough," he said. "Turvy, if you would see Judith back to her closet, please."

"Judith?" Mary asked as the slimy, sinew-covered skull and spine were wheeled out still wriggling and snapping.

Dr. Sleaford chuckled. "'Subject Seven' sounds so much more ominous, don't you think? 'Ooooo, tell me what I want to know or I'll sic Judith on you!'? It wouldn't do at all." His long, pale face turned solemn again. "Sir Angus *will* sic Judith on you, though, I assure you. Unless you tell me who sent you."

He paused hopefully, but neither Mary nor Hawksworth were any more inclined to answer.

"Fine, I'll stop," Dr. Sleaford said with a shrug. "It's just that we've never had prisoners of such obvious quality—not alive, at any rate—and it saddens me to think of what awaits when Sir Angus arrives."

"And when might we expect that?" Mary asked.

"Oh, there's no telling. He's quite busy with the recoronation, you know—or I assume you know. We sent word that we'd captured more spies, but I can't even be sure the messenger got through, with the streets as they are. Frightful out there, isn't it?"

"No more than in here," Hawksworth said.

Dr. Sleaford looked hurt.

"What we do, we do for England," he said. "Styles, we'll give the lady our deluxe accommodations, I think. The gentleman can wait here."

Styles—an unshaven brute of a man who outweighed Mary by at last ten stone—blanched.

"You don't mean for me to actually *untie her*, do you?"

"That was the idea, yes. Do you object?"

"You didn't see her fight, Sir."

"Would you feel better if I stood beside you with a pistol pointed at her?"

Styles stared down at his toes. "Yes."

Dr. Sleaford rolled his eyes. "As if you'd do anything so uncouth as to attack your hosts," he said to Mary.

"Perish the thought," she replied.

The thought stayed very much alive, however, for Dr. Sleaford did indeed keep a flintlock trained on Mary as Styles wheeled her gurney down a short hallway to another chamber and, once inside, began loosening the straps around her wrists and ankles. Dr. Sleaford also had the good sense (or perhaps just the good luck) to keep himself half-hidden behind a formidable barrier—Styles—that would have slowed Mary had she lunged for the gun.

"Miss Bennet?" Hawksworth called out once Dr. Sleaford and his lackeys had left, closing and locking more than one heavy door behind them. "Miss Bennet, can you hear me?"

"Quite clearly."

Mary stepped to the small, barred window in the door of her cell. Peering out, she could almost see the door to the laboratory/torture chamber Hawksworth had been abandoned in.

"I'm not far away." She turned to take in her cell in its entirety and found she could no longer think of it as a cell. "In the most well-appointed dungeon I've ever been thrown in."

It was true, for not many dungeons boast of thick, embroidered carpets and floral-patterned wallpaper and gas lighting and crisp white linens on a four-post bed. The last occupant had been quite pampered, and Mary had the feeling he or she had spent a long, long time here, whereas her own stay was unlikely to stretch beyond morning, one way or another.

Mary started to say, "Mr. Quayle?" But that wasn't right. "Mr. Hawksworth" felt wrong, too. The man had always been "Master Hawksworth" to her. Yet he'd really only been her master a few weeks, years before. And the word itself—"master"—had a sour taste to her now.

"I don't know what to call you," she said.

"You may call me whatever you wish."

Mary licked her lips and curled her fingers into fists.

"Geoffrey?"

There was a moment of silence.

"Yes, Mary?"

"You are Nezu's agent. I understand that. Is it safe to assume that you told him everything I did yesterday? Everywhere I went and all I planned to do today?"

"No. That would not be a safe assumption. I told him nothing."

"Why?"

"I was afraid he would order me to stop you. Or, worse yet, that he would decide to stop you himself."

"I see. So Nezu has no idea where we are. We can expect no rescue tonight."

"That is correct."

Mary thought a moment, found her fists unclenching, and then said, "Thank you."

Hawksworth coughed out a gruff chuckle.

"I am not being sarcastic," Mary said. "You protected my freedom to act. Our freedom to act together. I am grateful for that."

"Then you are welcome."

"Geoffrey?"

There was another pause, this one agonizingly long.

"You have another question," Hawksworth said finally, his voice even huskier than usual.

"Yes."

"You want to know what happened eight years ago. How I could abandon your family during the Siege of Netherfield."

"And what became of you afterward. Yes. Will you tell me?"

"I suppose I'd better. You've waited long enough for an explanation, and putting it off any longer might mean you will never receive it at all."

Mary heard Hawksworth suck in a long, deep, raspy breath. He didn't just sound like a man about to launch into a long story. He sounded like a man about to launch himself into battle. Or off a cliff.

"I'm sure you know how it began," he said. "I was a vain man, but my pride was a pedestal of ash. For all my posturing, I was secretly terrified of the unmentionables, and even more terrified of my own weakness. So I gave in to it. I threw a soldier from his horse and fled. To my amazement, I made it through the stricken hordes surrounding Netherfield and Meryton. I'd almost left Hertfordshire altogether when I finally noticed the scratch on my left hand. I thought I'd escaped unscathed, untouched by the dreadfuls. I hadn't. The skin was barely broken. There wasn't enough blood to coat the head of a pin. Yet that was enough. The whole arm would have to come off. How I raged to find my perfection stolen from me . . . even as you and your sisters were dying, for all I knew. And I realized then that it wasn't just my flesh that had been poisoned. It was my soul. No doctor with his saw could save me from that. It would fester within me every day I remained on earth. Unless I cleansed it."

"So you turned back."

"I turned back. I rode again through the herds of unmentionables choking Hertfordshire, toward the battalion of His Majesty's army we knew to be on the move from Suffolk. And this time, I received much, much more than a little scratch. I saw whole chunks of myself go down the gullets of the undead. But I found the column. And with it was my mistress, the head of the order that had given me my training: Lady Catherine de Bourgh. She attended to my wounds with her own sword. I've remained in her service ever since. Yet always I've dreamed that, one day, I might somehow redeem myself in the eyes of your sister Elizabeth and your father and you, too, Mary. For it was the Bennet girls of Longbourn who showed me what a true warrior is."

"You already redeemed yourself when you rode back through the dreadful swarms. If you hadn't done that, my entire family would have been wiped out."

"And how many more might I have saved if I'd never fled to begin with?"

"None. You simply would have died with us when Netherfield was overrun."

"Still—"

"You have no debt to repay," Mary said firmly. "No lost honor to regain. You were defeated in the first battle against your fear, that is all. In the end, it is clear, you conquered it. The man I have come to know these past days is a brave and honorable one."

Hawksworth said something so quietly Mary couldn't make it out, and after a moment he cleared his throat and tried again.

"Thank *you*."

"There is no need for thanks. It is simply the truth."

At that, Hawksworth laughed.

"Oh, Mary. In some ways, it was you I dreaded facing again the most. You always seemed so certain about everything. So unwavering in your judgments. I did not think you would understand or forgive."

"You changed, Geoffrey. We all can. Sooner or later, we all must."

"You sound very sure of that."

"Indeed, I am. Because, as always, I am right."

They both chuckled softly and then fell quiet again for a long while. Mary didn't find the silence awkward. It was merely a pause in a conversation she knew they would carry on again someday, provided they had other days.

"So," she finally said, "I find I harbor an unsavory suspicion." She surveyed the chamber again, noticing now how deep ruts had been worn in the carpeting. Someone had done much pacing here. "It is not particularly patriotic."

"You are thinking of the other prisoners Dr. Sleaford mentioned."

"Yes."

"Some would be our predecessors, of course. Spies sent by my mistress."

"Yes. But there was also the one who was kept *here*."

And then another voice, squeaky and weak, chimed in from somewhere farther down the hallway.

"And there's us," it said.

CHAPTER 32

Elizabeth and Mr. Bennet had no more luck with their search than Kitty had. They found (and did away with) two small flocks of unmentionables roaming freely through the darkened streets. They did not find Mary.

"Perhaps she and Nezu's spy ran off together," Mr. Bennet joked grimly. "I'd rather it were that than. . . . "

He lapsed into silence, and Elizabeth placed a hand on his slumping shoulder.

"Remember the Second Battle of Bridlington? When all those drowned fishermen began marching out of the sea?"

Mr. Bennet smiled at the memory. "And Mary started trawling them up in their own rotting nets. How proud I was of her that day."

"As you should have been. Mary is a skilled and resourceful warrior. What peril could London hold when she's defeated the worst Hell has to offer?"

Mr. Bennet nodded, though Elizabeth could tell it took some effort for him to keep his smile in place. She was glad her words could comfort him, even if only a bit, for they did absolutely nothing for her.

When they returned to the house, Kitty came darting out of the drawing room.

"Oh," she groaned when she saw them. "No Mary?"

Elizabeth shook her head.

"And no Nezu?" Kitty asked.

"We didn't know we were supposed to be looking for him," Mr. Bennet said. "How is it you managed to lose the man?"

"I don't know," Kitty mumbled. "I mean . . . he thought it best that we search separately."

"Well, I wouldn't worry about him," Mr. Bennet said, and Kitty brightened a bit, obviously anticipating the sort of reassurance Elizabeth had given their father not long before. "He is unworthy of your concern. Now, I'll wait up for Mary. You two turn in. Tomorrow you'll need to be at your best for the MacFarquhars . . . not to mention the king."

"I'll wait with you," Kitty said, walking with her father toward the drawing room.

He stopped, spun her around, and pushed her toward the stairs with a firm, "Good night."

Then he was off.

"Kitty," Elizabeth said, but it was too late. Her sister was already bustling toward the staircase.

"Good night, Lizzy," she choked out without looking back.

Elizabeth knew it wasn't just Mary her sister was worried about. She recognized the signs, and she would've liked to talk to Kitty about the risks she ran affixing any affection whatsoever to a man such as Nezu. By the time she reached the bottom of the staircase, however, her sister's bedroom door was already slamming shut above.

It was for the best, perhaps. Their father was right: The next day would be pivotal. It wasn't the time to stir up more turmoil. It was time to rest. If one could.

As it turned out, she couldn't. Elizabeth lay awake for hours, unable to sleep or even meditate. It was impossible to clear her mind with Mary still missing. And how could she worry about what Sir Angus would think when her connection to her husband—the man all this manipulation and duplicity was meant to save—felt so fragile?

There had been no response to the letters she'd sent to Rosings. Even if there had been, Darcy would have been replying to lies. He had no notion what she and her family were undertaking on his behalf. What would he make of the fact that she wasn't by his side? Not knowing the truth, he might judge her ill. Yet knowing the truth (and hating, as he did, deceit of any kind), he might judge worse.

"My good opinion once lost is lost forever," he'd said years before. And though he'd been a different man then—younger and prouder and more intractable—Elizabeth couldn't help but wonder how much that old implacability might yet live in him . . . and whether it could ever be directed at her.

As the night wore on, there were occasional distractions from these troubling thoughts, but none that Elizabeth welcomed.

Wails and shrieks in the streets. Someone barring the front door—and, in the process, locking Mary out, and perhaps Nezu, too. An hour or so before dawn, Elizabeth even heard a not-so-distant volley of musket fire. That was a sound that hadn't rung through One North in many a year. The situation must be desperate indeed if an officer, in the process of saving the respectable classes, would risk upsetting them.

London was consuming itself from the inside, like a stillborn dreadful chewing its way through its mother's womb. And that was the very image that haunted Elizabeth's dreams when sleep did finally overtake her. It was almost a relief to awaken to the thumping boom of blasting cannons.

Elizabeth rushed to the window and threw aside the curtains. There was no zombie horde in the streets, however. No pitched battle being fought outside their door. Instead, Elizabeth saw the usual gentlemen and ladies and workmen and servants going about their business with, if anything, a merrier air than usual.

Then she heard the bells, and the cannons roared again.

It was Recoronation Day. George III was reclaiming his right to rule. The Regency was over—and maybe, just maybe, England would return to its former glory.

London wasn't tearing itself apart. It was celebrating.

Yet the Shevington household remained immune to the festivity. When Elizabeth came downstairs, she found a subdued Kitty and a subdued Mr. Bennet at breakfast, while a subdued (though living) Nezu conferred in quiet tones with the staff (who were never anything but subdued).

Mary had never returned, nor had her escort.

Nezu was sending his fellow ninjas to scout for them, but no more was to be done just then. Elizabeth forced herself to drink a cup of tea and eat a piece of toast, and then it was time: The Bennets needed to dress for the recoronation.

Elizabeth took no pleasure in picking out her gown and gloves and slippers, beautiful though they were. Kitty emerged from her room looking resplendent in creamy white muslin and a feathered headdress, yet she seemed broody, too.

"Pearls would compliment that gown perfectly," Elizabeth said to her in the hallway. "As would a smile. For Bunny's sake, at least."

"How can I smile when Mary's disappeared? I wasn't so worried last night, but now? That she hasn't even sent word seems . . . "

"I know. Yet we must retain our faith that she will return to us. We can't give the MacFarquhars any hint that anything is amiss."

"I understand." Kitty put on a broad, ghastly grin. "Will this do?"

Elizabeth heard footsteps behind her, and she turned to see Nezu coming up the stairs.

"The MacFarquhars have arrived," he said to Elizabeth alone. His eyes never strayed even that fraction of an inch required to take in Kitty as well.

So it had been all morning. Him never looking at Kitty. Kitty never looking at him. Any other time, Elizabeth would have wondered what had happened between them. Not now, though. Not today. There was no spare capacity in her for caring. It was all occupied elsewhere.

"We'll be right down," she said.

When she turned toward Kitty again, all trace of her sister's mock grin was gone.

It was back a few minutes later, though, as Kitty and Elizabeth and

Mr. Bennet climbed into the MacFarquhars' landau. It even looked almost natural, especially after Kitty spotted Brummell adorned for the occasion with a huge red and white striped bow.

"And here I thought you were doing us a great honor," she said, "when it turns out people are bringing their pets!"

"Oh, poor Brummell's going to have to wait in the carriage." Bunny threw an exaggerated sidelong glance at his father. "*Some people* don't think it would be dignified to bring a rabbit into Westminster Abbey. Yet you'll be seeing any number of lap dogs, leeches, and old bats in there!"

Kitty popped off with a dutiful "La!" while Elizabeth and Mr. Bennet put on identical looks of polite, tight-lipped pseudoamusement. Sir Angus was in no mood to tolerate his son's foolishness, however.

"What you will be seeing—and mingling with—is the very crrream of Britain," he said after a moment's dour glowering Bunny's way. "Just to be in such company when His Majesty is recrowned is enough to conferrr rank and respectability."

This proved a little too blunt, even for one as fond of plain speaking as Sir Angus. He'd laid bare their quid pro quo—the Shevingtons' financial help for a lift to the upper crust—and his broad face flushed as he cleared his throat and turned to the driver.

"To Westminsterrr!"

The driver cracked his whip, and the landau rolled off through streets that were alternately deserted and crowded with roisterers, splashed with bunting flapping in the breeze and scarlet splotches drying on the cobblestones. There were long lines at all the inner gates as Londoners and tourists by the thousands wound their way south toward Westminster and St. James's Park. Yet the checkpoints all appeared undermanned, with but a handful of sentries to watch the masses pass.

As he had during their first carriage ride together, Sir Angus lectured the Shevingtons incessantly. But he wasn't calling attention to points of interest this time. Instead, he seemed intent on distracting the party (or perhaps just himself) from the soldiers' tense, sweaty expressions and the bloody Zed rods some of the hoi-polloi carried like canes and the occasional head lying on its side in the gutter. All this passed by unnoticed, or at least unremarked upon, as Sir Angus described the pomp and circumstance (and yet more pomp) to come: the coronation procession from Westminster Hall; the stately raiment of the king and Prince Regent and high steward and high constable and high this and high the other; the Ceremony of the Challenge with the king's champion; the Ceremony of the Chop with the king's slayer.

"You do us a great honor by escorting us to Westminster," Elizabeth said to Sir Angus, cutting off a lengthy discourse on the wig the king had specially made from the flowing locks of slain girl-dreadfuls. "I'm surprised you are able to do so, given your special relationship with His Majesty. Doesn't he need you at his side?"

"No. I was with the king all night, and when I left him this morning, I was satisfied that he was in perfect health. His recovery is complete. He stands as rrready to rule as everrr a man was."

"How much do we have you to thank for that?" Mr. Bennet asked. "Until only a few months ago, the king was in complete seclusion."

Sir Angus pursed his lips and narrowed his eyes.

"I cannot claim sole credit for His Majesty's recuperation," he intoned gravely. "Though perhaps I will find, one day, that the rrresponsibility is all mine."

Elizabeth found the man's words so cryptic, she wasn't certain she'd heard them correctly. Indeed, it was becoming more difficult by the second to hear anything beyond the ringing of bells and the huzzahs of the throngs.

The carriage was pulling up in front of the long soldier-lined walk to the abbey's main entrance, and covering the lawn and streets around it was a vast sea of people. Many waved red and white pennants, some appeared drunk, most were grinning, and every last one of them seemed to be bellowing, "Long live the king!"

It was a little shocking, all this enthusiasm. George III hadn't been a particularly popular monarch, reigning as he did over the coming of the dreadfuls and the resulting isolation and chaos. England had lost its colonies, found its once-great navies unwelcome in any port, and could do nothing but watch as Napoleon Bonaparte put half the world under his little heel. The king's one accomplishment had been siring a son—George IV, the Prince Regent—who would prove so debauched and profligate that his subjects would grow nostalgic for his father.

It was nothing Elizabeth felt like cheering. The rest of England clearly felt otherwise, however, and as she started toward the vaunted gray arches of Westminster Abbey, with Sir Angus on one side and her father on the other, the happy roar of the crowd grew so loud she almost worried it would deafen her.

"We must hurry," Sir Angus said as they swept by the crimson-liveried guards keeping the mob at a respectable distance. "These accursed crrrowds have made us quite—"

A brown blur shot past at ankle level.

"No," Sir Angus moaned.

His son said the same thing, only much, much louder.

Brummell was streaking up the red carpet toward the abbey.

"It's the noise!" Bunny cried as he and Kitty dashed after the rabbit. "The poor darling's terrified!"

"As he should be," Sir Angus grated out, the look on his face making it plain that *he* was what Brummell should fear most.

The crowd noticed the chase now, and the din grew even louder, swollen by guffaws and catcalls. The clamor disoriented Brummell all the more, and the rabbit darted left, then right, before doubling back and streaking between Bunny's feet.

Kitty, of course, was graced with quicker reflexes than young MacFarquhar, and she swooped down and snagged the rabbit by the tail before it could pivot and carry on again up the carpet. She promptly plopped Brummell into Bunny's arms and then turned to beam at Sir Angus.

"Our engagements are always so invigoratingly *eventful*, aren't they?

I wonder what shall happen next?"

"Why, it can't be!" a woman said.

Her voice filled Elizabeth with ice-cold dread.

A stately couple up ahead, nearly at the abbey doors, had turned to take in the confusion, and now they started back the other way, toward the Bennets and the MacFarquhars.

Elizabeth knew with the inevitability of death what two words the lady would say next. They were, in fact, the title the woman had once hoped to gain for herself.

"Mrs. Darcy?"

Walking toward them were the former Miss Caroline Bingley and her husband, the earl of Cholmondeley.

Mr. Bennet leaned in to whisper in Elizabeth's ear.

"Should I kill her? I know you've always wanted to."

"It doesn't matter now," Elizabeth replied. "It's over."

"I almost didn't recognize you with your hair that intriguing new shade," Lady Cholmondeley said as she drew near. She glanced over at Kitty with the same malicious smile she'd once worn when finding every opportunity to slight Elizabeth before Darcy and her brother Charles. "There's no mistaking your family, though. They've always been so very *memorable*. Where is your husband, pray? Escorting Lady Catherine, perhaps? Or is he still at Fernworthy, welcoming our newest niece into the world?"

"Lady Catherine. . . de Bourrrgh?" Sir Angus said through teeth clenched so tightly it was a wonder they didn't splinter.

"You mean Mrs. Darcy hasn't mentioned her connection to such a lofty personage as Lady Catherine the Great?" Caroline said. "That is so like her. I've always known her to be humble. Perhaps the result of her humble upbringing."

"That's it," Mr. Bennet growled. "I *am* going to kill her."

But it was far, far too late for that.

"Guards!" Sir Angus stabbed a finger first at Elizabeth and Mr. Bennet and then at Kitty. "Arrest these imposterrrs in the name of the king!"

CHAPTER 33

"Minoru!" Darcy called out as he backed away from his cousin. *"Kyabeji wo otose!"*

Drop the cabbages!

There was a loud thunking sound as a shoot opened in the holding pen on the other side of the dojo and a load of blood-smeared cabbages dropped into the zombie trough.

Anne's "friends"—Romeo and Juliet and Mercury and the rest—spun around howling and began staggering across the sparring floor toward their darkened paddock, which wasn't so darkened anymore, Darcy noticed. Something within glowed with the soft white light of a living thing. Darcy took a step toward it, drawn half by worry that one of his aunt's ninjas had fallen down the cabbage shoot, half by a hunger that suddenly stabbed his gut.

Anne reached out and clamped a hand to his arm.

"It's the cabbages," she said. "Everyone assumes the stricken are drawn to them because they look like brains, but that's not entirely true. You see the luminescence, don't you? It's the same for turnips, potatoes, and carrots, too, I've found. They're not really satisfying to eat, though, and mushrooms and fruits don't have the spark you'd see in a handful of sand. It's puzzling."

When the last unmentionable was back in the pen, furiously stuffing cabbage into its rotting maw, a section of nearby wall rumbled and began sliding to the side. A moment later, the zombies were again sealed in their vault to await the next round of target practice or the next visit from Anne.

Darcy could hear the ninjas outside unbolting the dojo doors. He jerked his arm free and began moving toward the nearest one.

"I understand," Anne said serenely. "It is a difficult thing, letting go of the past. Yet I know you will eventually come to accept the way of things. Accept *yourself.* And me. It is but a matter of time . . . and we will have all of that we need."

Darcy stalked out and grabbed the first ninja he saw.

"Where is Lady Catherine?" he demanded in Japanese.

"I do not know."

Darcy had a hold of the man by the tunic, and he twisted his fists into the rough black fabric and lifted with all his might. To his surprise and satisfaction, he had more of it than he thought.

The bottoms of the ninja's tabi boots lifted off the floor. Just an inch or so, but enough to make the right impression.

"You fear incurring your mistress's wrath?"

Darcy brought his face so close that the two men were practically rubbing noses. The ninja's life-light wasn't just something Darcy could see now. He could almost taste it.

He tried to ignore the fact that his mouth had begun watering.

"Fool," he spat, giving the ninja a shake. "Tell me what I want to know or Her Ladyship will never have the chance to punish you, for I will have already snapped your spine in two." Darcy cocked his head to the side and leaned down toward the ninja's neck. "Or perhaps I should simply bite you."

"The Highest One is hunting in the wood near Badgers Mount!" the man cried. "Please, tell her it was Yoshio who told you! He calls you 'He-Demon' and says we should kill the both of you."

His wide eyes darted toward the training hall. Toward Anne.

With a grunt of disgust, Darcy threw the ninja aside and stomped off toward the road.

His strength may have been returning, but the walk was still long and wearying. Badgers Mount was three miles beyond the borders of Rosings—taking his aunt far enough away, Darcy realized, to give him lots of time alone with his cousin. So it had been all week. Even with an ailing nephew to look after, Lady Catherine had been out hunting every day. Because the real game had been afoot at home.

Normally, Darcy would have taken a horse to go look for her, but he didn't trust himself with so much animal, so much glowing life, so close. Even the sheep grazing in the fields seemed to him like an endless buffet stretched out before a starving man, and it took a painful act of will not to stray from the path when he saw an untended chicken coop.

Was this what he had to look forward to? Licking his lips as he thought of chomping into livestock? Pulling the wings from butterflies and befriending corpses, like Anne? *With* Anne, in fact . . . and without Elizabeth? If so, his supposed salvation had been his damnation. He would have been better off dying back at Pemberley.

And then, just as he reached the most secluded, heavily wooded stretch of road yet, Darcy heard it: the high, breathy voice of a child singing softly. Something about it captivated him, entranced him, and he left the road and followed the sound into the forest.

The voice grew louder as he made his way through the thicket, and it wasn't long before Darcy saw its source. A girl, perhaps seven years of age, her golden hair in pig-tails, was singing to herself as she skipped around a flower-shrouded glade. She clutched a bouquet in one hand, and every so often she would stop and pluck another handful of dandelions or poppy blossoms, her song never faltering.

I'm lonesome since I crossed the hill
And o'er the moor and valley
Such heavy thoughts my heart do fill
Since parting from my Sally.
I seek no more the fine and gay
For each doth but remind me

How swiftly passed the hours away
With the girl I left behind me.

Darcy stopped in the shadows, half-hidden behind a gnarly old oak, and simply watched for a while. It was the purest picture of innocence he'd ever seen. And, oh, the light of this child! It was blinding, yet he couldn't look away. He found that he longed to be closer to it. To bask in its warmth. To *take* its warmth and make it his own.

Slowly, stumblingly, almost as if sleepwalking, he stepped out from behind the tree and started toward the meadow.

The girl stopped singing and skipping and stared into the forest. She wasn't looking at Darcy, though; her back was to him. Whatever had silenced her was on the opposite side of the clearing.

Darcy followed her gaze and felt, for a moment, as if someone had left a stray mirror propped up among the trees and brush. A tall dark-haired man was lurching toward the glade, eyes fixed on the little girl.

When his doppelgänger stepped into the sunlight, Darcy could see the green tint to his skin and the bloat that was starting to swell his belly and, most notable of all, the chopping knife through his neck, the handle sticking from one side, the blade's tip from the other.

The zombie gurgled and loped toward the girl.

She turned and ran . . . for all of three seconds. Then, inexplicably, she stopped beneath the jutting branches of a huge yew tree. A dozen more strides and the unmentionable would be on her, yet she didn't so much as twitch, let alone scream and flee.

The horror of what he was about to see finally snapped Darcy from his trance, and he cursed himself for having brought no weapon from the house. He frantically scanned the underbrush for a rock to throw or a fallen branch to use as a bludgeon, but there was nothing near at hand and no time to keep looking.

He had just enough strength to lift a ninja off the ground. He had to hope that was enough to stop a hunger-crazed zombie.

Before Darcy could take a step toward the girl, however, she shot straight up into the air, as if the Almighty Himself had finally taken mercy on one of the strange plague's victims-to-be and plucked her from harm's way. Her ascent to heaven ended a bit prematurely though—just beneath a particularly sturdy branch some twenty feet off the ground. Even the unmentionable looked surprised. But that didn't stop it from positioning itself beneath the dangling girl and jumping toward her, making hopeless swipes with its stiff arms.

The little girl began twirling in a slow circle, and Darcy finally noticed the thin rope from which she was suspended. It was secured around her chest, the line obscured by the high waistline of her dress. The rope was knotted in the back and, when slack, would have been hard to distinguish from the off-white muslin against which it hung. Darcy could see now how the other end ran down a series of ring bolts hammered into the tree and disappeared into a thick tangle of juniper bushes just beyond the trunk.

"Looks like this one's alone, m'lady," the girl said. She sounded remarkably bored for someone gazing down at a leaping dreadful intent on grabbing (and eating) her feet. She amused herself by trying to drop flower petals into the creature's upturned mouth. "No need to worry about scaring off the rest of the herd."

"I will be the judge of that," the juniper bushes seemed to say. They sounded exactly like Lady Catherine de Bourgh.

The zombie stopped its futile clawing at the air and turned toward the new voice.

"Now look what you've made me do," the juniper bushes said, and the unmentionable's head promptly exploded, spraying bloody pulp in every direction. The rest of the body topped over backward as straight and stiff as a felled tree.

"Oh, dear," the little girl sighed, inspecting the gore dripping from the hem of her dress. "Those stains will never come out."

Lady Catherine emerged from the bushes carrying her still-smoking elephant gun.

"You are becoming a most impudent girl. And if there's one thing I don't tolerate long, I assure you, it's impudent girls. If you want your sixpence—and you *don't* want a thorough English beating—you will hold your tongue next time we have a dreadful so . . . "

In one smooth swirl of motion, the lady tossed aside her rifle, drew twin flintlocks from the bandolier criss-crossing her stalking gown, and spun around toward the thick oak Darcy had been hiding behind. She kept her pistols pointed at it a full minute before the little girl spoke again.

"Are we hunting trees now, m'lady?"

"I thought I heard something," Lady Catherine said, holstering her pistols. "You will now only receive a groat for the day, Miss Flynn. And when I bring you down, I shall have to clap you once upon the left ear."

"Yes, m'lady," little Miss Flynn grumbled.

Lady Catherine peered into the forest again for a long, silent moment before lowering her zombie bait back to earth. She had indeed heard something, of course. Some*one* who'd slipped away, bound again for Rosings.

Darcy had changed his mind about talking to his aunt. There was nothing more to say. His reaction to Miss Flynn had shown him as much.

Elizabeth was right. He was tainted, befouled, beyond redemption. He could never again be what he once was. And he wouldn't allow himself to become like Anne.

There was a special case in his aunt's trophy room. It held two swords. One, Lady Catherine always said, she would use to disembowel herself if she were ever bitten by one of the sorry stricken. The other was for her second—whatever comrade or ninja was on hand at the time—who would use it to lop off her head, in accordance with tradition.

Darcy would have no second. He was and would be utterly alone. That wouldn't matter, though. He was strong enough again, both in body and in will.

He could commit hara-kiri all by himself.

CHAPTER 34

Elizabeth had just been exposed as the fraud she was before what seemed like half of England, and a part of her didn't mind. In fact, that part of her—it felt like a very large part, actually, perhaps as much as ninety-nine percent—wasn't simply ready for the yeomen of the guard outside Westminster Abbey to throw themselves on her. It was anxious for it. Anxious to *fight*.

There was just one problem: The guards weren't obliging. Even as Sir Angus railed on about the charlatans in their midst, the nearest soldiers just peeped at each other sheepishly around their pikes.

"If these people are imposters," one of them said to Sir Angus, "who the flippin' heck are *you*?"

"I am Sirrr Angus MacFarquharrr, personal physician to His Majesty the king."

"Poppycock!" Mr. Bennet roared. "You're nothing of the kind, you rascal!" He stretched out an arm and pointed at Sir Angus just as Sir Angus had pointed at him and his daughters a moment before. "He's the imposter! Seize him!"

"But—," Bunny began.

Mr. Bennet swung his arm toward Sir Angus's son. "And his accomplices!"

"A-a-accomplices?" the young man stuttered. He looked down at the squirming rabbit he was clutching in his arms.

But it wasn't Brummell Mr. Bennet was accusing.

He jabbed his finger at Lord and Lady Cholmondeley next.

"They're the frauds here, not us!"

Lord Cholmondeley puffed up his chest—which took much doing, it being a slight and concave little thing—and demonstrated why his speeches had become such favorites of both the Whigs and the more waggish Tories in the House of Lords.

"Thith ith outrageouth! Thethe people theem to be here under falthe pretentheth, tholdier, and I demand that you theithe them thith inthant!"

The nearest guard served as spokesman for all.

"Huh?" he said.

"Arrrrest them!" Sir Angus translated.

The guards shared more miserable glances.

"I'm sorry," one of them said. "I don't think we can arrest anybody without orders."

"We're from the 36th Foot Infantry," another added. He sneered down at his puffy-sleeved gold-trimmed tunic. "We ain't used to all this beefeater rot."

"'Today, you are a fence,' the color sergeant told us," yet another soldier threw in. "'So much as bat an eye as the toffs trot by, and you'll be digging latrines,' pardon *mon Français*, 'until it's George the ruddy Fortieth mincing into Westminster.'"

Elizabeth despaired of ever being attacked.

Sir Angus and Bunny also seemed to give up hope that the guards would actually guard anything other than the perfect straightness of the lines in which they stood. Each MacFarquhar turned to the woman he'd been escorting toward the abbey not long before.

"Who are you?" Bunny asked Kitty, looking hurt.

"How darrre you?" Sir Angus asked Elizabeth, looking like he wanted to hurt her.

Before either sister could reply, there was a blast of not-so-distant trumpets and the rumble of approaching drums, and the mob sent up a deafening cheer.

The king's procession had almost completed its short march from Westminster Hall to Westminster Abbey. The guards wouldn't be able to play fence much longer: Any second, George III and the Prince Regent and two hundred assorted nabobs and attendants would start down the very path the Bennets and the MacFarquhars and Lord and Lady Cholmondeley were clogging.

A burly bald man in the crowd reached out to tap one of the soldiers on the shoulder.

"'Ere. Why don't you just drag off the lot of 'em?" he suggested helpfully. "The whole barmy bunch. That way, you'll know you got the right 'uns even if you got the wrong 'uns, too."

"'The whole barmy bunch'?" Lady Cholmondeley fumed.

"Thuch intholenthe!"

"Ain't a bad idea, Thommo," the soldier said to one of his comrades. "I'd rather have the color sergeant mad at me than the flippin' king."

Finally, Elizabeth thought.

She went into a fighting stance.

Not that there would be any escape for her and Kitty and their father. There were at least thirty soldiers standing at attention between them and the street, and even if they should reach the end of the gauntlet, what then? One direction would be blocked by the procession. The other would be lined with yet more soldiers.

Resistance would be futile—but perhaps it would also be satisfying. If Elizabeth had to accept defeat, she would do so on her terms, not Lady Catherine's or anyone else's.

And then Lord Cholmondeley spoke again.

"I thay, that'th not my driver."

He was gazing, brow furrowed, back at the street. His carriage had returned, apparently, for Elizabeth saw a sleek black barouche adorned with silver molding and an especially ostentatious crest.

Nezu was in the driver's seat. Even more surprising, not to mention baffling, were his companions.

Sitting beside him were two small, mangy dogs.

"Oh, bra-VO!" Kitty said with a grin. "He really is the sneakiest little fellow, isn't he?"

"Yes, yes. Quite the slippery devil," Mr. Bennet said. He turned to Elizabeth. "The better part of valor?"

Elizabeth nodded. "So it would seem."

She and her father had exchanged these words on only a few occasions, the last more than four years before. "A true warrior does not know the word 'retreat,'" Master Liu had told his pupils again and again. So this is what the Bennets said to each other instead when the time came.

Time to run away.

Elizabeth had taken but a single step toward the carriage when a meaty hand clamped down on her wrist, dragging her to a halt.

"Oh, no," Sir Angus said. "You'rrre not going anywherrre."

"Quite the contrary," Elizabeth replied. "I think I'm finally getting somewhere."

She broke his hold, grabbed *his* wrists, and sent him spinning into the nearest row of soldiers. Half a dozen men went down together in a furiously cursing tangle.

Mr. Bennet, meanwhile, had begun running down the opposite line, smacking soldier after soldier with the butt of a pike he'd wrestled away. A pair of patriotic onlookers separated themselves from the gasping, cringing crowd to try to catch him, but Kitty leapt between them and threw her legs out straight to the sides in a perfect scissor kick. Both men went flying back into the roiling throng. Kitty landed nimbly and carried on after her father without missing a step.

After a few more kicks, punches, and pike-butts to the side of the face, the Bennets were clambering into the barouche.

"Goodness," Mr. Bennet said. He was already busy holding off soldiers with his pike but managed to jerk his chin to the right. "We seem to have disrupted the king's little parade."

About fifty yards away, where the road curved southwest around the abbey grounds, Elizabeth could see what had to be the beginnings of the king's procession. It was either that or an attention-starved theater company attempting an impromptu performance of *Romeo and Juliet*, for everyone in the street was clad in the frilled collars, ballooning breeches, and gaily colored hose of Elizabethan courtiers. If that was the case, however, the show was going very badly, indeed: Half the players were in a mad panic, shoving their way to the front or into the goggling hordes along the road while the other half gaped at them in confusion.

"I used to fear that the Bennets would end up infamous, but I had no idea we would manage it so spectacularly," Mr. Bennet said. "After today, they shall burn us in effigy once a year along with Guy Fawkes."

"Let us focus our attentions on the here and now," Elizabeth said as she kicked back a soldier trying to climb over the barouche's mudguard. "There is still the little matter of getting away."

She drew her ankle dagger—the only weapon she'd brought—and hurled it into the hand of another guard reaching for the horses' bridles.

"Gaaaahhhh!"

"Sorry!"

"Well, obviously we can't get through the procession," Kitty said. She turned toward the other end of the street, which was rapidly filling with soldiers and civilians rushing out to see what was causing all the trouble. "And how would we ever clear a path through that?"

"I shall show you," Nezu said. He'd been keeping the horses steady with a gentle but firm tug on the reins, letting the scruffy mutts, with snarls and snapping jaws, drive off soldiers who came too near. Through it all, he'd remained utterly still, utterly silent.

Now, however, he sucked in a deep breath and tilted his head back and opened his mouth wide.

"Dreadfuls!" someone yelled.

"What a coincidence," Nezu said. "That's just what *I* was about to say."

Then there were more shouts, all coming from the direction of the procession.

"Unmentionables!"

"Bogies!"

"Runnnnnnnnnnn!"

The soldiers tried to heed this last call by turning and hurrying toward the king's cavalcade. The crowd, on the other hand, surged away from the screams, sweeping most of the soldiers along with them. Within seconds, thousands of shrieking people were fleeing Westminster Abbey.

Nezu gave the reins a snap, and Lord Cholmondeley's carriage joined the stampede.

"Do you think there really are dreadfuls back there?" Kitty said.

Already it was impossible to tell what was happening where the panic had begun. People running, shoving, falling onto one another—that's all Elizabeth could make out. If any of those doing the running and shoving and falling were dead (or about to be), she couldn't say.

"From what we've seen lately, it wouldn't surprise me," Mr. Bennet mused. "Though I do wonder how they could penetrate so deeply into the center sections."

"What of the king and the Prince Regent and the rest?" Kitty asked. "Should we go back for them?"

"You see how it is." Mr. Bennet pointed at a soldier being swept past them backward by the current of the scurrying mob. "I doubt we could get back even if we wanted to. Not in time to be of any help."

"But—," Kitty began.

"Before you decide, consider this," Nezu said. "I know where Mary Bennet is."

"Where?" all three Bennets said in chorus.

"She is being held prisoner in Bethlem Royal Hospital."

"The spy you had following her finally returned?" Kitty asked.

"Not entirely."

"'Not entirely'?" Mr. Bennet grimaced. "Someone sent you his head?"

"He's talking about the dogs," Elizabeth said. "I thought they looked familiar."

Mr. Bennet blinked at the mongrels perched next to Nezu.

"*They* told you where Mary is?"

"They're extremely well trained," Nezu said. "A few biscuits and a map, and all was made clear. Miss Bennet and her escort have been in Bethlem since yesterday afternoon. Ell and Arr here would have reported to me sooner, but the journey from Twelve Central to One North was not an easy one without their master."

"Really?" Mr. Bennet gazed at the dogs in wonder. "I'm surprised they didn't just hire themselves a cab."

Ell and Arr were sitting up especially straight now, looking rather pleased with themselves.

"So," Kitty said, "what do we do?"

"What we should have done a long time ago," Elizabeth told her. "What I should have been doing all along."

A group of young men started climbing into the carriage, apparently intent on commandeering it for themselves. Elizabeth paused just long enough to crush their fingers and flatten their noses and generally do whatever necessary to send the invaders flying. When she was done, she dusted off her hands and smoothed out her gown and finished her thought.

"We act like warriors."

CHAPTER 35 (AN ASIDE)

Mr. Anthony Isaac Crickett of 23 Crabtree Row, Bethnal Green, Two East, London, did not lead an especially noteworthy life. A miserable childhood in a Whitechapel workhouse was followed by an adulthood stoking furnaces at the Hackney Crematorium & Glue Factory that was (fortunately) slightly less miserable but (unfortunately) rather brief.

Not that Mr. Crickett died an especially noteworthy death. When cholera swept through Two East (as it already had through Twelve and Thirteen Central and half the Souths), he succumbed to it, at the age of twenty-five, no sooner than most of his rookery neighbors, yet no later than most as well.

Under normal circumstances, that would have been the end of Mr. Crickett and whatever chance he ever had at leaving some kind of legacy. Not so in the Age of the Dreadfuls! Mr. Crickett had no family to see to his beheading after he hacked out his last breath in his tiny garret apartment. (Even if he had, that would have been no guarantee his corpse would have been properly attended to, for the cholera was mowing down entire families at once with one sweep of the scythe.) So the strange plague gave Mr. Crickett one last go at making his mark, and he seized the opportunity with both hands—and promptly tore it limb from limb. Anthony Isaac Crickett would finally be, for the first time in his quarter-century tenure on earth, something rather special.

No, he wasn't the first dreadful to discover that London's new sewers were as comfy-cozy as any mausoleum or cave or well or pit. He simply slithered in through an accommodating storm drain and made himself at home, as did scores of his fellow unmentionables. Nor was he the first to find, once a few pesky metal grates were broken through, that the sewer system made a most excellent thoroughfare, running, as it did, under all the walls and gates and watch towers of the stratified city above. It wasn't even he who first noticed that the Glow was flowing in great rivers through the streets to pool in a vast new ocean of light—of *life*—not far from where the sewers emptied: that venerable old cesspool known as the Thames.

In all these matters, Mr. Crickett was merely doing in death as he'd done in life. He mindlessly followed his fellows, going where they went, acting as they acted, eating as (and now *whom*) they ate.

Which was how he eventually came to be chasing the Archbishop of Canterbury up and down Abingdon Street with a half-eaten liver hanging from his mouth. Like all the unmentionables that had come streaming out of the sewers a few minutes before, Mr. Crickett was crazed with lustful hunger. Never had the Glow been so intense, so abundant, so free for the taking. All around was a veritable zombie smorgasbord, and all Mr. Crickett wanted to do was eat *eat EAT*!

The liver he'd plucked from the mangled corpse of a standard bearer, but the brains had already been dashed and eaten, and there was simply too much fresh meat still running around on two feet for him to think of settling down to savor his meal. So on he raced after the brightest lights—the scattering remnants of George III's recoronation procession and the multitudes gathered to watch it pass by.

Mr. Crickett settled on the Archbishop because he was an old man, moving slowly. But when the clergyman looked over his shoulder and saw that a zombie wished to pick him off the buffet tray, he yelped, threw off his heavy ceremonial robes, and immediately doubled his speed. The archbishop proved quite spry after that, weaving around abandoned sedan chairs and scepters and flags and swords of state too heavy with gold scrollwork and jewels to be of real use to anybody. He was wily quarry as well, trying to dissuade Mr. Crickett both by throwing things back at him (his Bible, his high-peaked mitre, his false teeth) and by drawing the dreadful close to possible distractions (this or that writhing body being ripped apart in the street, a flock of altar boys precariously perched in a walnut tree, et cetera.).

Yet Mr. Crickett never wavered, and at last his resolve was rewarded. When the Archbishop tried to duck inside the abbey, he found himself trapped outside with a small group of survivors. The reason: Those inside—"nobles" every one—had locked the doors.

"Let me in! It's me! The Archbishop!"

"How do we know you're not a dreadful?" a man asked from the other side of the door.

"Because I'm talking to you, you cretin!"

"Sorry. I really don't think we should take the chance."

"I demand sanctuary!"

"He led one right to us," said a pretty if rather sharp-featured woman, and she pressed herself close to the short, slight gentleman beside her. "And now others have noticed!"

Indeed, Mr. Crickett was closing in on the Archbishop, with a clutch of unmentionables right behind him.

"God have merthy on uth!" the little gentleman called to the gray heavens. "God have merthy on our poor thoulth!"

And it was here that Mr. Crickett finally separated himself from the vast ranks of the unremarkable and took his first step toward Destiny.

"Go, Brummell!" cried one of the entrées-to-be as the dreadfuls moved in. "Run, my one true friend!"

A shard of hot, white radiance seemed to break off from the man and shoot like lightning along the ground. All the unmentionables but one ignored it.

Mr. Crickett was that one. He was experiencing something rare indeed in zombies (and not always easy to find in people): curiosity. The Archbishop was forgotten—which worked out fine for Mr. Crickett, it turned out, for the clergyman and those around him were set upon by so many dreadfuls, each creature managed but a mouthful or two before more of the undead shoved their way in for a taste.

Mr. Crickett didn't get so much as an eyelid or a fingernail, for he'd left the abbey doors behind. The bolt of life-light was zigzagging away, and he was intent on catching it. It didn't have the soft, pinkish hue of that most cherished delicacy, brains, yet it burned with a brightness he found irresistible.

As prey, it proved as quick and canny as the Archbishop. It changed direction frequently. Whenever possible, it shot under or through obstacles Mr. Crickett had to go around. It even doubled back on its trail once, shooting between Mr. Crickett's legs as he fumbled for it clumsily.

Eventually, though, it began to tire. Its turns weren't as sharp, its sprints weren't as fast, but Mr. Crickett remained as fresh as ever. Which wasn't all that fresh, as far as his body was concerned (he had about him both the color and something of the smell of gorgonzola cheese), but he certainly wasn't growing fatigued. He could chase the light for the next week without slowing.

Yet just as he could finally grab for it, at the very moment he felt the first dull tickle of fur work its way up his dead nerves, the light swerved again and was gone.

Mr. Crickett stopped and turned. There was no light behind him. All he saw was a great long swath of thick red and gold fabric, like a carpet so luxurious no one would ever dare set foot on it. Why such a thing should have been dumped in the middle of the street was just the sort of question a dreadful wouldn't think to ask itself, thinking not being on its agenda at all. Which is why the large hump in the middle of the dumped-carpet-thing didn't capture Mr. Crickett's interest either . . . until it spoke.

"Ahhh!"

"Oh!"

"What was that?"

"I don't know!"

"It felt like a dog."

"Why would a dog be—?

"Shhhh."

"Right."

Mr. Crickett didn't understand the words, but he knew what they meant. Meat!

He threw himself upon the lump and bit down with all his might.

"My head! Something's biting my head! Make it stop! Make it stop! Nooooooooooo!"

These, to an unmentionable, were the sweet sounds of success, and Mr. Crickett bit down with all the more gusto. He didn't even notice when a rabbit and, shortly after, a portly dark-haired man scampered out from under the robe he was chomping on. For a robe it was they'd been hiding under—one so long that, just a quarter hour earlier, its train had been carried by eight pages, each boy the eldest son of a powerful lord.

Brummell shot away to the north. George IV, the Prince Regent, didn't shoot away anywhere. A dozen dreadfuls were on him before he could run ten feet, and within a minute his fine clothes were ripped off, his skin was stripped away, his copious insides were no longer inside him, his bones were broken apart and redistributed in every direction, and his head became the centerpiece of a spirited tug of war between three unmentionables.

Through it all, Mr. Crickett gnawed on. There had been no blood at first. The fabric was too thick for a quick, clean bite. But with some diligent munching and clawing, Mr. Crickett was able to chew through to—and then into—the man beneath. The robe muffled both the screams and the radiance that would have attracted more zombies, so Mr. Crickett didn't have to share his meal with anyone.

He had the brains of George III, last English king of the house of Hanover, all to himself.

CHAPTER 36

"What is your plan?" Nezu asked Lizzy as they peeked around the corner at Bethlem Royal Hospital.

Of course, he hadn't bothered asking Kitty if she might have a plan. That would require him to talk to her, something he had been avoiding all day. Kitty wasn't insulted, though—or wasn't *more* insulted, at any rate. It was natural to assume Lizzy was in charge, the way she'd been acting. Clearly, she would no longer be following Nezu's lead. He had to follow hers or be left behind.

Bedlam wasn't the first destination she'd insisted on. Once they'd escaped the screaming, stampeding masses around Westminster, they'd hurried to the Shevington house in One North. There, Lizzy, Kitty, and Mr. Bennet made ready for combat, changing into battle clothes and collecting their weapons, while Nezu mustered his staff of servant-ninjas.

"It's a good thing we're not worried about making the wrong impression any more," Kitty said once the entire party—the Bennets, the dogs, Nezu, and half a dozen black-masked ninjas—had crammed into their stolen barouche and set off for Twelve Central.

"I doubt if there's anyone of influence left to judge us," Mr. Bennet said, gazing off at an especially thick column of black smoke rising to the south. "That's Westminster Abbey, if I don't miss my guess. It would appear that someone knocked over a candelabra or brought down a chandelier in all the uproar. I daresay the whole of high society is, at this moment, being either roasted alive or eaten."

Even as he spoke, another black pillar rose into the sky, not far from the first.

The checkpoints between sections didn't slow them down much, for they'd been abandoned, the gates left up. The soldiers had either been ordered to Westminster or simply deserted. Whatever the case, a steady stream of dirty, shabbily dressed people was pouring from Twelve Central, some pausing to loot half-heartedly as they made their way out of the city.

"You'll turn that thing around if you have any sense!" a toothless old woman shouted at them as their carriage rolled under the watch towers.

"What do I need sense for?" Kitty called back, waving her battle axe over her head. "I've got this! La!"

No one else laughed. Even if they'd begun to, they would have stopped soon enough. What they found in Twelve Central shriveled up every "La!" Kitty had left in her.

Filth, decay, emaciated bodies dumped everywhere—some of them beginning to get up again. Nothing Kitty had ever witnessed on the battlefield chilled her half as much as this.

No one spoke again until they reached the hospital and Nezu asked Lizzy for her plan.

"Attack," she said.

"That is your plan? 'Attack'?"

"The time for guile is long past."

Kitty was watching Nezu closely—she couldn't help herself—and so she caught the glance he threw her way even though it lasted little more than a second.

"Perhaps you are right," he said. "Very well, then. The hospital does not seem to be heavily guarded any longer. I will send Ogata and Hayashi ahead to—Miss Bennet?"

Lizzy was already drawing her sword and walking away.

"HAAAAIIIIIEEEEEEEEEEEE!" she cried, and she broke into a sprint, bound for Bethlem Hospital's front gate.

"I see," Nezu said. He slid Fukushuu from its scabbard and dashed after her. *"Tanoshimou ne!"*

"Ii desu ne!" the ninjas all roared as they raised their weapons and followed.

Ell and Arr put up their heads, howled, and then joined the charge.

"Kitty," Mr. Bennet said, "one of us needs to stay here to look after the horses, and—"

"I agree." Kitty took off running. "So good of you to volunteer!"

Just before she unleashed her battle cry ("HOOOOOOOO-YYYAAAAAAAAHHHHHHHH!") she heard her father spit out a livid "Blast!"

He didn't miss much, as it turned out. At least, not at first. The only resistance the raiding party met outside was purely verbal.

"No!" the lone gatekeeper gasped when he saw Lizzy and the others approaching. He threw himself to the ground with his hands over his head. "Just keep going! Ignore me! I'm not important!"

Lizzy smashed through the gate, with Lady Catherine's assassins (and Ell and Arr) at her heels. Seconds later, Lizzy was crashing through a window into the hospital, and Nezu and the ninjas did the same (adding somersaults to their entrances, of course). Kitty chose to enter through the front door, pausing, on a whim, to try the knob rather than burst through with a butterfly kick.

The door was unlocked. As Kitty stepped inside the hospital, Ell and Arr scampered in with her. It took her eyes a moment to adjust to the darkness, but she could make out a great swirl of chaotic activity, and there were many shouts and wails and whimpers. She bobbed and weaved, her axe ready to parry and chop, until her eyesight returned enough to tell her she hadn't plunged into the middle of a battle. This was simply Bedlam.

The inmates seemed free to roam wherever they pleased; there were cells aplenty in sight but the doors to all were open, and the long hallway before Kitty was filled with giggling, weeping, yelling, whispering, shuffling, dancing, babbling, barking people. Many were half-dressed, some weren't dressed at all, and not one of them appeared even remotely sane.

Lizzy stalked through them so wild-eyed with bloodlust, she fit right in.

"At last, I am ready to *fight*, and this is all I find? Where are the keepers? Where are MacFarquhar's lackeys?"

Ell and Arr barked and went bounding up a nearby stairwell.

"They smell the Man," Nezu said, hurrying after them.

"The who?" Kitty asked as both she and Lizzy followed. The stairs wound upward in a spiral, allowing her to see nothing of Ell and Arr but their tails.

They seemed to be wagging.

"Their master," Nezu explained. "I've never known his real name. To me, he's just—ah!"

They'd reached the top of the stairs, and there he was: the Man in the Box. Or at least Kitty had to assume the Man was there. All she could see was the Box. It was halfway down a long hallway, past several heavy opened doors, and it looked much the worse for wear. There were scuff marks and deep gouges along one side, as if it had been pried open,

"LIZZY SMASHED THROUGH THE GATE, WITH
LADY CATHERINE'S ASSASSINS AT HER HEELS."

and the whole thing sat at a precarious angle thanks to an especially wobbly wheel.

Surely, the Man was inside, though, for Ell and Arr ran up and licked at the narrow slot that ran across one panel. Kneeling next to it, speaking softly, was Mary.

Both Kitty and Lizzy called her name and ran down the corridor toward her. Mary had never been the most demonstrative of the Bennets (unless she was demonstrating disapproval), yet she smiled while suffering through her sisters' hugs and kisses.

"I do hope you weren't worried about me," she said.

"Not for a second!" Kitty replied, even as she quickly wiped away the moisture that had collected under each eye.

"It would seem we had little cause for concern," Lizzy said. She looked around the hall, which was dingy and dark and fed into rooms that appeared even dingier and darker. "I can't say we find you in the most cheerful of places, but you seem to have made yourself right at home."

"Oh, it was a bit uncomfortable at first," Mary said. "But we made do."

She looked down at the Box fondly (or so it seemed to Kitty, much to her wonder) just as Ell and Arr slipped back into the harnesses attached to it. Both dogs then sat happily at attention, ears pointed, mouths open.

"Miss Bennet," the Man in the Box warbled in his rough, husky way. "If you would be so kind?"

"It would be a pleasure," Mary said.

She ruffled the bristly fur on Ell and Arr's backs and then gave each a pat on the head.

"Good dogs," the Man in the Box said.

"Uhhh, Mary?"

Kitty popped her eyes wide and nodded at the box.

"Proper introductions will be made at a more suitable time," Mary said. "For now, let us simply say that this is Mr. Quayle, and he is a friend. And there are others you should meet as well." She turned to call down the hall. "You can come out now! It's safe!"

For a moment, nothing happened. Then one small shape emerged slowly from a shadowy doorway at the end of the corridor. A little girl. A boy followed her. Then a man, then a woman, and so on, until ten people were shuffling shyly toward them. They all had dark faces and sunken eyes and dirty clothes and the stooped postures and cringing steps of those who've come to accept mistreatment and misery as their lot.

"They keep inmates so young here?" Kitty asked, appalled.

Mary shook her head. "These aren't inmates like the ones downstairs. They weren't committed. They were snatched off the streets of Twelve North."

As the prisoners drew closer, Kitty could see that some looked Indian, some Mohammedan, some African. Not one had blonde hair or blue eyes or fair skin.

There were terse mutters in Japanese, and Kitty glanced back to find Nezu's ninjas joining them in the corridor. Lizzy didn't even seem to notice.

"For Sir Angus's experiments," she said grimly.

"Yes," Mary said. "They can't tell us much about them, though. Only a few speak English, and some no longer seem to speak at all."

The children were only a few feet away now, and Lizzy stepped forward and knelt before them. The other prisoners shrank back as she approached, and Kitty couldn't altogether blame them. They obviously had little reason to trust those they should meet in Bedlam, and Lizzy seemed to be struggling in her attempt to project gentleness and warmth. A murderous rage was bubbling just beneath the surface, and it wasn't clear if it could mix with maternal tenderness or would, instead, boil it away like steam.

"Can you tell me your name?" Lizzy asked the girl.

She was thin yet still chubby-cheeked, with long black hair that reached almost to her tiny waist.

"Gurdaya," she said.

To Kitty's surprise, the girl's accent was more North London than

East Indies. Her family might have come from far away—before foreigners stopped coming to England at all—but she'd grown up right here in the capital.

"How long have you been here, Gurdaya?" Lizzy said.

"I don't know. A long time."

Lizzy held out her hands and nodded at the girl's arms. They were bony and bare, uncovered by the filthy smock the child wore, and Kitty could make out several ugly splotches on Gurdaya's skin.

"May I?" Lizzy asked.

Gurdaya meekly put her hands in Lizzy's.

Elizabeth turned the wrists and leaned this way and that to get a better look at the child's scars. Never in her life had Kitty heard Lizzy gasp, but she heard just that now.

"They let a—let one of those *things* bite you?"

Gurdaya nodded.

"When?"

"Weeks ago. Maybe months." Gurdaya shrugged, less out of uncertainty, it seemed, than resignation. She took back one of her hands from Lizzy and pointed at a row of pockmarks on her upper arm. "They make me bleed, too. Then they take it."

"They take your blood?"

A boy, perhaps nine or ten years to Gurdaya's seven or eight, stepped up beside her. He had the same café au lait skin and round cheeks and London accent.

"They take blood from us all," he said. "All of us who don't develop infections or . . . change. They had our parents here, too, at first. They didn't last long."

"I'm sorry," Lizzy said. "So, so sorry. But they won't hurt you anymore. That's done. I promise."

She let go of Gurdaya's hand, stood, and turned to Mary. She'd sheathed her sword, but Kitty noticed her hand grip the hilt.

"Where are they?" Lizzy growled.

"Most are in here."

Mary led her to one of the doors nearby. Kitty slid in beside them, staying close to Lizzy. It was one thing to slaughter your prisoners when they're zombies. If Lizzy did as she seemingly intended, that would be something else entirely.

"My, what a lovely cell," Kitty said as they peered in through the small bar-striped window. The room beyond was pleasantly appointed in the style of a gentleman's bedchamber. The furnishings were far more elegant than the occupants, however. Half a dozen rough-looking men lay strewn about on the bed and chairs and floor. Some were conscious, some not. All were bruised and bloody.

"This was my accommodation for the night," Mary said. "I traded it with my hosts only an hour or so ago."

Kitty cocked an eyebrow at her. "You couldn't escape before then?"

"The door is too sturdy to kick down, and picking locks is a Shinobi skill, not Shaolin."

"Fortunately, I was able to talk her through it," the Man in the Box said.

"Might I remind you," Nezu broke in, addressing himself (again, the twit!) to Lizzy alone, "the dreadfuls are swarming, London is aflame, and we still haven't found what your husband so desperately needs. I would think a little more alacrity is—"

"Yes, yes," Lizzy snapped. "What of it, Mary? Have you found anything that looks like a cure?"

"Far too much that does. Sir Angus's laboratory is overflowing with elixirs and powders and the like. Which is why we've been trying to get a little help narrowing the search."

"This way," said the Man in the Box, and with a few simple quavery commands to Ell and Arr, he led them into a chamber of horrors, complete with blood stains on the floor, gooey splatters on the ceiling, and a man seemingly about to be consumed by a wriggling gristle-covered skull and spine.

"Hello!" the man said, sounding remarkably chipper for someone tied to a table with a zombie tethered inches away. "My goodness! So many friends you've brought with you. Were they hoping for a tour? I'm afraid we don't do those anymore."

"This is Dr. Sleaford, Bethlem's assistant administrator," Mary said. "I believe he knows where the cure is, but he refuses to tell us, even with Judith here as inducement."

Kitty waved her battle axe at the skinless, limbless dreadful snapping its teeth at the doctor. "Judith?"

Mary nodded. "She was introduced to us yesterday under much the same circumstances, though Dr. Sleaford's position and ours were reversed."

"And he won't talk?" Nezu asked. He'd stopped just inside the doorway, his ninjas spread out beside him.

"Oh, he will talk. Most pleasantly. What he won't do is answer questions." A rueful expression came over Mary's face. "He doesn't seem to believe that we would let the dreadful bite him."

"What good am I to you if I'm dead?" Dr. Sleaford said, and he said it pleasantly, indeed. "True, I don't know anything about this supposed cure you're looking for. But there is a serum that can slow the progress of the strange plague. Such a thing would be worth thousands, tens of thousands even, if made available to the public at large. Release me, and I will share its secrets with you."

Lizzy stepped close to the gurney on which the man lay.

"Dr. Sleaford, I will ask you politely *once*, and with fair warning: My husband's life hangs in the balance. Where is the cure?"

"I am sorry, Madam. But I swear to you, I know of no cure."

"I see."

Lizzy reached out and gave Judith's trolley a nudge forward.

The zombie promptly sank her teeth into Dr. Sleaford's right arm.

"Ahhhhhhhhhhhhhhhhhh!"

Lizzy caught Kitty's eye and jerked her head down at the dreadful, which was munching away happily on the doctor even though the masticated flesh had no throat to travel down.

Kitty pushed back Judith's cart, raised her axe, and brought the heavy blade down flat across the creature's skull with enough force to crush it. A great gooey geyser of rotting brain squirted onto the floor, and Judith was at last not merely dead, but *dead*.

Lizzy leaned in beside a still-screaming Dr. Sleaford and brought her lips to within an inch of his ear.

"Now *your* life hangs in the balance. Tell me where the cure is, and you will get the first dose."

"Over there! In those drawers! The top one, the top one!" Dr. Sleaford lifted his head and strained for a look at his arm. "How much of me did she get?"

"Not much," Kitty said, appraising the man's wound with a cocked head. "Only a chunk about the size of an apple."

"Ohhhhhhhhh!"

"Well, a small apple. Maybe just a lime."

Lizzy opened the drawer Dr. Sleaford had indicated and pulled out a small glass tube with a needle at one end and a plunger at the other.

"It looks like a poison dart," Kitty said. She glanced over at Nezu. "The sort of thing your lot would like."

Nezu still wouldn't meet her gaze, but he wasn't wearing his usual look of stoic remoteness. He looked pained, strained, like a man fighting some great inner battle. Or perhaps stifling a belch.

"It is an invention of ours," Dr. Sleaford said. "The Sleaford Needle."

"The other one calls it the MacFarqwand," said Gurdaya, who was peeking into the laboratory through Nezu's legs.

The ninja turned and shooed her away.

"Sleaford Needle, MacFarqwand, call it what you will," Dr. Sleaford said. "It is a device that allows us to safely make subcutaneous injections, if that means anything to you. Now will someone at least staunch the bleeding? I'm starting to get all soppy here!"

Lizzy looked at Kitty and nodded.

"Hands only."

Kitty unfastened the straps around the man's wrists and helped him sit up. She then handed him a hankie, which he pressed to his wound.

"Thank you. That's so much better." Dr. Sleaford looked down at his arm and winced. "I shall probably need a tourniquet. Honestly, did you have to let Judith bite me so hard?"

Lizzy lifted a small dark vial out of the same drawer from which she'd produced the MacFarqwand.

"The *cure*?"

Dr. Sleaford nodded and began explaining to Lizzy how to administer what he called the "vaccine." A moment later, she was filling the MacFarqwand's glass tube with black liquid from the vial.

"More," the doctor said. "More. There. Stop."

"So much?" Lizzy asked. "That's half the vaccine. Is this all you have?"

"I'm afraid so. It is not easy to make. Now, if you please?"

Lizzy brought the needle toward the man's arm.

"Wait," Mary said.

Lizzy froze.

"Oh, please!" Dr. Sleaford wailed. "You're going to torment me now? That's just cruel!"

"I merely have one more question, while you're still inclined to be candid," Mary said. "Your former lodger across the hall: It was whom I thought?"

"Yes! Yes! Now can we get this over with?"

"By all means," Mary said.

Lizzy jabbed the needle into Dr. Sleaford's arm and pushed down the plunger. Slowly, the blackness in the tube disappeared. When it was gone, Lizzy pulled the needle out and said, "And now you are cured? As simple as that?"

"Now I *might* be cured. The vaccine is still experimental."

"But it worked on the king," Mary said.

Dr. Sleaford sighed. "Please tell me you'll be discreet about that."

"The king?" Kitty said. "You mean *our* king?"

"Well, I certainly didn't mean Nebuchadnezzar."

Mary looked rather proud of her attempt at wit, but all she got from Kitty was a blank stare, and Lizzy stared off dreamily at nothing.

"Of course," Lizzy said. "That's why the king was kept out of sight all these years. He wasn't mad. He was here, in secret, under guard. Stricken with the strange plague. And the serum that was keeping him from becoming an unmentionable . . ."

She looked over at the doorway. Nezu no longer blocked it, and Gurdaya was back, peeking in warily from the hall.

It had always been a mystery why the plague never spread beyond Great Britain. It had something to do with their island isolation, some said. A peculiarity born of the purity of English blood.

And now, looking into Gurdaya's dark, sad eyes, Kitty understood where the cure lay: in the blood of foreigners.

"It is abominable," she said.

"I might concede you the right to judge me," Dr. Sleaford said, "if your sister hadn't *let a dreadful bite off half my arm*."

"Oh, you didn't lose half. An eighth, at most."

"None of that matters now," Lizzy said.

"It matters to me," the doctor grumbled.

Lizzy ignored him. "We have the cure and we know how to use it. We must get it to Rosings immediately."

She turned back toward the tabletop on which she'd left the vaccine. Nezu stood there now, the vial in one hand. With the other, he drew Fukushuu.

The other ninjas—all six of them now spread out around the room—drew their weapons as well.

"Oh, yes. The cure is going to Rosings," Nezu said, slipping the little stoppered bottle into a coat pocket. "But you and your sisters will be staying here, Elizabeth Darcy. Permanently."

CHAPTER 37

"Finally," Nezu heard Ogata mutter.

"We should have slit their throats a week ago," Hayashi whispered back.

"We didn't have the whatever-it-is then," Ishiro said. "The thing the mistress wants."

"Well, thank Death that Nezu has it now," said Ren. "I cannot *wait* to kill that little fool who's laughing all the time."

"Oh, yes! Her!" said Momoko. "I would've gutted her already if Nezu hadn't—"

"Shut up, all of you," Kenji said. "The time to strike draws near."

And he threw Nezu a glare that added, *Why do you still talk to those we must kill?*

Nezu was thankful the ninjas ringing the room spoke no English. That he'd been educated, hand-picked for "improvement" by Lady Catherine, had always set him apart from his fellow assassins. He was Shinobi, but he was also English, in his own way, and that made him an outsider even in a clan of outsiders. This was going to be difficult enough without them knowing just how far outside he'd almost strayed.

"Nezu," Kitty said.

He forced himself to look at her, but it was difficult gazing into her eyes. He could see too clearly the pain of betrayal in them. So he tried to focus on her nose. It was such an admirable nose, though—not dainty or buttonish, but slightly bulbous in a way that seemed proud, unapologetic.

He tried looking at her chin.

"What is the meaning of this?" Kitty said.

"Isn't it obvious?" Elizabeth Darcy replied for him, and Nezu was grateful for the excuse to look elsewhere. "Lady Catherine has not been helping us. She has been using us, and now our usefulness has come to an end. She has what she wants—Darcy and the cure—and now vengeance shall be hers as well."

"Nezu," Kitty muttered, stunned, "how could you do this to us?"

She didn't add "to *me*," but Nezu could hear the accusation in her voice.

He raised his katana a little higher, looking at it rather than her.

"My father gave this sword to me. I named it Fukushuu—Revenge—after he died." He gazed at Elizabeth Darcy. "It was you who killed him. He was one of the ninjas sent for you at Pemberley after your marriage to Mr. Darcy."

"And you would blame her for that?" Kitty said. "Wish revenge upon her because she defended herself?"

She took a step toward Nezu that forced him to look at her once again. Or look at her left ear, anyway.

What a fine ear it was. . . .

"You fool," Kitty said. The words came out sad rather than spiteful. "If you wish to hold someone accountable, choose the woman who threw away your father's life on a petty vendetta."

"Lady Catherine is my mistress. I have sworn my life to her, as did my father."

Nezu dragged his gaze away from Kitty's ear and found himself looking into eyes that reflected distress but not despair. Even now, he could see hope and love and *life* in Kitty Bennet. Everything that had always been lacking within himself.

"Duty and honor cannot be ignored—you know that," he said. "We do what we must. We obey. We avenge."

"Not always," the Man in the Box said. "Sometimes, we change."

Nezu had almost forgotten the Man was there. It would have been easy to do. If not for his dogs, he could have been mistaken for a small cabinet on the other side of the laboratory.

When Nezu looked his way, he saw the barrel of a gun protruding from the bottom of the Man's box.

It was pointed at Nezu.

"You side with them?" he said.

"I do. As should you."

"Kore de ii no?" Hayashi said. *"Douka shimishita ka?"*

What's going on? Is something wrong?

Kenji was more assertive. *"Shizuka ni shiro dare ka o korose!"*

Shut up and kill somebody!

But Nezu preferred to take first things first. Priority number 1: not dying.

He threw himself into a somersault, vaulting high enough to run a few steps on the ceiling, then flipped over and landed on the opposite side of the room, behind the Man and his gun. By the time he had his feet planted firmly again, everyone else was in motion.

Momoko and Ogata were bounding along opposite walls, hurling throwing stars, while Mary Bennet matched them bounce for bounce, catching every star they threw and whipping them right back. Hayashi and Ishiro, meanwhile, were rushing the Man in a pincer movement, arcing in on each side, their long sai daggers ready to plunge through the top of the wooden box and into the head just beneath. Ell and Arr intercepted them in midair, latching onto the men where they could inflict the most damage—or the most pain, anyway. And Elizabeth Darcy was dodging poison darts from Ren's blow gun as Kenji charged Kitty twirling twin kama scythes.

"Lizzy! Trade!" Kitty shouted, throwing her battle axe toward her sister.

Elizabeth tossed up her katana.

The weapons crossed in midair. Then each woman snatched down her new weapon and went on the attack.

Elizabeth sent the axe spinning end over end toward Ren while Kitty leapt feet first into the wall and sent herself rocketing across the room—straight at Nezu. She only barely missed both Kenjis' swiping scythes and Dr. Sleaford, who was busily undoing the restraints that still held down his legs.

"I'm sorry about your father," she said once she'd landed in a crouch before Nezu.

He jabbed at her with Fukushuu as she straightened, but it was a half-hearted thrust, easily parried.

"The past is the past, though," Kitty went on. "We can't live there. We have to live here. *Now*."

Again, he sent Fukushuu at her heart, and again she easily turned the blade aside.

"We can honor what lies behind us without being a slave to it," Kitty said. "It's time you faced what could lie ahead. You wouldn't have to do it alone, you know."

Nezu's thrusts started coming more quickly now, yet Kitty kept deflecting them. She kept talking, too.

"You once asked me how I could be a warrior and remain so human. I suppose it's because I never saw the two things as mutually exclusive. And so what if they are? Then I would be neither a true warrior nor a true lady. I would be something for which there is no label. And I wouldn't care. Just call me Kitty!"

"You are babbling," Nezu said as his blade clanged again and again against hers. "If there is some point to all this, I cannot make it out."

"Then allow me to make it as clear as possible."

Kitty lowered her sword, then dropped it.

"*You* can decide what you are, Nezu."

Behind her, the room was still a chaotic swirl of hacking and punching and kicking and biting and dying. A gun went off. Someone screamed. A bloody hand landed at Kitty's feet. Yet she remained utterly still, even though with one swing of Nezu's sword, she would be dead.

"If you truly must obey your mistress, if you truly must have revenge, then you can start with me," she said. "But if you choose to follow your own path . . . well, you can start that with me, too, if you like."

Nezu looked into her eyes.

She smiled.

He threw himself forward, thrusting out his katana as far as he could, sinking it deep into soft belly flesh.

"Omae aho ya de . . . ," croaked Kenji, who'd been rushing up behind Kitty with his scythes raised high.

You are such *an ass.*

As the man toppled over sideways, Nezu simply let go of his sword handle, and Fukushuu dropped away with the dead ninja. Then Nezu slipped a hand into his coat pocket, pulled out the vial containing the cure, and handed it to Kitty.

"Thank you," she said.

Nezu looked down at Kenji's crumpled, bloody body.

"I am no longer Shinobi," he said. "I do not know *what* I am."

"Oh, that's simple." Kitty wrapped an arm around his. "You're one of us!"

She started leading him from the laboratory, and he numbly noticed the black-wrapped torsos they were stepping over as they went. All the other ninjas were dead.

"It appears the doctor escaped in the confusion," Elizabeth said as she and Mary and the Man and his dogs followed Kitty and Nezu out.

"He could cause trouble for us," the Man said.

When they were all in the hallway, they found Gurdaya and her brother kneeling beside a closed door. The rest of the prisoners had fled.

"You are free to go," Mary said to them.

"Go where?" the girl replied.

The sounds of slurping and munching could be heard from the other side of the door.

"What's in there?" Kitty asked.

"Barry," the boy said.

"Barry?"

"Subject *Six*," Gurdaya explained.

"It sounds like he's not alone," Nezu said.

"That's because he's not," the boy said.

There was an especially loud crunch from inside the closet.

No one bothered asking the children if they'd seen where Dr. Sleaford went.

"You know what?" Elizabeth said to them instead. "I think it's high time you two went on holiday, don't you? How does Hertfordshire sound?"

She held out her hands.

The children took them.

CHAPTER 38

Darcy's strength faded during the long walk back to Rosings, but his resolve did not. When he reached the manor house, he went straight to the trophy room and retrieved his aunt's hara-kiri sword—the one he would use to gut himself.

He would do it in his room, he'd decided. Immediately. Daylight was fading, and his aunt would be back any minute, covering the miles on her white charger much more quickly than he had on foot. He didn't want her or his cousin interfering.

Even with Lady Catherine's treatments, his world was lost to him forever, and if Anne was anything to judge by, his humanity would soon follow.

A "life" of half-death and obscene appetites . . . and without Elizabeth? No. Time to die. It would be his final gift to his beloved wife: a widow's freedom to fight. Perhaps he could make her happier in death than he had in life.

He paused for one last look through the trophy room's long picture window. The grounds hadn't changed in nearly thirty years. He could almost see himself out there, engaged in a round of Stricken and Slayers with Anne. Even when they were children, she'd been good at playing dreadful. He never had any idea she was near until she leapt out from behind a stack of cannonballs or a topiary shogun and "ate" him.

And then there she was, doing it again. A glance away and back, and the grounds were deserted no longer: Anne was halfway to the house from the dojo. Perhaps she'd been visiting her zombie friends again, biding her time until her cousin chose to join her little salon of the undead. Darcy would see to it that she had a long, long wait.

He started to leave, intending to hurry to his room and do what he had to quickly, but a flurry of movement on the lawn turned him toward the window yet again.

A man on horseback had ridden around the side of the house and was approaching Anne. His presumption was extraordinary. His appearance was shocking.

He was a big heavy-featured man with a sweaty face, bristly chin whiskers, and fiery eyes. The luminosity Darcy could see around him seemed to ebb and flow, strobing from almost blinding bright to a dull gray glow.

As Darcy watched, the man slid from his saddle, shoved a hand under his dust-covered coat, and produced a stubby pepper-box pistol—which he proceeded to point at Anne.

Darcy raced from the room, and seconds later he was bursting out of the servant's entrance at the back of the house, his aunt's suicide sword still clutched in one hand. The man swung his gun on him as he came closer, and it occurred to Darcy that there might be no call for hara-kiri after all. Perhaps the stranger would spare him the trouble.

"Stay back!" Anne cried out when she saw Darcy. "This needn't concern you!"

She looked even paler than usual—a feat on order with the Atlantic growing wetter.

The woman could walk among unmentionables without a care, yet this man, whoever he was, seemed to fill her with fear?

Darcy kept approaching.

"What is the meaning of this?" he called to the man. "Who are you?"

"He is a lunatic, that is all," Anne said. "He rides out here from Sevenoaks from time to time to spew his fantasies of persecution. He's no danger as long as we—"

"I am Sir Angus MacFarquharrr," the man said firmly (and with a burr as thick as a Highlands porridge).

"I know that name." Darcy stopped just ten yards from the man, close enough that a lucky shot, even from his inaccurate little pocket pistol, might well kill him. "You're telling me that you're the physician in charge of Bethlem Royal Hospital?"

"See! I told you!" Anne exclaimed with a triumph that was but rouged and powdered panic. "He is mad! For God's sake, Fitzwilliam, get away from here before he becomes agitated!"

"'Fitzwilliam,' you say?"

The Scotsman raised his bushy eyebrows. He held himself with a pinched stiffness Darcy recognized—he was injured somehow—yet he managed to muster a small smile.

"I have heard of you, too, Sirrr, and I see why your wife was inclined to act with such recklessness. There are now *two* stricken underrr Lady Catherine's roof, if I don't miss my guess . . . and no one makes betterrr guesses about the strange plague than I. Mrs. Darcy's efforts will all be for naught, howeverrr. She will be here any minute—I knew she'd be bringing the prize to your dearrr old auntie, and I just managed to slip by her party on the road. When she arrives, you will have her rrreturn to me that which she has stolen."

"But—," Darcy began.

"No buts, Sirrr. You see . . . "

The man used his free hand to pull open his coat. On his left side, just below the ribs, his waistcoat and breeches were soaked with blood.

" . . . now *I* need the cure just as much as you two."

"He's lying," Anne said. "It's some kind of trick."

"A minute ago, you told me he was mad. Now he's trying to trick me?"

Anne simply stared back at Darcy, her lips pressed tightly together. That's when he knew. This *was* Sir Angus MacFarquhar, and everything he said was true. Which meant that everything he'd read about Elizabeth was false—lies he'd been *meant* to find.

Darcy's head and shoulders slumped, and suddenly it seemed like a struggle just to keep the sword in his hand.

"How could I have been so blind?"

"All right, yes. We've kept a few things from you," Anne said. "But it was for your own good. Sir Angus, tell Mr. Darcy how his wife went about acquiring the cure. How she and her sister set out to seduce you and your son."

Sir Angus started to open his mouth, but Anne just kept on talking.

"She revealed her true self, Fitzwilliam. She is a liar and a schemer and a jezebel. And even if she is bringing the cure here for you, she is unworthy of you."

"My wife," Darcy said, and just those two words brought back some of his strength, "is so thoroughly magnificent, I wonder now if *I* am worthy of *her*. As for lying and scheming and seducing, it isn't Elizabeth you describe. It is you who have revealed your true self . . . and it is vile."

Darcy had often wondered if his cousin hated him for refusing to marry her; now he had his answer. Anne didn't just look hurt or angry. Her face contorted into a grimace of such deep and bitter malice, he almost expected her to act like the dreadful she half was and throw herself upon him, clawing and biting.

"I don't know what kind of grotesque family squabble I've wandered into here," Sir Angus said. "But . . . oh, thank Christ. Finally!"

A landau was rolling toward the house. It, like Sir Angus, was splattered with mud and dirt that spoke of a hard, hurried ride down the road to Kent. It seemed unusually crowded, with two men in the driver's seat and three ladies in the back clustered around a large black box. Two dogs leaned out over one of the doors, their tongues lolling.

Darcy would have puzzled over the meaning of it all, only the sight of one of the passengers shoved every question from his mind.

"Elizabeth!"

She was smiling back at him . . . until she recognized who stood just beyond him, gun in hand. A minute later, the whole motley band—Elizabeth, her sisters Mary and Kitty, their father, Nezu the ninja, the box and its harness dogs—had left the carriage and was slowly approaching Darcy and Sir Angus and Anne.

Elizabeth seemed to recognize the sword in Darcy's hand, and her frown deepened.

"You are well?" she called to him.

"Well enough," Darcy replied with a shrug. "Certainly, I am better now than I have been."

Seeing you, he meant. *Knowing that you still love me.*

He wanted so desperately to say the words to her. Yet he didn't know if he'd ever have the chance.

"That's farrr enough!" Sir Angus barked. "Any closerrr, and your husband's condition is going to worsen irreversibly."

The Bennets and their friends stopped about forty paces away. Elizabeth was carrying a small wooden box, but no one else held anything. Everyone seemed to be unarmed, though Darcy knew better than to rely on "seemed to." And so did Sir Angus.

"You," he said to Anne. "Go to them."

"Me? Why?"

Sir Angus waved his pepper-box at her. "*Go.*"

Anne threw another quick, hateful glance Darcy's way and then set off.

"You have the vaccine and the MacFarqwand?" Sir Angus asked Elizabeth.

She raised the box in her hands. "I do."

"Fine. Then you'll give that to Miss de Bourgh, and she'll bring it to me. The rest of you will stay rrright where you are. I've seen enough of your foreign tricks."

"Sir Angus," Kitty said. "Is Bunny all right?"

"My son is dead, Miss Whateverrr-Your-Real-Name-Is. Torn apart by dreadfuls along with all the royal family and most of London. As farrr as I know, the only ones to make it out of Westminster alive are me and that accursed rrrabbit."

"The royal family? Eaten?" Darcy said. "You can't mean it."

"Oh, aye. I do. I do not know what the future holds for England, Sirrr, but for now I can tell you this: It's every man for himself."

By then Anne had reached Elizabeth, and the two women stared into each other's eyes. After a long, silent moment, Elizabeth handed over the box.

"Bring it here now, Miss de Bourgh," Sir Angus said, "and we can put an end to all this unpleasantness."

Anne turned and started toward him.

"Though I have been wronged, I am not an unreasonable man," Sir Angus went on as she came closer. "There should be enough of the vaccine in that vial to cure two. Once I've taken my dose, you can decide who gets the otherrr . . . so long as I am free to go. Do you accept those terms, Mr. Darcy? On your honorrr as a gentleman?"

"I do."

"*I* don't," said Anne, and she stopped halfway between Elizabeth and Darcy.

Sir Angus muttered a word Darcy didn't think had ever before been uttered on the grounds of Rosings.

"You want to make sure you get the cure first," he said more loudly. "Is that it?"

"What makes you think I want to be 'cured' at all?" Anne snarled back.

She opened the box and drew out a vial of dark liquid.

"Careful!" Sir Angus cried. "If anything happens to that, none of us will be rrrid of the plague!"

"Exactly!"

Anne brought up her hand as if she meant to dash the bottle to the ground.

"DON'T . . . YOU . . . DARE!"

Anne froze.

Lady Catherine de Bourgh was riding around the dojo on her huge white stallion.

"He rejected me, *Mother*," Anne said, and Darcy realized he'd never heard her use the word. She made it sound worse than the one Sir Angus had mumbled under his breath a moment before.

"Again," Anne continued. "For her. Even after I told him everything."

"Then he will answer to me, and we will set all to rights once you're both cured."

Sir Angus cleared his throat and waved his pistol in the air. "Excuse me? Aren't you forgetting someone here?"

"Not at all," Lady Catherine said, and the ninja who'd been slithering up behind Sir Angus popped to his feet, snatched the gun from the man's hand, and rammed a kunai spike through his neck.

Sir Angus had more to say that wasn't particularly polite, but the words were hard to make out, what with him gasping for breath and choking on blood. As he fell to his knees, his hands pressed uselessly to his scarlet-spurting neck, the rest of Lady Catherine's ninjas—twenty in all—hopped up behind him.

"Now," Her Ladyship said to her daughter, "once we've attended to our other guests, we can administer the serum to you and your cousin and set about living happily ever after."

Anne narrowed her eyes at her and then turned to Darcy. He let the expression on his face say it all.

Never.

"You can all burn in hell!" Anne shrieked.

She was going to throw the vial this time, there could be no doubt.

And if it didn't shatter upon hitting the ground, she would smash it under her heel.

She brought up her hand—and screamed as a throwing knife pierced it through the wrist. Both the box and the vial tumbled from her grip.

They were but inches from the ground when a diving Elizabeth caught them. She rolled forward into a crouch and then opened her curled fingers.

She looked up at Darcy and smiled.

The bottle was unbroken.

"Shinobi!" Lady Catherine roared. *"Totsugeki shirou!"*

Ninjas! Attack!

Darcy couldn't help but notice that his wife's smile grew even wider.

CHAPTER 39

To Elizabeth's surprise, when Lady Catherine whipped out a brace of matching flintlocks, she didn't immediately point them at her.

"If there is one thing I cannot abide," Her Ladyship said as her assassins rushed toward Elizabeth's family and their newfound friends, "it's ungrateful help."

And she took aim at those new friends—Nezu and Mr. Quayle—and pulled the triggers.

Nezu was a moving target, bouncing and weaving toward his former comrades with a retractable bo staff in his hands. The shot intended for him went wild.

Mr. Quayle, on the other hand, wasn't nearly as nimble. There was a *thunk*, and a hole appeared in the side of his little crate.

"No!" Mary cried. She started to kneel next to the box, but there was no time. The first wave of ninjas was almost upon her, and she was forced to whip out the nunchucks she carried in a back-scabbard and go on the attack.

Mr. Bennet and Kitty were wading into the battle, too, but Elizabeth couldn't follow their progress. Lady Catherine had tossed aside her pistols and somersaulted from her saddle, drawing her katana just before landing. She started stalking toward Elizabeth as Anne staggered away, a dagger still stuck through her wrist.

"Wait for me in the dojo," Lady Catherine called after her daughter. "I shan't be long."

Elizabeth quickly tucked the vial back in its box with the MacFarqwand (which was also still in one piece, she was relieved to see). Then she stood and reached over her left shoulder. She was wearing a back-scabbard as well, only hers held a sword. She'd assumed—even *hoped*—this moment would come before the day was through.

It was time for her final duel with Lady Catherine de Bourgh.

"Wait!" Darcy called out, running to intercept his aunt. "There is no need for—!"

Her Ladyship caught him by surprise with a sudden, savage side kick that sent her foot deep into his midriff.

"I am extremely displeased with you," she said as he stumbled back a step and then collapsed.

The kick barely set Lady Catherine off her stride, and she carried on swiftly toward Elizabeth.

The old woman pointed at the box.

"Give me that, and I will make your death a quick one."

"There is something you should know before you try to take it," Elizabeth said. She slid the box into one of the oversized ammunition flaps on her battle gown and then jerked her head toward Sir Angus. The man was stretched out flat on his face, either dead or moments from it. "He was mistaken. Only one dose of the vaccine remains. You cannot save your daughter and your nephew both. The happy ending you sought is impossible. And always has been, I might add."

"Impudent wench," Her Ladyship growled, and she covered the last twenty feet between them in a leap, her sword pointed at Elizabeth's face.

Elizabeth dived aside with not a second to spare. Lady Catherine seemed even quicker than the last time they'd fought—and Elizabeth knew herself to be slower.

When Her Ladyship spun around and charged her again, she was smiling smugly. She began slicing at Elizabeth with big, arcing swings of the sword even as she talked.

"You know you cannot defeat me. I can see it in your eyes. I have been campaigning against the dreadfuls these past four years while you have lived the life of a gentleman's wife."

She lunged at Elizabeth.

"A gentleman's."

She lunged again.

"Useless."

And again.

"Wife."

Each time, Elizabeth only barely blocked the blade stabbing at her. Lady Catherine wasn't just fast, she was strong.

And she was right—about Elizabeth's abilities, at least. Elizabeth wasn't half the warrior she'd been four years before, and it had taken all her skill to defeat Lady Catherine then.

Still, Her Ladyship was four years older, and she hadn't been young to begin with. That had to count for something, didn't it?

Elizabeth went on the offensive—but found, after just one thrust, that the old woman had worked her sword under hers and almost ripped it from her hands with an upward jerk. By the time Elizabeth had regained a solid grip, Her Ladyship was whirling up before her in a beautifully executed twist kick that planted a heel against the side of her face.

Elizabeth stumbled back, blinded by pain.

"Do you need any help, my dear?" she heard her father call out through the ringing in her ears. "Usually, I'd be the last person to intrude in a private duel, but I'd be happy to make an exception for—ahhhhh! Never mind! I find I am quite unavailable after all!"

"Lizzy! Look out!" she heard her husband shout, and she instinctively rolled to the right. She wasn't quite quick enough, however, and Lady Catherine's blade raked across her left shoulder, barely missing her throat. Before she could get her feet solidly under her again, Her Ladyship's came flying in, and she took double blows to the side that sent her sprawling.

Elizabeth hit the ground hard. The breath was knocked out of her, and her sword popped out of her hands. But her first thought was of the vaccine. She put a hand over the box, feeling it through the rough fabric of her gown.

It hadn't shattered. She could only pray that its contents hadn't either.

By the time she rolled over to look for her sword, Lady Catherine was looming over her, the tip of her katana just inches from Elizabeth's nose.

"Don't do it!" she heard Fitzwilliam call out. "Kill her and you're killing me!"

His voice was too far away. Too strained and weak.

"This is for your own good," Lady Catherine replied without taking her eyes off Elizabeth. "The good of us all. You corrupted this great family when you introduced something so base and common into it. I shall simply be cutting out the infection."

"Noooooooo!" Darcy bellowed as his aunt brought back her sword for the death chop. And then a strange thing happened to his cry. Rather than diminish, it strengthened and multiplied, becoming a whole chorus of howls.

Dreadful howls.

A herd of zombies was bursting from the dojo. In the midst of them, to Elizabeth's astonishment, was Anne de Bourgh.

Lady Catherine was astonished, too—which was why Elizabeth was able to swing up her feet and send them smashing into the old woman's knees. There was an extremely satisfying *crunch*. Her Ladyship wailed in pain and made a clumsy swing with her sword, but Elizabeth was already rolling away backward.

When Elizabeth sprang upright a second later, she found Lady Catherine hobbling toward her using her katana as a cane. Behind her, the zombies had reached the first of the wounded, and a few stopped to feast on ninja tartare. The rest swept on toward them—with Anne in the lead.

"Please don't think I'm not enjoying our fight to the death," Elizabeth said, "but I do wonder if we should postpone it."

"Pah," Lady Catherine sneered, and she drew a throwing star from her sleeve and whipped it at Elizabeth's head.

Elizabeth dodged it easily.

Her Ladyship almost lost her balance and fell over.

Elizabeth began backing away quickly, and nearly every other living person was doing the same. The Bennets, their friends, the ninjas who'd been trying to kill them (and vice versa) just moments before—all were falling back toward the house. Fitzwilliam, too, though it wasn't the house he was headed toward. It was his wife.

"Elizabeth," he said when he reached her side. "I can't tell you how—"

"Duck, my love."

They both stooped low, and another throwing star went whizzing overhead.

When they straightened up again, Anne and her unmentionables were but steps from Lady Catherine. Elizabeth expected a handful to fall on Her Ladyship, and she prepared herself for those who would keep charging on.

She had no more knives or swords. Her last weapons would be her hands and feet. Her *self*. And that felt somehow right.

"You come back here this instant!" Lady Catherine said to her. "I am not finished with—"

Teeth bit deep into the stringy flesh of the lady's neck. But that wasn't what put the look of horror on her face. It was looking over to find her own daughter chewing and swallowing.

"I should have known!" Anne said as the dreadfuls—all of them—fell upon Lady Catherine and began doing as she'd just done. "You taste bitter, Mother! Bitter bitter *bitter*!"

Then she threw herself into the churning mass of cadavers fighting for another morsel. There were more than a dozen dreadfuls, and it didn't take long for the pack to reduce Lady Catherine the Great to bloody scraps.

It took long enough, though. By the time they were through, Elizabeth and the rest were ready. When Anne started toward them, face as smeared with her mother's blood as the day she was born, Fitzwilliam brought up the crossbow borrowed from his father-in-law and pulled the trigger. This was a family affair, and it seemed only right that he should end it.

The rest of the unmentionables were another matter, however. As Anne fell back, brain jellied by the bolt through her forehead, the Bennets and their new allies—the now mistressless ninjas—charged them together.

Elizabeth and Fitzwilliam were with them. The gentleman had laid down the crossbow and picked up a dead ninja's sword. The lady did the same, after finding a safe spot for the box in her pocket—and the vial and needle that remained perfectly preserved inside.

"This is how it should be," Elizabeth said as the two of them hacked and slashed at the undead together, husband and wife fighting side by side. "How it should have been all along."

Her husband spared a glance her way and, seeing the grim satisfaction on her face, spoke in the tones of one making a solemn vow.

"Then this is how it *shall* be," he said. "Ever after."

CHAPTER 40

"It simply isn't done."

Mrs. Bennet had used that phrase more than once in her time. She'd

"THE TWO OF THEM HACKED AND SLASHED AT THE UNDEAD
TOGETHER, HUSBAND AND WIFE FIGHTING SIDE BY SIDE."

heard it often enough as well (or at least had it said to her, which isn't necessarily the same thing). Yet as common as it was, Mrs. Bennet couldn't imagine it meaning anything much longer. Not when so much that supposedly wasn't done was *being* done right before her eyes.

It started with a letter from Lizzy. She was sending a pair of young friends to Longbourn, and Mrs. Bennet was to look after them until the Darcys, God willing, could collect them. The "God willing" might have seemed ominous had Mrs. Bennet paused to reflect upon it. Pausing and reflecting weren't her strong suits, however, and anyway she had mysterious guests to prepare for—an aristocratic couple of the highest quality, most likely. For who else would such as the Darcys be friendly with? The good silver and china would have to be put out and the linens changed and fresh flowers arranged and the grounds swept for dreadfuls. (Nothing made a worse impression than unmentionables pawing at the windows with their filthy worm-nibbled fingers.)

What Mrs. Bennet hadn't anticipated was how very young her visitors would be . . . and how very, *very* foreign. She'd been shocked when they stepped off the stagecoach from London, but it made sense when she discovered they were orphans. Mr. Darcy always did have a taste for exotic servants. Why Lizzy would describe her newest scullery maid and stable boy as "friends" Mrs. Bennet didn't know, but (once she was past her initial surprise and disappointment) she was happy to help them prepare for their new duties. Soon they were busy dusting and mopping and mucking out horse stalls.

When Mrs. Bennet received word from Lizzy to bring the children to Pemberley—where, it seemed, nearly all the family would be gathering to "recuperate"—she assumed things would soon be back to normal. (Again, there was no pausing or reflecting on what, say, anyone needed to recuperate *from*.) She would ferry the orphans to the Darcys' estate, they would be hustled off to their new lives below stairs, and that would be that.

Only that wasn't that. *That*, in fact, turned out to be something very different, indeed.

The children, it was quickly made plain, weren't to be servants at all. They were guests. And that wasn't the only or even the greatest shock in store for Mrs. Bennet.

For one thing, Lizzy was going out "on patrol" with Mr. Darcy every day. And in that horrible, drab old battle gown of hers—with a sword belt wrapped around it!

Well, what could Mrs. Bennet say to her daughter but "It simply isn't done." And "It's just not done." And "It is not done." And "The wives of gentlemen don't do such things." And many another variation. Yet day after day, Lizzy strapped on her "katuna" (or whatever it was called) and rode off with her husband, the two of them looking so giddy you'd have thought they were children again. Which also wasn't done! Respectable married couples weren't supposed to look so happy. It wasn't dignified—and it made things so much more awkward for everyone else.

As if that weren't bad enough, Kitty had fallen into the habit of taking lengthy country walks with an aloof little Asiatic named Nezu. When Mrs. Bennet complained about their long strolls and frequent unchaperoned "sparring sessions," Georgiana Darcy volunteered to keep them company—along with the young ninja *she* seemed to have grown close to during her recent tour of Scotland. It was scandalous!

Normally, of course, Mrs. Bennet could have counted on Mary to join her in self-righteous censure, but she was too busy nursing her box. The homunculus inside had been injured during some sort of kerfuffle at Rosings (the details were sketchy), and Mary had appointed herself as his caretaker. Each day, she pushed him out onto the lawn and sat with him and his two scruffy mongrels, reading aloud to them or feeding grapes one by one through the narrow slot in the man's crate. More than once, Mary had hinted that she and her "Mr. Quayle" had something to tell everyone, once his strength had returned. Mrs. Bennet could guess what the news would be. They already had one invalid in the family in Lydia's husband, the charming Mr. Wickham, so what was one more? At least a cripple was better than a ninja.

Mrs. Bennet knew better than to expect Jane and her husband, Mr. Bingley, to share her shock at all these improprieties. Although they were two of the most respectable and upright people anywhere, they were also among the most unassuming and pliant. Why, within minutes of arriving at Pemberley, they were letting their twins, Mildred and Grace, tear off with the little brown foundlings. True, the orphans were nice enough, polite and eager to please and awed to find themselves being treated with such kindness. Yet they still struck her as so different, so alien, so . . . so . . . well . . .

"So brown," Mrs. Bennet muttered.

"What was that?" her husband asked.

They were taking a morning constitutional around the grounds when they came across the children laying siege to a gamekeeper's shack that was standing in for a cave full of zombies.

"Oh, I was just admiring Gurdaya and Mohan's . . . unique coloration."

Mr. Bennet gave the children an appraising look—and a salute and a "Carry on!" when they noticed him staring their way.

"They seem more sienna to me," he said. "Perhaps mahogany."

"And 'Gurdaya' and 'Mohan,'" Mrs. Bennet went on obliviously. "What kind of names *are* those, anyway?"

"I believe we've discussed that at least five times. They are Punjabi."

"Well, what's a Punjabi?"

Mr. Bennet nodded at the children. "They are."

"You keep trying to tell me they're English."

"They are."

"They can't be both."

"Whyever not?"

"You can't be two different things at once!"

"Oh? I often find myself simultaneously amused and appalled . . . usually during our walks together."

"You're awful." Mrs. Bennet lowered her voice, even though the children were forty feet away and no longer paying them the slightest bit of attention. "You don't think Lizzy and Mr. Darcy mean to *keep* them, do you?"

"Gurdaya and Mohan? I have no idea."

The children's game was grinding to a halt amidst much squabbling. No one would put down their saber (they all carried real ones, handed out by Lizzy, along with zed whistles to blow if they spotted a dreadful) and try to eat the others. After a moment, Mohan finally agreed to be the unmentionable, and soon the girls were running from him shrieking with laughter.

"Wouldn't it be nice," Mr. Bennet said, "if Jane and Bingley's brood had friends to play Stricken and Slayers with whenever they came to visit?"

"Stricken and Slayers. Oooo." Mrs. Bennet gave a theatrical shiver. "How I hate that game. I always have, from the day you first introduced it to my little angel Jane."

They'd set off up the hill toward the house, but Mr. Bennet glanced back at Gurdaya and Mohan and his granddaughters. And he smiled.

"Who knows, Mrs. Bennet? Perhaps this generation of children will be the last to play it. I suspect the strange plague won't haunt us much longer. We're closer to a cure than you might think."

"Really, Mr. Bennet! I don't see how you can be so cocksure about the future! We don't have a king, the government is in disarray, half of London has burned again . . . including some of the nice parts this time! Oh, what will become of us? What will become of England?"

Mr. Bennet rapped the ground with the tip of his sword-cane. "It's still here."

"Oh!" Mrs. Bennet stopped and turned to glare at her husband. "Not everything is a suitable subject for your sport!"

"I would disagree," Mr. Bennet replied mildly. "But, more to the point, I wasn't joking. England will survive. Though it will be a different England."

"The kind where one's married daughter runs around with a sword collecting mahogany orphans, you mean? Or where one's unmarried daughters engage in disgraceful relations with the most inappropriate of men?"

"Yes. That kind."

"Mr. Bennet!"

"Mrs. Bennet, you may as well rail against the turning of the leaves or the rising of the tide. The dreadfuls came, and we looked to the East and to the deadly arts to save us. And save us they did—even as they changed us. England could have died, or it could become something new, and live. I, for one, am glad the latter path prevailed."

"But I don't want a new England! I want my old England! Some things were not meant to change! Some things should be eternal!"

"The change—that is all that's eternal. The rest of it . . .and us . . . ?"

Mr. Bennet shrugged and started toward the house again, his pace slowing as the ground rose steadily beneath him.

Mrs. Bennet wanted the last word, of course. So she had it. Even if, strictly speaking, it wasn't a word.

"Hmph!"

She crossed her arms and set her feet and threw back her head, as if to make herself into a statue—the very embodiment of the everlasting, unaging, unchanging England she so believed in. She would stand there forever, mute monument to all that was timeless and true.

"Forever" lasted about twenty seconds. Then the sun broke through the morning clouds and a shaft of light shot down upon Mrs. Bennet and she realized that she was thirsty and a little overheated and really, really needed to sit down and massage her corns.

"Wait! Mr. Bennet, wait for me!"

And the old couple carried on up the hill together as, down below, the children began a new game all their own.

THE END

JOURNEY TO REGENCY ENGLAND— LAND OF THE UNDEAD!

THE CLASSIC MASH-UP NOVEL

Pride and Prejudice and Zombies

By Jane Austen and Seth Grahame-Smith

ISBN 978-1-59474-334-4 • $12.95

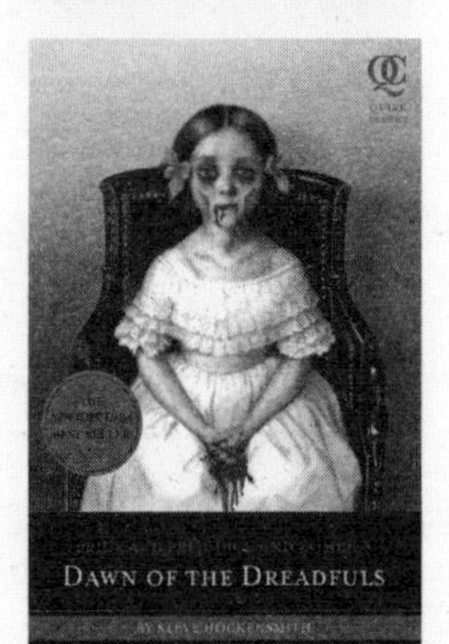

A MOST PECULIAR PREQUEL

Pride and Prejudice and Zombies: Dawn of the Dreadfuls

By Steve Hockensmith

ISBN 978-1-59474-454-9 • 12.95

A THOROUGHLY APPALLING SEQUEL

Pride and Prejudice and Zombies: Dreadfully Ever After

By Steve Hockensmith

ISBN 978-1-59474-502-7 • $12.95